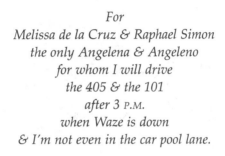

For
Melissa de la Cruz & Raphael Simon
the only Angelena & Angeleno
for whom I will drive
the 405 & the 101
after 3 P.M.
when Waze is down
& I'm not even in the car pool lane.

An ocean's garbled vomit on the shore
Los Angeles, I'm yours.
—Colin Meloy, The Decemberists
"Los Angeles, I'm Yours" (*Her Majesty The Decemberists*)

Royce Rolls *

MARGARET STOHL

FREEFORM BOOKS

LOS ANGELES   NEW YORK

* Loosely based on The Notebook of Teen Celebrity Bentley Royce—
which was loosely based on the Lifespan Network's Rolling with the
Royces *character Bentley Royce—which was loosely based on the
teen Bentley Royce—who was loosely based on genetic material
acquired as a zygote. These are their (the Bentleys') stories.*

All rights reserved. Published by Freeform, an imprint of Disney Book
Group. No part of this book may be reproduced or transmitted in any
form or by any means, electronic or mechanical, including photocopying,
recording, or by any information storage and retrieval system, without
written permission from the publisher. For information address
Freeform, 125 West End Avenue, New York, New York 10023.

First Edition, April 2017
10 9 8 7 6 5 4 3 2
FAC-020093-17123
Printed in the United States of America

This book is set in American Typewriter, Avenir, Century Gothic,
Officina Serif, Palatino, Wingdings/Monotype; KG God Gave Me You/
Kimberly Geswein Fonts; Modern Love/Resistenza.es

Designed by Marci Senders

Library of Congress Cataloging-in-Publication Data
Names: Stohl, Margaret, author.
Title: Royce rolls / Margaret Stohl.
Description: First edition. | Los Angeles ; New York : Freeform, 2017. |
Summary: "A famous-for-being-famous LA family stars on their own reality
show, but the sixteen-year-old daughter wants out"—Provided by publisher.
Identifiers: LCCN 2016039353 | ISBN 9781484732335 (hardback) |
ISBN 1484732332 (hardcover)
Subjects: | CYAC: Reality television programs—Fiction. | Family problems—
Fiction. | Fame—Fiction. | Celebrities—Fiction. | Los Angeles (Calif.)—Fiction.
| BISAC: JUVENILE FICTION / Humorous Stories. | JUVENILE FICTION /
Family / General (see also headings under Social Issues). | JUVENILE FICTION
/ Mysteries & Detective Stories.
Classification: LCC PZ7.S86985 Ro 2017 | DDC [Fic]—dc23
LC record available at https://lccn.loc.gov/2016039353
Reinforced binding

Visit www.freeform.com/books

One

THE WRECKAGE IS FOUND
May 2018
Grunburg Residence, Huntington Palisades
(Toyopa between Chautauqua and Sunset)

On May 4, 2016, in the early hours of the morning on one of the better streets of the Huntington Palisades,[1] Talullah Kyong-Grunburg (thirteen-year-old daughter of Lifespan Network president and chronic insomniac Jeff Grunburg[2]) saw the news on her Tumblr feed @AllHailMemeOverlord.[3]

Sixty seconds after she texted her dad from her upstairs Tahitian-sea-grass-wallpapered suite, he was on the phone in his downstairs Balinese-bamboo-bookshelved office.

The next twenty-four hours were a blur.

---

1 JG suggests "BEST?" But remember, these notes are just his SUGGESTIONS—after all, you're THE WRITER! Nobody can take that away from YOU! ☺ —Dirk

2 Per JG: Could we swap out CHRONIC INSOMNIAC for "POWER-HOUSE PLAYER" and/or "TOP TINSELTOWN EXEC"? (Note: JG prefers both!) ☺ —Dirk

3 Pls. include tumblr pages, digital posts & twitter feeds per LIFESPAN's social media mandate! And RE your GREAT Q—how much MORE MEDIA is "TRANSMEDIA" than "MULTIMEDIA"? It's N/A: we're now saying "ULTIMEDIA." (GREAT Q, THO!) ☺ —Dirk

THE LIFESPAN NETWORK

To: Daniels, Dirk (ddaniels@lifespan.com)
From: Grunburg, Jeff (jgrunburg@lifespan.com)
cc: Diaz, Barry (bdiaz@lifespan.com), Pearson, Pam
(ppearson@lifespan.com)
Subject: Problem
Date: May 4, 2018 [3:14 a.m.]

Lifespan Network Department of Publicity
Media Pull: ROYCE
Priority: High

Guys, are you seeing this?

Dirk, get me our guy at LAPD. Let's all assume damage control until we see how the story plays out.

Barry, get Marketing ready to pivot from A Very Special Wedding Special to A Very Special Funeral Special, just in case.

Pam, identify Lead Mourners. Headliners only. Key message is "Golden Ticket Event." I'm seeing Taylor Swift in a duet with one of the little Obamas. (How old is Hil's grandkid again?) And, it goes without saying, bagpipes. (Does the Pope play bagpipes? What can the Dalai Lama actually do? Could we get Lin-Manuel Miranda to take a sick day? Let's take a run at their agents, either way.)

Or—new direction—we hire the cast of Amazing Race to sing "Amazing Grace"? (Same #amazingrace hashtag either way, you seeing it?) They have to find their way to the funeral in a new Ford C-Max? Winner gets to shovel the first dirt or whatever? There's something there, stay on it.

All of you, I want reports on the hour. We're either totally screwed or we just won the lottery.

JG

JUNE GROOM MEETS DOOM—
ROYCE ROLLS OFF MULHOLLAND CLIFF
WEDDING DAY FOUL PLAY? LAPD WON'T SAY

AP: Los Angeles, California

Via Celebcity.com

Bentley Royce, celebrity daughter of the Royce reality television dynasty, and T. Wilson White, heir apparent to the Whiteboyz music label as well as fiancé to Royce's older sister, Porsche, are presumed dead this morning, following the discovery of burning wreckage in a cliffside ravine off Mulholland Drive.

The vehicle, a white late-model Audi, is registered in the name of T. Wilson White, who appears to have given the wheel over to his teen companion. According to witnesses, these were the only two people in the car. Royce allegedly lost control of the Audi just after 1 a.m., only hours before White's much-anticipated wedding to Royce's sister was scheduled to take place. That ceremony was to be televised as the season six finale of *Rolling with the Royces*.

According to sources, White and Royce were returning home from a wedding rehearsal dinner at the exclusive Soho House in West Hollywood when their car veered off the winding mountaintop road made famous by the death of Hollywood bad boy James Dean, dubbed "Deadman's Curve."

A low-profile yet high-ranking music producer (known

in some industry circles as "Whitey"[4]), White avoided the limelight much of his young life, though in recent months he often appeared in the public company of his future bride. His swift rise to the top job at the Whiteboyz label, upon the announcement of his father Razz Jazzy's impending retirement, came as a surprise to many.

In contrast, seventeen-year-old Royce's turbulent teen troubles were often documented on her family's show. Her own relationship with the media was legendarily uncomfortable.

No further information has been provided at this time. "But I can say that the ceremony has been postponed," confirmed *Rolling with the Royces* producer and spokesperson Pam Pearson, "due to the absence of the groom."

Veteran detective Harry Connolly, working with the LAPD's Homicide Special Section, has refused to address overwhelming media speculation that the incident was not a simple accident.

The balance of the family now remains in seclusion at their luxury home[5] in Beverly Hills' Trousdale Park gated community. The Royce family has yet to release a public statement. White's parents have still not surfaced since their sudden move to an unnamed South American

---

4 *JG isn't LOVING the nickname. ☹ Could we bring in a few writers & tweak? We have a line on the guy who came up with "Beliebers" and "Roycers" if that works for you? ☺ —Dirk*
5 *Per JG: The "Beverly Hills Post Office" neighborhood is now considered "luxury"? (Jeff is laughing.) ☺ —Dirk*

destination earlier this year, prompting rumors of a tax evasion investigation.

The Lifespan Network issued the following comment, via network exec Jeff Grunburg: "Today the Lifespan family has lost one of our own. We are shocked and saddened by the events of the past twenty-four hours, and urge everyone to withhold judgment until the investigation concludes. We ask to be allowed to grieve in public [*sic*] at this difficult time." The now-canceled wedding ceremony is rumored to have cost in excess of $3 million, the bulk of which was paid by corporate sponsors, including Porsche Royce's own cosmetics line and the Lifespan Network.

One of the biggest family success stories in Hollywood, the Royces (Porsche Royce; her mother, Mercedes; younger sister, Bentley; and younger brother, Maybach) rose to fame as the stars of their hit reality television show (known to fans as *RWTR*).

Now concluding its sixth season, *RWTR* is currently the most popular serialized cable program in the 18-to-24 age bracket, recently edging ahead of the hunting season cooking show and cable newcomer *Duke of Ducks*.[6] *DOD* was rated a mouthwatering first across all age demographics until Porsche Royce's wedding coverage emerged to pluck the feathers from its crown.

#Roycers, as fans of the show are known, are also making their way to the Trousdale gates, leaving offerings of

---

6 *No, no, no. Do not mention* Duke of Ducks. *This is a Duck-free zone. (Jeff is not laughing.)* ☹ *—Dirk*

notes, flowers, candles and stuffed animals as they hold vigil in the memory of lives and loves lost so young.

(Disclosure: Celebcity is a fully owned subsidiary of the Lifespan Network, which is a fully owned subsidiary of DiosGlobale.)

Follow @celebcity for breaking details,
or www.celebcity.com.

Eleven Months Earlier

THE FABCASTER FOUR REPORT: FAB OR FAIL?

AP: Beverly Hills, California

Via Trendcaster.com

ROLLING WITH THE ROYCES
FAIL

Lifespan needs to put down this dog of a show! Witchy mama Mercedes should unleash her flying monkeys; big sis Porsche is a D-list D-iva wannabe Marilyn; little sis Brat-ley needs a spanking (or military school); MayBach MayNot get by as just the CGB (cute gay brother) for much longer. What season even is this now? Fifteen? Fifty? Yawn! *RWTR* is one docu-(un)follow that has us running the other way!

PRO TIP: Try New Reality Channel's popular new hunting-season cooking show *Duke of Ducks* if you're on the hunt for a laugh, starting with the show's slogan: "This isn't just gun violence, it's DELICIOUSLY FUN violence!"[7] Joelynne Wabash, the eldest daughter in the reigning duck-decorated Wabash family, is a hoot to watch as she skins animals—then eats them! No wonder this show is the newly crowned King of Cable.

Follow @fabcaster for all the latest on Fab or Fail.

---

7 *Per JG: "Fun violence is not what will happen if this* DOD *refer-ence doesn't come out."* ☹ *—Dirk*

Two

THE FAMILY HIATUS
June 2017
Young Hollywood's "HELP IS IN THE CARDS"
Casino Night
(Chateau Marmont on Sunset, west of Laurel Canyon)

Looking good, Porsche! Work it, girl! Oh yes, thank you, Lord! Bentley! Bentley! Over here! Why so serious? Mercedes! This way, hot mama! Maybach! Bach! Bach! You got a smile?

The cameras kept flashing, but Bentley barely heard the paparazzi anymore. After years of red carpets, they were white noise. If she didn't try to pick out one from the next—if she didn't look at their faces—the effect was almost soothing. It was sort of like how the freeway could sometimes sound like crashing waves, if you didn't listen all that closely. Bent was an expert at tuning things out, especially when it came to the three people standing next to her.

She closed her eyes and felt a sudden pinch on her left hip, stinging like a wasp. She twisted away, but it was too late. Her mother's gel manicure—color conveniently entitled "BLOODRAWN"[8]—could, in fact, draw blood.[9]

---

8 *Per JG: Network wants to pair this scene with Porsche's product line, Cuties by Porsche cuticle cream and Pores by Porsche facial mask. Pls pump up the product profile! ☺ —D*
9 *Per JG: Network wants Cuticle Approval over hand models, after last month's unfortunate "Fat Cuticles" incident. Jeff claims he is "Cuticle Switzerland." Pls advise. ☹ —D*

"Ow!" Bentley yelped. "Retract your claws already."

"Tongue! Out!" her mother, Mercedes, said through her teeth. "Where's my favorite angry teen?"

"My mouth gets tired, *Mercedes*," Bent muttered. They weren't allowed to call her "Mom," especially not on a red carpet.

"Do you think *Miley* ever says that to *her*—*Tish*?" Mercedes pinched harder. She was gifted at scrubbing the m-word out, even midsentence.

"*Miley's Tish* doesn't control her life. If *Miley* sticks out her tongue, it's because she wants to."

Bent's sister, Porsche, glanced over at her. "Told you, B. Should have worn the Spanx. Less to grab."

Mercedes hissed behind her pursed red lips (her signature selfie trout pout), "Stand up straight! *Long necks* are *swan necks*! Remember the *golden string*—it runs from the top of your head right down to your toes!"

"Are you finally admitting we're your puppets, Mercedes?" Bent's little brother, Bach, the only boy in the family, snickered.

Mercedes ignored him. "Now for the smiles, everyone—"

Bentley sagged, despite any imaginary golden puppet strings. "Make me."

"I told you we should have used the back door," Bach said under his breath.

Porsche stuck out her lower lip even further (her signature selfie baby trout pout) and gave a quarter turn, angling her butt carefully to the left, so as to only expose its good side. (All cheeks, both upper and lower, had good and bad sides, according to Porsche; only amateurs forgot about their second pair.) "And *I* told Mercedes we should have left you both home."

Rude, Bentley thought, wondering why after all this time a classic jab from her big sister still got to her. Even though she knew Porsche was right—Bent and Bach weren't easy to manipulate into camera bait and paparazzi candy, and they didn't thrive off flashbulbs the way their mom and big sis did—it still didn't mean Bentley liked it that way. At times like this, she'd observe Porsche's stoic elegance and marvel at the way each camera flash, each intrusive holler, seemed to actually make her sister grow taller, more radiant, as if she were *feeding* off the harsh paparazzi vibes.

Truthfully, Bent envied it. While the paparazzi and attention and fame strengthened Porsche, it degraded Bentley. The spotlight only made her feel smaller—inside and out.

"Bentley—" Mercedes repeated. The stinging at Bent's waist intensified, and now she regretted agreeing to wear matching Balenciaga leather jackets along with her brother and sister. Bent's was cropped so that it exposed a good three inches of hip flesh that she desperately needed to keep out of her mother's talon reach.

"You know if you make me bleed, we'll actually have to buy this jacket," Bent said, blinking as the cameras flashed in her face.

Mercedes loosened her grip on her youngest daughter.

Bent raised her eyebrows, trying to dislodge her face from her own signature Bentley selfie-sulk. She sometimes got stuck that way. "And I was being serious, by the way.

Make me smile. I can't. I can barely breathe. These jeans are like four sizes too small."

Mercedes retracted her claws, and the four Royces stared out at the flashing bulbs in relative silence. Every bright flash left a negative imprint on Bent's eyes.

FLASH! The people became silhouettes.

FLASH! Now they looked almost like skeletons.

FLASH! Someone moved between them. Something.

FLASH! Blinking, Bentley looked again. This time, she thought she saw a hooded figure, dark and still in stark contrast with the surging crowd.

Weird.

She rubbed her eyes. The figure wore sunglasses and stood hunched over, as if trying to be small, unnoticeable. But Bentley had noticed—even just that stance was so out of place, it had made her stomach flip. No one in this crowd wanted *not* to be noticed, and trying it only achieved the opposite. Nobody knew that better than Bent.

Bentley blinked again, and just as quickly as it had appeared, the figure vanished. *Even weirder.*

But she forgot about it a moment later, when she heard the familiar melody begin.

"Landlord's mad and getting mad-der, ain't we got fuuuuuuuuun?"

"Mercedes, no." Porsche shook her head almost imperceptibly. "No singing allowed." The singing stopped.

Mercedes Royce had the worst voice of any human on the planet, and all she had to do to get any one of her children to crack up was to sing a line from any song, ever.

Though Mercedes's good looks and firecracker person-ality were why she had been cast in the short-lived trailer park makeover show *TRASHPIRATIONAL*[10]—along with the fact that she was already living as a single mother in the same Southern Utah trailer park where they were shooting—her earsplitting voice was the reason she had been the first one voted out of the double-wide. (Even if she had won the shooting range challenge *and* nailed the dem-olition derby, *dangit!*) Still, her first short stint on television had taught Mercedes to use what she had, and if what she had was a face that made people look and a voice that made them laugh, then so be it.

All of which was why, as usual, her silence was short-lived.

"Times are bad and getting bad-der, ain't we got fuuuuuuuuun?" Mercedes intoned again, sounding like a wounded animal.

Bentley started to giggle, in spite of the paparazzi. Mercedes never looked away from the cameras the whole time she was singing. She could sing the entire national anthem without moving her lips or opening her mouth; after years of practice, she was just that good.

"The rent's unpaid, dear, we haven't a buuuuuuuuus . . ." Bach chimed in, through his own clenched smile.

"But smiles were made, dear, for people like uuuuuuuuuus . . ." Porsche gave up, picking up the tune despite her own

---

10 *Per JG:* "Trashpirational! *I still remember that theme song!* 'With that camo wedding dress, you're my trash-pir-a-tion! In that mon-ster truck hot mess, you're my trash-pir-a-tion!'" ☺ —*D*

pouty pucker. Now Bentley was laughing in earnest—but even she couldn't resist joining in.

"In the mean-time, in be-tween time, ain't we got fuuuuuuuuun?"[11]

The Royce offspring broke character at the same moment, and as Bach threw back his head and laughed, Bentley grinned affectionately, and even Porsche dropped her forehead against Mercedes's shoulder. Only Mercedes held it together, as usual.

The cameras exploded to catch the spontaneous moment of Royce family togetherness.

Just as Mercedes had planned.

An hour later, sitting in the VIP room off the main bar at the Chateau Marmont, Bentley Royce was in a great mood. Truffle french fries in little paper cones were *never* a bad thing. And the cozy-candlelight, slouchy-vintage-hipster vibe of the Chateau Marmont didn't get on her nerves as badly as most event venues. Plus, there were no cameras now that they had gotten inside—and better yet, Mercedes had disappeared with Porsche to stalk Jeff Grunburg and pitch ideas for season six.

Bent and Bach were on their own for a few precious minutes. Hence the fries—hence the lack of *mandatory* mingling—hence not being made to take a lap around the

---

11 *"I Like Big Butts" could also work here, per JG. It's his ironic karaoke song. Pls consider.* ☺ —D

room like a Westminster beagle—and hence Bach's current run at the poker table, playing his hand between the two cutest boys in the room without a single lecture on how gambling was bad for his CGB image.[12]

But not one of those things was the reason for Bentley's current mood. She had a better one: as of tomorrow, *Rolling with the Royces* was on hiatus.

Hiatus—the few months when any television series, including theirs, wasn't shooting—was like summer vacation, only better. Hiatus meant no budget, so no show. No show meant no cameras. No cameras meant no hassle. No hassle meant no blowouts and no flatirons and no Spanx and no ab crunches. No panic over a zit the size of Mount Olympus, or even double pinkeye from an only allegedly hygienic lash-dyeing brush. (*It so happens!*)

During hiatus, as far as *RWTR*'s production team was concerned, it didn't matter what you wore, what you said, what you ate, or whether or not you worked out. (So long as you still looked good, said nothing too terrible, and hadn't gained a pound by the time you were back on camera.[13] Vicious cycles were *way* more vicious in Hollywood.)

Whatever.

Pam the Producer didn't want to have to deal with the cast during hiatus, but that was her only rule. If you crossed

---

12 "CGB" *Jeff wonders if we've sent this through trademarks, suggests we go for universal rights to "cute," "gay" and "brother" separately as well? Pls revise to include.* ☺ —D
13 *JG points out if B had gained the weight B would never be back on camera. Delete as obvious/superfluous?* ☹ —D

her, she would make certain you got the earliest call times possible for the entire next season.

Tonight was the Royces' last gig of the season—the annual *HELP IS IN THE CARDS* Children of the Angels Hospital fund-raiser, sponsored by none other than DiosGlobale, the parent company of Lifespan.

Bent hadn't wanted to come, but her brother and sister and mother had insisted: Mercedes for the networking, Porsche for the photo op, and Bach for the cards themselves. (Tickets-wise, Lifespan had contributed at the *FLUSH* level, and *RWTR* at the *FULL HOUSE*; even if the Royces themselves hadn't given *JACK*, Mercedes had still managed to use their show to talk their way in. That was just how the Royces rolled.)

Bent had caved in the end, for Bach's sake. It was their unspoken agreement, as the two lesser Royces. They were the wingmen beneath each other's painstakingly TryCycle-sculpted wings, usually. (Bach: "I prefer Wing-gay.") Tonight, though, Bach didn't need her. Not at a poker table.

If Porsche bloomed on the red carpet, Bach came to life behind a deck of cards. As long as he had a deck in hand, his life was as perfectly fitted to him as his vintage plaid jacket or his hipster T-shirt, which was soft and faded and advertising a trendy Mexican beer he didn't drink. (All of his James Perse T-shirts were tailored; Bach insisted on it, after reading in a magazine that Jennifer Aniston did the same thing.) It was the same outfit Bach had worn for *Vanity Fair*'s Young Hollywood shoot, and it worked. Girls and boys alike had crushes on Bent's brother (including their publicist, which was probably why Bach had made the issue and Bent had not). Bach took it all in stride, the same way he did everything. The fact that he only liked boys somehow never stopped everyone else under the sun from trying, and he was fine with it.

Fine? He's great. Relax. It's all good, B. Even this party.

But after thirty seconds of trying to convince herself of that—while simultaneously avoiding eye contact with the producer's son she'd been set up with for her "Awkward First Date" episode, as well as the alcoholic child actor who had once been cast for her "Sixth Grade Bully" episode, not to mention the whole *RWTR* App team—Bentley gave up.

"Yo, bro." She tugged on his T-shirt to get his attention. "This is boring."

Bach didn't answer. He was too preoccupied with his cards, studying them like vital digits that had previously been missing from his hands.

"Hello? Remember me? Your sister? Favorite person ever?"

"Bach said *I* was his fave person ever," said the still-struggling star of two critically acclaimed but financially insolvent big-screen YA adaptations. He sighed melodramatically.

"Whatsup, B?" Bach said, not looking up even the slightest bit.

Bent leaned on her brother's shoulder. "We're *kinda* supposed to have each other's backs at these things—that's the deal, *right*, B? And you're *kinda* leavin' me high and dry here, sailing away on your own little poker lifeboat and leaving me to drown."

"Translation: get off my floating door, *Leo*," laughed the cleft-chinned son of a famous vampire-novel writer.

"Whoa, those are two very opposite metaphors, B," Bach quipped, still studying his cards. "Wanna pick one? Are we in subzero waters or on dry desert land? I'm just trying to follow the narrative."

"*Boom*," said the YA heartthrob.

"*Ouch*," said the vampire son.

Bentley twisted her brother's ear. "Does it matter? I die a painful death either way."

Bach pulled his head away from her, finally looking up. "So dramatic! Come on, B, it's not that bad. I don't know— go sit by yourself and stare off into the distance like you're thinking about something mysterious and important."

"Why?"

"Why not? Nobody's ever mad at a beautiful girl choosing to spend time alone in a room full of people. They just assume she's cooler than they are, and move on."

"So you're saying I'm the beautiful person in this scenario?" She pinched his side, just like Mercedes would.

"I am if it'll make you leave." Bach rolled his eyes and shooed her away with a hand of cards and a tough-love smile. "Go be aloof. Somewhere else."

Maybe he's right, Bent thought, scanning the room for the perfect corner escape. Maybe tonight sitting alone could be her *thing*. As a Royce, she always had to have a thing—something, anything to feed the tabloids for the next morning. It didn't matter what it was, not really. A haircut. A flirty look. A script, accidentally on purpose held to show the title. One or another small clue to their imaginary life away from the cameras, even if only invented *for* the cameras.

You didn't have to shoplift a necklace or shave your head—you didn't even need rehab or an adoption. Not yet. After a while, though, there wouldn't be enough nipple slips in the world to stave off sliding into obscurity and nothingness. And according to Mercedes, nothing was worse than nothingness.

Bentley eyed a marble ledge near the bar. *Could work. Good lighting for important and mysterious thoughts.* She made her way toward it, imagining her new favorite headline: WHY SO SERIOUS, BENT? (REALITY STAR PONDERS NATURE OF REALITY AT CHATEAU MARMONT FUND-RAISER.)

Dream on, Bent. She sat down. She knew she'd never read that headline, because the truth was this: Bentley Royce was a smart girl with a mind of her own, but nobody, especially not the tabloids, cared about that.

All they cared about was that she was beautiful. They cared about her creamy skin and heart-shaped face, her bronzed breasts and the bubble butt that constantly threatened to burst through her ivory-white Rag and Bone jeans. They cared about her coffin-shaped acrylic nails and the blond *millennial* bob (as Phillip from Hair and Makeup called it) that fell to her shoulders, tipped at the ends in a rainbow of pinks and purples and blues, inspired by the time she had used a box of markers on her all-but-abandoned Bratz doll. (At least that was what the script had said, for the "Bentley's Rainbow Hair" episode.)

Everyone cared about Bentley's beauty, and to be honest, so did she. But she couldn't shake an unsettling feeling deep inside, a sense that ultimately her looks didn't matter as much as everyone seemed to think they did.

Because another, less-often-spoken truth was this: anyone could be beautiful if they went to the right people and had the right stylists and the right vegan chefs and the right trainers at their beck and call, day and night. That's what most people didn't understand about Hollywood. Anyone could be the Royces. Mercedes had realized it, and that's why it was the four of them who actually were the Royces, and not some other family.

There had to be more to life than fame and good looks, and anyone with half a brain could come to that conclusion. But knowing that didn't stop the anxiety that came flooding every time Bentley let this thought cross her mind.

Anxiety because the third and final truth crossing her mind at that moment was a secret one—and a painful one. It was something she had tried not to think almost as often as she'd thought it. It was something nobody knew, not even Bach.

The truth was, Bentley wanted to find out what there was to life outside the world of *Rolling with the Royces*, and to find that out she dreamed of the one thing she could not ever do.

Bentley Royce dreamed of going to *college*.

She winced at even thinking the word, it was so forbidden in her family. Almost cringed, really. But she also knew it didn't matter, because she'd never get to go, not in this lifetime and not in this version of reality—not if she stayed a prisoner to her television show and the television girl all of America expected her to be.

Dream on.

Bent stared past the crowded bar, out through a pair of glass French doors. The glittering city sprawled well beyond Sunset Boulevard, illuminating a bruised purple sky and a few lonely-looking palm trees on the horizon.

She thought of her mock college application essay back at home, gathering dust under a sea of hair extensions where hopefully nobody would find it:

Q: Discuss an accomplishment or event, formal or informal, that marked your transition from childhood to adulthood within your culture, community, or family.

She knew her response by heart.

A: My name is Bentley Royce. I know you already know my name, though I appreciate you pretending not to.

It's the little things.

I generally don't write about my family unless I want to read every single word I say online, but I'm going to make an exception because: college. I know, right? Why would I want to go? Why do I need to go? Seeing as I've already reached the pinnacle of American culture: I'm a celebrity.

Celebrities don't go to colleges. Sure, the "smart" ones do—Natalie Portman, Claire Danes, Hermione. Matt Damon, or maybe he was a janitor at one? Whatever. I'm not about to get into Harvard or Yale or Brown, or even be a janitor at Harvard or Yale or Brown. Let's be serious.

And anyways, I'm not that classy. Not Claire classy. Come on. My family is on a reality show. I mean, sure, we're on magazine covers, and maybe my sister's face and breasts are on everything from panty hose to lipstick—but let's face it, none of us are about to accept an Academy Award any time soon.

We're famous for being famous. Untalented. Self-promoting. The kind of celebrities real celebrities raise their eyebrows at. I know that. I'm not stupid. And anyways, maybe they're right, the eyebrows people. Not that I care.

Look, I just want to get out of here.

So: how did I transition from childhood to adulthood within my culture, community, or family? I'm pretty sure you know this, too, but since you asked, I'll answer. I transitioned from childhood to adulthood within my culture, community, or family when I got my period on live television at age twelve.

Is that classy enough for you?

Unfortunately, as you also probably know, I was in a swimming pool. With that year's Teen Choice Awards

Breakout Star Justa Beatbox. It looked like a shark attack, and the cameras were rolling, and Mercedes—my mother—wouldn't let them stop, even though I was furious.

Because the footage was gold. Literally. A picture is worth a thousand words, and by words I mean dollars, and Mercedes cashes them out as quickly as you can say unauthorized *In Touch* cover. That's my mama.

Back then, I was still a pretty private kid. I didn't even speak to anyone outside my own family until third grade.

And then that episode aired. Suddenly, I wasn't just famous; I was the most famous twelve-year-old in the world. Paparazzi followed me everywhere—coming out of the orthodontist with new headgear, shot with a long-range camera through the window of my bathroom when I had to pee, drinking mild sauce straight out of the packets at Taco Bell.

Mercedes didn't stop it. She went after it. I found out later from my sister that Mercedes used to call paparazzi and tell them where we were going and when we would be there. Go ahead and judge. Mercedes doesn't care.

You might think my mother is an attention whore, but if we're being honest, she's way past that. She's an attention pimp. Mercedes is jealous of police sirens if they're not headed her way. She sulks when the Jumbotron camera stays on the actual Dodgers at Dodger Stadium. Mercedes Royce is as hard as her new boobs and twice as tough. She's every bit as sharp as her snakeskin stilettos and way more dangerous.

So, anyway, yeah . . . my transition moment?

BENTLEY GROWS UP!

I made the cover of *People* magazine, huddled in my towel, red-faced and scowling.

Mazel tov.

I'm almost seventeen now, but I'm still the middle sister in the second most famous family on reality television (you gotta love a duckmeat Sloppy Joe!) and I'm your average, everyday Beverly Hills girl. I sleep with a Bible next to my bed. I bring my own lunch that the housekeeper has made. I drive myself to school, except when I can get my brother or my sister to take me.

Only my car is an actual Bentley, when I can stand to drive it (Mercedes never was one for subtlety), and half the time it's full of cameramen and chased by paparazzi.

My lunch is sushi, extra shiso leaf, easy on the rice. (Bread? What is bread? I haven't seen a sandwich since preschool.)

And the Bible by my bed? Don't be stupid; it's not the King James. It's the one from Production, the BENTLEY BIBLE, the rule set for the Bentley character on the show, the one based on me. The one I play in TV "reality."

So I don't forget what I'm like.

So I don't forget my character, i.e., TV Me.

So I remember to BE BENTLEY.

That's how Pam Pearson, our producer, says it to me. "I need a little more Bentley from you." And she's dead serious. Then my little brother, Bach, will usually kick me and hiss "Get Bent," which sometimes makes me feel better.

At least, it used to. I'm not so sure anymore.

People keep telling me I'm supposed to feel lucky. I've had the advantage of growing up full-time, full-on Royce. That's how Mercedes says it. Advantage. I never had to not be famous. I never had to know anything else. My mom gave us A Better Life.

That's what this is, in case you couldn't tell.

Sometimes I have to remind myself.

Here's what a better life gets you. A season four arc: WHY, BENTLEY, WHY? You know, the episode where the LAPD picked me up for shoplifting from Entrada Beachware? Three thousand dollars' worth of crappy overpriced polyester knockoffs made in China and sold to losers who'd pay $500 for a jungle-print caftan.

WHY, BENTLEY, WHY?

Seriously. It's a really good question, even if nobody wants to know the answer, which is this: because it was in the script. Because it's my job. Because it's in the Bentley Bible next to my bed. Because Porsche is the Pretty One or the Rising Star, and Bach is the Funny One or the CGB, and Mercedes is the Tough One or the Hot Mom. (Just don't actually say the m-word.)

And because I'm the Troubled One or the Basket Case.

The tabloids all say I'm going to die young and have a tragic funeral. Excellent. Live fast, die young, and leave a good-looking corpse—just like the postcards at Farmers Market say. That's me. I'm the rich kid bad girl of every mother's nightmare—the one who stays out too late and parties too hard and recklessly endangers other people. That's my part, anyway. At least it's hers. BENTLEY'S.

So why college? Maybe I want to read books without having to hide the covers behind fashion magazines. Maybe I want to learn things beyond the calorie count of a juice cleanse. (Trust me, you don't want to know.) Maybe I don't even want to be famous anymore. Maybe I never did. Maybe I'm tired of being Lindsay Lohan meets James Dean. (Also? They never met.)

Maybe you shouldn't believe everything you read or watch.

Maybe it isn't real, maybe it's just reality TV.

Maybe all I'm saying is, when it comes to my family and my show and my life, I think it's time to renegotiate my contract.

I want out.

WHY, BENTLEY, WHY?

Why not?

"Um, what are you doing?" Bentley looked up to see her big sister looming above her, hands on hips, parting the crowds at the Chateau Marmont bar. Porsche did not look pleased.

So much for people leaving a beautiful girl alone to sulk in private, Bent thought. I knew that was too good to be true.

She scowled at her big sister. "Um, I'm sitting down? Is that allowed?"

"It's not, and you know that. Not when the show's on the bubble. We are *this close* to getting kicked off the air. When we're anywhere other than our own home, we need to be . . ."

"Making a scene?" Bent asked. It wasn't really a question.

"Basically, yes. There's only so much I can do, Bent. You gotta help me out. Talk to people, fall down the steps, make out with the bartender, I don't care what, just as long as it's anything other than sitting in the corner like a sack of potatoes."

Bent knew her sister was serious: potatoes were the biggest insult the carb-conscious Porsche ever resorted to. "But—"

"But we can't afford to have any deadweight. Tonight I'll even take the heat for Bach letting his little poker problem show. Can't you, I don't know, find some girl to kiss?"

"That's Bach's job. Well, except for the girl part."

"Job? You want to talk about jobs?" Porsche shot her a withering look. "If the show gets canceled, we are over, do you understand that? Over, as in *no job, no future*. As in *kicked to the curb*. That's what happens when the bubble pops. So get your cute little butt up, okay? Time to rally. Get it together or get out."

Bentley glared at her sister as she walked away. She couldn't tell if Porsche was being paranoid—like the time she thought Kim Kardashian was trying to copy her nude lip—or if what her sister was saying could really be true. Bent couldn't imagine a world where *RWTR* wasn't on the air—was it even possible?

She wondered.

Hiatus hit right around the same time that networks like Lifespan made their programming decisions for the next fall. Winners got picked up. Losers got cut. And this year, for the first time ever, it wasn't clear in which category the Royce family belonged.

This year there was talk. Speculation. Whispers and Rumors, even. The word on the street was that the numbers were off.

But if *Rolling with the Royces* was actually canceled, it could only mean one thing:

Freedom.

What was so wrong with that?

Three

Given the choice between getting it together and getting out, Bentley almost always opted for the latter. Now Bent slipped through the crowded exit of the VIP tent, eyes on the ground, oversize Celine sunglasses on, even in the darkness.

Ten minutes, she texted Bach as she fled. *Then Uber.*

Fifteen, he texted back.

Deal.

She made it undetected down the tile staircase and out to the dimly lit grounds of the hotel. At the bottom of the stairs, she bumped into none other than Talullah, Jeff Grunburg's scrawny preteen daughter, clomping slowly along in what had to be her mother's Louboutin Pigalle pumps, four inches too high and three sizes too big.

"Hiding, Royce?" Talullah asked, her nose in the air. "Great idea. You do more of that, you guys are sure to be toast." She teetered on her heels for a moment—

Bentley caught her with one hand. "You okay there, kid?"

"*I'm* fine." Talullah straightened up. "But if *you* want

that renewal, Bent, you gotta give the people something to talk about. Something to remember." The kid sounded like a forty-year-old studio head, which wasn't surprising, given that her custody arrangement meant she spent three nights a week with one.

Bent shrugged. "Who says I want that renewal?"

"Yeah, right. Only everyone in this room, including the waiters," Tallulah said, clomping off toward the valet. "This is Hollywood. We can smell desperation."

Bent called after her, "Maybe that's just the truffle fries!"

Only laughter floated back through the air. Bentley shook her head. She was glad to see the mini Grunburg go.

Given the choice—mindless mingling versus being entirely alone—Bentley would always choose being alone, even if Porsche wanted her to stop playing wallflower and start playing wild child.

Even if twelve-year-olds like Tallulah Kyong-Grunburg agreed with her.

Even if Tallulah's father was saying it too.

If anything, the longer Bentley thought about it, the harder the idea was to shake: if acting out would help them get the show renewed, she was more determined to withdraw than ever before.

Why shouldn't she?

After all, being alone might get the show canceled, and if the show were to be canceled, she might get to go to college.

Being alone might give her a chance to figure out what BEING BENTLEY was actually supposed to feel like.

Being alone would at least make it easier to unbutton the top button of her pants and slip off her shoes, and she was currently contemplating both.

Freedom.

The word lingered in the back of Bent's mind as she made her way out into the deserted hotel grounds. The brick-paved pool deck was now dark and mostly empty— except for the shadows it afforded the occasional illicit smoker. It was much quieter out here, even if the striped cushions that covered the wrought iron chaises were damp to the touch. After trying a few seats, Bent found what looked like a strategic spot in the very darkest part of the yard. Perfectly dark, perfectly out of sight from any casual passerby.

Perfectly perfect.

Bent was the queen of the hiding place when it came to Hollywood parties. She had sometimes resorted to ducking into a coat closet, a bathroom stall, or even a service kitchen when it was really bad. But tonight wasn't that dire. It was early summer, and the evening air was warm enough to make it pleasant. Plus, half the paparazzi seemed to have fled, which could only mean Beyoncé had posted a selfie from an identifiable club somewhere in town.

Thank you, Queen Bey.

Bent could easily wait for Bach out here. She dropped her bag—and her guard—

and flung herself—

"You mind?"

RIGHT ONTO A PERSON—?!

Some sort of warm, unsuspecting person, from the feel of it.

It was a body, and it was moving, and Bentley was so startled she found herself yelping, and then shouting—

"WHAT THE—"

Bentley rolled awkwardly off what felt like a leg, or maybe a hip—and landed in a heap on the brick patio floor next to someone's shoe. For a moment she panicked, imagining a crime about to happen, remembering the hooded figure with hidden eyes in the crowd of paparazzi.

There's your headline, Porsche—

Then Bent's rational mind returned. She was being stupid and she knew it. She tried to pull herself together—or at least up off the ground.

A guy—unfamiliar, at least as far as she could see in the lightless yard—sat up on the chaise. He looked to be vaguely her age, but that was all she could tell in the shadowy yard. Only one thing was clear: he was not hooded, nor was he wearing sunglasses. So, not a criminal—at least not at first glance.

Bentley sighed, relieved—and only slightly disappointed.

There goes your headline, Porsche.

"Maybe you should try that one," the stranger said, pointing to the chair next to him. "It's just a guess, but I think this one's taken."

"No, really?" Bentley could barely manage to get the words out as she crawled up onto the next chaise. She tried to calm herself down, taking a deep breath. Her heart was still shouting. "Wow. I'm sorry," she finally said. "That was super embarrassing, even for me."

She heard a sound like a laugh in response.

"Yeah, you probably say that to all the guys you randomly sit on by hotel pools in the dark."

"You got me there," Bent said, still poised on the edge of the chaise. She fought off the urge to flee, which wasn't easy. Judging by the heat coming from her face, she was probably the color of a humiliated strawberry.

I could look for a closet to hide in. Maybe a pool house. Wherever they keep the towels around here . . .

"Don't," he said.

"Excuse me?" She didn't dare look his way.

"Run for it."

"Ha," she said. *HA? Why did I say that? Who says that?* "I wasn't."

"Good. You don't have to." He paused. "I mean, you can if you want to, whatever."

"Super. Thanks for the clarification." Despite every screaming cell in her body, she took a breath and sat tentatively back in her chair.

"That came out wrong," he said a moment later. "Sorry. I'm really bad at this."

"Not that bad," Bent said. "I mean, objectively speaking, you're not the one who just sat on a faceless stranger in the dark or anything."

"Yeah, well. That's a low bar."

"Not for some of us." Bent sighed.

He laughed. "See? I did it again. I don't mean to be rude. I just hate parties. I suck at all the *blah, blah, blah*."

"I don't know. You're *blah, blah, blah*-ing okay right now, I guess."

"How about you?" he asked.

Bent pulled her legs up to the chaise beneath her. "Me? I'm *great* at *blah, blah, blah*-ing, and I *love* parties."

"I can tell," he answered, gesturing to the empty pool surrounding them. "You're some kind of face-sitting social butterfly."

She laughed. "So why are you here, then?"

"Why is anyone here?" he asked.

Bent shrugged. *Good question.* "To be seen?"

There was a beat of silence. "To see someone."

Right. Of course you are. Let me guess—a size negative 2 with an expensive blowout? It only threw Bent off for a moment before she pulled it together. "Yeah, well, I'm just here for the poker," she said. "Obviously."

"Obviously."

Bent could hear the crickets in the bushy overgrowth that framed the pool area.

Then the stranger spoke up again. "Makes me wish I played poker—it would have been less boring in there."

The more he spoke, the more his voice sounded familiar, but she couldn't be sure. Bent shook her head in the shadows. "Not me."

"Is your brother still at the tables?"

She looked his way, startled. "You know Bach?" There weren't usually Roycers at these things, but she'd learned to be guarded.

Do I know this guy from somewhere? Is he one of Bach's minions?

A flicker of light drifted past them—a candle, floating in the pool. Now she could see that the stranger had dark hair, slicked back behind his ears as if he'd just gotten out of the shower. Still, his face was mostly turned away, and she gave up trying to catch more than just a passing glimpse.

"Is that his name? Bach?" The boy shrugged. "I don't really know him. He lifted some poker chips off me back there, that's all." He laughed.

Oh. Right.

She hadn't noticed anyone in particular at the poker table. Not outside of Bach and his boys.

As if this whole conversation wasn't already embarrassing enough.

Good thing it's dark.

"Yeah, well. You have to watch out. My baby bro is kind of a card shark," Bent said. It was true. "How did you know he was my brother, anyways?"

Because you watch us on TV every week? Because you've seen us play chess in our pajamas? Because you really liked that one episode about the swimming pool?

There were so many different creepy answers to that question, and she had heard them all. For a second, she almost wished the guy had been a criminal. It would at least have been a first.

"I saw you guys laughing together, and he looks like you." The stranger grinned—or frowned. It was honestly hard to tell in the dark. (She could see his teeth flash in the moonlight, however. They were admirably white, even for this town.)

Does this guy really not know who I am? Whoa.

"How long are you going to wait for him?" the boy asked. "I'll keep you company."

Bent shrugged it off, though she was pleased. "We landed on fifteen minutes, but who knows? You don't have to wait with me. You should probably save yourself."

"But then I'll feel guilty when they find your skeleton fused to that lounge chair in a hundred years."

She sucked back a laugh. "Fine. Let's make a run for it. Get out of here while we still have a shot. Cabo? Uber south to the border?"

"Not Cabo, Tulum.[14] Better surf." He nodded—then sighed. "But too far. Morongo? Pechanga? Hit the Indian casinos? Since we both obviously love cards so much."

She pretended to consider it. "Too skeevy. How about Marfa, Texas? Art hipsters and grilled cheese? Texas is close to Mexico."

"If you're a drug runner," the boy said. "Now that's skeevy."

"Hey, it's a job. All jobs suck, don't they?" Bent sighed.

---

14 *JG is in favor of the Mexico references. Great for DiosGlobale product placement. Could Bentley work in a reference to some of the more popular Luchadores here? Esp the ones DiosGlobale has contracts with? Pls revise.* ☺ *—D*

Especially mine. "Not that I'm complaining—but okay, I'm complaining."

"If you're an aspiring drug runner, I'm sorry. I didn't mean to knock it. Sounds like solid, gainful employment." He looked around the pool patio. "At least you have a future."

"Don't you?"

"Not according to my dad. Not if I don't apply myself. Like sunscreen or something." People took sunscreen very seriously in this town.

"Ah. Dads. That's the one problem I don't have. Mine is Mer—*my mom*." Bent stumbled on the word. Then she was struck by the silence; she usually got a knowing laugh when she referenced Mercedes, but this guy didn't say a word. *Really? Nothing? You don't really know who I am?* She kept going. "You and your dad fight much?"

"Nope. Not since I took off."

The sound of breaking glass echoed over the patio, followed by drunken laughter. The fools were all inside—*she'd come out here to escape them, hadn't she?*—and yet something about this boy's voice made Bent herself feel as foolish and giddy now as she had felt at her first Kids' Choice Awards.

"Idiots," he said.

She stole another glance at his face, what she could see of it. "Are you laughing? I can't tell."

"And?"

"And nothing. I just wondered."

"Ah."

"At least you're smiling. I think I heard it."

"You got me. Hold on—lean in."

Bent leaned toward him and smelled the tiny blast of sulfur just as she heard the match strike. He held it up between their faces, and they looked at each other.

It was a quick look, nothing more. They only had a few seconds before the match burned all the way down to nothing.

But there you are, she thought. The match only threw off a bit of light, but it was enough to get a partial sense of him. A glimpse of half a tanned face with angular bones, like he'd been drawn with a messy charcoal. Black hair. Luminous blue eyes. It's you, she thought, even though she was certain they'd never met.

Bent wasn't sure what she was feeling, or even thinking. She couldn't think of how she would know him, or anyone else he could be—at least, not who would be at this party.

"Ow," the boy said, dropping the match to the brick pool deck. He waved his hand in the cool night air.

That was when Bent remembered that the boy had seen her, too, and she found herself beginning to blush. "What do you think?" She tried to sound playful, but inside she was freaking out. "I mean, about me?"

He sat back in his chair. "Deep."

It had sounded like he was teasing, but she couldn't be sure. "Deep?"

"Yeah. You look deep. Anything wrong with that?"

Now she was the one trying not to laugh. "I guess not. It's just—I haven't heard that one before."

"You look like you've got a lot on your mind."

"I do."

"Yeah? A lot of something deep?"

"Sort of. I'm thinking about—" *What am I thinking about? Lifespan? Mercedes? Second chances?*

"Poker?"

"Change," Bent said, surprising herself by answering truthfully. She wasn't going to see him again. There was no reason not to confess all, here in the shadow of the Chateau.

"What kind of change?" He sounded intrigued.

She thought about it. "A paradigm shift. Or maybe a sea change—is that what it's called? Whatever's bigger."

He held up a fist. "I called it. *Deep.* Also, what are you talking about?"

She tried to tap his fist with hers, but she couldn't see it and missed entirely. "When everything changes. A brain departure. An experiential rupture. A transcendental experience. A mind journey."

"You mean like Burning Man?" He was teasing now.

Bent shook her head. "No. I'm talking about a *journey* journey. Where you go away. From this."

"This pool deck?"

"This everything." She knew she sounded melodramatic, and she didn't care. It was how she felt.

"Okay, *Frodo.* Anywhere in particular?"

She took a breath. It was her big secret, and yet here she was, laying it out in the dark to a perfect stranger. "College."

There. She had finally said it to someone, even if it was someone she hardly knew.

"College?"

"Next year. I think I want to go to one." The words sounded strange now that she had said them out loud.

"Not to be rude, but that was sort of anticlimactic." He was chuckling.

"Rude! Very rude! I bared my soul to you, and you're *laughing*?" Bent scolded. She could feel her face getting hot.

"You're right, I'm sorry. Okay. College. So why don't you just go?"

Why don't I?

This time next year, I could be graduating high school and going to college. I could live in a dorm in anonymity. I could eat in a dining hall and do laundry with quarters. I could be like everyone else.

It was something she'd only seen on TV (and everyone knew *the college years* of any high school series sucked) but there it was—and it was what she wanted.

If only.

She sighed, coming back to reality for the moment. "Maybe I will. I'm working on it. Getting there, I think. But I kind of have this weird job that gets in the way."

"Right. I forgot. The aspiring drug runner."

"Yeah, no."

He paused for a second, apparently thinking. "Are you an actor? I mean, seeing as this is Hollywood and all?"

This is crazy. He looked at my face and he still *didn't recognize me.* It was a thrilling thought, and a burst of nervous electricity spread down her spine.

"Sort of," Bent said, keeping her voice even. "Are you?"

"Me? No. Never. I can barely even handle acting like myself. Not to mention acting my age, or acting responsible, or acting like a grown-up. I'd be the world's worst actor." He paused. "But you are one. Okay. That's cool. I'm down with that."

"Also good to know," she said. As she did, she realized she meant it.

"So—you can't just take time off, or whatever?"

"Not really. Not yet. Not take off, I mean, like you did. But I want to—I mean, I hope to."

"What's stopping you?"

"Things. My job. My family. I'm not sure. A lot of stuff is kind of up in the air right now." Please, god, let that be true, Bent thought. "But I was thinking I might still apply to some schools, anyway. I'll be a senior in the fall, and most applications aren't even due until December." Saying it somehow made it seem real.

"Yeah?" the boy asked, but he didn't sound like he knew a thing about it, or cared. "My family would love it if I did that, but I'm not sure I'm what you would call college material."

"Ah. Sucks for you," Bent said.

"I mean, I'm smart enough," he said, a little defensively, which she thought was cute. "I think."

Look at that. He cares what you think of him—how is that not adorable? It's not not *adorable.*

Bent nodded. "I get it. How do you really know, right?"

The cushions squeaked, as if he was settling in. "I figured I might go someday. I mean, I read books. And I like comics," he volunteered, as if that was some kind of evidence of intelligence.

It is.

"Marvel or DC?" Bent asked.

"Marvel, Wolverine, and that's not a real question." *Ding, ding, ding!* "You?"

"Black Widow, and I'll read any spy novel," Bent said.

"Also LA noir. Like, old detective stories," he said. *Right answer.*

"And history books, about wars and military strategies," Bent offered.

"Exactly. And survival narratives. The nonfiction ones," he countered. *Three for three!*

She raised an eyebrow. "Where people live off the land?"

"Is there any other kind?"

"So, zombie apocalypses?" She held her breath. This one was important.

He scoffed. "How else will you know the many uses of duct tape?"

My perfect man.

Bent sat up. "What about toxins and venom and, you know, lethal mold."

The chaise sighed as the boy rustled next to her. "Hey, you should always know what could kill you. That's my policy, anyhow."

"Solid thinking." She tried again. "What's your take on the Big One?"

"Don't get me started." He sounded almost cheery now. "Every sewer pipe in Southern California is going to burst. Everyone in that room back there will suddenly be deprived of their private toilets." They both started laughing at the thought, and he reached for her in the darkness, all the way from his chair to hers, touching her arm with one tentative hand. "So just say all that to a college. I'm sure they'll take you."

"Right? How could they not?" She could feel the goose bumps spreading under his fingers, and she wondered if he could feel them too.

Don't move your arm.

He moved his arm.

Damn it.

"Now you know my big secret," Bent said. "You probably think I'm crazy."

"Of course you're crazy. You're a television star."

"I didn't say television. I also didn't say star." She raised an eyebrow, even if he couldn't see it.

"Okay, starlet."

"Starlet *on hiatus*."

"Another clue. Actress. TV. Hiatus. Zombies. You play a corpse on *Throne of the Undead*?"[15]

"So, so close," Bentley said, smiling in the darkness.

---

15 *Per JG: Could we change this reference to a Lifespan show? Greatest American Ninjacats or similar? ☺ —D*

They sat in comfortable silence now, not really talking and not really minding. The sounds of the party floated down the stairs toward them. She imagined the room. Bach flirting and winning at the tables in back. Porsche flirting and posing for the paparazzi out front. Mercedes flirting and hovering around Jeff Grunburg and his minions.

HA HA HA HA HA. Bent could almost hear her mother's assault laughter now.

Upstairs, everyone would be moving around one another like little schools of fish, where lots of tiny ones feasted off one big one, no matter how they all pretended not to. Nobody would be looking at anybody they were already talking to. What was the point?

Bent gazed up at the stars, what she could see of them in the city sky, which was dark now. *Why do this? Why bother? What does it matter to anyone? What is this?*

The boy moved in the chair next to her.

I can't go on a regular date. A regular person couldn't handle the cameras. I wouldn't expect them to—and I wouldn't do that to them.

She heard the chair scrape as he adjusted it.

Would he want to be with me? What did he see, when he lit that match? Who does he think that girl is?

Then it didn't matter, because Bent saw Bach appear on the stairs and sat up. "I have to go." She stood. The boy stood up next to her. She had hoped standing up would shed some—*any!*—light on his face, but it didn't. His features stayed hidden in shadow.

Oh, come on.

Bent lingered for one last second. "And you were wrong, by the way. I'm no starlet. My sister's the star."

"Ah," said the boy. "There you go. There's the real crisis."

"Why is it a crisis?"

"Because to me, you're the star." And with that, he leaned forward and pulled her by the hand toward him—

Then kissed her cheek, his lips soft and warm in the night.

She felt her face catch fire, turning pink.

It was the sweetest, most unexpected moment of her seventeen years, and she didn't want him to ever stop.

He stopped.

Damn it.

"What's your name?" Bentley breathed.

"Asa," he said, not letting go of her hand. "What's yours?"

"You'll figure it out," she said with a smile. Bent couldn't bring herself to say it. Her name would break the spell— and she was still enjoying the revelation that someone could like her whether or not she was *BEING BENTLEY*.

"I will?"

"Everyone does, eventually." She let go of his fingers as she pulled away, running across the damp bricks until she reached the stairs.

She looked back and smiled. He still hadn't moved. She turned and took the stairs two at a time.

In her hand was his matchbook.

Four

"Mercedes is late," Bentley groused.

Bach shrugged. "Of course Mercedes is late."

Bent stared across the white-linen-covered bistro table at her sweating brother, who looked as miserable as she felt. Santa Ana winds were blowing in from the desert today, which made the air in the café unbearably hot and dry, even in the shade of the white canvas umbrella over their heads. Regardless, Production had refused to scrap the shoot.

"Production" meaning Mercedes.

So here they were, shooting where the Royce family meetings were always shot: the semi-fabulous rooftop restaurant on the fifth floor of the Beverly Hills store of Barneys New York, known for its killer view.

"It's hiatus," Bentley groaned. "Why did she make us come back and shoot a stupid family meeting two weeks into hiatus? When the season's over, it's supposed to be over, right?"

"Right," Bach said, leaning forward in his chair.

"Hold still," Ted (camera one) said, shoving a mic inside Bach's shirt collar. Ted was a good guy; he had once come to school with the younger Royces on Grandparents and Special Friends Day. (Mercedes no longer spoke to her own parents and didn't really do *friends*, special or not.)

"What did you have to cancel today, Ted?" Bent asked the hulking cameraman. She tried not to look at his pit stains, which now reached almost down to his waist.

"Me? Had a tee time with the crew at Rancho Park." Ted shook his red dreadlocks (Dred Ted, that was what Bach and Bent had first called him) and puffed out his pink cheeks beneath them. "No big." That was all Dred Ted had ever said for five years now regarding Mercedes and her last-minute production changes. Dred Ted was a wise man.

"I was supposed to be surfing." Bach shook his head as Ted dropped the mic cord down his back. "Some guys from my poker club were meeting up at Zuma."

"You don't surf," Bent said, annoyed at the mention of her brother's poker habit. In the two weeks since the benefit, he'd played every day. He was acting like Porsche did when she fell off the Diet Coke wagon. One day she had given it up—the next, you opened her car door and all the empty soda cans fell out.

"I might have surfed. I like cute boys in wet suits." Bach shrugged. "Now I guess we'll never know."

Mac (camera two) held up a mic. "Your turn, B. Let's get you wired up."

Bent leaned forward in her distressed wicker chair. Mac pulled out the tails of her shirt (Ulla Johnson) and ran the cord up her back over her bra strap and bare skin, just as he had most days for the past five years. He knew (and didn't care) that her bra would be some kind of horrible running bra, just the same way that she knew (and didn't care) that his fingernails would be black with motorcycle grease. That was the nature of the bond.

Beyond Mac and Ted and occasionally JoJo (camera three), if anyone's underwear managed to show, there was no one left to notice; the restaurant patio was full of tables and empty of customers, except for Bentley and Bach. Even though it was Sunday, and even though the deck was normally crowded, no restaurant turned the Royce family away—not when they were filming. If the network used the footage, the social media payoff would be huge; people would drive in from as far as Phoenix or Salt Lake City, just for the photo op.

So the tables were held, and the regular people were turned away, making it clear that unknown social media followers who may or may not ever show up to eat were somehow ten times more important than real customers who were already waiting outside. LA ran on invisible rules like that. Sure, there was a whole lot of talk about the freedom of food trucks and taco shacks (*carne asada is not a crime!*)[16] and how you could wear sneakers (*Golden Goose!*) and jeans (*size zero!*) into any restaurant in town—but that was only if you were young and hot and as toned as a free-range chicken.

Or if you happened to be a part of the Mercedes Royce Show.

In a few minutes, Mercedes would be able to pretend to

---

16 *It is to us vegans!* ☹ —D

enjoy the view of sky and palm trees and hills—and, thanks to Mac and Ted and JoJo and the rest of the *RWTR* crew—nobody else would.[17]

"I see you broke out the man-bun today," Bent said, looking back at her brother. "That's new. I mean, for you." Bach's longish gold-brown hair was pulled up and out of his eyes in a kind of stubby, perspiring ponytail that sprouted like a damp mushroom cap on the crown of his head.

Bach reached up to feel for himself. "I know, I know. I'm pathetic. I was going for less of a man-bun and more of a man-doughnut. Seeing as every guy in the room when we were at the Chateau last time had one."

"Not the whole flock." Bentley grinned. Talking about the party sent a secret thrill down her spine. She reached her hand into her pocket and held on to Asa's matchbook, a pleasant reminder that meeting the mystery boy had been real, not a dream.

And that it—he—the night—had been amazing.

Even if I can't find him on Instagram or Snapchat or Facebook or Twitter or anywhere, she thought, even if he hasn't found me yet either.

She took the matchbook out of her pocket and held it between two fingers. In blue cursive letters it read *Philippe's*. She wondered where Philippe's was, and if she could find him there. Her search of the matchbook's origins had turned up few suitably glam A-lister alternatives; all

---

17 *Per JG: So we'll need to hire a fake camera crew to follow our fake/real Royce family around while our real camera crew follows the fake crew around? Budget note for pilot. —D*

she'd found was a bar in Kyoto, a restaurant in New York, and a chef in Montreal.

"Fine," Bach said, mistaking her smile for a laugh, feeling for his hair. "So it's more like a man mini-doughnut."

"Try doughnut hole," Bent said, still smiling.

"Stop. I'm already starving." Bach looked at Ted. "Where *are* they?"

"Five minutes," Ted replied, holding up his walkie. "Pam just got a sighting on *MRSDIVA*." Mercedes drove a massive white Mercedes SUV that looked like an ambulance; the crew tracked her (for their own safety, Bentley thought) by her unmistakable vanity plate. At least it was better than her convertible, which had the plates *MRSMERC*. The Mercenary Royce nickname had sprung up as soon as she'd brought it home.

"Wow. Five minutes? That's almost punctual for her. You know those reality show divas," Bent added, in a lame attempt to improve her brother's mood. (Diva jokes were his favorite.)

"Yeah, yeah. Easy on the reality, double down on the diva," Bach said, with a melodramatic sigh. "Today I starve while last time we shot here I had to eat lunch six times back-to-back. Order, fight, pee, change, repeat. The Diva isn't just late, she's cruel."

"The Diva giveth and the Diva taketh away," Bentley agreed.

And then, as if they'd somehow conjured her up themselves, the Diva was upon them—and the easy camaraderie of cast and crew instantly vanished.

"Is this the setup I asked for, Teddy?" Mercedes stepped into the center of the deck, JoJo (camera three) scurrying after her. "Is Mac going to tape down these cables? Someone's going to die here, and I'm going to get sued, and you're going to get fired—and not in that order." The crew went scrambling until her path was clear and the surrounding white umbrellas were tipped up, just so. Once satisfied, Mercedes launched herself toward the table, sat, and dropped her bag at her feet.

"God, this weather. Can we set up fans or something? Blow the haze away? *Pam?* Where's Pam? And where's my drink? *Hello?* Do none of you even *show up* until I get here?" Her minions went running, which was what she expected and more to the point what she felt she *deserved*, Bentley knew. Greatness demanded effort, her mother liked to say, not just from herself but from everyone around her.

Effort was an understatement—but great Mercedes Royce was.

Today, if not exactly dazzling, she was something in all white, even in the bleak heat. She was shining. Glaring, maybe. It was her signature color. White suit jacket. White fitted pencil skirt. Cristophe salon blowout. Chunky eighteen-karat collar and cuffs. Rings on her fingers and bells on her toes, Bentley thought. That's my mama.

Mercedes picked up a waiting mic from the table, tucking the cord expertly behind her lapel, before Ted could take a step toward her. She looked back to the doorway expectantly. "Come *on*. What are you *doing* in there?"

Cue the sister.

Porsche, smacking her lips and waving a lip-gloss wand, followed in her mother's path with less commotion but no less magnificence. As always, Porsche *nailed it* when they were shooting. Her fitted black Dolce dress—everything black, that was Porsche's go-to color—dove down between the truly exceptional breasts she had gotten for her sixteenth birthday. Her face was equally impeccable, with utterly flawless, Cleopatra-perfect makeup, and—beneath her enormous custom Parisian sunglasses—about as much eyeliner. Her mouth was drawn with a vibrant rose, huge and lush and glossy.

There was no denying it. Porsche Royce was a marvel, even to her little sister. She was the very definition of femininity, like the armless lady statue in the Louvre. (The one on the stairs that they'd rushed by on the way out, when Bach had to pee.) Or like the ancient whatever fertility goddess on the slide from Bentley's art history class. On days like today, my sister makes most women seem like men in comparison, Bent thought.

"How do I look?" Porsche pursed her glossy lips.

"Hideous," Bach said.

"My thong is totally riding up my crack," she said, unfazed. With that, she dropped her Lippies by Porsche lip-gloss wand and jammed on her mic.

"Lovely," Mercedes said.

As Diva Number Two sat back, Mac and Ted and now JoJo circled the table with their handhelds, getting into position.

Producer Pam lurked in the doorway, muttering into her headset as a row of waiters lugged fans out to the patio, per Mercedes's request. (*As if they really could blow the haze away!*) "Quiet on set," Pam called out, raising one hand into the air. The waiters froze in place. "And we're rolling."

A waiter in an entirely different uniform and with significantly more chiseled cheekbones—probably played by an out-of-work actor—scurried over, holding a tray of drinks.

Mercedes smiled flirtatiously at him. "Wow, that was fast."

Porsche made a point of ignoring him; she only flirted with herself, or at least people more famous than she was.

"Sweet shackles, Mercedes." Bach looked his mother over. "Jingle all the way, babe." Bach was improvising, as usual; he never bothered to read the scripts ahead of time, which drove his mother insane—also as usual.

"Is that any way to talk to the woman who keeps you in Rag and Bone?" *Another classic m-word dodge.* Mercedes glanced around to make sure the cameras were still rolling, and then grabbed Bach by both cheeks. "Darling boy. *Kiss, kiss.*" But they were just words. No actual kisses were exchanged. There was entirely too much lipstick involved for that.

She reached for Bent's hand across the table, giving it a quick-clawed squeeze. "Sorry to keep you waiting, *lovey*. The paparazzi chased me all the way here. I swear they're trying to kill me."

"Whatever," Bad Bentley said, rolling her eyes per the script—though today's write-up had been pretty sketchy, even for the *RWTR* writers' room. Probably because: hiatus. What the hell were they even doing here on what should have been their time off? She hoped the crew was getting paid time and a half.

Porsche kissed the air in Bach's direction, as well. He waved her off lazily. "Kiss, kiss to you, too, big sister."

She tossed Bent her lip gloss. "New color. Lippies by Porsche, Summer Salmon."

"Ew." Bent wrinkled her nose (which wasn't in the script, but in fairness, Porsche's endless product placements never were either). "*Fish*-gloss? Gross."

"It's a *color*," Porsche said, now irritated.

"Plain iced tea," the waiter said, putting a glass of murky brown liquid in front of Bach. He enunciated carefully as he spoke, which was always what happened when an extra landed a speaking part; they sounded like GPSs. "Muddled mint lemonade," he continued, placing a glass of white-and-green fizz in front of Bent. The Diet Cokes he slid silently to Mercedes and Porsche, which meant Pam was paying by the line.

Bent picked up her mint lemonade and waited for the latest salvo in the war between her mother and herself over the extra three (*two? one?*) pounds she carried on her bubble butt, which had become one of this year's recurring story lines.

Mercedes clucked. (It was her on-camera *disapproving mother* sound.) "Drink tea, not lemonade, Bentley."

Bent shrugged. "You know I don't like plain tea. It tastes like wood." She stuck out her tongue. Bach kicked her under the table, which he did every time she gave in and stuck out her tongue, as instructed by the Bentley Bible.

"Nothing tastes as good as skinny feels," Mercedes said sternly. It was one of her favorite lines, and she had a habit of adding it to every script.

"God, listen to yourself," Bentley said, scooting her chair farther away from her mother in annoyance. (Another beloved on-camera #RWTR joke.)

Bach drank from his glass. "Skinny doesn't taste that bad. You get used to it." This time, Bent kicked her brother beneath the table. *Suck-up.* He already *was* skinny—damn him and his Adderall.

"Is that my Diet Coke? Did nobody order me extra ice?" Porsche ate like one of Satan's hounds guarding the entrance to hell. Strips of flesh and Diet Coke or water, depending on whether she was on or off the soda—her own personal crack.

Nothing else entered her body.

"It's the weather," the fake waiter said apologetically, before disappearing in search of ice that could withstand a Santa Ana wind—and a possible second performance. (Bent doubted he would find either.)

"So let's cut to the chase. Why are we here, Mercedes?" Bach was already shuffling a deck of cards in one hand, beneath the tablecloth. He looked nervous, and Bent realized she was nervous too.

Right from the start, when Mercedes had landed them the show, Porsche was the anointed alpha dog; Bent privately thought of her mother and sister as *Thing One* and *Thing Two*. Everything was about the two of them, and they were a fierce doubles act; if the Royce family was Under

Mercedes, it was also About Porsche. Which was a pretty scary feeling for the other people in the family—for your own life to never be about, well, *you*—to be B- or C- or even D-listed by your own flesh and blood. Whereas other families maybe had favorite children, the Royce family had *stars* and *additional cast members*. Which, as bad as it might be, *felt* even worse—at least for the additional cast members.

Bach kicked her under the table. *Focus, B. They're filming.*

"Yeah, what he said. Let's get this party started already," Bent said. "Before we melt." She didn't feel like making a Bad Bentley face, and couldn't think of a rude enough comment, so she just tried to slurp her lemonade as loudly as she could.

"Absolutely. You're here," Mercedes finally said, sitting tall in her seat (*Golden string, Mercedes! Golden string!*) ". . . because I have News."

Hmm. Also not in the script.

"Please say syndication." Bach was momentarily intrigued. "Please, *please* say syndication."

Porsche snorted—*not* one of her approved on-camera sounds—and put down her Diet Coke with a thump. "Are you kidding? Syndication? *Dream on*, guys."

"*CUT!*" Mercedes yelled.

Mac and Teddy looked at Pam, and then slowly lowered their cameras.

JoJo kept filming. (It was Lifespan policy to keep one camera rolling, in case Jeff Grunburg wanted to go through the footage later. Privately, Mercedes felt like this was just another tactic in the psychological war the two of them waged on each other, the ongoing battle of who worked for whom.[18])

Mercedes turned on Porsche. "Really? *Dream on?* You just couldn't keep that one to yourself?"

Bentley raised an eyebrow. *Mercedes snapping at Porsche? Is there a crack in the Great Wall of Diva?*

"It's his fault." Porsche glared at her brother. "We've been off track since we started. If you for once ever learned the script—"

"Yeah? At least I'm not the reason we just had to stop shooting." Bach scowled.

Porsche rolled her eyes. "What was I supposed to say? *Syndication?* At the rate we're going, that will *never* happen. This isn't *Duke of Ducks.* I'm not Joelynne Wabash. We don't have a secret family recipe for duckloaf. We'll never be syndicated."

"We don't know that," Mercedes began.

"Don't we? Then how come we haven't even heard a word about *next* season yet?" Porsche started to stress-frown, and then realized what she was doing and took a breath, massaging her face with her fingertips. (Stress wrinkles, Bentley knew from her sister's daily lectures, went *deep.* Maybe even the *deepest.*)[19]

"Well, that's why we're doing something about it,"

---

18 *JG points out that the* RWTR *contracts are perfectly transparent on this point, and suggests this addition: "Even if it was clear to* LITERALLY *everyone else that Jeff Grunburg was the boss of Mercedes Royce." (He'd also suggest bolding.)* ☺ —D

19 *JG asks: How deep? JG is concerned, will circle back on this. (I'd actually like to know too.)* ☹ —D

MARGARET STOHL * 61

Mercedes said calmly. Only she wasn't calm, Bent knew. Mercedes never bothered to make herself *sound* calm when she actually *felt* calm.

Uh-oh. That's not good.

"Doing? Doing *what*? There's nothing we can *do!*" Porsche, unlike her mother, was practically wailing. "We're getting boxed out. Everyone's so busy *not* talking about it and *not* picking up when we call and *not* asking us for favors and *not* inviting us on their planes, it's almost like they're rubbing it in."

Bentley looked at her sister. "Not to be negative, but would it really be the worst thing in the world? If we were, you know, cance—"

"*Don't say it!*" Porsche shrieked. "Don't put those vibes into the atmosphere! If you say it, it could happen, and then what would we do?"

"Go back to our regular lives? Go to school? Get jobs? Contribute to the greater good of society, for a change?" Even before the words left her mouth, Bent knew that she was pressing her luck.

"*What?*"

"*Bentley!*"

Both Mercedes and Porsche looked like they'd been struck. Bentley sighed. At least she could give them that to agree on. Even if it meant Bach's foot was now digging into her ankle.

Mercedes recovered first. She leaned across the table and clutched Bentley's hand. "I know why you feel you need to say these *hateful* things, Bentley. I know you're *terrified* on the inside that the *unspeakable* will happen, and that you don't know what you'll do if you have to go back to *regular* life."

"Okaaaay," Bentley said. She looked back at the cameras, because Mercedes was definitely doing her on-camera voice. Ted's and Mac's green indicator lights were still off, though. Only JoJo circled around Mercedes now. She's getting primed, Bent thought. This is just the lead-up. Proceed with extreme caution.

Mercedes kept going. "But we *are* going to make it. I *promise* you that. *Literally* nothing else in our life matters, not to me. Because I am your *mother*."

Bent and Bach locked eyes. Mercedes had used the m-word.

"Wait. *Literally* nothing?" Bach asked.

Kick, kick. Bent answered him beneath the table.

"But you're right, Porsche. We've got to up the stakes for next season if we want to stay in the game. Joelynn Wabash is this year's headliner, that's true. That's also part of the reason why I want you to meet someone. A very special someone." Mercedes looked at Pam. Pam's arm shot up, and the cameras went back on.

An ambush, Bent thought. Not in the script, but Pam's in on it. Then she caught the look on her sister's face—which was shock. *Wait—Porsche's as clueless as we are? How is that possible?* Since when did Mercedes start keeping Porsche out of the loop?

It wasn't possible.

Porsche recovered seconds later, just as all three cameras began to move in on the family. She made a point of adjusting her face so it stayed out of the sun—or rather, the direct line of both Mac's and Teddy's shots—while she pulled herself together. "You know I hate surprises, Mercedes."

"Well, you're all going to love this one," Mercedes said, looking mischievous. "He's just in the other room. I've invited a very special boy to come live with us. A beautiful baby boy. And we're going to raise him as a Royce."

The cameras swiveled for the reaction shot (which, as it turns out, was not one they would have missed—no matter where they were positioned on the patio).

"*What the hell, Mercedes?!*" Porsche knocked over her Diet Coke and staggered to her feet, dripping wet.

"*A WHAT?!*" Bach looked at his mother blankly.

"*The hell?!*" Porsche said again, this time more loudly.

"*A BABY?!*" Bach said, incredulous.

"*MERCEDES! YOU CANNOT TAKE CARE OF A BABY!*" By the time Porsche got the words out, she was shouting.

Not Bentley. She said nothing. She didn't know what to say. She had never in her life seen her sister turn on her mother like that. When Mercedes drove, Porsche rode shotgun. When they sat in a restaurant booth, it was always assumed that Porsche got the seat next to her mother. And the spare Birkin. And the second producer credit. And the extra Emmys ticket . . .

It's not possible, Bent thought again. Thing One and Thing Two aren't supposed to fight like this. The Divas were . . . the Divas. The stars were the stars.

And yet here they were, her sister screaming at her

mother as if she were something lower than an additional cast member.

Bach slammed his hand on the table with mock excitement. "*Of course* Mercedes can't take care of a baby. Which is why this whole angle is *genius!*"

"Oh, please," Mercedes said.

"*Nothing* about this is genius," Porsche barked.

"Oh, yeah? You know what's *really* going to move the dial on our ratings? When *our mother* is arrested for *reckless endangerment of a baby!*" Bach started clapping. "Well played, Mercedes. Even for you, well played."

"You're being rude." Mercedes drew herself up, pushing back her seat. She looked straight at Porsche. "I don't deserve this, and I'm hurt, really. Have a little faith. I know what I'm doing."

"*'I know what I'm doing'?!*" Porsche began laughing hysterically. "*Says the adoptive parent of my new baby brother?!*"[20]

"You might as well at least *meet* the poor thing. Especially since we had Production drag him *the whole way* from *Ojai* along with his *team*. You have no idea, the *paperwork*." Mercedes sniffed.

Porsche and Bent and Bach were speechless.

"Stay there, I'll bring him out. We can pick it up with a new reaction shot." Mercedes rushed back to the patio door, motioning to Pam. "Probably *joy*, right? Or maybe *surprise*? Pam? What did the writers say? Do we need to do more

---

20 *Per JG: Remind Marketing—prime opportunity to promote our BigBoxBaby megastores! —D*

than *joy*?" Mercedes disappeared into the restaurant.

"Joy should cover it," Pam said, as if nothing strange was happening at all. Then she turned to the Royce kids. "Can you guys give me joy?"

"Seriously?" Porsche looked at their producer, disgusted.

"Do I *look* like I'm joking?" Pam did not. (She never did.) She bent over the table now, leaning on the back of Mercedes's empty wicker chair. "It's hot. It's hiatus. We're now in time and a half." She raised her head and stared straight at the three remaining Royces. "So can you please *get it together* and *give me some freaking joy*? GIVE. ME. SOME. FREAKING. JOY. That's *all* I want to see or hear from *any* of you."

The siblings stared. Bent's heart was pounding. She didn't know what to think if even Pam was losing it now.

Pam stood up straight again. "I need more Bentley. More Bach. And you, Porsche?" She looked serious. "Dial it down. I need way less Porsche for the rest of the day, okay? Okay."

Less Porsche. Two words that had never been said before. Porsche was so surprised, she didn't say anything at all.

"Fabulous." Pam turned back toward the patio door. "Quiet on set." Her arm flew up. "And . . . we're *rolling*. Bring him in!"

They could only hear Mercedes's voice at first. "Come here, Hope. Come with Mama, Hope. That's what I'm calling you. My sweet baby Hope."

Mama? Impossible.

Mercedes emerged in the doorway, calling over her shoulder—but to what, Bent couldn't tell.

"Hope! Come here, hot stuff. Come give your new *big sister Porsche* a big kiss. She *really, really, really* wants to meet you."

Bent held her breath—

As the three cameras swung around in the direction of the newest member of the Royce family—

As Mercedes lifted up what appeared to be an orange-and-brown leather Hermès leash—

And as an enormous feathered creature waddled out behind her.

"*A DUCK?*" Bent said, choking on the words.

"*IT'S A DUCK?*" Bach shouted.

"*WHAT THE DUCK?!*" Porsche howled.

Mercedes smiled. It was a duck, all right—and not just any duck. Hope the Duck was the size of the turkey they'd eaten at the LA Country Club last Thanksgiving. To be honest, Hope was just a few webbed feet short of being the size of a Smart car. He was no gentle turtledove either.

"Hope is from Joelynne Wabash's wild game supplier. Get it? He's *Duke of Ducks* royalty," Mercedes said proudly. "Take that, Joelynne. This is one feathery fricassee you'll never lay your lips on."

Nobody said anything. Not in words, anyway.

QUAAAAAAAAAACK!

The approach of mother and duck was accompanied by a chaotic chorus of flapping and fluttering and feathers flying.

Bent stared at the thrashing animal. "I don't . . . I can't . . ."

"Oh my god," Porsche said. She sunk back down into her chair and started to cry. "That's it. I can't do this. I give up. It's over."

"Don't talk like that. You'll scare *Hopie*." Mercedes yanked the leash harder. "He's part of our family now." As if in answer, Hope hopped up onto Mercedes's empty chair and scrambled to the top of the table, knocking over Bentley's (almost full) lemonade glass and stepping straight into a plate of soft (completely untouched) butter— narrowly missing Mercedes's Diet Coke.

QUAAAAAAAAACK!

Porsche cried harder. Bach put his arm around his sister. "It's okay, P." He patted her back. "Everything will be okay."

"Stop crying! I said stop!" Mercedes was getting frustrated now. She couldn't handle this many emotions in one day. "This will work. *I'm telling you!* Hope is going to fix everything. You just aren't seeing it yet!"

Porsche snapped. "Give up, Mercedes! How *desperate* do you think this looks?" She sprung to her feet. "You think people are just going to buy that we're suddenly *duck people* now? Well, *they won't*! Because *we're not*! We're *nothing*! We're not getting another season and we're just as *pathetic* as *everyone thinks we are!*"

"*Not everyone,*" Bach began, standing up—but Bentley pulled him right back down into his chair. This wasn't a fight for *additional cast members* like the two of them. Not when the Divas were facing off.

"Do you have a *better idea*?" Mercedes was starting to lose it herself.

"Better than making us *a joke*? *A low-class, white-trash joke?*" Porsche hurled back. "Of course I do!"

"*GREAT! PITCH ME! GO ON, DAZZLE ME!* Since you suddenly know everything—what's *your idea*, Porsche? What's your *big high-class trash-don't-stink million-dollar idea*? If you've got one, by all means *let's hear it!*" Mercedes's voice grew louder as she spoke, until she was shouting. Porsche was clearly caught off guard.

"*WELL?!*" Mercedes roared.

"*NOW?*" Porsche was blushing. "I don't know—I guess—*Oh, come on*, Mercedes, it doesn't work like that. I'd have to brainstorm—storyboard—consult—that kind of thing takes time—" She looked at her brother and sister for help.

"Sure," Bent said from the table.

"That's what I've heard." Bach tried his best to be supportive. Of course, neither sibling had ever been asked to pitch or storyboard anything before.

Mercedes yanked the leash in front of her. "*Of course* you've got *nothing*! You *complain* and *complain*, but do *any* of you ever *do anything*? *No! Never! Why should you?*"

"I'm at *every meeting* you're at, Mercedes!" Porsche's eyes narrowed. The worst was not yet over, it seemed.

"And I'm the *only one* who actually *does what it takes* to *help* this family!" Mercedes was as red-cheeked and emotional as Porsche now. She yanked the leash again.

QUAAAAAAAAAAAAACK!

The panicked duck couldn't take it anymore. It flung itself into their faces, flapping its wings and stomping its flippers and as a result upsetting nearly every drink, breadbasket, salt and pepper shaker, and bowl of artisanal sugar cubes on the table in one spin around the center.

Bach rolled out of his seat. Bentley pushed her chair away from the table. Porsche screamed. *"HELP?* This is your idea of *HELP?"*

"At least I'm doing SOMETHING!"

"You think this is something?" Porsche was apoplectic. *"What do you think I've been doing all this time? I thought my Lippies Line would save us—but my entire product line is tanking! I've got a twenty-million-dollar budget shortfall, and you're buying the family a pet duck? Wake up, Mercedes! You guaranteed my loans. We're not just going to lose the show—we're going to lose the house!"*

QUAAAAAAAAAAAAACK!

Hope the Duck must have mistaken Porsche's scream for the sound of an enemy predator, because its beak shot toward her heaving chest with the power and precision of a martial artist.

QUAAAAAAAAAAAAACK! QUAAAAAAAAAAAAACK! QUAAAAAAAAAAAAACK!

Bentley's heart stopped. She couldn't listen to another word. She felt herself pulling away, letting the chaos of the rooftop restaurant dissolve around her. Before she knew it, she was plugging her ears. She couldn't bear it. Her whole world—everything she'd thought she understood, every fixed point of her known, dependable universe—had all just gone into free fall.

"Bentley"—Bach leaned in toward her, a look of genuine concern in his sparkling green eyes—"I think we're losing it. What are we supposed to do?" He sounded shocked, like he'd been slapped in the face, which was increasingly likely, given the flurry of avian and human limbs.

Do?

How was she supposed to know?

Did Bach think this was in the Bentley Bible? Because it wasn't—and that was about all she knew for certain. They were off the map, in uncharted Royce family waters.

This is what's going on, she wanted to say. *The Royces are not all right.*

Each person in their family was even more terrified than the poor, thrashing duck in front of them now—and *that* was what really scared Bentley.

If Mercedes and Porsche are like this now—what will they be like if we don't *make it?*

If we do *get canceled? If we have to move?*

How could they survive that?

Bentley had no clue. She didn't know what to say or even think. Instead, she found herself beginning to hum.

Times are bad and getting badder, ain't we got fun?

She closed her eyes, blocking out her screaming mother and her crying sister and her thrashing duck brother and her dumbstruck human one.

In the meantime, in between time, ain't we got fun?

She imagined her mother driving the RV down the dusty I-15, singing to stay awake while the three of them lay on the bed in the way back.

The rich get richer and the poor get poorer . . .

She could picture Porsche running ahead of her into

the Dairy Queen. Mercedes laughing, carrying Bach on her hip, behind them. Counting out enough nickels and quarters and dimes at the register for four chocolate-dipped cones. Bent could hear the sound of the coins hitting the counter—hitting and falling and rolling right across the sticky aluminum steel. They sounded like love.

Ain't we got, ain't we got, ain't we got fun?

Porsche screamed—and Bentley opened her eyes just in time to see Hope the Duck attack again.

"STOP THAT!" Mercedes yanked its leash. Now the duck whirled around, this time going for Mercedes's gold-studded Hermès collar, shrieking as it did.

"Watch out—" Bach yelled.

"OH, NO YOU DON'T! NOT THE HERMÈS!" Mercedes swung her purse at it. *"THINK AGAIN, YOU FILTHY ANIMAL!"*

QUAAAAAAAAAAAAACK!

The leash went flying. The duck went flying.

Porsche knocked it back toward her mother, who swung again, smacking it clear into the air with a single adrenaline-powered surge.

QUAAAAAAAAAAAACK! QUAAAAAAAAAAAACK!

Hope the Duck spun into the cloudless blue sky. The cameras swung to track it.

"No—no, no, no—" Bentley shouted, suddenly realizing what was happening. She lunged after Hope again—the leash only a fraction of an inch from her outstretched fingers—

But it was too late.

They all watched—Royces and crew alike—as the poor

duck went soaring over the stone balustrade that edged the rooftop of Barneys.

The cameras stayed on it.

It arched into the sky and desperately began to flap—

If only ducks could fly.

At most, ducks could get off the ground a few feet, then settle down. They certainly couldn't carry their weight this high in the air—especially not with the additional heft of the leather Hermès collar and leash—oops!

QUAAAAAAAAAAAAAAAAAAAAAAAAAAAAAAAAA AAAAAAAAAAAAAAAAAAAAAAAAAAAAAAAAAAAAA AAAAAaaaaaaaaaaaaaaaaaaaaaaaackkkkkkkkkkkkkkkkkk . . .

Mercedes, Porsche, Bentley, and Bach stood helplessly by as Hope plummeted five stories down. It was right then that Bentley Royce had an epiphany, and not just that her family needed to make a rather large donation to the ASPCA.[21]

She had no choice but to face two facts—and they stuck with her the whole time she winced and waited for the inevitable thud.

First, someone had to do something. Even if keeping *Rolling with the Royces* on the air was no easier than teaching a duck to fly, it was the only chance they had.

And second, the Royce family had finally hit rock—

THUD.

Bottom.[22]

---

21 *Jeff's daughter Tallulah "Saved Animals" as her Mitzvah project, so JG will have Tallulah (or T's assistant, Felicity) get back to us with notes on which groups to mention here! (Expect Post-its; T has Felicity drive them over most afternoons. One at a time.)* ☺ —*D*
22 *Reminder: pls destroy this footage. It can never surface. Ever. Anywhere.* ☹ —*D*

DUKE OF DUCKS SPIN-OFF *DUCK CAKE WARS* GREENLIT; *ROLLING WITH THE ROYCES* ROLLS DOWNHILL

AP: Beverly Hills, California

Via Celebcity.com

What's better than a reality television cooking show based on duck hunting season? A reality television cooking show based on duck hunting season AND high-fructose corn syrup consumption—two time-honored American pastimes rolled into one!

Further proving that more is more, and that when it comes to Hollywood, success always has a formula, cable's latest reality cooking show offering, *Duke of Ducks*, has just announced that a duck-themed cupcake contest spin-off is in the works for the fall lineup: *Duck Cake Wars*, starring *Duke of Duck*'s own Joelynne Wabash!

"I love cupcakes and hunting season and just getting out there and doing my public-speaking stuff, so this is a dream come true," said Joelynne Wabash (rocking beaded bangles and matching bead-and-feather earrings, both by Walmart), who will now be moving to Hollywood for her new show. "And this is a big middle finger to everyone who told me I'd never get famous unless I got braces."

Teeth aside, when you're hot you're hot, and when you're not you're not, and unfortunately for Hollywood's longest-running reality cabler, *Rolling with the Royces*, there isn't even a duck on the menu—unless you count the lame duck the show has become in the Lifespan lineup.

"I'm confident the Roycers will come out to support

us for a sixth season, just as they have for the past five," Mercedes Royce said, in a statement issued by her representatives. "Lifespan is part of our family, and the definition of family is the people who stand by you throughout the ups and downs. Isn't it?"

Jeff Grunburg, Lifespan's top exec, was unavailable for comment at the time of printing. His assistant, Dirk Daniels, did say this: "*Rolling with the Royces* is all about THE JOURNEY. And of course THE FEELS. And the CLIMB." When pressed for clarification, he had no comment.[23]

(Disclosure: Celebcity is a fully owned subsidiary of the Lifespan Network, which is itself a fully owned subsidiary of DiosGlobale.)

Follow @celebcity for breaking details,
or www.celebcity.com.

---

23 *I feel this statement was perfectly self-explanatory.* ☹ —*D*

Five

Bentley knew better than to leave important moments to her mother and sister. That was why she now stood, digital tablet in hand, trying to wedge her way into the green-light meeting on the other side of this conference room door. Mercedes and Porsche had just walked right through it, but Jeff Grunburg had blocked her path the moment Bent had tried to follow them inside.

"Sorry, kid. This one's not open to the public." Jeff smiled a very Jeff smile, which was to say not so much a friendly expression of emotion as an aggressive baring of teeth. Beyond the frosted glass door, Bent could hear the other executives in the room laugh. (Mercedes said they were Jeff Grunburg's human laugh track.[24] She said all Top Execs wanted one, the same way they wanted a personal bathroom in their office, as if crapping on people and crapping on other things were all related.)[25]

"Bentley! What do you think you're doing?" Mercedes

_____

24 *Jeff prefers the term "direct reports."* ☹ —D
25 *Per JG: Think of it as an executive parking spot, only for asses.* ☺ —D

looked horrified from the other side of the door. "You and Bach can wait for us outside, like always."

"I'm not *the public*," Bentley said, glaring down at Jeff. (She was a good two or three *man-buns* taller than he was.)[26] "And I just need a minute."

"Well, that's a minute more than you've got," Jeff said, activating his human laugh track. As he spoke, rage began bubbling inside her chest, until her whole body shook. She lowered the tablet in her hand so he wouldn't notice.

Calm down. You want him to think of you as a grown-up? Act like a grown-up.

It was up to Bentley now. Porsche and Mercedes had been with the Royce money managers every afternoon, and from the way they fled to their separate rooms (Mercedes to the master suite, Porsche to the pool house) the moment they got home, it didn't seem like anything had been resolved.

Which had left them little time for working out season-six story line pitches.

Enter Bentley.

The Royces were a televised train wreck, and they were in desperate need of a mechanic. As a result, like any responsible, concerned passenger, Bentley had been forced to reconsider her priorities. Frankly, the more Bent thought about what her family would be like when and if they were left on their own—when and if the cameras had moved on—the more she realized the scenario could only ever be one of unspeakable horror. The Royces were not a *normal*

---

26 *Jeff feels this comment is sexist and suggests you replace "taller than he was" with "too tall." Or similar.* ☹ —D

family, and they would never be cut out for *normal* life. There was no plan B. There was only plan Bentley.

Bent stood tall *(Golden string! Golden string!)* and eyed Jeff Grunburg. "If you don't have one minute, then I guess you're going to miss out on all my *killer* story line ideas for season six."

"Your killer story line ideas? For season six? I don't know which part of that is funnier!" Jeff himself was laughing now. "Okay, kid, you got me. That's *hilarious*." It actually wasn't.

"I'm not going anywhere until you at least listen to my ideas," Bentley said.

He didn't appear to be moving out of her way, so she took a deep breath and dug in. "The problem with our show is that it's gotten predictable, right? So how about the whole arc for the upcoming season is *RWTR: RELATABLE*. And that's the basic idea. It's about *real reality*. The Bentley character stops acting like a jerk, and the Porsche character stops acting like just a dumb bombshell, and maybe the Bach character finds true love, and the Mercedes character goes to work in a real job, as the CEO of Porsche's Lippies line. . . . I don't know, we could do, like, family therapy, get a dog or something . . ."

Jeff was laughing so hard, he had tears in his eyes when Porsche darted back out through the door to her sister's side, blocking his view of her. Porsche lowered her voice. "What are you doing, B?"

"I've been brainstorming," Bent said stubbornly, holding up her tablet. "You guys need me in there, now more than ever. I can help, just like Mercedes said. So let me."

Porsche shook her head at her sister sadly. "I think that's the sweetest thing anyone's ever tried to do for me, Bent." She glanced over her shoulder, back into the conference room. "Also probably the stupidest."

"I'm not an idiot." Bentley stood her ground, or at least her doorway. "I've been on this show as long as you guys have."

"But you've never been in one of these rooms, and that's a different thing. And especially now, with this whole *Lippies* mess . . ." Porsche shrugged.

"But you don't have to do it alone. You can't," Bent said, because she knew it was true.

Porsche reached for Bentley's hand—but grabbed her by the wrist. It was how the big sister and the little sister had always held hands, how Porsche had pulled Bent safely through a thousand parking lots and across a thousand playgrounds. "I need today to go well. We all do. So in three seconds, I have to shut this door, and you have to let me."

"Porsche," Bentley began. "Listen."

"Two," Porsche said, firmly.

"I can do this."

"One. Sorry, B."

Jeff Grunburg cleared his throat behind Porsche. "Are you coming, Porsche?" He reached for the open door with one hand and looked at Bentley, irritated. "I thought we wrapped up this conversation. Is there a problem? We have a lot to get through."

Porsche smiled at him. "You know kids."

"I know Tallulah," he said, looking tired. "And she tells me I'm the immature one." The laugh track went off again, in the background.

"That's hilarious," Porsche said, trying to bring up a smile.

"Believe me. You wouldn't want to face Tallulah in this conference room," Jeff said. "You'd lose. We all would."

HA HA HA HA HA—Mercedes's artillery-fire laugh floated through the open door. Jeff held the door for Porsche, who disappeared back inside the room without looking at her sister. Then he slammed it shut.

Bent could still hear the muffled laughter from the other side. It seemed Jeff's laugh track had decided she was the joke of the day.

Maybe they were right.

Here she was, stuck out in the lobby on the wrong side of the most important door of her family's life. Utterly and completely powerless.

An hour later, Bentley and Bach were still sitting in the low leather chairs in the lobby of the sleek Lifespan building.

"Are you all right, B?" Bach put his hand on her shoulder. "You look like you're going to be sick."

"I feel like it." She looked up from the University of Southern California website open on her iPad, and noticed for the first time that day that Bach didn't look so good either. His green eyes were red around the edges and supported by dark, puffy crescent moons. "What's up with you, Bach? When was the last time you slept?"

"What are you talking about?" He rubbed his face and smiled. "I sleep. I slept last night."

"For how long? What time did you come home?"

"Uh, I dunno. A normal time? What's with the third degree, Bent?"

"You just seem out of it. Did you go to some awesome party and not invite me? Because that's what it looks like, and that would be rude. A direct violation of our code."

"Sorry, sorry, it was a boys' night out," he said, seeming oddly relieved. "I'll let you know next time, promise."

"Were you gambling, Bach? You smell like smoke, you know."

"I do?" He lifted his T-shirt to his nose. "What does smoke have anything to do with it?"

"Oh, please, I've been to the casinos. It's like a ten-thousand-square-foot ashtray in there."

He laughed. "Okay, I might have been gambling. But why not? Yolo, right? And besides, a little poker never hurt no one."

She eyed him suspiciously, then smiled. It felt nice to have a real conversation with a real person who she really cared about. Oh god, she thought, the highlight of my day is now scolding my little brother for playing cards? What has my life become?

She felt almost physically ill as the facts of "reality" life rushed back in.

Ever since the fateful D-day (which of course meant

Duck Day, but they had now been legally advised never to speak of *the incident* themselves, unless they wanted to incite the ire of every animal rights group on the planet), one thing had become perfectly clear.

If the show went, her family was going with it.

Twenty million dollars was a lot of green, but the current crisis wasn't just about the money, and it wasn't about the failing product line.

Bentley didn't know why she hadn't seen it before. It was all so obvious now. What could someone like Mercedes Royce do, for example, without *RWTR*? Bentley tried to imagine her mother's future starring vehicles.

RESOLUTIONS WITH THE ROYCES?

High Concept: Every New Year's Day, Mercedes screams scathingly supportive comments—like *"FRIED rhymes with DIED for a reason, you know!"*[27] or *"NOTHING tastes as good as SKINNY feels!"*[28] or *"COBB SALAD? COBB is the CHEESE-CAKE of SALADS!"*[29]—at total strangers instead of her own daughter. (Probably a no-go. Bent somehow doubted that watching someone berate strangers would be as satisfying as watching someone berate their loved ones.)

RUNNING WITH THE ROYCES?

High Concept: Mercedes keeps her face on bus stops and

---

27 *Do not remind Jeff about his Fatty Liver. He gets really upset and then I have to spend hours rejiggering the proportions in his chia hemp mulberry amaranth mix!* ☹ —D
28 *Jeff seems skeptical that anyone feels differently? Delete as obvious?* —D
29 *It so is. Even vegan cobbs are the vegan cheesecakes of vegan salads!* ☹ —D

billboards across the country—two of her favorite places to see herself, when not on the cover of a magazine—by running for public office. Hijinks ensue. (Unlikely. Bent suspected her mother's past as Southern Utah's most infamous demolition derby bookie might rule this one out. Mercedes had always had a hard head for numbers and a shrewd eye for opportunity—give or take a duck or two.)

REBOOTING WITH THE ROYCES?

High Concept: Mercedes goes back to the trailer park and revives *TRASHPIRATIONAL.* (Possibly. It would depend on the statute of limitations on money laundering. And also if the town had a hotel now, aside from the one in the gas station where Mercedes had allegedly given birth to Porsche.)[30]

None of this was helping. The main question still remained unanswered: Who would Mercedes boss around slash terrify, when and if *RWTR* wrapped?

Who besides the three of us?

Porsche's future was no clearer. How would she promote Lippies by Porsche without the show? (Originally, she had wanted to call the line Lippsche by Porsche, pronounced Lipp-Shh!, but nobody could pronounce it. Other products they couldn't pronounce? Clothesche by Porsche, her ready-to-wear line, and Yogsche by Porsche, her ready-to-sweat line.)

And Bach? Without the show to distract him, how long would it take her brother to get his butt kicked at every

---

30 *Per JG: Has someone actually pitched this to Original Programming? Promising reboot potential, no?* ☺ —D

casino in North America, including all 479 Indian gaming operations? (Bent had googled it, just to be certain.)

To be honest, it was all so horrific to imagine that Bentley (like everyone else in her family) now tried to avoid doing so at any cost. Between Mercedes's love of the spotlight and Porsche's love of her product lines and Bach's love of the poker table, free time was not something anyone in her family needed.

What they needed was a season-six renewal.

But as Bentley sat in the lobby of the Lifespan building— humiliated and rebuffed—in the back of her mind she was already starting to unravel.

She clicked her iPad off, hiding away the USC website, and shoved it deep into her bag. She was embarrassed that she'd even thought about it. Not to mention that she'd gone and told her crazy college escape plan to a perfect stranger.

No matter how perfect he seemed at the time.

She tried not to think about it again.

It—or him.

With everything going on, meeting a boy in the darkness of the Chateau Marmont seemed like something that had happened a whole lifetime ago. Asa was now even more out of reach than the dreams she had confessed to him.

And she couldn't even think about college now. The family was in crisis, and as much as Bentley might person-ally want the family *reality* show to end, she did not want the family to end *in reality*.

Which is why it was so maddening to just sit here in the lobby while their future was being decided in the next room: Whether or not they would be canceled, after five straight seasons. Whether or not they would go off the air for the first time since Bentley was twelve and Bach was eleven. Whether or not their entire family was about to be fired . . .

She glanced at the door.

"Don't even think about it," a voice said. Dirk from Development[31] (also known as the Dirk, in Bentley and Bach–speak) spoke without even looking up from his phone, on the other side of his desk. "Strict orders. No one in or out."

The Dirk was blond and tanned and so healthy-looking, it was creepy.[32] His eyes followed Jeff Grunburg desperately, at all times—as if the Dirk was somehow trapped underwater and Jeff was his only air tank. He seemed more *enslaved-blond-robot-race* than human,[33] Bentley thought, and she tried not to look at it—er, him—when she didn't have to.

Instead, Bent looked at Bach. "We have to do something," Bent said again, as she had for days now.

"Yeah, well, you let me know when you come up with it." As usual, Bach had his cards out, and his fingers were flying faster and faster as he shuffled. He'd dressed up for Lifespan just like his sisters, as much as he could, per Mercedes's instructions. It was hard to know exactly what to wear to their first *you're-all-probably-fired* meeting. Bent

---

31 *I'm here! *Waves* So exciting!* ☺ —D
32 *Thank you! (Boot Camp five mornings a week on the beach! The boots really add to the burn, esp. when they fill with sand!)* ☺ —D
33 *It's actually my sculpted bone structure—I get "hot robot" a lot. #genetics #thanksmom* ☺ —D

could see he'd gone with hipster layers—and a T-shirt that said *LIBERATED*. *(Ha-ha. Very funny.)*

She wished for the thousandth time that Lifespan had never decided to expand her brother's appeal to the straight-teen-boy demographic (not to mention, to launch the *RWTR* line of branded card decks) by giving her brother poker for a hobby. If only they could have stuck with the whole *MEET A CUTE BOY AT PRIDE* arc . . .

If Bent could, she would roll back the tape and erase the day Bach had come home from school to find *The Beginner's Guide to Texas Hold'em* left waiting on his bed. *Jerks.* It had taken only days for the Mulholland Hall Poker Club to spring to life at school. Now it was his fixed place in the social scene; all his friends played—gay or straight, cis or trans, hipster or hipless. That wasn't the problem. The problems were the people he played against who were definitely not his friends—and the degree to which his fingers almost seemed to itch when they weren't touching his cards.

As Bent watched her brother now, she tried not to think about those 479 Indian gaming facilities he had yet to play. *And three times that many, if you count the whole country.* . . . But that problem would have to wait, at least until she solved this one. Bent could tackle only one family crisis at a time.

I'm no Joelynne Wabash, she thought grimly.

"What?" Bach looked at her. "Why are you staring at me?"

"I'm not. It's nothing. Just—they should have let us go in with them. That's all." Bent strained to see over the thick wall of frosted glass that separated the two rooms.

So Jeff Grunburg was in there. And the silver-haired man she recognized as Fred Tinker, chairman of the Lifespan board. And then Porsche, and Mercedes. Bent couldn't make out the other heads, which was frustrating. *Who are they, the ones deciding our fate? Who gave them that power? Why can't it be us?*

"That was never going to happen, you know that," Bach said. His fingers paused. "You think we're really going to get the ax?" For the first time, he actually sounded worried.

"Who's getting the ax?" An old man, bent at the shoulders and slightly swarthy-looking, sat down in the white chair-cube next to them. He seemed to have come out of nowhere. Though the man's face was as lined as an old stone, his shirt was white and crisp, and his tan linen jacket was pressed and neat. Above his jacket, his eyes were an improbable light blue, and his thin-lipped smile was encouraging. He looked friendly, almost familiar. Still, she cursed herself. Every alarm in her head was ringing. She should have known better than to have this conversation— any conversation, really—in the lobby of Lifespan.

"I'm sorry. Never mind. You two were talking. Don't let me interrupt," the man said. He pulled a pink ticket out of his pocket. His hand was shaking, and the ticket wagged in the air. "I'm just here looking for the fellow, you know . . ." He made a fist on top of his head, the universal sign for Dirk's man-bun.[34]

"The Dirk." Bent laughed in spite of herself. She looked up to find the lobby desk empty. The Dirk must have gone

---

34 *Is that true? Adorable!!!* ☺ —D

outside to tend to one of his many Twitter accounts.[35]

"He forgot to stamp this, and then the valet wanted thirty-eight dollars. Can you believe it? Thirty-eight US dollars. For parking a car." The old man scoffed.

"He didn't forget. The Dirk never stamps anyone. You have to be Tom Cruise to get a validation from him. Literally." Bentley shook her head.[36]

"Oh yeah?" Bach grinned and slipped a book of validations out of his jacket pocket. "How many do you need?"

"Bach," Bentley hissed.

"Where did you get that?" The man looked surprised.

Bach shrugged and tossed it to him. "I lifted it from the counter when Dirk was on the phone."

The man looked interested. "So you're a thief by profession?"

"More like a professional idiot," Bent said.

"I was only messing with him," Bach said. "The Dirk guards these things like they're gold."[37]

"Yes, I imagine so. Thirty-eight dollars' worth of gold. I am forever in your debt," the man said, counting out his stickers as he shook his head. His teeth were as white as his shirt when he smiled.

"No problem," Bach said.

The old man stood to go. "You've missed one. An easy one. Black jack to red queen. There." He pointed at Bach's solitaire game. "It's staring you right in the face."

---

35 *Shhhh! Can't disappoint my fan base!* ☹ —D
36 *coughs* *Lin-Manuel Miranda, and I gave him an extra twenty mins.* ☺ —D
37 *Because they are.* ☹ —D

"You like cards?" Bach moved the jack of clubs to the queen of diamonds.

The man smiled. "I dabble in the occasional game of strategy. A poker man, myself."

"Me too," Bach said, dealing another card.

He nodded. "Then I have one piece of advice for you, my young friends. Never bet on the obvious."

Bentley raised an eyebrow. "What do you bet on?"

The old man put his hat back on his head. She hadn't realized he'd had one. "The inevitable," he said.

"Which is?" Bent looked at him.

"It's not about what's already on the table. Anything but that. Those cards are already played." His eyes glinted. "It's the opposite. It's about what's waiting in the hand. What will be on the table three turns from now. The inevitable."

"How do you know what's going to happen three turns from now?" Bach asked.

"Simple. You can't. Not unless you make it happen."

Bent frowned. "So you cheat? That's your advice for winning at cards?"

"Not winning. Playing. Taking control of the game, rather than getting played. Choosing your own cards, rather than accepting the ones you are dealt. It's not the same thing."

"Cheating works too," Bach said with a grin.

"I suppose you're right." The man smiled back. "If you're a scoundrel or a wastrel or a reprobate." He shrugged. "No judgment. I've known a few."

"I did choose my cards," Bentley said. "I came up with a whole season's worth of cards. Great cards—but the people I was playing with wouldn't even listen to what I had to say."

"They wouldn't? Why not? Or should I say, *Why, Bentley, Why?*" The old man grinned.

Bentley turned red. "Very funny."

Bach frowned at him. "You watch our show?"

"No. Of course not." The hunched man smiled unapologetically. "All I care about are *Luchadores*."

They stared.

"Mexican wrestling," he said, trying again.

Bent and Bach exchanged a confused glance.

The man sighed. "Americans. That's why I'm here. To get Lifespan to distribute more of it. But I know about your show. People talk. I read things. The internet, for example."

"Right," Bentley said. "Because the internet is where all the truth is kept."

"I apologize. You were saying? The cards, in your hand?" The old man looked interested.

She shook her head. "I had ideas. Cards I could have played. But it doesn't matter anymore. We're probably getting the ax, remember?"

"You don't need permission to play your cards, *linda*. They're your cards. Nobody gets anything other than the cards they deserve, not by the end of the game," the old man observed.

"So now you think we deserve to get sacked?" Bach looked depressed.

"That's not what I said at all. And, speaking of cards . . ."

The old man pulled a worn business card out of his pocket and dropped it on the table. It landed neatly atop

Bach's discard pile. "That's mine. In case you ever find yourself in need of validated parking. In Mexico City." He smiled.

The old man picked up his hat. "For what it's worth, I hope this ax of which you both speak falls on someone else."

"Or how about, on no one at all?" Bentley asked.

"Nonsense. An ax always falls. And so it should." He smiled. "Why else would we have axes? But of course, you are both far too young to know that." He held up his parking ticket. "And too kind." Then he nodded, straightened his hat, and was gone.

Bentley picked up the old man's business card, straight out of the discard pile. It was handmade, just a white paper rectangle inked with the old man's name and a phone number. It looked like he had used some kind of fountain pen. That was it.

"Congratulations, young Jedi," Bach said. "You just got full-on Yoda'd."

She thought about what the old man had said. What was the *inevitable* move, when it came to the Royce family?

Think three moves ahead. Bentley barely knew what was going to happen three episodes from now.

Nobody gets anything but the cards they deserve. Did she even have any cards?

Bent pulled off her jacket and stared more closely at the game in front of her. "Shut up and deal me in."

Now she reconsidered her *RWTR* pitch for next season. Why had she thought the truth was the answer? Or the relatable? Since when was real reality anything anyone wanted to watch?

Maybe she had been going about this the wrong way. Maybe she had been trying to play the wrong cards. Maybe she had to rethink her entire strategy. Maybe she had more in her hand than she realized.

Slowly she began to formulate a plan.

Lifespan wanted Bad Bentley? They had no idea how Bad that Bentley could be.

Bent would give Jeff Grunburg the performance of her entire life.

No. More than that.

Bent would give Lifespan the performance of her entire series.

Because Bentley Royce now knew what she had to do. She had one hand around the proverbial Hermès leash, and even though Hope the (dead) Duck was (metaphorically) dangling, she refused to let go.

"You're sure?" Bach looked at her.

The expression on her face was all the answer he needed.

He began to deal again, this time for both of them. Bent looked down at her freshly dealt hand. The answer suddenly seemed so obvious.

If I play my cards right, I can get my family renewed for another season and *get the hell out of here.*

Look out, world.

It was time to double down on Being Bentley.[38]

---

38 *Per JG: Poker circuit cameo? With Bach Royce limited-edition decks? Talk to Simran in Short-Form.* ☺ *—D*

Six

Bentley hadn't planned on working during hiatus, but if their renewal was on the line, it was time to #TURNITUP. It had been a month since she had made the decision to go full-on Breaking Bad Bentley, and by the time she got in the car on this particular hot July night, she felt like she was ready for battle.

Maybe it was the war paint plastered all over her face. Maybe it was the stranger-danger adrenaline coursing through her body. Maybe it was the head-to-toe Balenciaga leather armor, or the thigh-high leather stiletto boots. (The filmy pink gauze tutu that some stylist had selected for her to wear over all of the above wouldn't be much help in the event of battle.) Either way, she had come to fight, and fight she would.

Bent slammed the door of Mercedes's SUV, sat down on the plush seat, and turned to her perfectly made-up big sister. "Bad Bent, ready to roll."

"Really? A tutu?" Bach looked at her in the rearview mirror. Driver Dan had the wheel (he was the Royce family driver; nobody knew his real name), and Bach had insisted on going along for the ride.

"Ask me if I care what's on my body right now. Go on. Ask me," Bent said.

Bach smiled and looked away. "That's my girl."

Bent turned to Porsche, who was still expertly applying lip liner. "Boi? Really? That's the name of the club?"

"Yeah. So? What were you expecting?" Porsche looked amused.

"I dunno," Bent admitted. The Death Star. Waterloo. Normandy Beach, Bentley thought. The Titanic.

Bentley Royce's Last Stand.

"Hey, what are you looking at?" Porsche craned her neck to try to see what was on Bentley's phone.

"Nothing," Bent said, turning her phone facedown in her lap. "Let's get this party started."

Bent's opening salvo came long before they got to the club itself, which was a nondescript building, painted black and white, with the silhouetted photo of a skateboarder stretching three stories high. She checked her watch. "Pull over. We can't arrive before midnight."

"Why? This is a vampire hangout?" Porsche, redoing her lip liner, already sounded bored.

"Now that I've finally looked at it, I can tell you the Bentley Bible is pretty strict on that point. Bentley Royce never shows her face anywhere until the party is peaking."

"How does she know?" Bach asked from the front seat, trying not to laugh.

"Apparently she just does," Bent said, staring out the window. "Maybe it's a pack-animal thing. Like how wild wolves know wild wolf . . . stuff."

"Look at you," Bach said. "Bad Bentley's a wild thing."

"I get it." Porsche nodded. "I like it."

Ted knocked on the window, holding his handheld camera. Tonight, he and Jojo had followed in their own car. "Give me a count when you're ready for us, guys."

"I guess that's it. Boi," Porsche called up to the front seat, holding up her phone. "I'll get the Snap vid."

"And we are . . . rolling," Bach said as Porsche swung her phone toward Bent.

Bent smacked her lips and started to open the door, then slammed it shut. "Wait."

"What's wrong?" Porsche asked.

"Selfies first," Bent replied. "Almost forgot." Bach laughed out loud.

"Excuse me?" Porsche raised an eyebrow. "*You're* voluntarily posing for a picture?"

"Hey, I'm all about the follow-through—" Bent held up her phone and stuck out her trademarked tongue, while Porsche did her pout.

"Go you," Porsche said, picking up her bag. "Leveling up your selfie game."

"Remind me to give you your *RWTR* merit badge when we get home," Bach said from up front.

"Oh, I'm just getting started." Bent typed into her phone. "Adding location—on. There we go."

"What?" Bach looked curious.

"Gotta give the paparazzi a chance to catch up." Bent dropped her phone into her clutch, which was a Vuitton frog so tiny that it barely even held that much. "One more thing," she said.

"Did you step in something?" Porsche looked concerned as Bentley grabbed one stiletto heel and began yanking on it.

"If that's a new look, I'm not seeing it," Bach said. "But it's disturbing."

"I'm going for drunken party girl train wreck, right? I mean, she is? Bentley?" Bent yanked harder.

Porsche looked amused. "That's the general idea. So?"

"So Bentley needs a stagger, but I won't remember to do it all night, and someone will catch on. Only one way to be certain." Bent pulled as hard as she could—until the stiletto heel popped off. "There. Now she'll walk like a drunken sailor."

Bach was impressed, if still anxious. "Are you nuts?"

"Possibly, but I'm just going by the book here."

"Who wrote that thing, LiLo herself?" He shook his head.

Even Porsche looked envious. "Yeah, really. The Porsche Bible really just has the color for my highlights, my sizes, and the names of my BT." Porsche's BT was her Beauty Team, whom Bentley and Bach privately referred to as the Death Eaters.

"I have to admit, it was all pretty inspired." Bent reached for Teddy's jacket, which hung over the seat in front of them. She grabbed a pack of Marlboro Lights.

"*Gross,*" Bach said.

"It's not like I'm really going to smoke them. *God,* that would be so disgusting." Bent tapped out a cigarette. "Anyways, this is LA, not New York—the Bentley Bible just says to light and hold."

"This feels like act one of every teen movie ever." Bach shook his head. "And I predict this will somehow end with me paying you to pretend to be my friend so I can become the most popular gay at John Hughes High."

Porsche looked her sister up and down. "I almost feel a little queasy seeing this. It's *so* not you, B."

"It is now," Bent said gamely. "The new me."

"Next thing you know, you'll be angling for the up-skirt shot," Porsche said.

Bent turned red. "What? No. No way. That's where I draw the line. The underwear stays on."

Porsche shrugged, pulling a compact out of her bag. "I thought you were going for train wreck?" She checked her lip gloss again.

Bentley stared at her sister. She couldn't tell if she was teasing or not, and Bent found herself wrestling with the impulse to open the door and run for it, as fast as she could—even with only the one heel. "That's more like a train pileup."

"Go big or go home. That's what Mercedes would say." Porsche shrugged. Bent knew Porsche was just goading her, but she also knew her sister had a point. Still. There was headline far, and there was headline *too far*.

Wasn't there?

No, Mercedes would say. *There isn't.*

"Forget it," Bach said from the front seat. He was already unbuttoning his pants. "I'm wearing clean boxers. I'll do it."

Bentley and Porsche looked at him like he was insane.

"Not you! You're the good one. The CGB! Don't let her take you down with her!" Porsche looked at Bent. "No offense."

"None taken." Bent sighed, because her sister was right. "But, Bach, I think that's the nicest bullet anyone's ever almost taken for me."

"You're welcome." Bach threw his jeans over his left shoulder, and then there he was. Sitting in the front seat in his polka-dot Italian silk boxers. Thank god the windows were tinted.

"I've got an idea," Bent said.

Five minutes later, Porsche looked over her sister, studying her from head to toe. "Wow, you really are taking one for the team."

Bentley took a breath. "Porsche, you still filming this?"

"Oh, right. Yep, here we go." She raised her phone so that it stared straight at Bent.

"Oh my god, I'm sooooo drunk, you guys!" Bent grinned and lurched at her sister, who rolled down the window.

(Bentley had never been that trashed, but she'd seen plenty. Between high school and Hollywood, she probably knew enough to administer a Breathalyzer with courtroom-admissible precision.)

Porsche was trying gamely not to laugh. "That must be Boi," she said brightly. "Looks hoppin'."

"*Boi meet girl!*" Bent burst into laughter. "Get it? The club is called *Boi*? And me, I'm a *girl*?"

"Got it," Porsche said. She patted Bent's head protectively. "You sure you're up for this, cute thing?"

"*LIPPYTIME!*" Bentley said suddenly. "Mushy Melon me!" She puckered her lips. Might as well throw in a little product push, seeing as the failing family fortune depended on it.

"Musty Melon," Porsche said, but still, she handed Bentley the gloss gratefully.

Bent sniffed it. "*Ummm. Yuuuummmmmmmy.*"

Porsche pinched her sister's cheek. "Let's do this."

Bach covered his face in the front seat, and Bent couldn't tell if he couldn't bear to be seen or if he couldn't bear to watch what was about to happen. Probably both.

Porsche ducked out of the car first, long legs unfolding in front of her. The noise swelled, both the screaming and the shouting of the paparazzi calling her by name, as it always did. The flashbulbs were blinding, almost deafening. Porsche turned back toward the car door. "Well? Are you coming?"

Well? Am I?

Bent hesitated. She thought of college: Would these

pictures jeopardize her chances of being accepted? Would *this* be the headline that pushed her over the edge, the one that cost her a future shot, however far down the line, at four years of Royce-free freedom? It might, she knew that. If not this headline, then the next one, or the next. But she also knew it was a chance she had to be willing to take.

In the middle of her fake-drunk, single-shoe, cigarette-in-hand delirium, Bent had a moment of perfect clarity: tonight was a sacrifice, her sacrifice, and she had to make it. She had no choice. She had to have faith. It was now or never.

She could feel Bach looking at her (between his fingers) from the front seat—and Porsche watching from outside. She could even feel Mac and Teddy behind the cameras—and then the overwhelming energy of the crowd that had gathered around the car.

This is what you came to do. So do it.

Bent's off-balance stilettos hit the pavement, teetering.

Turn it up, Royce.

She stood up, blinking in the light. She wore nothing but Bach's boxers, one Balenciaga jacket, and one broken stiletto heel. She looked like a homeless person, or an idiot, or maybe a movie star.

Judging by the swelling roar of her name and the number of flashbulbs going off, it worked like a charm.

Bach shook his head. Porsche looked shocked. Driver Dan looked straight ahead as always. Ted and JoJo got it all on film.

Bentley held up the cigarette by her face, coughing. Then

she took a step—and fell right over. The crowd roared, and she smiled at the asphalt.

She rolled onto her back, staring up at the cameras and the streetlights and beyond that, the stars.

Judge me, she thought. Judge me and hate me and watch me and need me. I'm yours for as long as you want me.

Take that, Grunburg.

And then: If this doesn't do the trick, nothing will.

Tallulah Kyong-Grunburg, wearing tie-dyed pajama bottoms and a Four Seasons Hualalai T-shirt—a hotel she had a particular soft spot for ever since she'd made a *killing* in chocolate eggs at the resort-wide Easter egg hunt, along with Judd Apatow's youngest daughter's friend's youngest sister—checked her Tumblr feed and froze.

She picked up her cell phone and hit a rapid succession of buttons. The phone rang, echoing up the stairwell outside her room—which meant her father was downstairs watching Korean soap operas to try to fall asleep.[39]

His voice came through the receiver. "Go to bed, Lulu. Your mother wants you at your advanced origami tutorial in the morning before school tomorrow."[40]

---

39 *Jeff asks if you could swap out for "reviewing potential foreign market drama acquisitions," or similar? ☺ —D*
40 *Recycled? (Jeff would like you to indicate in text.) We're a green network! ☺ —D*

"Yeah, you know what origami is, Jeff? *Folding freaking paper.*"

Her father sighed on the other end of the line. "Lulu, I'm not getting in the middle of this. You know your mother says Stanford wants one of two things—"

"I know, I know. The bleeding edge and the obsolete. Google or the marimba. Or maybe a podcast about the marimba."

"Exactly. Now tell me, what's more obsolete than *paper*?"

Lulu rolled over on her Pratesi duvet. "So Justin Brammer learned how to beat paper out of tree bark for his application. Big deal. Marguerite Vendermeier built a whole boat. Am I suddenly going to have to grow a pair of sea legs, too?"

"Instead, how about you finally open the pamphlet about this Illuminated Manuscripts summer camp thing?[41] Your mom wanted me to talk to you. It's in Alexandria, but we could upgrade you all the way to Athens. Do you want to come downstairs for a face-to-face?"

"I'm good." Tallulah waved him off, her eyes glued to the laptop perched on a pillow next to her. "Gotta run. Check out TMZ. I just sent you the link. You're going to want to get in the middle of *this*. And *you're welcome.*"

She hung up, turning her attention back to the headline that lit up the center of her screen, and smiled. Tallulah was

---

41 *Per JG: See Manuscripts Museum, Biblioteca Alexandrina, for more detail. Could be good for the Tallulah character. (Also for Tallulah.)* ☺ —D

always impressed when someone had enough sense to take her advice.

BAD BOI! BENTLEY ROYCE BOOTED FROM CLUB—IN BOXERS!

She reached for the open bag of Hint of Lime tortilla chips she kept under her bed, where a stash of carbs could remain safe from the prying eyes of that spy/babysitter she called an assistant. After twelve straight years of gluten-free, sugar-free, wheat-free, cruelty-free, GMO-free, joy-free, organic vegan living, smuggling junk food under her parents' noses was her one remaining passion in life.[42] (She wondered what Stanford would have to say about that.)

"Well played, Royce. Well played." Tallulah stuffed another chip into her mouth and hit REFRESH. "I gotta admit, I didn't know you had it in you."

---

42 As you know, JG has begun AGGRESSIVE litigation vs. his home air purification system manufacturer re the removal of processed food smells along with any allergens, thus limiting his ability to parent effectively. Legal says to stick a pin in this chap. ☹ —D

BENTLEY GETS BOOTED FROM BOI—
HOLLYWOOD HOTSPOT REJECTS ROYCE

AP: Beverly Hills, California

Via Celebcity.com

It looks like Bentley Royce is Hollywood's latest Boi toy. The long-troubled teen reality star hit the club scene with her big sister, Porsche, last night.

Already stumbling on her way inside the celebrity hot spot, bad-girl Bentley could be seen partying from the moment the car pulled up near the entrance to the late-night venue off Sunset Strip.

Once inside the VIP area of the club, a popular haunt among young Hollywood's A-listers, Bentley was said to be dancing on the tables before the night was done. Wearing only boxers and a leather jacket, it was unclear what look she was going for.

Porsche Royce, telling waiting photographers she had an audition in the early hours of the day, left well before the younger Royce. Bentley's personal party showed no sign of stopping; when things reportedly got a little too out of hand, and management approached the wayward teen about cleaning up her act, an alleged altercation resulted in Bentley beating it out of the club.

Loyal little brother Bach Royce, the only son in the second-most-famous family of reality television, appeared to claim his sister at the end of the evening and see that she made it home. (Despite recent rumors about the youngest

Royce sibling and the poker table—Bach Royce is the founding member of the Mulholland Hall School Poker Club—it's clearly Bentley who remains the wildest child in the Royce family.)

The following tweet was issued by the verified account of @TheBentleyRoyce in the early hours of the morning.

"ROYCERS: 'If everything seems under control youre just not going fast enough'—Mario Andretti @TheBachRoyce @ThePorscheRoyce @Real_Mercedes #RWTR6 #Lifespan"

(Disclosure: Celebcity is a fully owned subsidiary of the Lifespan Network, which is itself a fully owned subsidiary of DiosGlobale.)

Follow @celebcity for breaking details,
or www.celebcity.com.

Seven

It was Saturday, and Bent was sitting up in bed, furiously typing on her laptop—at least she was, right up until the moment Porsche stormed in and pulled her lilac embroidered duvet and sheets clear off her. (They were, as Mercedes liked to brag, the same sheets made for the Queen of England, who was said to carry a single set from castle to castle in Louis Vuitton trunks, they were so expensive.)

"Go away, Porsche." Bent clicked quickly out of her Word document and onto Celebcity.com.

Porsche pulled her sheets harder. "Where have you been the past few days? I've been trying to talk to you."

"Nowhere."

Project #TURNITUP seemed to be working. Two weeks, three boutique openings, one Vegas club birthday, three late nights in West Hollywood (and as many unflattering headlines) later, Bentley was crashing hard and burning harder.

At least, she was trying her best to.

@TheBentleyRoyce had more followers than ever.

She had guest DJ'd at Tricky Dick's while slurring and calling every single band by the wrong name—which was an extra-tricky feat, considering it was Beatles Night.

She had walked down Rodeo Drive wearing a feather boa and dragging a tiny stuffed dog on one end of an Hermès leash. (Apparently Hermès leashes, especially ones covered with microscopic duck feathers, were more difficult to return than Mercedes had imagined.)

She had thrown up on the tram to the Getty Museum from the parking lot in front of a fifth-grade field trip. (To be honest, she had gone with fake vomit plan B, the old thermos of cream of tomato soup mixed with yogurt. The performance was Emmy worthy.)

She had hung out with her fancy relatives, including her cousin Royce Blakely (apparently Mercedes wasn't the only Californian who believed in aspirational naming), whose dad was, like, a congressman or something. Royce was a nice guy, but his older brother Mason was pure trouble, and Bentley knew Mason would be up for primo partying. Still, she couldn't even remember how she had gotten home, and that was after dumping shot after shot onto the bar floor. (Uber? Had to be.)

But after all that, frankly, Bentley Royce was exhausted.

Porsche stepped on Bach, who had been snoring peacefully on the carpet, his face wedged halfway beneath the personalized beanbag chair Bentley had kept since sixth grade.

"Ow," Bach said, opening one eye.

Porsche pinched Bentley with one hand while kicking Bach with one foot.

"Wild night?" Porsche bent to pick up an empty can

of cocktail peanuts, eyeing remnants of a late-night chess game scattered across the floor. She kicked Bach in the ribs again—yanking Bentley's ear.

"What?" Bent groused again, slapping her laptop closed.

"Get in the car," Porsche said. "Now."

"Why?" Bent mumbled, and attempted to lie down instead. "It's summer. I'm busy."

"What she said." Bach didn't open his eyes.

"Well, change of plans. Now you're going to get off your butts, both of you, and meet me in the garage." Porsche raised her voice. "You too, Mercedes."

Mercedes had stopped in the doorway behind them, next to Donielle, her Pilates instructor, who was following her out to the gym in the pool house, as she did every Tuesday, Thursday, and Saturday morning. "Why?" she asked.

"Why? Because I want you to meet someone. Get dressed." Porsche went to open Bent's closet. "Try to look decent. It's important."

"Wait! I'm up—" Bent tried to stop her sister, but it was too late.

Porsche slid the mirrored door open, revealing two obviously new bags of clothes from Ralph Lauren. "What's with the Ralph, B? The whole preppy thing? You going rogue? I don't think Pam would consider Ralph Lauren your approved wardrobe."

"Which is why I've never worn any of it." Bent tried her best to shrug it off. "I made some joke online, and they sent me some horrible samples. It's nothing."

Bach sat up, rubbing his head groggily. "Why are you

still talking? Who are we meeting? Tell me it's not a duck."

"Maybach," Mercedes warned.

"No. I'm not getting a pet." Porsche cleared her throat. "Or maybe I am, I don't know. I guess that depends on your definition."

"What?" Bentley rubbed at last night's eyeliner smudge.

Porsche took a breath, sitting down on the bed next to Bentley. The intimacy of the move startled Bent, who couldn't remember the last time she'd seen her sister in her bed.

"Wait!" Bach crawled up next to the two of them and lay down again, using Porsche's leg for a pillow. "Okay. Now you can tell us."

"Porsche?" Mercedes was impatient. "What's going on here?"

Porsche put an arm around her brother and sister. "I'm getting engaged," she said, barely pausing to deliver the news. She squeezed them so hard, Bent almost yelped. *"Surprise!"*

"EXCUSE ME?" Mercedes gaped.

Bentley's jaw dropped. "What the—"

Bach scrambled to his feet. "You're not serious."

"Now. Car. All of you. We have a meeting with Jeff Grunburg at the network in fifteen minutes. Code Red."

"Wait, Porsche," Mercedes blurted. "We have to talk about this. You can't just—"

But Porsche was out the door.

The Porsche SUV (the one Porsche used to drive the family around, not her beloved two-person coupe) shot out of the driveway, with the third Porsche (the girl) sitting behind the wheel.

"Why? What do you mean, *why*? Why *wouldn't* I get engaged? Somebody has to do something to save our family's neck. Our neck and our show and our house—not to mention a factory full of lip gloss in Shenzhen."

"You mean, something aside from Bent lighting herself on fire for every paparazzi in Hollywood?" Bach asked. As always, a team of paparazzi-driven cars swooped up along-side the SUV.

"Yes, Bach. Something aside from that." Porsche sighed.

Mercedes was white-faced. Bach was red-faced. Bentley didn't know how to react.

"You can't just get married," Mercedes said. "It's not that simple."

"Actually, it is. I am getting married, and this is how we're getting renewed." Porsche slammed the car out of reverse and into drive. "I'm kind of into the whole idea, if you want to know the truth."

"Roll down your windows!" the paparazzi shouted to try to reach the Royces, to get a rise out of them, to get a juicy photo op. The Royces automatically tuned them out.

SCREEEEEEEECH—

"And the simple fact is, we don't have a choice. So get with the program. This family is about to throw a wedding, like it or not."

A wedding.

As the words sizzled and popped like a lit stick of dynamite, the car rounded another curb.

SCREEEEEEEECH—

Bentley found herself holding her breath. She couldn't believe it was actually happening.

In the backseat, Bach's cards went flying. "Walk me through this again. You're getting engaged . . . to be married."

Porsche sighed. "Yes, Bach."

"But—to a person?" Bach asked again. "This family cannot get any weirder." He shot Bentley a look.

"Ridiculous." Mercedes shook her head.

"Bentley!" The paparazzi honked from the next lane, continuing their campaign of harassment. "Hey, Bent! Give us a smile! Bentley! We know you're in there! Is it true you're off your meds?! Are the rumors true, Bentley?!"

Meds? thought Bentley. What are they talking about? And why were they shouting *her* name? They never shouted her name when Porsche was around; it had always been Bent's sister they wanted.

Then it hit her: the plan was working. Operation Train Wreck was attracting exactly the type of attention she needed.

Great, she thought, her stomach sinking. Just great.

SCREEEEEEEECH—

Porsche glared. "I'm getting engaged—to a person—and everything's going to change." Her eyes flickered over to her mother. "It's not ridiculous. I've outlined things. I've made a plan. A beat sheet. A whole season arc. Are you excited for me? Say you are. I am."

Mercedes looked out the window. More silence. Bentley could tell *excited* was probably not the word. *Furious* might be a little closer.

Porsche spun the wheel, annoyed.

SCREEEEEEEECH—

"I'm pretty sure this is when you start squealing and tell me I'm going to make a beautiful bride," Porsche said, sounding bitter.

"What are you doing, Porsche?" Bentley leaned forward in her seat with a frown on.

"More importantly, who?" Bach looked equally disturbed.

Porsche sighed. "Whitey."

Mercedes sounded disgusted. "Whitey who? That's not a name. What are you marrying, a cat?"

"Actually, that's not a bad idea," Bach said. "I mean, if that cat was cute. Do you know how many hits cute cat videos get? It's *bananas*."

Porsche ignored both of them. "I'm not an idiot. His people came to Pam—"

"How do I not know about this?" Mercedes was furious. "And Pam does?"

"They all knew you'd make it personal."

SCREEEEEEEECH—

"It's my child's wedding. It's *personal*, Porsche."

"Oh please, Mercedes." Porsche rolled her eyes. "This is *me* you're talking to. Cut the crap. It's only *personal* because it wasn't *your* idea. It's *my* wedding, and I'm fine with it, so maybe you should let it go." Porsche looked in the rearview mirror for help, but neither Bentley nor Bach said anything.

Nobody knew what to say.

A moment later, Mercedes sat up in her seat. "Hold up—*THEY? ALL?* How many people know about this, Porsche?" *Before us.* That was the implication.

"Nobody. Hardly anybody. Like, ten? Twenty? Thirty, max? Just Casting—and Production, obviously—and then we had to check it all with Marketing—and I guess Sales."

"And Jeff?"

SCREEEEEEEECH—

Porsche didn't seem to know how to answer. Bentley thought her sister must have sensed, correctly, that it was a trick question.

But Porsche just shook her head. "Twenty million dollars is a lot of money, remember? I'm telling you, Mercedes, it's a solid proposition. I talked to Casting. I had them check him out. And I told Pam to put together a Wedding Bible for today's pitch meeting." She sounded defensive. (Bentley wished for a fleeting moment that her sister would also drive that way.)

"Let's get back to the cat groom. Could this cat also walk down aisles? Or wait—ride a Roomba down one?" Bach looked at Porsche. Bent knew he was babbling because he was nervous. "Or maybe wear a tiny bride's veil?"

SCREEEEEEEECH—

Bent looked at her sister. "Seriously? You got your fiancé through *Casting*? So you could *pitch* your wedding?"

"That's not where I got him, obviously," Porsche said. "He reached out to Bernie, through the agency. Bernie passed it along to me."

Mercedes frowned. "You met your fiancé through your *agent*? And you told your producer before your family?"

"A catnip bouquet? A little kitty tux, with a hole cut for the tail?" Bach suggested. Porsche reached over and flicked him in the head.

Mercedes was in shock. "And you're telling us this *now*? On the way to meeting the *network* about it?"

Bent realized her mother was shaking.

"You know what you're like." Porsche sighed. "I knew if it wasn't your idea that saved us, you'd freak. Like you are right now."

Mercedes pulled an ecru-colored cosmetic bag out of her ecru-colored Birkin bag and unzipped it. (Her stylists had agreed that when accessorizing her all-white signature ensembles, nude and ecru were the best option for her secondary leather highlight colors.) She found a jar of gummy melatonin and popped two into her mouth.

"It's nine in the morning, Mercedes. You know those are for sleeping, right?" Bent took the jar away from her mother.

"They better be." Mercedes said. "I'm out of Xanax, and I'm trying to put my nerves to sleep."

SCREEEEEEEECH—

Bent braced herself against the door.

"Honest to god, Porsche"—Bach put his hand over his heart—"I fear for the lives of all drivers when you're behind the wheel."

"Stay with us, Mercedes," Porsche snapped. "You have about ten minutes to get on board before we start selling it to the channel. Especially since the ceremony's going to be televised live as our season finale." She glanced over at her mother, who was silent.

"Really? You have nothing to say?" Porsche looked like she wanted to reach across the clutch and slap her.

"Give me a minute," Mercedes said, staring out the window. "I'm thinking."

"Think faster." Porsche tightened her grip on the wheel. "I had the network run the numbers, if that helps. You know what we stand to make on this? Do I have to tell you? We're talking Lippies money." She said a number. It was staggering. The effect on the car was the same as if she'd opened her mouth and puked gold: everyone sat up, startled.

"That's *all* Lippies money?" Bach sat up. "Really?"

"Is that even possible?" Bentley said incredulously. "In *one year*?"

"Close enough," Porsche said, looking back at Mercedes again.

Mercedes clamped her lips together. Bent could almost see the wheels turning in her mother's head. As Porsche's mother, the news was horrifying. As Porsche's manager, it was thrilling. As the guarantor of Porsche's (and thus the family's) massive mountain of debt, it was probably all of those things at the same time—exponentially.

Finally, Mercedes sighed.

"We'll need to rebuild the entire product line around the wedding," she said. "And we won't have a lot of time."

"But?" Porsche asked.

Mercedes looked out her window, thinking. "Here

Comes the Bride. Here Comes the Nail Polish. Here Comes the Foundation and the BB Cream and the Home Facial and the Bubble Bath . . ."

"Here come the sponsors," Bach said. "They'll be lining up."

"As will the magazine covers. Here come the wedding magazines," Bentley said.

"And the Lippies! Here Come the Lippies," Porsche added, looking relieved.

"Here comes the money," Mercedes said, finally starting to smile.

That was it. They all knew then that it was over. Mercedes was on board. Bentley didn't know whether to laugh or cry. She looked at her phone.

Eight minutes.

That was all it had taken her mother to sell her first-born to someone she'd never met. It had to be some kind of record, even for a family like theirs.

"Aren't you sort of skipping one thing?" Bach said seriously.

"What's that?" Porsche asked.

"We have no season six yet?"

Porsche looked at her little brother in the rearview mirror. "You leave that to me. Step aside. Here comes the freaking bride, baby."

Porsche sounded like the Terminator, and Bent shivered. She wouldn't want to be Jeff Grunburg right now.

On the other hand, she wouldn't want to be this Whitey person either.

But the person she most didn't want to be was her sister, and that wasn't something she could bear to think about at the moment.

"You," Grunburg said, the second he saw Bentley. He pointed to her. "Keep it up and you might get your own line of boxers. Even Tallulah's been impressed. That's a first."

"Thanks," Bent said. "In fact I've been thinking . . ." But he had moved on.

That you're a giant loser.

But at least she and Bach had been allowed inside the room for this pitch. Porsche's doing, Bent was sure.

"So, let's hear it," Jeff said, turning back to the room. "The Wedding Pitch for season six. Dazzle me."

Dazzle me. It was one of his favorite lines, probably because it made everyone else so uncomfortable. (Bentley wondered if there were actual statistics somewhere—hard data—that showed the degree to which hearing the words *dazzle me* impacted the dazzler's ability to dazzle anyone at all.)[43]

"Let's go over the basics," Pam said briskly. She was not remotely dazzling and did not seem to care. As the producer of *RWTR*, she ran the production meetings, which is what this technically was. Pam was all about the basics. From her plain navy T-shirt to her awkward jeans to her unfortunate dishwater-brown hair, it was easy to see why she'd built a

---

43 *Jeff & I would also like to see these stats, if we do end up tracking them down.* ☺ —D

career out of keeping cameras pointed away from herself.

"The basics?" Mercedes raised an eyebrow. "Starting with the groom?"

"It's all there, in the folders in front of you," Pam said.

Jeff flipped his open. Everyone else in the room—production teams from both the Lifespan Network and Whiteboyz music label—did the same.

"Pass," he said. "I don't care about the basics. I want the rush, the sting of the shark bite.[44] I'm not feeling dazzled yet. Talk to me." He looked up, impatient. "You want season six, sell it to me."

"That tone—" Mercedes began. (Somewhere around season two, she seemed to have decided that when it came to Jeff Grunburg, the only strategy was to never agree about anything, and put up with even less—which made these meetings potentially difficult but also sometimes hilarious. When people took notes in this room, they were mostly for the purpose of recounting *Grunburg v. Royce* skirmishes on social media.)

Porsche interrupted. "It's *fine*, Mercedes." She cleared her throat, looking nervous. The faces at the long, oval table in the conference room looked back at her skeptically. "Well, T. Wilson White is the son of Razz Jazzy White, one of the most financially successful music producers in Hollywood," Porsche said, as if that explained anything.

"Sorry, honey, when I said sell, I didn't mean you." Jeff

---

44 *Per Jeff: he's filed paperwork to trademark his name for that rush: "the shark bite." He'd like you to include here, if possible. (His lawyers will contact you for remittance.)* ☺ —D

looked at the Dirk, who stood at the door. "Bring him in. Jazzy Junior. The groom."

"Send him in," Dirk called into the hall.

Porsche stared intently at the doorway. "You mean—now? Here?"

"You got a problem with that?" Grunburg grinned. "Say it now or forever hold your peace, sweetheart. Boom!" The human laugh track sounded off.

Bent slipped her arm through Porsche's. Mercedes kept her eyes fixed on the door. Bach's foot was tapping compulsively beneath his chair.

And then he appeared in the doorway.

The man my sister is going to marry, Bentley thought. T. Wilson White. Whitey, who is not a cat, but who might as well be.

"Hey."

Bent's future brother-in-law stood at one end of the conference room, while Porsche sat at the other. The air suddenly went electric, and when Bentley glanced at her sister, Porsche's bare arms were covered with goose bumps.

Bent was startled—until she looked down and saw that the remote for the air conditioner was sitting in Mercedes's lap—and was now set to fifty-two degrees Fahrenheit. As usual, if anyone was going to assume control of the *dazzling* situation, it was going to be Mercedes.

But as she shivered, Bent studied the reason for the meeting as closely as everyone else did.

The guy looked like he couldn't be much older than Porsche—a tall, lanky street kid, dressed like a rapper. He played it that way too—even now, as the room stared.

He stared right back.

His pants were low, his high-tops were high, and the neck of his plain white T-shirt was so covered with chains, he might as well have been Mercedes during a Fashion Week accessories show. A black bandanna hung from the back of one pocket.

Mercedes leaned toward Porsche, whispering, "Does that *mean* something?"

Bent leaned toward Mercedes. "Probably that he sweats a lot." Porsche rolled her eyes—but Bentley noticed that she didn't look away.

He was ripped; beneath his T-shirt, his biceps looked almost like one of those cut guys who hung out in Muscle Beach. For all anyone knew, maybe he was. The whole effect was Manhood with a capital *M*, Bent thought, which meant basically, that he was the male version of Porsche Royce. In that respect—which was pretty clearly substantiated by the way everyone in the room was now staring at both of them—it was a match made in heaven.

Bentley was impressed. Bach whistled.

"Jazzy Junior," Grunburg said. "I'm Jeff Grunburg. I take it you already know your future in-laws."

The guy looked around the room. His eyes rested briefly on Bentley—then Bach and Mercedes—but when he saw Porsche, he smiled.

"Hey, Sweet Thing," he said affectionately.

"Hi . . ." Porsche said, struggling, ". . . Thing."

Whitey laughed and crossed the room to give her an

awkward kiss—which she only made more awkward by turning her cheek to him. Then he nodded and held out a hand to Bentley. "Hey, li'l mama."

"Hey." Bent didn't know what to do with his hand, so she fist-bumped him.

"Good one." He grinned, moving past her.

Bach held out his hand to Whitey. "Mr. White."

Whitey shook it. "Bro-ham."

Finally, he smiled at Mercedes.

"Hey, Big Mama," he said, somehow not intuiting that those were her two least-favorite words in the English language. The resulting hug was so stiff, Bentley was afraid her mother was going to shatter.

"Whitey," Mercedes said, trying to compose herself.

He didn't seem to notice, though, and dragged a chair over to squeeze in next to Porsche, who still seemed to be blushing from the whole ordeal.

"*Whoa, whoa!* Tone it down, you guys. All this love in the room, it's too much for me. And you two! Your chemistry is just off the charts," Grunburg said. The laugh track went off again.

"Like your mouth?" Mercedes shot back. The laugh track began to rumble—until Jeff's glare silenced them.

Whitey put his arm around the back of Porsche's chair protectively.

Jeff got up and strolled over toward the couple in question. "Is it just me? Are you guys thinking what I'm thinking? Because I'm not sure I'm feeling it. I'm not seeing *headliners* for a multimillion-dollar wedding here."

"Yeah, well. Maybe I'm not feeling *this*. I kinda feel like I'm in a police lineup or something." The rapper shrugged.

"Do you have a lot of experience in police lineups?" Grunburg didn't smile.

"Do you have a lot of experience being a dick?" Whitey sighed.

Jeff glowered. Mercedes looked shocked. Bach just seemed spooked. Bent froze. The room was quiet.

Until Porsche giggled.

The giggle grew louder, until Bentley was caught off guard by the simple sound of her sister laughing. When had she last heard that? She tried to remember, but she couldn't. More to the point, though—why was she hearing it now?

Does my sister actually like this guy?

Porsche sighed, smiling at Whitey. "Oh my god. You're insane. That was hilarious."

Whitey pulled on a curl of her hair, as if they were both sixth graders. "Weirdo." Then he began to laugh at her.

"If you two are finished . . ." Grunburg began.

Whitey waved him away. "We're finished. It's all good. Kidding, right, Grungeburg?"

Mercedes gasped, and the Royces laughed harder.

"Grunburg," said Grunburg stiffly.

Whitey didn't seem to be paying attention. "And you can call me Whitey, riiight? Everyone else does. Except my moms, but you don't want to know what kinda names she calls me, unless you want me to start cussing in here, Iceberg—"

Jeff growled. "Grunburg."

Whitey nodded and ran his fingers back and forth through his choppy blond hair until it stood straight up. "So you guys want to ask me some stuff?"

"Just a few questions," Jeff said. "Like, why have *dicks* like us never heard of you?" The laugh track laughed—but this time none of the Royces joined in.

Pam looked like she didn't know what to do. "If we could just get back to the folders—"

But Whitey stopped her. "Why haven't you heard of me? You really want to go there?" Whitey sighed. "Because you're old, Funbag."

The laughter stopped.

"His name is Grunburg," the Dirk said, finally. "Jeff Grunburg."

"Can we actually get through this, boys?" Mercedes asked.

"All right." Whitey shrugged. "You don't know about me because my moms never wanted me to have anything to do with music. She made a deal with Pops that he wouldn't bring home his job. Last year, though, Pops decided he was too old to run the label. He's stepping down, and he wants me to step up. He and my moms want to see the world, do the things they never got to do while Pops was always in the studio. Our publicity clowns gave him some advice about *transitioning* and *continuity* and *stability* and all that shizz—"

"Oh right, *that shizz*," Mercedes said, in spite of herself.

"And one of them suggested I needed a relationship," Whitey went on. "He thought hooking up with someone like Porsche would do that for me." He smiled at Porsche. "I mean, hey, I'm not complaining."

Porsche looked away, hiding her lips behind her hand.

Jeff looked at Pam, who nodded.

"It's true. He's a story. He's having a moment. He's also the new face of Whiteboyz. He's never even given an *interview* before. Think about that," Pam said.

Mercedes already was. "So it's a true whirlwind romance. Maybe even love at first sight. Stranger things have happened. Who are we to judge what goes on between two people?" She stared at Whitey, like an artist eyeing a bowl of fruit.

"Preach." Whitey grinned.

"Porsche's marrying a family friend. Someone who gets it, and gets us. With similar interests, both professionally and personally," Mercedes said, trying out the line for the very first time.

Pam took notes. "I could make that work."

"Perfect. So could I. Now, then," Mercedes said, raising her voice, taking control of the room. "Here's how we're going to play it. Bent, you're not losing a sister, you're gaining a brother."

"That's a fresh take," Jeff said. Mercedes glared at him. "Go on," he said warily.

Pam was furiously taking notes.

Mercedes looked at the ceiling as she put it together. "You're jealous at first, Bentley, because your beloved sister will be spending more time with her new fiancé than with you. So you'll be acting out. As usual. Looking for attention."

"Classic Bentley, at her finest," Bent said.

Mercedes turned to Bach. "Bach, it's harder for you. You've never had a father figure, you know."

"Oh, I know." Bach smiled. Bentley could tell by the way he held his arm that he was shuffling a deck of cards beneath the table.

"And you live in a world dominated by strong women." Mercedes looked at him. "Don't."

"I didn't say anything," Bach protested.

"But Whitey will start doing manly, brotherly things with you. Courtside Lakers seats. Dodger Dugout Club. Guy stuff." Jeff shot Bach a look.

"As opposed to *gay* stuff?" Bach raised an eyebrow.

To be fair, Jeff had never seemed to have a problem with Bach's sexuality, excepting a brief phase when Jeff had wanted Bach to start an a cappella group "like that gay kid on *Glee*," and had been disappointed to learn not all gay boys could sing. Jeff's many competing biases against ugly people, fat people, old people—not to mention most women his own age—seemed to frame more of his thinking than any problem he might have with the LGBTQIA+ community. Jeff Grunburg was fine with all people of all races, genders, and sexualities, provided they were young, attractive, and painfully thin. That had always been Jeff's idea of the LA melting pot: a world where all the realistic bits had melted right off.[45]

"Awesome," Bach said, since there wasn't much else he could say. "I love sweaty boys."

---

45 *Can they do that now? Like Coolsculpting, but with heat? Will have to ask my guy!* ☺ —D

"We like manly. Manly is money." Jeff nodded, in spite of himself.

"I get it," Bach said. "Sweaty boys *with* money."

"Hey," Whitey said. "You do you, bro."

"This is touching." Mercedes rolled her eyes. "Can we get back on track?"

"Absolutely." Pam spoke up. "There's a multi-episode arc we've been playing with about Whitey and Bach going go-karting in the Valley, if the sponsorship comes through."

Bach raised an eyebrow. "I don't know which part of that sentence was more disturbing. *Go-karting* or *Valley*."

"I only heard *sponsorship*," Jeff said. The room started to laugh. Mercedes glared, and Whitey offered Bach an air fist bump. Bach looked on, amused.

And the circus rolled forward.

The rest of the morning went on like that. Mercedes composed her daughter's love story, while Jeff Grunburg raked Romeo over the coals. Mercedes pitched take after take on true love, while Jeff Grunburg tried time and again not to be dazzled.

They were formidable adversaries.

As the actual inquisition continued, the rest of the room turned over every detail of Whitey's life: his spending habits (predictable), his hobbies (fitness, training, and fitness training), his vacations (Cabo for surfing, Iron Man Triathlons), his cars (imported, see spending habits), his wardrobe (*flip-flop hip-hop*, or in other words, the official uniform of Los Angeles), and his education (irrelevant).

Finally, Jeff checked his watch. "I have a golf meeting in

a half hour. Can we cut to the chase, lovebirds? The bathing suit competition?"

"Excuse me?" Porsche said.

"The visuals. Let's do the visuals," he said.

It was the final humiliation in an already humiliating day. If Jeff Grunburg sounded petty, it was because he was. He didn't lose gracefully, and Bentley was slowly beginning to realize that was what this meeting felt like to him. A loss. He really had been planning to cancel the show, and now it looked like the tide was turning against him. He didn't know how to handle that—at least, he didn't know how to handle it like an adult.[46]

"The visuals," Jeff said again, snapping his fingers. "Get on with it."

"Oh no," Mercedes said, half under her breath. "You did not just go there."

Bent looked at Bach. Bach shook his head. Whatever was coming, it wasn't going to be good.

Grunburg gestured at Porsche and Whitey with one hand. "You. Yes, you. Stand up. Both of you. Show us your stuff. We need to see if it works."

Porsche stared in disbelief. She looked at her mother, who shrugged, disgusted. But Bentley already knew the answer. There was nothing anyone could do. There never was. If Jeff Grunburg wanted to do this, Jeff Grunburg got

---

46 Per JG: "Or he was just doing his job." ☹ —D

to do it. Twenty million dollars in debt and a factory in Shenzhen said he got to do it.

Bentley felt like throwing up.

Porsche stood, slowly, holding her hand out for Whitey. He took it, pulling himself up next to her while the room watched in silence.

"There," Porsche said. "Is that enough? Are you happy?"

"Does he make her look . . . *bigger*?" Grunburg glanced around the table, ignoring Porsche. "Do you see it? Anyone?" The room was silent. *Big* was the nastiest insult anyone ever said about anyone in this town, or this room.

"Excuse me?" Porsche trembled, outraged.

"You know, a little chunky. Maybe here, and down here?" Grunburg gestured awkwardly to his own hips. "You know. Like a *big* girl."

As the word hung in the air, Porsche looked like she was actually going to lunge at him. For a moment, Bent considered attacking the guy herself. Even Whitey now had an arm around Porsche's waist, looking like he was physically holding her back.

"I think they look fabulous," Mercedes spoke up. "And I think you've had your fun, Jeff. Let's move on."

It was a threat, and Grunburg heard it. He looked across the room at her.

Make me. That was the look on his face as he went on.

"Could you spin around, hon? Give us the view from behind? Think of the last royal wedding, you're competing with what was her name? *Pippi?* We've got to make sure you've got the junk in the trunk, you know, the gear from the rear."

The man was Satan.[47]

Porsche's face turned white and then red. Whitey was even redder. Mercedes's hands had tightened into fists. Bach was still as a ghost.

But it was Bentley who finally launched herself at Jeff Grunburg. *"YOU—WORTHLESS—ASS!"* She thrashed toward him. *"THAT'S—MY—SISTER!"*

Before Bent could reach him, though, she found a solid, bandanna'd mass in her way. "Sit down, li'l mama. I got this."

And with that, T. Wilson White turned and punched the top exec of the Lifespan Network in the face, so hard his chair toppled over backward.[48] In that one moment, Whitey became the single most (secretly) popular person in the room.[49]

Maybe even the company.

"You really are an asshole, Dickburg." It was a historic moment, and one that would grow with every retelling. But that wasn't what mattered.

What mattered was that when Porsche Royce pulled her fiancé in for a kiss—moments before he was ultimately kicked out of the building by security—it was the realest thing anyone in the room had ever seen.

---

47 *Per JG: "Or the head of a network?"* ☹ —D
48 *Per JG: "Reports of this incident are greatly exaggerated." He'd prefer you stick to the facts (his version).* ☹ —D
49 *Per JG: "*$#@!^&*%$#"* (Per Dirk: I'm staying out of this one!)* —D

It made Bentley think of *Rolling with the Royces: RELATABLE.*

So that was it. That was the big moment. The first moment Porsche Royce was crushing on her fake fiancé. And the first moment any of the Royces believed they could be renewed for a sixth season. Either way, there was no turning back now.

This ship had sailed, and there went the bride.

ROLLING
WITH THE
ROYCES
SEASON SIX:
LIGHTS,
CAMERA,
REALITY!

Eight

"Big news coming from the Royce fam! Don't miss out! Heart-heart-heart." Bent tweeted the words as she spoke them, then tossed her phone down next to the chessboard. "Oh my god, I think I just threw up a little in the back of my throat."

"Big news?" Bach looked up. "There is?"

Bent sighed. "There better be. Porsche and Whitey should just announce it already. The engagement."

"Why? What do you care?"

"The sooner they announce, the less time the network has to cancel us." All signs were pointing to the engagement story line having saved the day, but they still hadn't gotten the official green light from the network.

"Wait a sec. Rewind. Since when do you want us to *not* get canceled?" Bach stared at his sister in disbelief.

"I dunno." Bentley shrugged. "Since now, I guess. Things change."

Bach eyed her suspiciously—but his phone chimed, and he looked down to check it. "Uh-oh. Hold that thought. Jeff wants to talk to us." He took a breath. "All of us."

"Talk? His jaw must be getting better." They smiled at each other, despite everything.[50]

"Guess so. Either way, looks like they've made up their mind," Bach said. He held out his hand and pulled his sister to her feet.

"Either way, looks like we better run," Bentley said, grabbing her bag.

"Why?"

"Beat Porsche to the car before she can get behind the wheel."

He nodded. "I like your thinking."

"You know me. Three steps ahead," Bent said as they took off running.

Jeff Grunburg looked up from the hot-lunch line at Tallulah's summer school, where he was talking on the phone wearing plastic gloves. Felicity, Tallulah's nanny, was scooping kale salad for the students, while Dirk, who Bentley had come to think of as Jeff's nanny, was handing out orange wedges. A sign directly overhead read PARENT VOLUNTEERS ONLY—PLEASE DO NOT SEND FAMILY EMPLOYEES TO HOT-LUNCH LINE.

Tallulah sat between Felicity and Dirk, looking bored as she stirred the massive trough of FRanch[51] dressing in front of her.

---

50 Per JG: No comment. (His lawyers have advised him not to comment!) ☹ —D
51 FRanch = Organic Vegan Ranch-Free Ranch dressing substitute. Is that clear enough or do we need to provide nutritional information? Jeff doesn't want ppl to think he sends Tallulah to a school that endorses DAIRY! ☹ —D

"He's on the phone," she said as they walked up. "But you can have some kale salad if you want."

Jeff motioned to the Royces before covering the phone. "Give me one sec."

"Of course," Mercedes said. "So obnoxious," she whispered.

"You realize there's probably no one on the other end of that call," Bach said in a low voice.

Bentley laughed nervously, watching as Porsche and Whitey huddled together, whispering like they were here on a playdate. They weren't focused on anyone but each other, as if whatever decision Jeff Grunburg held for all of them wouldn't forever change their lives as much as anyone else's.

Which it would.

Lippies and Shenzhen and Fake Weddings and all.

But Porsche seemed strangely calm about the whole thing—while Bentley was holding her breath. She tried not to think about it as she waited with Mercedes.

Bach had taken a seat crammed in next to Tallulah with his cards, and was already teaching her how to play Texas Hold'em.

Jeff finished his phone conversation as if the Royces weren't there.

"You can go tell DiosGlobale to screw themselves. We're not giving them new numbers. They may be our parent company, but they're not our parents. Grandpa CEO can go . . . You know what Grandpa CEO can do. You tell him that for me. Better yet, do it to him."

He clicked off, looking annoyed. Then he glanced up

at Bentley, almost surprised, as if he were only just now remembering that they were there.

"Congrats, kid. You got it. You've been renewed."

"Really?" Bentley broke into a smile, in spite of the fact that the person she was smiling at was Jeff Grunburg.

"*Of course* we've been renewed," Mercedes snapped. "The new season is brilliant. I just don't know why we had to be dragged down to *Brentwood* to be given this information." The 405 freeway divided the west and east sides of the city; during certain times of day it would have been faster to cross the Mississippi River on a sapling raft. The most passive-aggressive thing someone could do was demand that you attempt that passage unnecessarily. As Jeff knew.

Message received, Bent thought. You may be renewed, but I'm still the boss.

Jeff smiled generously, ignoring Mercedes. "Between the wedding story line and the Bentley Royce train wreck, how could we say no?" He nodded at Bent. "Wreck yourself before you check yourself. I like the new Bentley."

Mercedes rolled her eyes, but Bent could tell how relieved she was. Porsche and Whitey smiled at each other, confident and calm, as if they'd never had any doubts. Neither Bach nor Tallulah looked up from their card game.

But Jeff kept going. Seeing Bach there with his daughter seemed to have reminded him of something else. "Just one more thing—Bach and the gambling."

All three Royce women stared.

"I know we were staying off it, but now I think we should let it roll. Play up Bach's addiction. Get a little edge in there. It's a big problem among American teens—"

"No," Mercedes said. "No deal."

"Forget it," Bent said fiercely. "Bach is off-limits."

"Why?" Bach said, finally giving up on his game. "If Bentley can throw herself to the feeding frenzy the way she has lately, why should it be any different for me? I mean, Porsche's *marrying* a guy. Mercedes offed a—"

"Don't!" Jeff and Mercedes said, in almost perfect unison.

Bach shrugged. "Seriously. What have I done for the show?"

"Bach," Bentley started.

He began to pick up cards from the table. "And don't say I'm the good one. Don't say I'm the cute gay brother. That's so condescending."

Nobody said anything—except Jeff.

"I agree. Bach's right. I'm not going to let you keep him sidelined because of your own *homophobia.*" Jeff grinned smugly and let a hand fall on Bach's shoulder. "I'm an LG . . . B . . . TZ . . . B . . ."[52]

"You already hit *B*," Bach said, amused. "But I appreciate you throwing the bonus *Z* in there. For all the Zesbians."

Jeff looked relieved. "I'm an ally, son. You know that."

"Oh, I know. I know exactly what you are," Bach said. He looked at his family. "Great. Then it's all settled."

"It's not," Bentley said. There was no way she was

---

52 *Jeff would also like you to know, as an ally, he has also always considered his private office bathroom all-gender. (Conceptually. Though only he uses it. #equality)* ☺ *—D*

going to let Bach become a casualty of the situation. Not if she could help it.

Jeff looked at Mercedes. "We can talk about it after we pick up this season's Emmys."

A load of hungry first graders walked up to the table. Jeff motioned to Tallulah, Felicity, and the Dirk. "Okay. Let's do this!" They went to work scooping salad.

Whitey broke from Porsche and casually approached Jeff. "Hey," he said, tapping him lightly on the shoulder, "now that we're going to be working together, I want to make sure we're all good. No hard feelings, eh, Pops?"

"No hard feelings." Jeff nodded, extending his hand to Whitey. They shook hands. Everyone saw, and all were pleased. Even Mercedes managed to lift both corners of her Restylane-filled lips.

What they didn't see was the moment after, when Jeff pulled Whitey in close enough for a whisper. "If you touch me again, I will *end* you."

Nobody saw it happen, and nobody heard it said.

Nobody except Bentley.

Then Jeff let Whitey go and looked out at the swarm of children, grinning. "All right, get out your cash. Throw in a Hamilton, and I'll let you cut to the front of the line. No, not the *Hamilton on Broadway* line."

Laughter and groans—but Bent didn't hear it.

She only heard her heart pounding in her ears as she followed her family to the car, wondering when he'd come for them, and whether or not she'd see him coming.

ROYCERS REJOICE: RENEWED
SEASON SIX! ON THE BUBBLE NO MORE!

AP: Beverly Hills, California

Via Celebcity.com

Flying in the face of every Hollywood pundit—and in the face of last season's uninspiring ratings—as well as rumors of a widening rift between production and network execs— reality television celebrity, talent manager, and producer Mercedes Royce announced via Twitter that *Rolling with the Royces*, the longest-running reality program on the Lifespan Network, would be renewed for a sixth season.

Earlier today, the verified account of @Real_Mercedes tweeted the happy news to her devoted army of #Roycers, the name given to the highly active Royce family fandom.

"ROYCERS: HAPPY TO SAY #RWTR JUST GREENLIT FOR S6! BIG NEWS CAN'T WAIT 2 SHARE! <3 U #RWTR6 @ThePorscheRoyce @TheBentleyRoyce @TheBachRoyce #Lifespan"

The verified account of RWTW star @ThePorscheRoyce (also credited as a producer) immediately tweeted the following response:

"ROYCERS: U KNOW ITS TRUE, WE'RE NOTHING WITHOUT YOOOOOOOU! #Blessed #Family #RWTR6 @Real_Mercedes @TheBentleyRoyce @TheBachRoyce #Lifespan"

Little brother Maybach Royce (@TheBachRoyce), the only male member of the Royce family, replied by tweeting a picture of a sexy manatee.

Younger daughter Bentley Royce, whose behavior in recent months has scandalized the tabloid world, shared this happy report, via her verified account, @TheBentleyRoyce:

"ROYCERS: oh my god ppl i just saw @ThePorscheRoyce eat a french fry #turnitup #celebrate #RWTR6 @Real_Mercedes @TheBachRoyce #Lifespan"

(Disclosure: Celebcity is a fully owned subsidiary of the Lifespan Network, which is itself a fully owned subsidiary of DiosGlobale.)

Follow @celebcity for breaking details,
or www.celebcity.com.

THE BENTLEY BIBLE
Rolling With The Royces: Season Six (Prospective)
A LIFESPAN NETWORK Property

NOT FOR CIRCULATION

CHARACTER: Bentley Royce

HANGOUTS: Urth Caffé, Barneys, Neiman's (shoe department only), Hugo's for breakfast, Brentwood Country Mart (Farmshop only, try to go when Reese Witherspoon is there at her corner table, IM*), Tacos Por Favor (taco shack near Bruckheimer, go during lunch, IM), Pressed Juicery, Rodeo Drive (pending featured branding opportunities.) [Note: Grunge Couture only. See Punk Rock exhibition poster from the Met added to Bentley's bedroom wall, for inspiration.]

COLOR PALETTE: Black/gray, if color—neon; dark, edge, iconoclastic, no subtlety.

FOOD: Grilled salmon on dark leafy greens (mandatory); Occasional featured items (cupcakes, ice cream, etc.) pending short-term sponsorship agreements. [Note: character will perform a reasonable facsimile of eating during every sponsorship period.]

SPLURGE SNACK: SheWeed Seaweed (Don't get excited, it's just seaweed enhanced with calcium for women!) or

TokyoPoppers (Microwave popcorn enhanced with matcha green tea powder). [Note: Per pending agreements.]

DRINK: IQH2O water (until further notice), free-trade coffees (will blur non-licensed brands), most iced teas (no lemonade added—NONNEGOTIABLE!).

SCHOOL SUBJECT: The Bentley character hates school, and most homework sessions should emphasize crumpling up pages and tossing them into the trash can, yet missing. [Note: Writers have been hired to generate homeworklike material to feed to paparazzi Dumpster divers.][53] Mulholland Hall has also signed a confidentiality clause regarding Bentley's grades; we can produce our own low-scoring "report cards" in support of season arcs.

UNIFORM: Skirt gets rolled up, socks get rolled down, oxford untucked & unbuttoned (three buttons) over a black tank, tie untied. Think Serena, not Blair.

BOOK(S): The Bentley character chooses not to read. If pressed, she should say "any magazine with Porsche on the cover" or "the book that inspired that one Steven Spielberg movie."

MOVIE: "Anything by Spielberg."

---

53 Per JG: "Ironic, since most of what our writers give us is garbage." "Ha, ha." ☹ —D

MUSIC: The stuff Justin plays me in private. [Note: Legal is still double-checking this; as long as you don't stipulate which Justin, it is likely to be approved.]

WORKOUT: Hot yoga, TryCycle [Note: favorite instructors TBD, pending agenting contracts with partner groups] or similar.

HAIR: Coloring determined by a Lifespan Hair & Makeup Consultant, per usual contract. [Note: three-color minimum established in Season Four will still hold until otherwise notified.]

NAILS: Unless for a particular shoot, nails will be black and groomed on set, pending weekly inspections.

BROW MAINTENANCE: Bentley Royce (the Actress) can choose, within Lifespan standards re: thickness/shape.

BRANDING: Per arrangement with the Network. [Note: Season Six is still TBD via our last word from licensing.]

COSMETICS: The Bentley character, aside from her trade-mark thick black eyeliner, features Lippies by Porsche along with all developing Porsche Royce product lines. [See Mercedes Royce, Amendment 42, 2014.]

HOBBIES: Negativity. Sarcasm. Mild depression. Blow-outs. [Note: Edgy. Curl goes out, not under, with added gel for spiky effect.] Trying out new looks. [Note: More specifically, trying ON new looks the *RWTR* style team has preselected. Also edgy.]

PRESCRIPTIONS: TBD/pending season arcs and/or Big Pharma sponsorships.

FRIENDS: Maybach Royce, "Gina from school," and other Featured Extra Cast Members as needed. [Note: Speaking and Not-Speaking.]

OPINIONS: The Bentley character thinks what you're listening to is "a total rip-off"; Facebook couple statuses are "so basic"; Instagram is for Mercedes and her friends; Snapchat is "what old people do to feel cool"; her school is "bass-ackward"; her mother is "ridiculous"; that nobody really "gets it"; hipsters are "god try a little harder why don't you"; nerds are "poseur much"; athletes are "so limited"; college is "sad and pointless." (Updated quarterly per Bentley Royce slang guidelines.)

LOVES: To hate (per market-driven trends). To party (at sponsored clubs). To shop (our sponsored brands). To stick out her tongue irreverently (per the Bentley character arc). Also, animals? (Great photo potential. TBD.)

*IM = implied meetings

Nine

"Slow down, Porsche!" Bentley clung to the door. "One of these days you're going to roll this car and kill us all."

Porsche careened around the corner onto Sunset Boulevard in her sleek black Porsche—jerking to a stop at the intersection.

SCREEEEEEECH!

"I don't know why we couldn't have picked a closer meeting. This drive is ridiculous." Bentley gripped her door handle. They were on their way to their usual Wednesday-afternoon appointment, and by now every photographer in town knew it.

"You know why we picked this meeting, B. Location, location, location. Besides, it's a great route for imagery. Green trees. Big houses. Famous street. I'll roll the window down in a sec, and it'll be a feeding frenzy. The headlines will hit before we get to the coffee."

"I know." Bent sighed. "I know." It was exhausting.

Porsche was very into imagery. It was never paparazzi or photos with her. It was only images and imagery, the way she imagined herself and how she could best project that image onto the world around her. The paps might have thought they were using her, but the joke was really on them.

Even though her engagement had yet to be announced, Porsche was on top of her game these days. She was getting (sort of) married, Maybach was playing up his poker habit for the cameras, and for now, Mercedes once again had her show. And Bentley? She was supposedly gaining a brother, not losing a sister—plus or minus a little acting out, for good measure.

That was all true.

The May (sweeps) wedding was six months out; the "Untitled Porsche Royce Wedding Special" green-light meeting with Lifespan had gone one fist short of perfectly, and full-scale preparation plans had been launched.

Whitey himself had come up to the house for two different planning dinners so far—both painful. Just because Mercedes had signed on to the wedding arc didn't mean she had to like it or him, and she didn't. While Bach and Bent tried to stay out of the bickering—eating their Café Gratitude acai bowls with record speed—Mercedes presided over the fledgling faux couple with more than a watchful eye. Each meal was an opportunity for a new precision strike, and they were all potentially lethal.

Like this: "You really need to wear lifts in your shoes, Whitey. Porsche cannot wear less than a three-inch heel, preferably four. Otherwise she gets *a little thick* around the ankles and you know what Jeff will say about that."

And this: "I've brought in Jacques, here, to teach you how to take a good couple's selfie. Your selfie game is *not strong*, Whitey. I mean, you don't even have an Instagram account. You'll have to set that up immediately, and then I'm really going to need you to practice with Jacques before we release you out into the wild."

And this: "You're going to need cute, loving, funny-but-not-too-funny nicknames for each other. I've hired writers. They're telling me *Booboo* is going to make a comeback."[54]

Whitey frowned. "You mean, like, *babe*?"

"Really? Babe?" Mercedes looked down at him over her reading glasses, which she never wore out of the house. "We'll get back to you. Stick with *Porsche* for now."

"Whatever you say, *Moms*." Whitey grinned, which caused Mercedes to make a small choking sound.

For his own safety, Porsche had dragged Whitey out to the pool house (next to the gym) after that. (She had claimed those two rooms plus bath as her grown-up bedroom the day she'd turned twenty-one.) She didn't venture back inside the main house until the next day.

But not everything about the Royce family had changed. Two months after getting their season-six pickup, the sisters found themselves in the same place doing the same thing that they had for more than a year.

Maybe Wednesday afternoons would always be this way, Bent thought—at least as long as *RWTR* was on the air. Even if Whitey was now in the backseat, sometimes. As he was today.

The light turned green, and Porsche floored the gas

---

54 Per JG: No BooBoo! Never a BooBoo! Lifespan isn't TLC! (Pls. revisit!) ☹ —D.

pedal. Whitey's head knocked against the side of the car. Things were getting intense (emphasis on the *tense*)—even for the Royces.

SHRIEEEEEEK!

They still knew relatively little about Porsche's mysterious future groom: he lived in Venice, on the canals near the beach, but Porsche had never been over there. He had dropped out of Santa Monica City College but seemed to have no friends from those days to speak of. He'd taken Porsche to meet everyone at the record label, but not to meet any of his clients. Porsche hadn't said anything, but Bentley knew she was a little worried.

In private, Mercedes, of course, was beside herself. "Who is he bringing to the table? Who are his guests at the wedding? Who even is this guy, aside from the son of some rich record exec? How do you know he's not just using you? He's not a celebrity gold digger?"

When the conversation got that far, Porsche usually lost it. "Because *that's us*, Mercedes. *We're* the celebrity gold diggers, remember?"

SCREEEEEEECH!

This time, Bent's head knocked against the window as Porsche slammed her foot on the brake and the Porsche swerved to a stop. On either side of them was a stretch of the clogged 405 freeway, but the bigger traffic jam was the one now following Porsche Royce. The car behind them, a banged-up puke-green Ford Fiesta, was wielding a telephoto lens. The dented Caddy fell into place behind it.

Bent watched in the rearview mirror. "Did you ever

think about what it's going to be like? Once you announce your engagement?"

"How big I'll be?" Porsche smiled into the rearview mirror, at Whitey. "How big *we'll* be?"

"Maybe a Bey and a half? A Double Bey?" He grinned at her. "Especially once Whiteboyz releases your new album." They'd been going to the recording studio together for weeks now. Unfortunately, Porsche's voice wasn't all that much better than her mother's or her brother's. Mercedes's gift for terrible vocal stylings was clearly a dominant gene.

"How big of a zoo your life will be?" Bent shook her head. "Or just how *bad* it's going to be?"

"If by bad you mean incredible, yes. Absolutely." Porsche smiled. She was actually starting to give off that weird glow, the one that belonged to brides and pregnant women, Bentley thought.[55]

It was creeping the whole family out.

Bent tried again. "By bad I mean bad, Porsche. The paparazzi will be hounding you constantly. As it is now, they're already jeopardizing our safety on a regular basis. Amp up the fame and you could get yourself killed."

"Oh, please. Name one celebrity who's been killed in a paparazzi-induced accident." Porsche swerved again.

SCREEEEEEECH!

"Princess Di," Bent deadpanned.

"*Dang*, B," Whitey crowed.

"Honey"—Porsche glanced over her sunglasses and

---

55 *I have that glow too, it's from the La Mer product line, right?*
☺ —D

into the rearview mirror—"I don't think I'll ever be *that* famous. Although, they do call us Reality TV Royalty, so I guess you never know."

She laughed. Whitey grabbed her hand and kissed it.

Bentley had to give it to her sister. The memories of their near cancellation already seemed forgotten. Porsche Royce had gotten everything she'd wanted this far in life, and she was right on track for getting everything else. Porsche was her mother's daughter, and for more reasons than just their matching Midnight Noir hair and terrible voices. When it came to the iron will to succeed, there was no mistaking the shared gene pool of mother and daughter, even if Bentley had escaped it.

Her sister had the Mercedes gleam in her eye. Bent wondered if the photographers were catching it.

By the time the Porsche pulled up in front of a nondescript gray building on Seventh Street in Santa Monica, the paparazzi had moved to a respectful distance.

They knew the score. Meeting days were always the same. The photogs had to stay on the far side of the parking lot no matter how many telephoto lenses they had crammed under their Windbreakers or stuffed inside their backpacks. Because today was one of the only things left in the sisters' lives that wasn't about the wedding.

It was true; every Wednesday afternoon, both Porsche and Bentley were spoken for. It was their day off, written into their contracts, due to some unspecified problem that had been covered lightly—very lightly—on the show.

Wednesdays were for AA.

It was unclear which one of them was the addict (in *real* reality, neither); all the tabloids knew was that *Rolling with the Royces* had done a brisk intervention episode, right after Bentley's sixteenth birthday party (again scripted, this time with even more painful casting done at Mulholland Hall, Bentley's and Bach's own school)—throwing around a lot of words like *supportive* and *holistic*, and decided as a *family* (or *production team*, depending on who you asked) that Porsche and Bentley would begin attending AA meetings. Before a more serious problem actually did develop.

Hence Bentley's fake trip to rehab, during which ratings had skyrocketed for an entire month. Porsche had started meetings with her the month after. She never could resist a spotlight, no matter the reason.

By the end of the summer, when no one had actually OD'd, the ratings went back to normal, and the girls couldn't help but feel they'd let the family down. But they were still chip-carrying members of AA.

The paparazzi, for the most part, behaved. In the beginning, one had tried to actually make his way into the meeting posing as an addict, but Lawrence, the strikingly good-looking trans guy who ran the meetings, had found him out (and kicked him out) within the first five minutes. Lawrence was good about ferreting out the paps. He was really into privacy—in life and in his meetings, just like most AA sponsors.

And things had quickly gotten easier after that; the

prying eyes had kept their distance once it became clear that the Roycers were sympathetic to the rehab story line. Blurry photos on the way in and out of the meeting were okay, at least in the eyes of the fandom; stolen spy shots from the front row were not.

Still, the Royce sisters kept going, if only for different reasons. Porsche liked to talk, and Bentley liked to listen. It didn't hurt, either, that half the words out of Lawrence's handsome mouth could also be read on the inspirational posters that plastered the walls of the meeting room.

Today, as they hurried to the door of the building, the paparazzi watched with more interest than usual. It was only Whitey who waved at the cameras now.

"Whitey," Porsche warned. "Not here. Not yet."

"What?" He sounded annoyed. This was only his second meeting, and he didn't know the ropes that well.

"Don't encourage them. Not until we announce our engagement," Porsche said.

"She's right," Bent said, annoyed.

"Aw, I'm just messin' around, darlin'." Whitey pulled his fiancé and sister-in-law in for a photo, zipping open his Adidas jacket.

On his T-shirt was a hot-red Porsche, the sports car. He grinned and made the sign of the horns with either hand, next to the Royce girls' heads.

Porsche giggled. "You're so bad."

Bentley glared. "Seriously?"

The paparazzi went nuts, and any Royce AA protocols were instantly suspended.

"DOES YOUR FRIEND HAVE A NAME, PORSCHE?"

"WHO'S THE NEW GUY?"

"YOU GOT A NAME, BRO?"

"Whitey! Lifespan will kill you. You know that's not allowed," Bent said, pulling her sister away. Pam had been very clear—until the announcement, the Royces were to say nothing about Whitey, confirm no rumors, give up no information.

As the three of them headed down into the basement of the building, the tall dark-skinned man (sporting a long-sleeve Heal the Bay T-shirt and the bone structure of a runway model) looked happy to see them. "Porsche! A vision as always! Hello, T.W. Glad you could join us again. And welcome back, B. One of these days we're going to get your mother and brother to drop in."

"Hilarious." Bentley kissed his cheek. "Looking good, Lawrence." No one was allowed to call him Larry. That was his only rule.

"What other people think of me is none of my business, B." He smiled. Lucky for you, Bentley thought. It's my whole life and my family's whole business.

Now the group leader drew his arm around her, kindly. "Tell me the headlines aren't true, B?"

"They never are, Lawrence." She let him hug her. The last thing she needed was a lecture right now. "You know that."

"I do. Just keep coming to meetings."

Porsche smiled. "Hello, *Lawrence.*"

"Hey." Whitey nodded, next to her. "Just letting you know. It smells like crap in here."

"He's right." Porsche sniffed. "Cigarettes." *Sniff.* "No, sweat." *Sniff, sniff.* "Camel Lights and sweat." She looked exasperated. "For goodness' sake, can't you get the smokers to stand by the back door? I can already feel my pores clogging. They're, like, *crying out* all over my face."

Lawrence sighed. "*Humility isn't thinking less of yourself,* Porsche. . . ."

"Save it." Porsche shoved him out of the way and stalked off toward the coffee table. Whitey lingered, hands jammed in his pockets. Like he wasn't sure what to do with himself.

Bentley looked at Lawrence sympathetically. ". . . *It's thinking of yourself less.*[56] And you might as well give up on that one, Lawrence."

"Never." He smiled charitably, even now. "*God is your copilot.* Yours, mine, and Porsche's."

"Actually, I'm her copilot now," Whitey said, over his shoulder, with a wink.

Bentley rolled her eyes and patted Lawrence's back. "Believe me. If Porsche was god's copilot, he'd switch seats or jump."

But there was no getting Lawrence to give up. Not even on Porsche. "We're all here to *surrender ourselves to a Higher Power.*"

"Yeah, that's not gonna fly. Porsche's self-esteem is steel-plated and sealed in Teflon. The thing's airtight." Bent rapped on his head. "Like a drum, Lawrence. Tighter than Mercedes's post-op forehead."

---

56 Per JG: Is humility aspirational enough for Lifespan? He isn't sure, will kick it up the chain. Let's stick a pin in that line. ☹ —D

Lawrence wobbled, and for a second Bent thought he was actually going to break character. But he sucked it all back in the moment the next broken-down former hippie producer stumbled up. "Brian! Are we *keeping it simple*?"

She'd never rattle that AA composure.

As Lawrence made it to the podium at the front of the room, Bentley followed her sister and Whitey to the very back.

He beamed. "Are you ready to get started? Because *if you want what you've never had, you've got to do what you've never done.* Am I right? Everyone? Are you with me?"

"Yes. . . ."

"You know it. . . ."

"We're with you, Lawrence. . . ."

The room mumbled and nodded. It was a stampede of mild positivity, Bentley thought. But it must have been enough, because Lawrence went with it.

He cleared his throat. "My name is Lawrence, and I'm an alcoholic."

"Hi, Lawrence," the room dutifully responded.

Bentley and Porsche looked at their phones in unison. Two synchronized swimmers treading water in the shallow end. *Forty-four minutes and counting.*

"Does anyone want to share?" As usual, Lawrence looked around the room. What happened next was less usual.

Whitey stepped up to the mic, or rather, T. Wilson White, as he introduced himself. He looked nervous. "I'm not really sure what to say. I've never—"

"Just say what you're feeling, Tomas." Lawrence was

eating it up. He hadn't had a first-timer step up to the plate in a while. "You can't open the door to a better place if you don't—"

"Don't what?" Whitey frowned.

Lawrence looked distracted. "Put . . . put all your weight . . . on the handle." He wasn't used to being interrupted.

"What handle?" Whitey looked confused.

Lawrenced blushed. "Your handle, I mean. Your metaphorical handle."

"Whoa, dude, come on. Let's leave my *handle* out of this."

Bent looked at Porsche, who was trying not to laugh.

"No—I—you misunderstand—" Lawrence stammered. Even their unflappable group leader was flapping in the face of Whitey.

"My handle? Like a trucker?" Whitey shook his head. "I don't know what you're talkin' about, man."

"Forget the handle. Just go on," Lawrence said. Now he was sweating. He rubbed the sleeve of his T-shirt against his forehead. "And remember, first names only."

Whitey nodded, clearing his throat. He looked directly across the room to where the two Royce girls were sitting. "So, like I was saying, I don't know—I've never done this before, but I met someone, and it's important to her. I mean, it's, like, one of her things, riiight? And she's important to me—well, I mean, she's going to be, I think, riiight—and so, yeah. I gotta push through it. Here I am."

Whitey's laying it on thick today. Bent wondered why.

"You're taking the first steps." Lawrence nodded. "Emotionally, you're a toddler."

"I guess so, riiight? Seeing as I first-stepped all the way into this dump, didn't I?" Whitey sighed. "This time around, it's important." He scratched his head, uncomfortably, or fake uncomfortably—it was impossible to tell. "She's important, I mean."

His eyes moved across the room, stopping on the last row.

"I don't know, I tell you, she's . . ." He made an exploding sound. "Blows my mind, L-Dog."

"It's Lawrence," Lawrence said, staring at Whitey as if he were speaking the meaning of life. "But go on."

"I love everything about her, to be honest. From her fancy-pants business-lady lip-gloss line down to the fact that she still keeps her childhood teddy bear next to her vanity mirror. It's adorable." He shook his head incredulously, unable to believe his good luck.

Bentley looked over at her sister. Porsche couldn't take her eyes off Whitey. She was completely frozen, transfixed, deer-in-headlights–style—except this was LA, so the only things you saw in your headlights were more headlights.

Had Porsche told him about not being able to let go of Binky the Bear? She never told *anybody* about that. Bentley had to consider the possibility that T. Wilson White represented more than just a business deal to her sister now—and that was a very troubling realization, even to the sister who was supposed to be the Troubled One.

It was just too cruel. If Porsche was really starting to like the guy, she was doomed. Fake marriages produced by fake reality shows didn't have the best track record, longevity-wise. Not compared to the longevity of a Shenzhen lip-gloss manufacturing plant.

And twenty million dollars was a lot of track record.

But it wasn't just Porsche feeling it.

As Lawrence pronounced him "committed" and "authentic," Bentley watched while her future fake brother-in-law came and took his seat next to Porsche. Bentley noticed that her sister adjusted her position so that her arm brushed up against his—and he did the same.

The way a couple sits.

It was the strangest thing, seeing them together like that. Not talking, not looking at each other, but somehow still a *couple*.

Though Bentley knew it was supposed to be fake, it didn't look fake—not even here in this shabby basement of a room, the one place where there could be no cameras at all. It was . . . alarming.

Very.

Just then, Bentley's phone vibrated loudly in her lap. The anonymous alcoholics around her all turned to see what the noise was about. She blushed a deep shade of red and grabbed for her purse.

"I'm so sorry," she said, fumbling with her phone, "I thought I turned it off."

The meeting picked up where it left off, and Bentley was able to sneak a glance down at her screen.

It was a message from Mrs. Reynolds, her high school English teacher. The subject read: YOUR REQUEST.

Her heart began to race. She had asked Mrs. Reynolds for a college recommendation letter—but that had been long before everything—before Whitey—before the show got picked up again.

Now here was the response. Bent wanted so badly to open the email right there and then, but she knew it wasn't the time.

There's never going to be a time. You know that. You made your call. Quit whining about it.

Delete and forget.

Lawrence's voice floated toward her from the front of the grungy room. *"Happiness is appreciating what you have, not getting what you want,* people. Say it with me." Bent pressed a button and closed her eyes, losing herself in the mumbling crowd.

Thirty minutes later, the three future in-laws stood together by the back door. Now the coffee cups were out and the cigarettes were lit, which meant freedom was at hand.

"How is this worth it? You spend a whole hour every week with these people? Most of them look like they still live with moms and pops. I mean, I love my moms, but . . ." Whitey shook his head over a paper cup of bitter coffee that tasted like it had been brewed in a toaster, or maybe even a toilet.

"You realize you're the one who keeps mentioning your

moms, right? Twice now?" Bent raised an eyebrow.

Whitey held up his hand in a high five. "You got me. Every boy loves his moms, am I right?"

"That's three," Bent said, leaving him hanging.

"Whitey, there's something you should know." Porsche looked over her shoulder to where their fearless leader was chatting up a (hot) hot yoga instructor. "We don't have a drinking problem. That isn't why we come."

"Yeah?" Now Whitey looked interested. Porsche had yet to show him how things really worked at meetings—or more precisely, after them.

Bent studied the alleged music mogul over a paper cup of her own. "Porsche's right. It's time. We can trust you. Walk us out, and we'll show you, Whitey." She clapped her hand on his back. His shoulder blades were sharp as knives.

"If we don't pass out from the smell first," Porsche said, pinching her nose and making a face.

"I hear you, Sugarplum."[57] He smiled at her. "You know, you're pretty cute when you're crabby."

Bent ignored both of them until she reached the door. "This is the payoff. Forty-five minutes of emo sharing, and this is what you get in return."

With that, she pushed the back door open dramatically. On the other side was nothing but an empty parking lot.

---

57 *Per JG: Sugar is considered a drug in this community; could he call her PLUMMY PLUM instead? FRUITY PLUM? PEACHY PLUM? Or similar. ☹ —D*

WHITEBOYZ HEIR, SON OF RAZZ JAZZY WHITE: IS HE ROLLING WITH THE ROYCES NOW?

AP: Santa Monica, California

Via Celebcity.com

Friends help friends stay sober—and from the look of it, celebrity sisters Bentley and Porsche Royce, stars of reality television's long-running *Rolling with the Royces*, have made a new friend.

Once again seen in the vicinity of their regular (if undisclosed) meeting of what appears to be a local Santa Monica–neighborhood Alcoholics Anonymous group, both girls appeared to be enjoying a quiet afternoon out with none other than mogul-in-the-making T. Wilson White, son of Razz Jazzy White, legendary founder of the Whiteboyz record label.

Never one for the cameras, the White family, aside from Razz Jazzy, has made a point of staying out of the public eye. Until this year, T. Wilson White didn't have a social media presence whatsoever. The Royce family less so; Bentley Royce, whose problem with teen addiction was briefly depicted on the show's low-rated fifth season, has virtually grown up on television.

Neither Royce had any comment on the appearance (other than the hand gesture the younger Royce made toward the paparazzi) excepting a cryptic tweet issued on the verified account of @ThePorscheRoyce:

"ROYCERS: minds are like parachute pants. They only work when u know how 2 open them. XO @TheBentleyRoyce @TheBachRoyce @Real_Mercedes #RWTW6 #Lifespan"

This meeting marked the eleven-month anniversary of the Royce sisters attending Alcoholics Anonymous.

(Disclosure: Celebcity is a fully owned subsidiary of the Lifespan Network, which is itself a fully owned subsidiary of DiosGlobale.)

Follow @celebcity for breaking details,
or www.celebcity.com.

Ten

LOST TIME
November 2017
Santa Monica Public Library, Santa Monica

"There ain't nothin' here." Whitey looked out from the back basement door to the empty parking lot in front of them. It bordered the distant street, and there wasn't a car in sight until you got all the way out to the black asphalt of the badly paved road.

"Exactly," Bentley said. "Also, nobody."

"See? No paparazzi. They're all waiting for us on the other side of the building." Porsche sounded like she was explaining the alphabet to a preschooler.

Whitey grinned. "All right. I get it. Now what?"

"Now? Lost time. We split up. Every Royce for herself."

"Hold on," Whitey said, looking from one sister to the other. "You just take off? Every week? Where do you go? A bar? A club? A hotel? Somewhere naughty?"

"That," said Bentley, "is the first rule of Lost Time. You don't get to ask, and we don't have to answer." Bent shoved on her Ray-Bans.[58] "Okeydokey, then. I'm off."

Porsche nodded, and they went their separate ways.

Since nobody knew exactly when AA began and

---

58 Per JG: We have an overall with Hipster Hut, so this brand may have to go. ☹ —D

ended—given the essential coffee and smoking[59] and mingling time on either end—Porsche and Bentley had developed a weekly routine for being Anonymous. Which is to say, they stretched the off-limits, off-camera "Meeting" time as long as they could, at least a good two hours.

Because, as it turned out, there really was something more anonymous than AA. There was PPP. *Plain Personal Privacy.* This was the ritual. This was why they kept coming back.

When Bent turned to look behind her this time, though, she saw that Porsche had paused at the intersection.

Don't do it, P.

"Well? Don't just stand there. Are you coming or what?" Porsche called back to Whitey, who looked like he didn't know what to do. He grinned and raced to catch up with her. Bent shook her head.

With a moment finally alone, Bentley opened the email from Mrs. Reynolds and smiled. She hadn't been able to bring herself to delete it, no matter what Lawrence had preached to the group.

Let me have my fantasy just a little while longer. It's just mine. It's almost the only thing I have left that's just mine.

And wasn't that what PPP was all about?

Once Bentley reached the street, it was only a quick turn down the sidewalk, past the parking lot, and straight into

---

59 *Not actual cigarettes though, right? Jeff feels that would be "too New York."* ☹ —D

the side door of a neighboring gray concrete building. She couldn't stop smiling.

The Santa Monica Public Library,[60] at Sixth and Santa Monica, was arguably the most architecturally significant space in the small seaside city. It was a sleek, modern fortress, though because it was in Santa Monica (*Soviet Monica*, according to Mercedes), the most homeless-friendly city in North America, it kept out nothing but the breeze.

Like a monument, Bentley had said. *To hobos,* Porsche had corrected her.

But it wasn't just the homeless who loved the library, though arguably they loved it best. Out-of-work screenwriters, LSAT tutors, nearby office workers, civic-minded seniors, and a surprising number of wounded vets—by the sound of the wheelchairs turning and the crutches clacking—had taken a shine to the vast concrete cubes of artfully contemporary space. The place was almost a town hall, only one where nobody was interested in any kind of meeting.

Loose ends. Loose people. Loose ponytails, though mostly on the men. It was the beloved, scraggly center of a less beloved, scragglier universe, even if that universe did sometimes smell like old pee. In other words, it was the perfect place for Bentley's own loose and scraggly purposes, whatever they might be during any Lost Time afternoon.

Bent didn't know what her sister did with her own stolen minutes—and she didn't even want to think about what

---

60 *A library? Full of BOOKS? Jeff wonders if this could become a comic-book store, food truck rodeo, improv workshop, modeling agency, beach club, or similar? Discuss!* ☺ *—D*

she and Whitey were doing with them now. That was the whole point. Private meant private.

Bent only paused once on the way through the door when she noticed that the newspaper vending machine on the sidewalk was stacked with copies of a local alternative press—the *Southland Weekly*—with her face on the front cover, along with her stumbling entrance into last night's club and a headline shouting LIKE A ROLLING ROYCE!

Oh, please. Not here.

She crouched in front of the vending machine, feeding in quarters until it opened wide enough that she could grab the entire stack—which she flung into the recycling bin as soon as she walked by. Not a single person in the building seemed to have one clue that, outside these walls, Bentley was famous—and she was determined to keep it that way.

First stop was the Bookmark Café, where she looked longingly at the sandwiches—not the wraps, which were, as far as Bentley was concerned, nothing but a cruel reminder of why bread was supposed to exist in the first place. But years of Mercedes's voice in her head wouldn't permit it. *If it's a carb, it's not allowed,* the voice threatened. *Simple as that.*

Even in my year of living dangerously, though?

Bentley smiled to herself and went in big—a latte and the most massive piece of chocolate cake she could find. For $3.99, it was four inches thick, striped with chocolate and vanilla icing, and probably four thousand calories.[61] Fortunately, Mercedes had never even thought of mounting a

---

61 *Jeff thinks we'll have to check with Standards about showing this.* ☺ —D

tirade against cake. Why bother? Who in this family—who in this town—would dare eat cake?

"Someone's hungry," Shane—a library patio regular, maybe some kind of aspiring cartoonist—cracked as she carried the cake past him to her table.

"You know it." Bent laughed. Just like (she hoped) a regular person would.

Thinking of her mother and how she would react to this debauchery made Bent force herself to finish every bite and lick every last chocolaty crumb. Because there, outside the café, in her little protected courtyard—her only company a man in a dirty USC sweatshirt and two sleeping bags, three gray-and-white pigeons, and a grove of Seuss-looking cactus palms—she was safe. Basking in the late-afternoon sun, a little high on sugar, sitting back and relaxing at her table, Bentley was in paradise.

Her second stop was just through the courtyard doors and up the staircase to the left. That was where she found the library's upstairs bank of computers, the one right next to the reference desk. She thought of it as her Santa Monica office space—just like the other guys at the computers did. Even if they slept on the sidewalk instead of beneath Frette sheets. Though the smell of occupational sweat and dirt was a little pungent at first, Bentley loved it. She was actually sad when she got used to it after the first five minutes, and didn't smell it anymore. She wanted to remember it—it was so different from the rest of her world.

Just like he was.

The guy's name was Venice, or at least, that's what she'd

always called him, because of a worn black hoodie emblazoned with the words VENICE BEACH ROLLERS that he never seemed to take off. He was her favorite of the library computer station regulars, and also the youngest; he couldn't be much older than she was, really. Bent wasn't sure what his story was. Some days he looked like he might be homeless, but his skin was softer, less weatherworn than the others who hung around. Maybe he was just a surfer. He was hard to figure out, and she liked it that way.

Venice looked up from his computer terminal and smiled. His face was warm and brown and his eyes were sea-colored. His hair curled choppy and brown around his face, almost to his shoulders. It hid his eyes with thick clumps. On humid days, it practically stood straight up, almost an Afro. On regular days, it hung down off his head like the unwashed do of a really messed-up girl.

Yeah, Venice *definitely* cut his own hair.

He watched her as she sat down, carefully, so as not to disturb his ratty skateboard, his ratty backpack, or the broken tripod strapped to his back for no apparent reason. One day she'd find out the story there, but not anytime soon. He mostly only asked questions, as if he himself knew better than to answer any.

Now Bent smiled back at him as she put her earbuds in, awkward as ever, and waved. Was it insane to be crushing on someone so far removed from her own reality? So mysterious and, in his own weird way, unattainable?

She wondered this for a moment, then thought: yes, insane, maybe, but also so predictable, and so Bentley. She grabbed one end of her earbud cord and pulled her phone out of her bag, and a blue matchbook went flying onto the table in front of her.

Philippe's. She remembered those matches and the boy at the Chateau Marmont.

Asa.

As if she could forget. When she looked at the matchbook, she could still see his face by the glow of the match's light, which was why she kept them.

You need therapy. You have therapy. Okay, you need more therapy.

Asa had been equally mysterious and unavailable, equally elusive. Her dream man, like he'd stepped out of some high-budget Italian menswear commercial. He had said more in that one night than Venice said in a month, but what did she really know about either of them? And what could possibly happen with either?

Talk about fantasies.

Asa the dream man had never reached out. Never emailed, never called. Never found her on Twitter or Snapchat or Insta. Maybe you should have given him your name after all, she thought for the ten thousandth time.

On the other hand, Venice, her cute but grungy library pal, was Asa's opposite in every way—and still, they weren't exactly chatting up a storm. She doubted he even had a smartphone.

Bentley had achieved the yin and yang of pointless crushes. This time, she was officially out-Bentley-ing herself.

There's a gripping story line for you, Mercedes.

She gave up and plugged into her phone.

Seconds after she had her earbuds secured, though, Venice reached over and pulled them out of her ears.

"Don't hide from the world, Sweet B." She couldn't help but smile every time she heard the pet name he had given her. "Come be a part of it."

"I'm here." She dropped her phone back into her bag. "I didn't know what to listen to anyway."

"Well, listen to me," he suggested. "Wednesdays at five, right? That's our time. Best time of the week."

"It's a date," she joked.

"Yeah, you wish. You'll have to fight these ladies off first." He grinned, gesturing to the rest of their computer table, where the other regulars, guys like Fox and Bulls Cap and the other guy whose name she always forgot, sat at terminals. She laughed.

Why did she feel so comfortable around him? Maybe it was because she had always felt like she had something in common with homeless people, just like she did stray animals, as weird as that sounded. Like them, she was missing a place to belong, or maybe just missing the kind of family that didn't want anything from you. What did they call that? Unconditional love?

Don't be so melodramatic. Bach loves you. Mercedes and Porsche do too, in their own way. So maybe there was more to it than that. Maybe it was his ocean eyes. *Not just the color of the water. The water on a sunny day.*

Or maybe it was the way he had called her Sweet B on the first day they met, before he even knew her name. She had looked to her wrist and realized she was wearing her Tiffany's bracelet engraved with a *B*, and couldn't believe he had noticed a detail so small.

He was like that about everything; he rummaged through the world of visible detail within the building the way the other guys at the computer table rummaged through the Dumpsters outside it. He'd noticed when a cat was stuck in the patio tree, even though everyone else had just walked by. He'd noticed when it was Ivy in the Teen Department's birthday, or when Robert at the Information desk had twisted his bad ankle again.

Most of all, he'd noticed her—the real Bentley, the secret one. Just as he was seeing her today. "Bad day?" he asked, looking her over now.

"You have no idea." Bent dropped her head down to the table momentarily.

"Try me."

"I can't. It's all too terrible."

"Lemme see." Venice pursed his lips. "Somebody stole all your stuff? You had to sleep outside in the rain? Didn't make it to the shelter before they ran outta grub?" He shook his head. "Wow, your life blows."

Bentley looked at him. "Yeah, you got it. How did you know?"

Venice laughed out loud. "Could be worse. At least your television pilot doesn't suck as bad as Bookman's here." Bookman was his name for Josh, the reference librarian, who was also an aspiring screenwriter, like roughly half the population of the city.

As if on cue, a scrawny guy with a curly mop of red hair looked up from the next terminal. "Quiet. Ven-man."

Try as he might, Josh was never all that funny. Even his supposedly funny hipster T-shirts weren't that funny. (Today's shirt had a picture of a library card made to look like an Amex card and captioned PRICELESS, and Bent was pretty sure that wasn't even a joke.)

"This is a library," Josh added.

Venice threw up his hands. "You kidding me? I thought this place was Disney Hall. Ah, day-um. I'm in the wrong place. Somebody call the conductor. Again."

"And my pilot isn't that bad," Josh grumbled.

"Have you ever been to Disney Hall, Venice?" Bent was suspicious. Any little clue was something. She knew he was educated; he'd once told her Cicero was named after a chickpea and that the Romans had invented the snow cone. He also seemed to randomly know about sailing—but then, he did like watching historical documentaries on the library computers, so who knew? Aside from the documentaries, the only movies he ever talked about were Star Wars films. And when he found his way into any pocket money, the first thing he did was buy chocolate cake (*her cake!*) from the downstairs café for the whole computer table. (Sometimes even Josh.)

But that was most of what she knew, after a year of talking with him, sitting by him, walking up and down the stairs for coffee with him. *A chickpea and a sailboat and Star Wars and a piece of cake.* That was about all he'd let slip out, which seemed like a clue in and of itself, though to what, Bent couldn't say.

Yet.

"Disney Hall? Me? Lots of times. For the opera. In my private box. *Barbara of Seville.*" Venice smirked. "Yeah, she's hot. Barbara."

"Barber," Josh said, still not looking up.

"That's what I said." Venice smiled. "Ask my boy Josh, the librarian."

He knows to make a *Barber of Seville* joke, she thought. Add that to the list.

Josh looked up from the reference desk, forgetting they weren't supposed to be talking. "I'm not *the* librarian. I'm barely even *a* librarian. Technically, I'm only a *part-time* librarian. Mostly what I am is a screenwriter."

"I know, I know." Venice sighed. "You've told us. A few times." He looked at Bentley. "I've been trying to help him, but he won't let me. He's really stuck."

"It's a thriller," Josh said. "Tricky stuff."

"Been sitting here next to screenwriters all year." Venice shrugged. "Read more thrillers over more shoulders than you ever will."

"He's got a point," Bentley said. "I always go to Venice with my plot problems."

He grinned at her. "See? Even Sweet B agrees."

Thirty seconds later, Josh was spilling the details of "DTLA"—his work in progress—and they were all three sharing one of Venice's highly polished Pink Lady apples. (Library food rules notwithstanding, Venice was famous for his apple-polishing skills. "Just takes time," Venice said, "not money. Not gear. Not even luck. Time, that's all you need to polish an apple, and I got plenty of that.") Now, the three of them stared up at Venice's screen as they ate.

"What are you reading?" Josh asked him.

GOING OFF THE GRID, the headline read, flashing on the monitor in front of them. YOU CAN BE YOUR OWN MAN.

"That's what I'm talking about," Venice said. "There's tons of this garbage out there. You gotta make it real. People who have to live on the street know. You can't just take off for south of the border and think you're gonna get there. That's like OJ Simpson taking off on the 405 with his trash in a bag."

"He's got a point," Bent said, though she had never had to live on the street. (She'd read plenty about getaways, though. They were one of her spy-book subgenres.)

"Really?" Josh looked skeptical.

Venice shook his head. "A guy like that—OJ, sure, but your leading man, too—thinks he's gonna drive to Mexico? He's not going to make it past Legoland. That was some bad plan."

So you know the opera and Legoland? Bent smiled to herself. It was more information than she usually got from him in a day. I should start keeping a notebook about him instead of my journal, she thought. *"CLUES TO VENICE."* She'd fill one page a year.

Thinking of the notebook reminded her. She leaned over and fumbled in her bag until she pulled out a book. *The Zombie Apocalypse Survival Guide.* She held it out to Josh. "Venice's right. Your character doesn't seem like black ops. He doesn't even seem like Black Widow. What's his tool set? Read the chapter on all the things you can do with duct tape. You can make pretty much anything into a tool or a weapon with duct tape."

Josh just looked at her. "Why do you know that?"

"Doesn't everyone?" Bent smiled.

"I do." Venice shrugged. "You can make a prom dress out of duct tape. I saw it in the news."

"See? Also typhoon pants," Bent added.

"Or a kayak." Venice nodded.

"A hammock."

"A toolbox."[62]

She smiled at Venice. "I see you're well versed in zombie apocalypse survival. That's good. I can't defend this place alone."

"I've got your back, Sweet B. You can trust me."

"Oh really?"

He shrugged. "Well, as much as you can trust anyone in a zombie apocalypse."

She pointed at him. "Exactly. See? That was a test, and you passed." She looked at Josh. "First rule of a zombie apocalypse. No trusting."

Josh took the book, shaking his head. "Duct tape," he muttered, scribbling notes on his legal pad. "Typhoon pants." He turned a page. "Trust."

Venice nodded. "Duct tape. Batteries. Magnets. Some solid cable. An old radio that he can strip for parts. That's more like it. Your dude's on the run, he's gotta prepare. He's

---

62 Per JG: Duct-tape-related product line tie-ins? Check with Lifespan Consumer Products. —D

only got one shot. Gotta know how to lay low and move out slow. Gotta put in the hours *before* the 405. And if we're talking about crossing a border, well, that's a whole other conversation. In that case, he's gonna need some friends."

Bentley leaned in. "How come you know so much about this stuff, Venice?"

Venice shrugged. "How come you got a zombie survival guide in your fancy bag, Sweet B?"

"No reason," she said.

"Me neither," he said, staring at the screen. "Maybe a person just needs to know they have options, you know?" Then he smiled at her. "Options and duct tape."

Bentley nodded, studying him. "Maybe they do."

They caught each other's eyes.

Then Venice leaned down and picked up Bentley's bag. "Your time's up, Sweet B. This is when you leave me."

She looked at her watch. "Damn it."

"Wednesdays at six. Worst time of the week," Venice said, reaching up to smooth a rainbow-tipped curl behind her ear.

"The worst of the worst." She felt herself blushing and took the bag from his hand. "See you next week?"

He nodded. "Like I said, it's a date."

She slung her bag over her shoulder and pushed past him.

"Hey, Sweet B—" Venice called out.

When she turned, he was right there behind her.

"Don't forget your matches." Venice pressed the worn blue book into her palm, letting his warm hand linger in hers until her cheeks were as shiny and pink as one of his famous apples.

PORSCHE EYES NEW PROJECT: COLLABORATION WITH WHITEBOYZ RECORDS IN THE WORKS?

AP: Beverly Hills, California

Via Celebcity.com

Could Lifespan reality celebrity Porsche Royce, currently film-ing season six of *Rolling with the Royces*, be the Whiteboyz record label's newest recording artist?

Royce made headlines yesterday when she was seen entering the studio with T. Wilson White, the son of rock impresario Razz Jazzy White.

This is the second time White has been seen in the com-pany of Porsche Royce in recent days. "Whitey," as he is known to friends, is new on the music-industry scene.

Considered by some to be heir apparent to the Whiteboyz Record Label and entertainment empire, White has suddenly been appearing in the public eye. According to several knowledgeable sources, White is known to have been an important behind-the-scenes factor in the success of his father's Whiteboyz label.

Should Royce in fact be venturing into collaboration with the music producer, it would mark her first foray back into the recording studio since her disastrous track "Drive Drive Drive," which was panned by critics and fans alike.

The verified account of @ThePorscheRoyce seemed to confirm the collaboration in a tweet posted earlier today:

"ROYCERS: Love being back in the studio. Baby I was born 2 rock! @TheBentleyRoyce @TheBachRoyce @twhiteywhite #RWTR6 #Lifespan"

(Disclosure: Celebcity is a fully owned subsidiary of the Lifespan Network, which is itself a fully owned subsidiary of DiosGlobale.)

Follow @celebcity for breaking details,
or www.celebcity.com.

Eleven

"You are a *horrible* human being." Porsche pointed at her mother with a long kitchen knife. "What are you saying, he's not good enough for me?" She turned the head of lettuce and went to town on a fresh side, almost as if she knew how to make a salad. (In reality, Porsche just liked chopping. It relieved stress, and on a good day, sometimes made her feel like part of the human race, or so she had once said to Bentley. "You know, almost like I'm one of those people who makes things or builds things, or, I don't know, *eats* things.")

"Yes," Mercedes said, slurping even more loudly. "Finally, I'm getting through to you. That's exactly what I'm saying. It's the little things. I have a good eye, you know. There's something off about him, like something's not quite right up there."

This was the battle raging around Bentley as she hunched over her copy of *Zombie Apocalypse* book one, trying desperately to block out the noise. She wasn't reading the book, she was writing in it, jotting down her emotional reactions to her family's drama and chaos as a coping mechanism suggested by her therapist, Dr. A.

All around her, the house was overrun with camera crews prepping for tonight's shoot—an elaborate setup involving a precarious cake tower, a dining room full of long-stemmed roses, and the crew of *Entertainment Tomorrow*, who had acquired the rights to the exclusive interview. The Royces had fled to the kitchen, which had now become a sort of functional backstage.

Bentley sat at the Sumatran-teak breakfast table across from her brother, scribbling in the margins of her book while Bach played his thirtieth game of solitaire in a row. (In an uncharacteristically parental move, Mercedes had banned poker in the house after seeing Bach's first-quarter homework grades.)

Porsche chopped iceberg lettuce at the kitchen island. Mercedes hovered over her usual mug of black coffee, slurping through a straw. (*Veneers!*)

Porsche grimaced. She hated mouth noises and had to leave the room if someone clicked a spoon against their teeth, ate a potato chip, or slurped. She had once asked a stranger on a flight to JFK to stop chewing ice, and he had been across the aisle.

Mercedes had a deathly fear of knives, as she had ever since their double-wide kitchen, when the sink was right next to the crib. After waking up to find Bach teething on a bloody potato peeler, she had never touched one again.

This was how they fought.

The more Mercedes slurped, the harder Porsche chopped, so as to drown out the noise. The more they did either, the more things escalated, and the more they argued.

Like now.

"Please." Porsche rolled her eyes, though it nearly cost her a finger. "Something's *off* about my fiancé?"

"*Fake* fiancé," Mercedes corrected her with a slurp.

Porsche hurled the knife toward the butcher block. "Is that the *BEST*"—*chop*—"*YOU*"—*chop*—"*CAN*"—*chop*—"*DO?*" *Chop*.

"You'll see. It'll all come out eventually. It always does." *Slurp! Slurp! Slurp!*

"*It?* What is *it*? Be a little more *vague*, why don't you?" *Chop! Chop! Chop!*

Mercedes pointed to her head with her straw, flinging hot coffee into her own eye. She blinked and kept going. "You want specifics? Pam and I were putting together your engagement press release for tonight. Turns out Whitey doesn't even know which Whiteboyz albums went *platinum*. That's not just stupid. It's *Wikipedia stupid*, and that's just *rude*. I mean *hello?* It's his father's company! Put in a *little* effort. *Lie* about it. Get out your phone and *fake* it. That's what *I* do when someone asks me about *you three*."

Bentley looked up.

"Exactly. You're one to talk," Porsche said, as she cleaved an iceberg head in half. "And *Wikipedia* stupid? You didn't know what a *meme* was until you were on one."

Bach snorted as he picked up a card.

Mercedes upped her game. *SLUUUUURP!* "If he's such a genius, then why didn't he go to college?"

Bentley sighed and went back to her book.

Porsche rose to the challenge: *CHOP CHOP CHOP!*

"Seriously? No Royces have *ever* gone to college! His dad went to *Stanford*. You barely got through traffic school!"

Bent sighed more loudly.

Mercedes: *SLUUUUURP!* "He works with his father. What does that mean, he couldn't get a job of his own?"

Porsche: *CHOP CHOP CHOP!* "I work with my *mother*! Is that what you think about me?"

Mercedes: *SLUUUUURP!* "I'm just not convinced that you need to rush into this. That you've considered all your options."

Porsche: *CHOP CHOP CHOP!* "What rush? Whitey went through Casting *six* months ago, Mercedes."

Mercedes: *SLUUUUURP!* "Why not a Kennedy? Or at least a Schwarzenegger? I'd be fine with a Spielberg."

Porsche: *CHOP CHOP CHOP!* "I was born in a gas station and spent my formative years in a double-wide. Whitey was born in Toluca Lake and spent his in a ten-thousand-square-foot house with a built-in grill and a smoker. I'd think you of all people could be a little less of a snob, *MISS TRASHPIRATIONAL!*"

Mercedes: *SLUUUUURP!* "Fine. What about a love triangle? The world loves a love triangle. *You* love a love triangle."

Porsche: *CHOP CHOP CHOP!* "We aren't going to get sponsors for a love triangle. You can't sell a product line around a love triangle. Bridal magazines aren't going to want to put a love triangle on the cover. I'm not torn between two *vampires* here, Mercedes. This is my *marriage* we're talking about."

"First marriage," Bach said, laying down another card.

"Exactly. First marriage. A girl only has *one* first marriage," Porsche said.

"Or a boy," Bach said, raising an eyebrow as he drew a card.

"Even more to the point. Why waste it on him?" Mercedes said. She punctuated the question with an extralong *SLUUUUUUUURP*, for emphasis.

"It's a werewolf," Bentley said, looking up from her book.

"Excuse me?" Porsche glared.

"It was a vampire and a werewolf. The love triangle," Bentley added.

"Ha! That's right." Mercedes slurped on. "And think about those magazine covers—and product lines—and corporate sponsors—for a *Love Triangle!*"

CHOP SLURP CHOP SLURP CHOP SLURP CHOP SLURP . . .

"STOP IT!" Bach slapped his hand on the table. "Enough of this! My god, you're *all* acting like children. How is it that I'm the youngest and I'm the only one who sees this?" He hurled his deck into the air, giving up.

As the cards fell, Mercedes and Porsche stopped to stare at Bach. Even Bent couldn't think of another time when her brother had so openly snapped. He was the chill guy. The easy buffer—not the snapper. Porsche and Mercedes, they were the snappers.

"I'm sorry, Bach." Bent sounded as helpless as she felt.

"It's not your fault," he said wearily, rubbing his face with his hands. "It's just another Diva Smackdown." But it didn't feel the same as usual, Bent knew. The stress of a family falling apart was clearly getting to all of them. She felt a troubling combination of shame and anxiety—a potentially toxic cocktail—and worried about her little brother even more than usual. . . .

Snapping had a way of spreading. Now Porsche shook her head, raising her knife to point it at her mother. "Now look what you've done!"

Mercedes slammed down her coffee. "Me?"

Porsche sent the knife clattering to the counter. "Mercedes! Stop trying to *produce* me! It's my decision, and I've made it. I don't know why we keep talking about this. You're not the bride; I'm the bride."

Mercedes rolled her eyes. "Oh, wait—*you're* the bride? Funny, I don't think anyone could have missed that."

Porsche whirled toward her mother, sending shreds of lettuce flying like confetti. "You know what this is? You can't stand that this whole thing was my idea. The wedding. It kills you that it's going so well, doesn't it? Is that what this is about? Why do you insist on punishing us?"

"*Us?*" Mercedes caught it quickly.

Uh-oh. Bentley ducked behind her book. Bach hid his face in his hands.

"US?!" Mercedes shrilled again.

No, Bentley thought. This is not happening.

Porsche looked frustrated, as if the answer should be obvious. "Us. Whitey and me."

Mercedes laughed. *HA HA HA HA HA!* Bent couldn't believe she was using her artillery laugh on her own family—or that she felt like she had to.

"What is wrong with you?" Porsche looked from her mother to her siblings.

Bentley closed her book, shaking with sudden anger. "We're the Us, Porsche. The four of Us. Just like we've always been."

Porsche hesitated, momentarily stunned. "You know what I meant."

"No." Bent shook her head. "No way. I'm not going to let you screw this up. Your fake groom doesn't get to be your Us. He's your season-six story line, remember? But that's all."

"It's not like that. It's not that simple. I don't know why you're talking to me like I'm a moron." There was a quaver in Porsche's voice. Bentley wondered: Could her sister be expressing genuine *sadness*?

"She's right," Bach said, calmly now. Bent could tell he wanted to be the rock, the thing that brought them all back down to earth. Someone had to be, and it was just as well, because what Bent had to say just might make her sister come completely unraveled.

So Bentley spoke slowly. "He's not real, Porsche. You've never met his parents, have you? You've never even been to that house you just told us about."

"His parents are traveling. He lives in Venice. I've been there," she said, defensively. "Three times."

"But that's not what it's like, Porsche," Mercedes said, trying to sound more levelheaded than she had all day. "Not when it's real. You just don't know the difference because you haven't found it yet. That's what I've been trying to tell you. Nothing about Whitey is real. Not for you. He's a gig. Like one of those actor waiters you can barely even stand to look at when we're taping a lunch scene."

"Shut up," Porsche said. "That's not true."

"You know what comes after season six?" Bentley asked. "Season seven."

"I know that."

"Then use your brain, Porsche." Bent tried to be gentle as she walked her sister through it. "You're the producer. If season six is your fake wedding, what do you think season seven is?"

"I *know*," Porsche said, in a tone that made it pretty clear that she didn't, or at least didn't want to.

"Your fake divorce," Mercedes said. "That's seven."

"I get it. It's fake. I hear you. Fake. Are you happy? *Fake, fake, fake.* Now. Can I go back to planning my wedding?" Porsche moved the knife down into the sink and turned on the water. When she turned it back off again, her eyes were blazing. "Has it ever occurred to any of you that you're the only ones who want this wedding to be fake?"

Mercedes stared. Bentley felt the blood draining out of her face.

"Porsche," Bach said, trying to intervene. "Stop. You can't be serious. This is, like, crazy talk."

"I can. You guys don't understand. I can and I have to. If I'm being honest, it's how I feel." Porsche took a breath. "I don't know what it means, and I don't know what will happen, but I know I want this part to happen. And instead of attacking me about it all the time, maybe you all could try to understand how confusing that might be from where I stand."

"That's enough," Mercedes said. "I'm not going to listen to this garbage anymore. Not from you."

"Excuse me?" Porsche looked like she wanted to slap Mercedes.

"Maybe, Porsche, you should consider the fact that *I'm* the one who gave birth to you in that gas station, that you've never met your father, and that everything I've ever done in life has been to make sure you didn't end up like me. I didn't name you *Chevy, Dodge,* and *Buick,* did I? And yet now here we are."

"Please!" Porsche snorted. "Look around. This isn't a gas station. We aren't trash."

"Right," Mercedes said. "Because this whole desperate mail-order-bride thing? Now that's what I'd call *classy.* Good luck with that. I just hope you get the right name on the cake."

Silence.

Porsche picked the clean knife back up and stabbed it into the butcher block as if it were a corpse. It made a low twanging sound, vibrating as she let go.

For a moment, Bentley actually thought her sister was going to hurl it at one of them. Because this conversation was over. It had to be. Porsche had reached her breaking point.

"Listen to me. You can get behind me—and my wedding and my future husband—or you can go sit at table sixteen by the bathroom." Porsche looked from Mercedes to her brother and sister. "That goes for all of you."

"Great," Mercedes said. "Looking forward to it. Closer to the exit."

"Save me a place," Bentley said. "I'm not going to pretend, Porsche. And I have a tiny bladder."

Porsche looked at Bach. He just shrugged. "It doesn't matter where I sit."

"Done," Porsche said. "I'm just glad it's all out in the open. I'm glad I know how you feel about it."

She raised an eyebrow defiantly.

"About *us*."

By seven thirty sharp, the Main House was ready for an eight P.M. (nine central) live airtime. The format was simple. The *Entertainment Tomorrow* interview was really just two things: (1) a (fake) surprise proposal—during a (fake) interview covering Porsche and Whiteboyz's new (fake) music collaboration—all on live television, and (2) a whole lot of talkie fluff.[63] That way, the footage could then be repackaged for an hour-long programming block. (With plenty of commercial breaks! From plenty of sponsors!)

First the interview had been picked up nationally, then internationally, and now anticipation was building as Porsche's small (large) nation of social media

---

63 Per JG: Could we swap "hard driving journalism" for "talkie fluff?" Pls. revisit! ☹ —D

followers awaited what they thought would be her new label announcement.

Ever since Whitey had first been seen out with the Royces, most of the tabloid world had been expecting it. Porsche Royce was going to be collaborating on an album with the Whiteboyz label. A few outlets had already guessed that they were also dating, but nobody was expecting *THIS*.

The surprise fiancé reveal angle had been Mercedes's idea—and it was a great one. The engagement wouldn't be announced until that night on the show, and then on social media, during the West Coast airtime. The fiancé reveal was the twist that would hopefully break the bank, and be replayed in every country on the planet, for years to come. As a result, *Entertainment Tomorrow* had paid stupid money—stupid millions—for sixteen minutes of bad hand-held from Teddy and Mac. Bad *exclusive* handheld video that was about to become their most-watched work, excluding maybe the wedding itself, if the predictions were right.

No pressure, guys.

Bentley watched from the portable monitors, back in the kitchen. Porsche had been in Hair and Makeup for most of the day. Now she looked as beautiful as ever. If you weren't her sister, and hadn't studied her face as intimately as you had your own, and for as long as you'd been alive, you might not have noticed that she had been crying.

But Bentley did, and she felt terrible. As the live interview went on, she only felt worse.

"What do you have to say to your millions of fans and followers, Porsche? This hunky young music mogul who you've been *collaborating* with, can we expect an album any-time soon?" A fabulous power-blonde with an inarguably good blowout held out a square microphone with a slick *Entertainment Tomorrow* logo.

She knew what she was doing.

"Obviously, what we care about is making music together," Porsche said, trying not to blush.

"Sweet, sweet music." Whitey grinned. "You know it."

Porsche smiled. "We've been really busy lately, haven't we, Whitey?"

"Aw, you know it, Fancy Face." He held his stomach. "Aww, man? Did you hear that? Think that was my stomach growling, on live television."

The journalist smiled, a twinkle in her eye. "Well, goodness! That's certainly not something you hear every day."

Porsche looked at the journalist apologetically. "Sorry, we did come right from the studio. I think neither one of us even had five minutes to grab a granola bar tonight."

"That's okay. I got this." Whitey whipped out his cell phone and punched a few numbers into the keypad.

Porsche looked from the journalist to Whitey, feigning confusion. "What's he—what are you doing? Whitey?"

Whitey smiled at her, putting his hand on her arm. Bent noticed that even now, his signature black bandanna was wrapped around his wrist. "Mercedes? Let me put you on speaker." He held up the phone. "Hey, Moms, you're on live television. Say hi to the planet."

"Hi, planet!" Mercedes's voice echoed out over the dining room.

"Listen, Sweet Pea and I are starving, and I wouldn't normally do this to you, but seeing as we're in your house, and we're kind of busy right now, do you think you could whip up a little something for us in the kitchen?"

"What are you doing?" Porsche said in pretend horror. "That's my mother, not a pizza delivery man!"

He winked at her.

The journalist looked captivated.

Now—still holding the phone, Mercedes stepped out into the dining room and into the interview itself. She was dressed to the nines in a sleek white Chloe sheath, with an old-fashioned apron tied over it. Holding up an oversize wooden spoon.

Whitey doubled over laughing. Porsche looked confused and embarrassed. "Mother!"

"Whip up a little something? Sure, Whitey. No problem. Easy peasy." Mercedes winked back at him. "Piece of cake."

"What is going on, *Tomas*?!" Porsche's face was turning pink now, and her eyes were bright. Surprised! Excited! Confused! Shocked! Embarrassed! This was like the comprehensive final exam for every emotion she'd ever learned how to do. She was *acting* so hard, she looked like she was in danger of popping something.

"Come here," he said to her. "Closer."

Porsche leaned forward.

"What's that on your nose?"

She touched her face, mortified. The interviewer laughed.

Whitey tweaked her nose, pretending to examine it. "Oh, that's nothing. Just a little frosting . . . Sweet Thing."

"Frosting?"

"Sweet Thing?" The interviewer beamed, as if she'd just trapped them in a world exclusive through plucky journalistic skill, instead of through millions of dollars.

Porsche blushed madly. "He knows I love it when he calls me that."

"WAIT A MINUTE! DID YOU SAY . . . LOVE?"

Mercedes waved the spoon over her head. "Bring it out, guys!"

Out in the hallway, Bent and Bach looked at each other. "That's our cue."

Pam tapped her headset. "And we're bringing out the cake. . . ."

Bach grabbed one handle of the massive rolling base, Bentley the other. "Holy crap," Bach coughed. It was like trying to push a VW Bug.

"Push harder," Bent whispered. Bach nodded, and they stared up at the cake, straining as they moved it slowly forward.

It had been molded and baked and frosted to resemble a towering stack of six Tiffany's boxes, all in pale blue buttercream, with the classic white buttercream ribbon. The whole stack was probably bigger than the Royces' Sub-Zero. The center box was made to look like it was open, and on a white chocolate disk in the very middle of that was a black velvet ring box—also open—to display what would forever be known as Porsche Royce's Engagement Ring.

In a matter of seconds, at least half the population of the planet (if Lifespan's *nice numbers* held) would be looking at the same seven-karat (that was the number Bent had heard from Mercedes), emerald-cut, platinum-set solitaire ROCK of a ring that looked to Bentley to be the size of a golf ball.[64]

"*HOLY CRAP!*" Bentley said, again, under her breath. "You could probably kill someone with that thing."

Bach nodded. "Like brass knuckles, only harder, right?"

"How will she be able to move her arm?" Bent stared.

"I don't know. Maybe she won't."

"Go, go, go," Pam said, holding her headset with one hand.

Bent and Bach went back to rolling the cake forward. The crew—Mac and Ted and JoJo—shoved the table from behind so they could pick up speed.

"Remember," Pam said, looking at Bentley, "I want joy."

"Joy." Bent nodded.

"Don't forget." Pam was dead serious, as always. "Give me some freaking joy."

Ted and Mac ran ahead to open the French doors. JoJo flipped on the hall light. Suddenly Bent could see the writing on the cake—bold silver and gold letters carved into the thick white curls of the largest piece of white frosting ribbon.

---

64 *Per Consumer Products: We've run into a snag with the "Porsche Royce Engagement Ring Pops" promotion—standard Ring Pops aren't large enough so we're going to have to special order Jumbo Ring Pops—ups the per unit price. Stay tuned!* ☺ —D

Will You
Marry Me
Porsh?

Bentley froze. She gasped.

"ARE YOU KIDDING ME? Bach, look!" She pointed with one hand, desperately trying to slow the rolling cart with the other.

But the cake only picked up speed toward the stage, where it would be caught on camera and broadcasted to the entire world.

"Her name! Look at the name—"

All Bentley could hear was Mercedes's voice echoing through her head, just as it had echoed through the kitchen itself a few hours before.

I JUST HOPE YOU GET THE RIGHT NAME ON THE CAKE.

"Porsh? Man." Bach was wide-eyed. "Someone's going to be *so fired.*"

Bentley could hear Porsche's screams in her head already. She could imagine the headlines. She could see the people laughing, in front of their streaming video and their televisions and their cell phones—

"No. No. No." Bent looked at her brother, desperate. "We have to stop this. We can't take it out there. PORSH? That's, like, I don't know, PORN meets HORSE—it's like Horse Porn. Is that even a thing?"[65]

---

65 *Standards has still not approved "Horse Porn." They're asking if "horse corn" could evoke the same basic feel? Better yet: "Horse Popcorn"? Potential snack foods tie-in? ☹ ☺ —D*

Bach made a face. "How would I know? I'm gay, I'm not a farmer."

"Bach! This is serious!" It was. But it was also too late.

The cake cart was rolling—

The French doors flinging open—

Spotlights hitting the cake—

Iconic Pop Star Slash Actress Treysi Sweet—a close personal friend of Razz Jazzy—began to sing an original song, "Sweet Thing," in the background. She'd written it just for tonight (and for an undisclosed sum that Bentley could only imagine would pay for more cat toys and matching friend-group nightgowns and cookie batter than a girl could ever dream of).

I JUST HOPE YOU GET THE RIGHT NAME ON THE CAKE.

The cart rolled onward.

Bentley could now see them all, clustered at the far end of the dining room, where it joined the foyer.

Treysi Sweet leaning down from the main stairwell (beatifically crooning)

Mercedes standing a few stairs beneath her (angry tooth-smiling)

Porsche at the very foot of the stairs (softly crying)

Whitey on one knee in front of her (always grinning)

I JUST HOPE YOU GET THE RIGHT NAME ON THE CAKE.

I JUST HOPE YOU GET THE RIGHT NAME ON THE CAKE.

I JUST HOPE YOU GET THE RIGHT NAME ON THE CAKE.

In that split second, Bentley knew what she had to do, and she knew she wasn't the one who could do it.

Only one person she knew could.

Bad Bentley dove toward the rolling cart.

She pushed off against the polished bamboo floor, hurling herself into the air, tumbling up and into the cart full of cake—

WILL

Reached for the frosted PORSH ribbon, fingers outstretched, as if the horrific word itself was her own personal Golden Snitch—

YOU

Caught the look of horror on her sister's face—the flash of anger in her mother's eyes—the eight feet of buttercream as it flew toward a kneeling T. Wilson White—

MARRY

(Treysi just kept singing. She was the consummate professional.)

Bent's hands made contact.

ME

Her hands clutched at the cake, exploding one cake box after another as she spun out into the tower.

PORSH?

The rest was slow-motion chaos. Bright lights flashing. Porsche reeling. Bentley shouting. Whitey lunging out of the path of the cart.

BAM!

The cake hit the stairs and went off like a bomb.

Bentley went tumbling, spread-eagled, into the full length of the most expensive cake ever to be produced by the illustrious Rosebud Cakes of Beverly Hills.

Everyone in the room—camerapeople and gaffers and producers and editors and makeup artists and hairstylists—were sprayed with sugar and buttercream and raspberries, but only Bad Bentley was maimed by it.

(And only Treysi Sweet remained immaculate.)

The cart toppled over on the marble foyer floor.

The room fell silent.

Bent lay back in a soft layer of jettisoned sponge cake, like a halo-shaped pillow, trying to catch her breath.

"What the hell just happened?" She opened her eyes to see Whitey standing over her with his cake-splattered face.

Bentley held up her hand and opened it.

Inside was a diamond ring the size of a golf ball.

He took it from her, a strange look on his face. Then he threw back his head and began to laugh.

Whitey turned to Porsche, who was pulling herself up on the bottom step of the cake-covered stairs. He tried to help her, but one high-top slipped in a puddle of frosting, and he wound up on the floor next to her.

Now he was laughing so hard, he was howling. Then the gaffers started laughing. Then the second grip, and the first AD, and the sound technician. Then the social media person, camera three, a producer, two assistants, and an assistant to those assistants.

Whitey was laughing so fiercely now, he looked like he

was crying. Porsche giggled, and cake got into her nose, and she began to snort-laugh harder.

Whitey fell back into a pile of cake on the floor, rolling from side to side. Porsche wiped a flap of cake from over her left ear and tasted it. "Cake? Do you know how long it's been since I've had cake?"

The room was convulsing now. (Even Treysi Sweet smiled. She was full of compassion.)

Whitey reached up and pulled Porsche down into the cake puddle with him, slipping the golf ball of a ring onto her finger.

"You never answered my question," Whitey said.

"Oh, I'll answer your question." Porsche smiled, pulling him back down into the cake. And the cameras rolled and the crew laughed and the champagne flowed and even the lifestyle journalist was found under the dining room table with Dred Ted—

It was generally thought to be the cutest proposal ever. More than twenty-eight million people in fifty countries and seven continents said so. (Even Treysi Sweet took a selfie with the golf ball rock.) They also said that Bentley was an idiot, except in many more colorful languages and idioms than that.

Only Bach knew the truth, and he'd never say a word, except to hand a cake-covered Bent a bathroom towel when it was all over. "You're a really good sister, Bent. Even if you don't have much of a future in horse porn."

She took the towel and rested her head on his shoulder.

YOU'RE INVITED TO THE ROCK-AND-ROLL, CELEBRITY, FASHIONISTA, HOLLYWOOD WEDDING OF THE CENTURY!

PORSCHE ROYCE & T. WILSON WHITE

STAR IN A LIFESPAN SPECIAL PRESENTATION
"ROLLING WITH THE ROYCES:
YOU MAY NOW KISS THE BRIDE."

COMING TO A TELEVISION NEAR YOU.

EIGHT WEEKS AND COUNTING,

DON'T FORGET TO WATCH EVERY WEEK AS
ROLLING WITH THE ROYCES' FAVE BRIDE
GETS CLOSER AND CLOSER TO
WALKING DOWN THE AISLE.

GUEST STARRING:
BENTLEY ROYCE AS BRIDESMAID
BACH ROYCE AS BEST MAN
MERCEDES ROYCE AS
THE MOTHER OF THE BRIDE
AND YOU AT HOME AS OUR SPECIAL GUESTS!

ENGAGED?! LIFESPAN DROPS A BOMBSHELL: PORSCHE ROYCE HEADS TO THE ALTAR—EXCLUSIVE! BENTLEY BOTCHES BIG MOMENT FOR BIG SIS

AP: Beverly Hills, California

Via Celebcity.com

Surprise! Porsche Royce, reality television celebrity, will be heading to the altar with music label heir and unlikely love T. Wilson White. It's a sudden development for a duo that flew so low under the radar they were thought to be collaborating on an album, rather than on coupledom.

White surprised his now fiancé with a tender television proposal during tonight's exclusive live interview with *Entertainment Tomorrow*. The very Royce proposal included tears, kisses, family and of course, little sister Bentley screwing it all up—sending a six-foot cake flying. Footage of White's proposal is now appearing on every major media outlet in the world.

"I was blown away," Porsche Royce said on her Tumblr page earlier this evening. "Too happy to speak. Also too covered in cake! Love you Bentley! Hope you get the frosting out of your ears! #blessed." The groom confirmed the news in a single tweet from his newly verified @twhiteywhite account. "Boom. Engaged."

"It's every mother's dream. I'm just so thrilled that Porsche and Whitey have found each other," Mercedes Royce said in a post on the official #RWTR fan site. "My children are the most important thing in the world to me, and anything that makes them happy makes me happy."

Bentley Royce tweeted "LET THEM EAT CAKE! ALSO: WEAR CAKE #KLUTZ" via her @TheBentleyRoyce account.

Bach Royce (@TheBachRoyce) tweeted only "IT'S TRUE!" No other details of the engagement were made available.

The internet was ablaze with reactions to tonight's episode.

"@RoycerFan um omg was that the big 1 cuz i'm dying here didn't c that 1 coming! #RWTR6 #OTPorscheWhitey"

"@PorschePeople crying who even is this guy #rwtr6"

"@Royatics speechless #rwtr6 #truelove #porscheboy"

(Disclosure: Celebcity is a fully owned subsidiary of the Lifespan Network, which is itself a fully owned subsidiary of DiosGlobale.)

Follow @celebcity for breaking details,
or www.celebcity.

Twelve

"That's ridiculous." Bentley glared at her phone from the passenger seat of Mercedes's car.

"What is?" Her mother flipped on her blinker.

"Porsche's engagement is *still* the lead story on *People* and *InTouch* and *Us Weekly*—but I didn't even get a mention from Perez. Not a word!" Bad Bentley had been working overtime, and she was more than a little annoyed.

"You? Since when do you care about Perez Hilton?"

"I let some One Direction clone give me a ride on a freaking Harley down Sunset Boulevard. We practically ran over half the TMZ crew. I mean, we gunned an engine in Perez's face. There are *Snaps* of it, Mercedes. Snaps."

Mercedes raised an eyebrow as she pulled her car into the parking lot. "I'm not sure I want to hear about that."

"Too late," Bent said. She tossed her phone into her bag. "All they want to write about is either the future Mrs. Whitey White—or the Duck Daughter baking up Donald Duckcakes. Joelynne Wabash is skyrocketing straight into Miley Cyrus territory."

Mercedes looked at her daughter strangely. "You know

what they say. Maybe you just need to leave it on the wheel."

"I need to leave it somewhere, all right."

"I can't believe Shandi is late," Mercedes griped.

"Don't worry. I reserved our bikes. And besides, the later she is, the less we'll have to sweat," Bentley replied.

Saturday was off to a bad start. Any Saturday that started off at TryCycle was off to a bad start in Bentley's opinion. But the holidays had whizzed by at record speed (yes, with Whitey over for Christmas Eve, and yes, with a camera crew) and it was time to get rid of the holiday love handles. So: spin class.

But Shandi was a no-show so far, and the beloved Tomme had quit the Beverly Hills TryStudio months ago, so there was no one to cover Shandi's slot. Rumor had it that Tomme (who didn't overwhelm you with choreography but whose arm repetitions were deadly) had gotten a small speaking part in a Blake Lively movie. Since Blake Lively was herself a TryCyclist, it was entirely possible— but either way, the fact remained that Tomme was gone and the Beverly Hills location had yet to recover.

Mercedes dropped her glasses into the locker.

Bentley narrowed her eyes. "Are your contacts in?"

"No. I didn't have time."

"Then you have to wear your glasses. You won't be able to see a thing."

"I sweat too much. They'll slide off my nose." Mercedes slammed the locker door. She was actually just too vain to wear her glasses when anyone could see them, even in a dark room during a workout class. So vain, in fact, that she barred the crew from all her workout sessions as well. She didn't want anyone catching any sort of jiggling on camera.

Bent shook her head. "Shandi's hard. You need to see for her choreography." TryCyclists were always talking about choreography, which usually just meant swirling your butt around in the air over your seat.

"I'll be fine. Shandi's no Tomme." Mercedes sighed as she grabbed her complimentary water.

"How would you know? You never even went to Tomme," Bentley groused, examining the water. It was plastered with custom For Your Consideration signs advertising *Blown*, a Lifespan show that one of the Lifespan producers who came to this TryCycle had up for some kind of Emmy.

"Of course not. He was the one with the arms, right?"

Bent nodded, holding up her water. "*Blown*? Wasn't that canceled?"

"Maybe too late to get it off the water bottles." Mercedes shrugged, checking them in on the seat chart at the counter. "You put us behind each other? How do you feel about staring at my butt for an hour?"

"Not all that great."

"Would you rather I stared at yours?"

Bentley grabbed a towel. "This day is only getting better and better."

"Shandi just called. She'll be here in five," said the perky, buff twentysomething behind the counter.

They headed into the studio, where candles flickered in

the darkness. Mercedes stumbled into the first row of bikes, then cursed as she gouged her calf on a spiked pedal in the second. By the time they got to the third row in the darkness, Bent was ready to flee, even if it meant her mother would never be able to find her way back to the one small square locker in the sea of identical small square lockers that hid her glasses.

It would almost be worth it for that alone.

As they reached their seats, Bent could hear her own stomach growling along to the whining steel-string guitar playing in the background. "We should have had breakfast." She sighed.

"We did." Mercedes stopped at her bike. "This is mine, right?"

"Yes. But seven blueberries and a tablespoon of chia seeds in half a cup of Icelandic yogurt is not breakfast."

"What were you expecting, toast?" Mercedes laughed.

My mother is cruel, Bentley thought. She jammed her foot onto the pedal of the stationary bike. "I don't see what's so wrong about two pieces of bread, that's all I'm saying. Bread is good for the soul."

"TryCycle is good for the soul. Bread isn't good for anything. It's just not necessary. And not even an *ancient* grain." Mercedes lowered the seat on the stationary bike in front of her. The TryCycle room was dark, but not as dark as it was about to be. She cocked her head and listened. "Speaking of ancient, what do you think? Is that sitar? Or the lyre?"

"I think it's the sound of my brain shutting down." Bentley shot a pleading look at her watch. They still had three minutes until Shandi's arrival, which was more than enough time for this conversation to go very badly.

"Don't be nasty," Mercedes said. "Just because I'm not a carbivore."

"You don't have to eat it. You just have to admit that bread has been important to every civilization for a thousand years," Bent said, hoisting herself up onto her seat. "Then I'll agree to disagree."

"Civilizations don't get the cover of *Teen Vogue*," Mercedes said, wrenching loose another knob on the bike.

"Neither do I."

"You won't if you can't get past this whole bread thing. You have to go for it. You're not getting any younger."

"I'm seventeen, Mercedes."

"Seventeen is old for a model."

"Then I guess it's probably a good thing I'm not a model."

"You have to start thinking about the future."

"I have. That's why I want to go to college." The words came rolling out before Bent could stop them, so she went with it. "I've already applied to UCLA, actually. I got a recommendation from Mrs. Reynolds, and she says it's not a sure thing, but I have a decent shot. I still don't know if I'll get in, but—"

"*Seriously?*" Mercedes looked like she had just been slapped in the face. "This is a joke, right? Because it's not in any of the projected story lines, not for season seven or even eight."

Bentley shook her head. She didn't know what she was doing. She didn't blame her mother for freaking out. To be honest, she couldn't believe she'd said any of it out loud. What the hell was wrong with her? Self-sabotage was not in the game plan. "I know. Forget it."

"I'm forgetting it," Mercedes said.

"I didn't mean it."

"I know you don't mean it. This is what you do."

"*Is it?*"

"*Even you* couldn't be that selfish. Not after everything we've been through. You're just acting out."

Bentley stared at her mother. This time, she was the one who felt like she'd been slapped. "I'm not *acting out* on anything. I'm just telling you how I *feel*. And what does that mean, *even me*? You think *I'm* the selfish one?" she said, busying herself with readjusting her handlebars.

"Exactly," Mercedes said.

There was no point trying to explain to her mother the irony of those particular comments, especially coming from her. Instead, Bent tried another line of questioning. "How is it selfish to want to get an education?"

"Where is this all coming from? You've never rocked the boat like this before."

"How about from the fact that literally everyone else in my school is going to go to college except for the two actresses, the art school kids, and the girl writing the eating disorders memoir?"

Mercedes glared.

"And even the eating disorders girl is probably going to the UCLA Neuropsych ward, so technically that's still a campus."

"Seriously?" Mercedes sighed.

"You knew I wanted this. You just pretended not to know," Bent said. "You never wanted to talk about it, and you didn't care if I did."

"What is there to say? What do you want me to tell you? You can go to college when we're in syndication." Mercedes laid her towel across her handlebars.

Wow, Bentley thought, now I know I was right to keep my college plans a secret. She pedaled on, telling herself that this was a good thing, that it meant she could trust her instincts.

She wasn't giving up hope yet.

Mercedes could say whatever she wanted now. There was now, and there was later. If Porsche and Whitey became as big as they wanted to be—as big as Bentley had every hope of them being—nobody would insist on needing Bentley on-screen for season seven. That was what she told herself, anyway.

Not even Mercedes.

"It's time, everyone. Let's leave it on the wheel." Shandi, their dreadlocked TryGuide, beamed from the spotlight, flopping her well-toned body back and forth as she cycled from a standing position on the stage at the front of the room. If Bent squinted, Shandi looked like some bizarre species of extremely happy, jumping fish.

"I've got a special treat for y'all, TryCyclists! Remember

our boy Tomme? He's going to come up on the stage and ride with me today. Get up here, Tomme-boy!" Shouts and cheers drowned out the end of the sentence.

Bentley sat straight up.

A muscular boy in all-black spandex and a black bandanna hopped up onto the stage.

Shandi beamed. "I know you've all heard the rumors, and guess what—they're true. Tomme's got a real acting gig, so let's be extra supportive and give him a big TryCycle welcome home."

The class burst into applause. Bentley didn't.

Tomme stood up on his bike, pedaling as fast as he could. He nodded his black bandanna'd head, rocking out in time with the music. "You guys ready for some killer arms?"

The class cheered. Bentley didn't.

She just held her breath and focused on his trademark black bandanna.[66]

Then the lights went even darker and the music went up and there was nothing else Bentley could do but stare at T. Wilson White as he completed a full forty-minute TryCycle routine not twenty feet away from her unsuspecting mother.

Mercedes tried to keep up with his killer arms, even if she couldn't focus well enough to see his face. If she could have seen, if she could have put it all together, then she

---

66 *Per JG: Could we price mass production of the signature "Whitey" Black Bandanna? Look into trademarking the color black, also bandannas? He says "There's something there." ☺ —D*

would also have known what only one other person in the TryStudio knew.

What Bentley knew.

That it was him.

That his acting gig was on *RWTR*.

And that the beloved former TryCyclist known as Tomme, he of the killer arms and the easy choreography, was also the fiancé currently known as Whitey.

"I am going to freaking *kill you*," Bentley hissed.

Tomme stood there in front of her, panicking.

He was frozen in place next to his locker with a half-toweled-off torso—and looked like he'd seen the ghost of his greatest enemy.

Only I'm not a ghost, Bentley thought. *Though you'll wish I was by the time I'm finished with you.*

"How could you do this?" She was shaking. It had taken her all of ten minutes to coax Mercedes to the car without her, saying she had forgotten her earphones. In the course of those minutes, she had not become the least bit calmer.

"You don't understand," Tomme said. "I can explain everything. Come with me."

"I'm not going anywhere with you."

He wagged his head toward a back room with a half-closed door, where Bent could just make out a mop.

"Let's go somewhere we can talk privately," he said. He pushed open the door. "Half my old clients are in this hallway."

Bent glared and followed him inside. "You were right. I don't understand at all. You're supposed to be marrying my sister. You're supposed to be the head of a major record label. You're not supposed to be *teaching spin class* at TryCycle. You're not supposed to be such a *giant idiotic loser*."

"I can see you're upset," Tomme began. Then the door creaked open a bit, as if someone was pushing it from the other side. Bent froze and grabbed Tomme by the arm. He swung the door slowly open—but no one was there.

Bent slammed the door again. She was pale. "Upset? Of course I'm upset. *MY FUTURE BROTHER-IN-LAW SLASH MUSIC MOGUL WAS TEACHING MY SPIN CLASS.* While my sister thinks you're doing, what? Golf?"

He nodded, embarrassed. "Eighteen holes at the Riviera."

"Make that giant, idiotic, loser *liar*." Bent shook her head. "What if Mercedes had been wearing her glasses?"

"I'm sorry, Bentley. It won't happen again."

"You're right. Do you know how I know that? Because I'm going to go right home and tell my sister everything. Then it won't happen again, because she'll never speak to you again—and good riddance!"

Tomme looked crestfallen. He picked his words carefully. "Is that really what you want? What about the show? What about the wedding? What about—Porsche?"

"Don't pretend you care about my sister." Bent was furious.

"I'm not pretending. I love your sister. I want to marry her."

Bentley slapped him as hard as she could.

The moment she did, the door creaked open and Tomme slammed it once more. "We're having a private conversation, here!"

Luckily, whoever it was walked away, but Bentley was officially miserable.

"Tomme. I don't know what to say."

"I know, I know." He rubbed his damp hair with his black bandanna, and Bent closed her eyes so the sweat wouldn't fly into them.

She didn't want to see him, anyway.

He looked like one of the small, drowned rats the pool guys dragged out of the Royce swimming pool with their long nets.

"This has to stop, Tomme. Now."

"We have to figure out a way to break up Whitey and Porsche," Bentley said to her brother, hours later, as they sat in the parking lot of In-N-Out Burger, mildly exhilarated off their successful (though temporary) escape from the camera crew.

"Hell *yes*, girl. Screw that jerk," Bach said, dumping ketchup on his fries.

"I'm serious. I'm done. It can't go on. This whole thing is getting out of hand." She moved a pawn on their travel chessboard and unwrapped her grilled cheese.

She wished she could tell Bach the truth. She wanted to tell him everything. Most of all, she wanted to tell him not just that their future brother-in-law was a fraud, but that he was also an idiot; if Tomme was stupid enough to try to lead a class at TryCycle, then other people were going to find out he was a fraud. And then all it would take would be one tweet, one Snap, one Instagram, and it was over. Everything. The wedding, season six, her entire existence.

And a factory full of Lippies.

Over.

Bach took a bite of his burger. "You think anyone's going to listen to us? In case you haven't noticed, you're not the one getting married. The bride's a big girl."

"Don't let her hear you say that." Bent smirked. Porsche had the trainer coming up to the house every day now.

"She knows what she's getting into. She can take care of herself," he said.

If you only knew.

Bach checked the board, moving a pawn before he bit into his Double-Double. "Besides, she'll kill you if you mess up her wedding."

His phone buzzed. "I gotta take this. I'm putting together a game—"

"Bach—"

But he held up a hand to silence her. "Yeah. I got it," he said into the phone. "We can handle one more guy, but that's it, Jake. One. Cash only. Yeah, we're changing things up a little. I'll text you an address when I have it."

He clicked off.

"Another game, Bach? That's not cool. You know it's getting out of hand."

He made a face. "God, you too now? I get enough of this unsolicited bullshit concern from Whitey."

"Whitey?!" Bent fumed. "Whitey does not have the right to worry about your gambling. I'm not Whitey. I'm your *sister*, your actual sister, your flesh and blood, and my concern is not bullshit. Unsolicited, sure. But bullshit, no."

When did everything get so complicated?

"Relax, sis." Bach shoved the rest of his burger into his mouth and swallowed. "Jeez. Are you going to move again or what?"

"I'm going to move. Of course I'm going to move. I'm just still trying to figure out what to do," Bent said.

As she said the words, she realized they were true.

It was her move, and she needed to make it.

"Well, you let me know when I'm up," he said, crumpling his wrapper and flashing her a wink that was less fitting for a little brother and more for a suave, professional gambler.

"Oh, you'll know," she said. "You'll definitely know."

But now he was back on the phone and setting up some other game and laughing, and she had plenty of time to contemplate the future and weddings and television and how to plot the perfect checkmate.

Thirteen

Maybe there was something to it after all, this hunting stuff. As Bentley made her way through the crowded ballroom of the Beverly Wilshire, she felt her adrenaline spike.

It was a rush, knowing that she had set out to do something dangerous. Something difficult. Something potentially life-altering—

"What are you doing here?" A voice from behind interrupted her.

"Nothing," Bent said, before she even turned around to see Whitey standing there in jeans and a black tuxedo jacket. She knew he'd be here; the Wilderness Society was one of his assigned causes. "Are you okay?" He looked so pale and jittery that for a moment she forgot she was here to take him down.

Whitey nodded. "I guess, sure. I'm here to 'hunt for hope'!" Bentley winced at the name of the event—what were the odds of a hunting-themed benefit coincidentally named after the Royces' own deceased—

Don't say it,[67] Bent thought. Don't even think it. Instead, she looked around the room and tried to make herself smile.

Whitey assumed the smile was for him and grinned back. "Hey, you clean up pretty nice, sis."

I do? she thought, feeling only a little guilty about her plan. Too bad I'm here to break up you and my sister.

She nodded, placing her hand on his arm gently. "Whitey, don't take this the wrong way, but you seem really . . . off."

"Off how, exactly?" Whitey looked spooked.

She tilted her head, looking him over. "I don't know. You're shaky, agitated. Like you've been hitting the Red Bull again. Maybe even . . . scared?"

He whistled. "You're good. I didn't want to say anything, but Grunburg's been up in my grill all night. I know I'm not supposed to touch the guy, but it's like he's baiting me, B, I swear."

"I believe it. The guy's a menace."

"Like he wants me to blow it or something."

"I'm sure he does."

Whitey frowned. "But that's not your problem," he said. "I'll shake it off, don't worry."

Then someone caught his eye, and he pointed to the stage, where Joelynne Wabash was already sitting at a round table.

"Check it out. Up front." The Duck Diva was wearing so many spangled sequins, you couldn't have missed her in a football stadium full of Christmas sweaters.

---

67 Per JG: Really, don't say it. ☹ —D

Bentley shuddered. "Joelynne? How could I miss her?"

"Not her, him. My buddy Sean." Whitey was actually pointing to Sean Slotkin, the (balding) head of the Reality Channel, Lifespan's rival company, who was standing there talking to the Duck Diva.

Bent looked at Whitey, confused. "How do *you* know Sean Slotkin?"

Whitey—or more accurately, Tomme—shrugged. "He's been in the front row of my Thursday-evening class for, like, two years."

"Do not tell me that," Bent said.

"Let's go say hi." Whitey smiled, putting his arm around her shoulders. "He's a great guy. Really strong core."

"What? No way."

"Why not?"

Bentley froze, struggled to swallow.

Because he knows you're a TryCycle instructor, dumbass? Because it will blow your cover, as I've tried to explain a thousand times? Because he's a tool, like they all are, and you're too stupid to even know it?

But she didn't say any of those things.

She knew she was going to have to act now if she was going to act at all. The plan in her mind was ready to be executed, but she couldn't help but feel a pang of guilt: Was this going to ruin things for her sister? Was it going to ruin Whitey's—no, *Tomme's*—life?

Does it matter? You came here to get rid of him, she reminded herself, *so do it.*

She forced herself to look Whitey—Tomme—directly in

the eyes. "Because he hit on me," she blurted.

"What?"

"Yeah. When I first got here. He, uh . . . he put his hand on my . . . butt." It pained her to say it, but it was all she could come up with. She just hoped he bought it.

He did.

Whitey's face dropped. "Oh, hell no. Nobody touches my baby sister-in-law without her permission. Screw that guy." He balled up his fists, cheeks turning red, and started to walk away.

One . . . two . . . three . . .

"Whitey, stop! Where are you going?" she called after him. *Protest. Make it convincing. You don't want him to get himself into trouble.*

"I'm gonna give that guy a piece of my mind. I can't let him get away with that—you may think this wedding is fake, Bent, but Porsche's family is real to me, okay? So I'm taking care of this. You don't worry."

Crap.

She felt like crap.

Big mistake, Bent! Abort mission! Abort mission!

What was she thinking? Whether or not Whitey was right for her sister, he was a stand-up guy who cared about her and her whole family—and sabotaging him now just wasn't a decent thing to do.

Those twenty-eight million people were right. You really are the worst sister in the world.

"Whitey! Wait up!" She tried to catch him, bumping

into waitresses with wild animal noses carrying carefully balanced trays of champagne as she made her way through the crowded room.

She closed the gap little by little, past wraps and shrugs and caplets and jackets, until she could make out his broad, cut shoulders directly in front of her.

"Whitey!"

She grabbed him by the arm—one of Tomme's infamous *killer* arms—and pulled him toward her.

"What—?" Whitey was startled, and so was the deer-nosed waitress standing next to him—and she shoved against him, and he against Bent—

Until there they were, face-to-face in the enormous crowd, arms around each other. She leaned up to whisper in his ear. There was no other way to do it.

CLICK CLICK CLICK CLICK CLICK

The sound of a thousand lens shutters sounded. The paparazzi covering the entrance to the ballroom went crazy—and Bent and Whitey turned around, looking like two guilty children, caught red-handed.

CLICK CLICK CLICK CLICK CLICK

Whitey backed away, and Bentley fled.

CLICK CLICK CLICK CLICK CLICK

But it was too late.

CLICK CLICK CLICK CLICK CLICK

There was a word in Hollywood for what it looked like they were doing, and it wasn't one Porsche Royce was going to want to see in print.

CLICK CLICK CLICK CLICK CLICK
It was canoodling.[68]

The next morning, Porsche yanked Bent out of her bed from beneath her comforter while she was still asleep.

She fell to the floor in her jammies. "What?"

"CANOODLING? ARE YOU FREAKING KIDDING ME?"

Bent's sister didn't let go of her arm. Right away, Bent guessed the news had been bad. She could tell by Porsche's iron grip.

"It's not how it—"

"YOU GOT A CANOODLING CAPTION? WITH MY FIANCÉ?"

"I know how it looks—"

"CANOODLING?"

"Okay, I see your point. That's bad—"

"Bad? It doesn't look bad. It looks terrible. Beyond skanky. Desperate, even."

"I was just trying to—"

"Trying to what? Trying to hook up with my *fiancé*? Is something going on with you two, Bent? Is that what this is about? Whose side are you on, here?"

"No! God! Yours! I'm on *your* side!"

"Your sister's right," Mercedes interrupted from the doorway.

---

68 *Per JG: Licensing tie-in opportunity: Canoodling Pasta? Canoodle the noodle? Canoodles and Cheese? Or similar? ☺ —D*

"She is?" Bentley looked up from the floor.

"I am?" Porsche frowned, dropping her sister's arm.

"Wait. You're taking her side?" Bent was suspicious.

"My side?" Porsche repeated, incredulous.

Mercedes folded her arms. "Of course I am. Any mother would. Bentley, you're getting out of control. That's it. I've seen enough. You're *grounded*."

Bentley stared. "I'm *what*?"

Porsche raised an eyebrow. "For real?"

Now Bach was in the room, leaning against the doorway in his infamous boxers. "What exactly does that mean, Mercedes? *Grounded*?" He looked amazed, almost delighted.

"You know exactly what it means." She didn't smile.

"If you want to be mad at someone, why don't you ground Whitey?" Bent groused. "This is so sexist."

"Because I don't care about Whitey," Mercedes said evenly.

"If I'm grounded, that means I can't go out in the public eye. I can't do my job. I can't do anything. That basically goes against everything you've raised me to believe in, Mercedes, so excuse me if I'm a little freaked-out here." Bent had never seen her mother act this way.

"You'll still be in front of the camera," Mercedes said matter-of-factly. "You'll just be doing what you're supposed to be doing. Planning your sister's shower, like the good bridesmaid you're supposed to be."

Porsche looked shocked. "I thought you hated Whitey. I thought you were opposed to this whole wedding thing."

"It is what it is. I can't stop it now." Mercedes turned

to Bentley. "But I can stop you. No. More. Parties. For the show, and for the family. That story arc is officially finished. I can't take another day of it."

Bentley was reeling. "Excuse me?"

Bach exhaled. "Oh, thank god."

Porsche rolled her eyes. "Finally."

Mercedes stayed on point. "And Bentley, this means no more Whitey, period. I don't care what your intentions were, you've set yourself up to look like an idiot."

"Yeah, I get that a lot," Bent said.

"It's not funny." Mercedes shook her head. "I told you T. Wilson White was a disaster waiting to happen. Porsche may be too far down the rabbit hole to save, but he's not going to take you down too. I'd sooner toss that loser off a balcony myself than let that happen." She didn't smile, and she didn't seem to be joking.

"Too soon," Bach said, shaking his head. "Poor Hopie."

"Way too soon." Bent nodded.

"Excuse me?" Porsche said, insulted. "That loser? Are you talking about my fiancé?"

Bent didn't know what to think.

On some level, she knew this—the grounding, the lecture, all of it—was the nicest, most maternal thing Mercedes had ever said to her—and yet, on another level, it was also the least Mercedes thing her mother had ever said.

What was happening to the Royce family?

Bent was stunned. She wasn't sure whether to laugh or cry.

So she did both.

BENTLEY DENIES CATCHING GROOM'S EYES
FAMILY FEUD OR MORE TEEN 'TUDE?

AP: Beverly Hills, California

Via Celebcity.com

Proving that a Royce can steal the spotlight from anyone—even Joelynne Wabash, the so-called Duchess of Ducks, headlining her own fund-raising event—Bentley Royce made the news again Saturday night, when she was photographed in close proximity to T. Wilson White, her sister Porsche's fiancé.

Though the troubled teen daughter of the *Rolling with the Royces* television family has long been photographed doing the wrong thing at the wrong time, canoodling with her sister's fiancé would represent a new low for the tight-knit family, even considering Bentley's checkered past.

Mercedes Royce, matriarch of the clan, took to Twitter to denounce the rumored Royce rift. In a statement issued via her verified Twitter account, @Real_Mercedes, she said:

"Media wants to see dirt everywhere but not everything is a scandal, @twhiteywhite is like a brother to @TheBentleyRoyce! There is no 'Royce Rift.' #GROWUP"

Bentley Royce herself said, via @TheBentleyRoyce:

"That's gross and you know what I'm talking about. #EWW @ThePorscheRoyce @twhiteywhite @TheBachRoyce"

Bach Royce said, via @TheBachRoyce:

"Seriously?!?!?!"

Porsche Royce turned the focus to her latest product, SisterLippies by Porsche—a line of blush said to work "not just for you but for when your little sister steals it from you!"

T. Wilson White's Twitter account focused mostly on his workout.

Developing . . .

(Disclosure: Celebcity is a fully owned subsidiary of the Lifespan Network, which is itself a fully owned subsidiary of DiosGlobale.)

Follow @celebcity for breaking details,
or www.celebcity.com.

Fourteen

Weeks later, Bentley sat in therapy trying not to fall apart. The adult coloring books Dr. A. kept offering her were not helping, no matter how soothing they were supposed to be. Bent could color for a week straight, and everything would still be a mess; in fact, she was currently as messed up as she was grounded.

Which was very.

Bent knew what had happened. Her problem had a name. A few, actually.

T. WILSON WHITE.

TOMME TORRES.

WHITEY.

She just couldn't bring herself to say any of those words out loud—and definitely not what she knew about them. She wasn't exactly sure how patient-shrink privilege worked, and for a moment she had considered unburdening herself—but it was too risky. She wouldn't even let herself think about it all, let alone talk about it.

Dr. A. cleared his throat. He fluttered his fingers and Albie got up, padded over, and nosed his aging, white snout into Bentley's hand. (Dr. A. was good with dogs; he was considering becoming a dog therapist—not just because the money was better, but the clients were apparently friendlier.)

Go away, Albie. I don't need your sympathy licks, Bent thought crossly, although she couldn't help it. She stroked his apricot-gold fur and immediately began to talk.

"What happened is something I can't tell anyone."

"Why not?"

"It's too terrible. I can't handle it. Especially because it's my fault."

"What is?"

"Everything."

Dr. A. looked interested. He tapped his pencil on his empty pad. "For example?"

"Bach is worse than ever. Porsche thinks I'm trying to steal her fake fiancé. Mercedes is so desperate, she's reading mommy blogs for the first time in her life. We're all falling apart, and I was supposed to be the one who was keeping us together."

"Sometimes falling apart is also progress."

"And sometimes it's just falling apart. Personally, I think we're looking at door number two."

"And? How does that all make you feel, Bentley? What do you want?"

To disappear.

I wish I could just disappear.

She didn't answer him, though.

Not out loud.

Instead, she stared into space.

That's what I want. I want to disappear.

"Bentley? Are you with me?"

"Oh, hi. Sorry. I was . . ."

"Have you ever considered pet adoption?"

"Excuse me?"

"I was just thinking, it might sound a tad extreme, but what if you had a companion, someone loyal, someone you could tell everything to, no matter what, and who would keep your secrets safe?"

"You're back on the pet thing again?"

"You've often spoken of relating to shelter animals, feeling like you have a lot in common?" Doc A. tapped his pencil on his yellow legal pad.

She looked at her therapist. "You're kidding, right?"

"Why would you say that?" He tapped again. "Why don't you head over there after our session and find yourself a confidant?"

She sat up in her overstuffed chair. "Because I have actual problems, Doc. Grown-up problems. Not kid problems. Not the kinds of things finally getting the dog or the cat you've always wanted can fix."

"Have you?"

"What?"

"Always wanted a dog or a cat?"

Really? "I don't know what I've always wanted, Doc."

"I think you do, Bentley. I think we all do."

She scowled at him. "Well, whatever that thing is, it better not need a leash. Let's just say, my family doesn't have too great a track record in that department."

"How do you know?" Doc A. asked.

Bent looked at him. "I was there."

"I mean, how do you know this won't help until you try? I think having a creature to care for will do wonders for you, not to mention it will love you unconditionally."

There it is again. Unconditional love.

Was she thinking about it because of therapy, or was it coming up in therapy because it was something she needed to think about?

Either way, she knew right then she would be visiting the shelter.

When she arrived home with two kittens, Bentley was, predictably, attacked. She had hoped Mac and Ted and JoJo would be around, shooting extra material up at the house—anything that could constitute some form of human buffer—but no such luck.

"You don't get to make those kinds of decisions alone, Bentley." Mercedes almost sounded like a mother. "When you live under my roof, you live by my rules. That's the way it has to be."

Wow, one good grounding and look at her go.

Suddenly Mercedes Royce was embracing parenthood with arms wide open. Her voice echoed all the way through the kitchen, where they were sitting, out into the dining room and the front hall, where stylists were putting together the next day's pull rack.

"Why? Because I'm a child?"

"Yes. And because you had no idea what you were doing, bringing home live animals." Mercedes shook her head. "They're going back."

"No, they're not. They're my therapy kittens. Dr. A. says—"

"Bentley Royce! I don't care what your therapist says. I'm your mother, and I say you will listen to—"

"Excuse me, *Mercedes*? You're my *what*?"

"Calm down, Bentley."

"Don't tell me to calm down. I don't have to calm down. And don't tell me I don't know how to take care of someone, because I do."

"This is all about that stupid rabbit, isn't it?"

Bentley froze. She hadn't even realized her mother remembered the rabbit. The fact that Mercedes did somehow made the whole thing worse, and it was all Bent could do not to burst into tears on the spot.

"It wasn't just *a stupid rabbit*. His name was Franklin, and he was *my* stupid rabbit, and I happened to love him. And you said we were going on television, and we didn't need stinky rabbit pellets piling up beneath his hutch—"

"We didn't."

"And I said I would keep the cage so clean that there wouldn't be any stinky rabbit pellets."

"It was just a rabbit."

"Not to me."

"I can't believe we're still talking about this."

"I can't believe I came home to find the hutch was empty and Franklin gone."

"If you're waiting for me to say I'm sorry, it's going to be a long wait." Mercedes wasn't backing down. "You wouldn't have been able to handle the responsibility. Another living thing, depending on you, all the time? Every day of its life—and yours?"

Bentley knew her mother wasn't just talking about kittens anymore.

"We couldn't afford it then, and you can't handle it now."

Bentley stood up. "Oh, wow. Okay." She was reeling, practically stumbling. Dr. A. always said she would know when she had reached her limit, and Bent had more than reached it. Bent had destroyed it. It was over. This whole charade called the Royce family had finally come to the end, at least as far as Bentley Royce was concerned.

This is the real bubble, and it's finally popped.

"Sit down," Mercedes began.

"Has it really been so terrible for you, all this time, *Mother*? Have we really been that much of a burden, *Mom*? Because I can just about buy my own kibble now, *Mommy*."

"No, you can't. You know your money is all in a trust until you're older."

"Still. Say the word, *Moms*, and we don't have to pretend to do this anymore."

Now it was Mercedes's turn to spring out of her chair. "That's enough. This conversation is over."

"It's not just this conversation that's over, *Momma*. Don't tell me I can't handle the responsibility, *Mommy*, because you have no idea what I can handle, *Mother*."

"Really?"

"Let's just say, you would be surprised." Bentley stepped between her mother and the No Kill cardboard cat carrier. "And if you come near my kittens, I'll be gone so fast, you'll never find out."

Bentley picked up the carrier and disappeared into her room before her mother could answer.

Mercedes hadn't ventured into her daughter's bedroom, or even tried to, in as long as Bent could remember. She usually hovered near the door, which was the unspoken protocol and as far inside as she ever came. Bentley didn't know—or couldn't remember—which one of them had decided it had to be like that, or when. That was just how it was.

Yet now there Mercedes was, two hours later, knocking on the door as if she was the sort of person who came into her children's rooms all the time.

"Bentley."

Bent didn't answer.

She had a few things on her mind and two sleeping kittens on her lap, so she wasn't exactly in the mood to go running to the door.

In fact, if Mercedes had asked, Bentley might have admitted she was counting down the minutes until midnight.

That was when the first of her college admissions

decisions was supposed to be posted, at least according to Mrs. Reynolds, her counselor.

Regular parents knew things like that—and if they didn't, they knew enough to ask. Not that Bent thought Mercedes would do either. And Mercedes didn't.

So Bent said nothing, and the door stayed shut.

Mercedes must have finally given up waiting for permission to come in, because eventually the door creaked open. "Hi," she said meekly.

Silence.

Bent hit REFRESH and stared at the screen. A kitten twitched in its sleep.

Mercedes slowly ventured into the room—deeper and deeper—and finally sat awkwardly down on the foot of the bed.

Bent ignored her, keeping her hand on the kittens and her eye on the clock in the top corner of her laptop screen.

Mercedes laid her hand on her daughter's forehead. It was a supportive gesture implying familiarity and family—the kind who touched each other. The kind you found on scripted television, with parents and grandparents played by people like Roma Downey or Stacy Keach.

In other words, it was not something Bentley had ever felt before. Not from Mercedes.

Not for years.

"I'm—I guess—really." Mercedes drew a breath and tried again. "I'm sorry."

Bent shivered beneath her mother's hand.

"I can tell something's on your mind. Do you want to

talk about it? You know you can tell me anything, Bentley."

Bent didn't know what to say.

Tell you what?

That I'm not going to get into college and that it doesn't matter because you're not going to let me go anyways?

That Porsche is falling in love with a TryCycle instructor pretending to be a music mogul, and I'm the only one who knows it?

That Bach has a gambling problem the size of Texas and nobody seems to care?

That I'm tired of Being Bentley, and tired of being told what to do?

That maybe growing up means coming up with my own story lines?

That you can't ground me and lecture me and expect me to suddenly take you seriously as a parent, after seventeen years of you not letting me call you Mom?

Should I tell you that?

That I don't feel like you love me, and that I hate myself for letting it get to me the way it does?

Do you really want to know, Mom?

Bentley sat up and looked at her mother. Really looked at her. Her expression was concerned. Her eyes were sad. The touch of her hand was gentle. But there was something else, something Bentley couldn't put her finger on.

It wasn't just her face that seemed different.

The way the collar tucks up from the soft gray V of her sweater. The small pearl studs. The pointed Tod's loafers. The neatly tailored, pressed pants.

Then Bent realized why she was confused, because she

realized what look it was that her mother was going for.

The word was *normal*. Practically *conventional*.

Almost—and this was most frightening of all—*maternal*.

These were not observations Bentley Royce had ever had about her own mother, not even once that she could remember. This was a development both strange and new—and beyond that, terrifying.

None of this was in the approved Mercedes Royce character bible. This was a character arc taken from the wrong network, maybe Family Programming, or some kind of Thanksgiving special.

If you believed it.

No, no, no—

There was no way to know what part of Mercedes Royce could be trusted. Jeff Grunburg didn't call her Mercenary Royce for nothing.

Bent thought about the family chessboard hidden under her bed.

Was it just another move? Could any of it be real?

Does she ever feel anything at all?

"Whenever you're ready," Mercedes said.

Bent didn't answer as her mother stood up, crossed the room, and pulled the door quietly shut behind her.

She nuzzled the two sleeping kitten heads with her face, holding still until she could feel their tiny hearts beat in a regular rhythm beneath their downy fur.

Bent looked back at her computer and refreshed the screen.

She couldn't wait another day to get out of the House of Royce, this house of insanity—this hall of mirrors. She was so crushed from the weight of pretending all the time that she could hardly breathe.

The Royces had rolled right over her, just like they did everyone. That was the problem with the Royces, especially Mercedes.

They just kept on rolling.

Even when the ground beneath the red carpet gave way to nothing at all.

YOUNGEST ROYCE GAMBLES WITH ADDICTION—
WILL TROUBLES SPREAD AS SISTER WEDS?

AP: Reseda, California

Via Celebcity.com

Bach (Maybach) Royce, the youngest son in the titular *Rolling with the Royces* clan, is reportedly facing legal troubles, according to numerous sources familiar with the teen's current situation.

Security footage recorded at a local area casino clearly shows Maybach Royce using a fake driver's license to access the facility's poker tables.

While the youngest Royce admits to playing poker socially, he has vigorously defended himself against media allegations of any degree of gambling addiction.

As mother Mercedes Royce and sisters Porsche and Bentley Royce are increasingly occupied with Porsche's upcoming wedding, some are speculating that Bach is in for harder times ahead.

"It could just be a case of falling through the cracks," said Los Angeles psychiatrist Dr. Barbara Kleinman-Weiss, who has not treated any of the Royce siblings, and who is not familiar with the show. "Or of a child wishing he could fall through the cracks. Or being afraid of cracks, generally. Or, of course, crack."

"A significant percentage of family members do admit to feeling some sort of mild depression attributable to being a member of a family," agreed Sarah Burnes, a research scientist at California State University, Northridge. "Beyond that, a significant percentage of nonfamily members do admit to feeling a certain degree of mild depression attributable to not being a member of a family. Either of these factors could be relevant here.

"Or the subject could just really like poker."

No representatives of the Royce family were available for comment.

(Disclosure: Celebcity is a fully owned subsidiary of the Lifespan Network, which is itself a fully owned subsidiary of DiosGlobale.)

Follow @celebcity for breaking details,
or www.celebcity.com.

Fifteen

FIFTY SHADES OF PINK
March 2018
Beverly Hills Hotel, Beverly Hills
(Sunset at Coldwater Canyon)

Bentley had been fake working on fake planning her sister's fake shower for more than a month. Since she'd been grounded by her fake mother, there hadn't exactly been much else to do to fill her off-camera hours, aside from going to the shrink and AA—and thus the library.

Every Wednesday at five, she wanted to tell Venice the truth about everything she was going through. Instead, she told him about the kittens. About how they slept on her bed and used a litter box in her bathroom. How they played with water bottle tops and shoelaces and paper. How they didn't want anything except the basics—food and water and scratches, so many scratches. (She didn't tell him she groomed them with the $150 Mason Pearson[69] hairbrush Mercedes had given her, or that it was especially satisfying.)

Venice had nodded and listened—he got it. "They get you out of your head." She'd smiled. If he'd known what was in her head, he'd also have known how impossible it was to escape it.

---

69 *Mercedes Royce has asked that we delete this detail from the manuscript. "That little . . ." Pls. revise.* ☹ *—D*

Every Wednesday at six she went home to proof enough of that: the House of Royce was still crazy, and her sister was still marrying the fraud that was Tomme/ Whitey. Bent tried to tell herself she'd been wrong to worry. She tried to think of the engagement as job security; sure, Porsche was marrying a fraud, but that was good television, wasn't it? The show would stay on the air, and her family would survive. And wasn't that all anyone cared about, anyway?

Bent wasn't so certain anymore.

Season six rolled onward, and Porsche's wedding sped toward them—and the shower that Bentley herself had helped fake plan was suddenly upon them, as the official start of it all.

Now, as she descended through the press gauntlet waiting in the driveway outside the Beverly Hills Hotel, Bent wondered if it would ever really end.

Bentley! Where've you been? Bentley, over here! Bentley, how'd things work out with your sister's fiancé? Come on, Bent? Where's the smile, gorgeous?

Porsche, who was all too aware that the *bride* was generally the center of attention at a *bridal shower*, hissed at her—"Don't speak, move!"—and Bent had been grateful to run ahead.

That was where the bridal aesthetic assault began.

There had never been so much *pink*—which Bentley had quickly learned was not the correct word—in one city block. The hotel, historically famous for its *coral blush* (and sea-foam-green) grandeur, was already the most retro pink hotel in Los Angeles on any normal Saturday. This was not one of those.

On this exceptional Saturday, the hotel was awash in an entire rainbow composed specifically of various gradations of *rose-colored* splendor. Porsche's combination Valentine's-themed bridal shower *plus RWTR* shoot *plus* product launch for Lippies by Porsche had demanded nothing less, and Lifespan had obliged.

When Bentley stepped through the golden doors that opened to the sunken ballroom occupying a large part of the hotel's lower floor, she was immediately confronted by an enormous pair of reflective *electric-fuchsia* lips that parted around a furry *red*-carpeted tongue, leading into the rest of the space.

Whoa. I don't remember fake planning that. . . .

The lips were momentarily so off-putting that Bent had trouble recalling the theme of her own sister's party—even after having sat through all the fake planning meetings. When Bent realized she was actually looking at a blown-up image of Porsche's own *roseate* plumped and pricked and primed lips, she almost couldn't bring herself to stumble through them at all. (Bach used the back door.)

Kiss the Bride, Valentine!

That was the theme. It also happened to be the name of the particular color of Lippies by Porsche Slick Stick that was launching today, in her own honor. *RWTR*'s set decorator had outdone herself.

With the help of a thousand *strawberry princess*–petaled peonies, a *neon-raspberry* step and repeat (bearing the Lippies by Porsche logo), *watermelon afternoon*–hued heart-shaped linen table rounds, *salentine rosato* heart-dotted netting chair covers, and oversize *bubblegum-and-berry* weather balloon hearts that had put Production back more than a hundred bucks a pop—the room looked like a four-year-old girl's dream prom, only if it were sponsored by Pepto-Bismol.

Plus, hearts.

As many as Bentley had been able to track down, from every online crafting site known to man. (Dr. A. would have been proud.)

Porsche herself, in a woven *azalea bloom*–toned sheath that had cost more than some normal citizens' cars, was absolutely magnificent. Nobody could argue with that, Bent thought. She wore her curls in a cascade to one side, her *magenta* laquered-and-clipped hair almost as glossy as her *sunlit coral* Kiss The Bride, Valentine! by Lippie'd lips. Bentley herself had accepted the *salmon-kissed* tunic her stylist had picked out for her with relatively little complaining (aside from noting that nobody had probably ever kissed a salmon), and even Bach had eventually managed a *warm flush* tie. ("Warm flush? Is that a card trick or an Arizona toilet?")

Not Mercedes, though.

She wore her *winter morning* all-white suit as if it were her battle armor, which Bentley knew it was. It wasn't clear that Mercedes was going to even make a cameo at Porsche's shower until that morning. While Porsche blamed Bentley for throwing herself at her fiancé, Porsche blamed her mother even more for *not* blaming Bentley too. But

Mercedes had never recovered from the *canoodling* headlines, and even now rarely acknowledged Whitey in public. So, while the fighting between bride and bridesmaid was bad, the fighting between bride and mother of the bride was worse. Much, much worse. Poor Bach just tried to keep his head down as he dodged the bullets.

"Stay by my side," Mercedes said as soon as she spotted Bentley.

"Where are you imagining I would want to go? The Lippies Testing Table? Or the Here Comes the Bride Makeover Tent?" Bent rolled her eyes. Ever since the grounding, she was never allowed out of her mother's sight, especially not in public.

"Very funny," Mercedes said, grabbing a glass of rosé champagne from a passing waiter. When Bent reached for one, she slapped her hand away. "Nice try."

Bach and Bent looked at each other. They'd been sneaking champagne since season one, and nobody had ever said a word.

Mercedes's new approach to motherhood had been a hot topic between them lately. Bach had tried to shrug it off. "What if it's legit? What if she's, I don't know, changing?"

Bent didn't buy it. "Mercedes? You can't fall for this parenting *shtick*. It's like Charlie Brown and the football thing. The minute you let your guard down and start thinking she's going to actually let you kick the football, she'll yank it away. That's what Mercedes does."

Now Bach had his cards in his hand. "I'm going to hide out on the patio. Less pink out there."

"No you don't," Mercedes said, grabbing him by the arm. "We have to do forty minutes. Right here where everyone can see us. That's what Pam said." She gritted her teeth. "Not a minute longer."

It was true; if Pam and the *RWTR* producers hadn't stepped in with a color-coded line graph that vividly detailed the potential impact on production costs of her nonattendance (as Mercedes was technically an executive producer on the show, these all impacted her profit-sharing percentages as well) she might not have come at all. Which didn't mean the next forty minutes were going to be pleasant.

Bach looked at Bentley, panicked.

Bentley pointed at a nearby waiter. "Mercedes, isn't that the fried chicken you love? Chef Ludo?"

Luckily it was, and so as the bride circulated the room—trailed by photographers—the mother of the bride stood by the nearest waiter, recklessly accepting paper cone after paper cone of Hollywood's favorite fried chicken, until Bentley began to worry that the splashiest headline to come out of Porsche's party was going to be something like MERCEDES ROYCE UPCHUCKS CLUCKS!

"Why don't we just find our table?" Bach finally suggested.

Bentley caught her sister's immaculately made-up eye as mother, brother, and sister moved through the ballroom. Predictably, the seating plan Bentley had (fake) spent the last ten days on had been abandoned. And, true to Porsche's threat, all three of them—Mercedes and Bach and Bentley

herself—not being sufficiently Team Whitey—found themselves at table sixteen, nearest the restrooms.

Point taken.

"How many minutes has it been?" Mercedes asked as
they sat surrounded by two D-list actresses (from *RWTR*
season two and season three), Porsche's high school acting
coach, and an alternate Death Eater from Porsche's Beauty
Team. In the last seat was Tallulah Grunburg, who held up
her Shirley Temple and winked at the exiled Royces. "To
family!"

"How many?" Mercedes said again, with a slightly
strangled voice. "Minutes."

Bent looked at her watch. "You don't want to know."
Thankfully, forks were already clinking on glasses as she
spoke. The toasts were about to begin.

"Oh, thank god," Mercedes said.

Over on the other side of the room, Porsche cleared her
throat and began to read off a notecard. "Thanks so much
for being here to celebrate our special day. The Kiss The
Bride, Valentine! by Lippies line is a very special product
to me, because it's my very first foray into Porsche Royce
Bridal, not to mention Here Comes The Lipgloss, and I
wouldn't have either today if it wasn't for my wonderful
fiancé, T. Wilson White."

Bentley and Bach kicked each other.

"Mazel tov," Tallulah said, holding up her Shirley
Temple again.

Mercedes drained another champagne glass.

Porsche held out her hand for Whitey to join her by the

mic. He kissed her fingers as he stepped to her side. She beamed and looked out at the crowd.

"This wonderful, strong, sensitive man is not just the *love* of my life, he's the *like* of my life. And while I've fallen in love before, I'm not sure I've ever liked someone this much."

Porsche's former acting coach, a tiny woman with red glasses and a severe geometrical bob, leaned forward and tapped on Bentley's arm. "Look at that. She's doing love. Love is *such* a tricky one. Porsche really couldn't do love *at all* when she studied with me. Now, look. She's nailed it. Great progress. Huge." The woman sat back in her chair.

Bent nodded, but she knew it wasn't true.

She knew it the same way she could tell Bach knew it, sitting bolt upright in his *salentine rosato* heart-dotted tulle-swagged chair.

The same way her mother knew it, even over her haze of chicken regret.

Her sister was a terrible actress.

Porsche wasn't *doing love.* She wasn't *doing anything.* She was just telling the truth. Even if the truth was the last thing anyone could ever expect from a reality show, or a reality star.

You've been such an idiot, Bentley Royce. None of this is going to work out.

You aren't going to save the show with a season six wedding and a season seven divorce.

Your sister's gone, all the way gone.

And now you have to do something—

Across the room, Porsche was unveiling a secret project, a special Lippie that she'd designed just for her groom. "It's called First Kiss, and I'm only going to wear it once, on our wedding day. Then I'll retire it forever, because you only have one first kiss with your first husband. . . ."

Awwwwww! said the room.

"Babe," said Whitey, sounding choked up.

"And I'm so happy it's you," Porsche finished. Then the future Mr. and Mrs. T. Wilson White kissed tenderly as the room broke into thunderous applause.

That was it.

This had to end.

The situation was now way beyond pink.

Things had gone Code Red.

Bentley threw her *watermelon afternoon* napkin down on the table in disgust, though she didn't know who she was more disgusted with, herself or her sister or the idiotic fake groom who had somehow managed to take her entire family down with him.

"I gotta go," Bent whispered to her brother, trying to keep her head lower than her toasting sister's sight line.

Bach looked at her like she was as crazy as she felt. "Go? Has it been forty minutes? We don't get to go—do we?"

"Something came up, and I have to meet a friend. It's important." She clapped her hand on her brother's shoulder. "Keep your eye on Mercedes." She grabbed her bag and slipped past him.

Hurrying away, Bent felt sick with regret, and not the

kind you get from too much fried chicken.[70] She had made a mistake. She had messed with her sister's heart and mind and now she needed to make things right.

She needed a new plan.

One service elevator, one kitchen hallway, and one loading dock later, she was on her way.

Bentley was still wearing her salmon party tunic when she climbed out of her Uber on Santa Monica and Seventh, at the Santa Monica Library.

It had begun to rain, so she pulled off her twelve-hundred-dollar shoes (free to her; at least her feet were sample size!) and took the slick concrete stairs of the library so slowly, they might as well have been wet cement.

Robert at the Help Desk offered her a mini water bottle.[71] She declined. Ivy in the Teen Section pointed out a poster for Movie Night. She kept walking. Librarian Josh waved. She ignored him.

Instead, she headed straight to the nearest empty monitor and flung herself into the chair in front of it. This wasn't Wednesday, and it wasn't five P.M., and she didn't know if any of the regulars would be there, but she didn't know how else to find them.

And she had to. She had to talk to someone.

---

70 *Tough call, Jeff notes. A chicken binge could be pretty regrettable.* ☹ —D

71 *Per JG: IQH2O water? Or similar. Check with sponsors!* ☺ —D

No.

Not someone—one person.

Him.

It was only five minutes until Venice rolled his chair up next to her. "What's going on, Sweet B? How's it hanging? You look—ruffled."

"Do you mean my clothes or my mood?"

"Both, kind of. Now that you mention it." He shook his head admiringly at the dress. "Those are some killer threads, though. You're . . . really . . . clean."

"Thanks," she said. "I guess I am."

"I've never seen you in here on the weekend," Venice said.

"What, do you live here?"

"I get around." He shrugged. "So? Lay it on me."

"Lay what on you? It's—it's nothing."

Venice shot her a look, then rolled his chair closer to hers, pushing back his damp hoodie a few inches. Brown curls came springing out.

He reached for one of her hands, then the other. His fingers were as warm as she remembered, and she exhaled.

Slowly, he leaned forward, until his forehead was almost touching hers. She could smell the ocean in his hair, like always.

When he spoke, his voice was low. "Baby B, you're wearing a party dress, you came running up the stairs in no shoes, and you don't even have your zombie book, okay? Whatever's going on, you didn't come here because it was *nothing*. You came here looking for me. So start talking."

She closed her eyes and let her forehead touch his. "I don't know how." Now she could feel his hair curling against her cheek.

"I've heard you talk, B." His arms came up around her shoulders, and Josh coughed in the background. Still, Venice didn't move. "I know you can do that."

Bent's heart was beating so loudly, she imagined he could hear it. She took a deep, steadying breath.

"I don't know how to say the things that matter, Venice."

I don't know how to say the things that are true, because no one I know wants to hear them. And it's been like this for so long, I can't remember a time when I did.

His words were so quiet now, they were practically a whisper. "Try. I think you can. I think you wouldn't be here if you didn't know you could trust me."

I know, she thought. I don't even know why I know that, and yet I still do. How crazy is that? Crazier than Porsche Royce falling in love with a TryCycle instructor? Who am I to talk?

Slowly, gently, Venice pulled his head back from hers, until she could see the blue-blue of his eyes. "I'm here for you, B. What did you come all this way in the rain to tell me?"

All this way.

She nodded, but the words caught in her mind.

All this way.

She pushed her chair backward, opening up the space between them. "How do you know how far I've come?"

"What are you talking about?"

"All this way. What way? Where did I come from?"

"I don't know, it's just an expression."

"Venice. Don't tell me to be honest with you and then lie to me."

"It doesn't matter. You can tell me." Venice pulled his hood back with one hand, exasperated. "This is about the guy, right?" he said. "Your sister's hitch? Whitehead? Whitesnake?"

"You know about him? Whitey?" Bentley's eyes went wide. "You know about me?" She stood up, grabbing her bag.

"Bentley—" He stood up too.

"I trusted you. I thought we were friends. I thought this was real."

He looked frustrated. "It was. It is."

She kept her bag between them. "One real thing. Do you understand what that means to a person like me? Do you know how important this was to me? How important you were?"

"Voices," Librarian Josh said from the reference desk.

Venice whispered. "Yes, I do."

"But you're a liar," she hissed back, still stunned.

"Am I?" Venice looked frustrated. "Have you been a hundred percent honest with me?"

Bentley stared at him. She knew it was over. She knew she already should have gone down the stairs. There would be nothing to salvage here. There never was.

"Would you give me a chance to explain?" Venice

whispered, tilting his head toward the reference room. "Come on."

Bentley followed him into the room. Josh stood behind the reference desk, watching with interest as they slipped past him and locked the glass door.

Josh knocked on it. "You can't do that."

"Five minutes," Venice said.

Josh gave up, pointing at his watch. *Five minutes.* He walked away in a huff.

Venice sat down at the small table in the center of the stacks and pulled out the chair next to him. "Time out. We have to talk."

Bent sat down.

She stared at him in disbelief. "You know everything? You know about the show too?"

He sighed. "Yeah, okay. I should have said something." There was a pained expression on his face now—not just embarrassed, but guilty. "Nobody here knows. Josh and the other regulars, they don't have a clue."

"How did you figure it out?"

"It was a newspaper kiosk, right outside the front door. There was a big headline, with your face on it, one day. It said 'Why, Bentley, Why?' And I thought, I have no idea who this Bentley is, but it must suck to have strangers talk like they know you. And when you walked over to the table and sat down that day, I knew right away it was you."

"Wow," Bentley said. "And I thought I was playing it so cool."

"Come on, B. Even your raggiest clothes cost a hundred times more than a piece of that cake you like so much."

She knew he was right, but it didn't make her feel any less betrayed. "Why didn't you say something?"

"Are you kidding? You would have bolted. At least, I would have, if I were you. And I used to be like you, you know? The big house. The fast cars. The pretty people."

She nodded. "I figured you had a story. You and your boats and your Latin and your operas."

Venice looked surprised. Then he drew in a breath. "Yeah, well, I did. Have a story. I mean, I do. A big one."

"And?" She looked at him expectantly. "Come on, it's only fair. You and the rest of the world watch my whole life story on the news every day. I should get to know at least the Twitter version of yours."

He shrugged. "The Twitter version is, my brain sucks. It fell through a wormhole, kind of. That's how I tried to explain it to my dad, anyways. Before I left."

"Yeah?" She was careful not to press him. For a year, he'd been as guarded about his life as she was about hers. She didn't imagine this conversation was any easier for him than it was for her.

"Oh yeah," Venice said. "My brain just sort of freaked out. Big-time. Started playing tricks on me."

"What tricks?"

He looked at her. "At first everything looked all wrong, and then it felt all wrong, and then it was all wrong. By the time I came out the other side—"

She smiled. "Of the wormhole?"

He nodded. "That's right, the wormhole. By then, I figured out that I was on my own. Because no matter where I went, that's how I felt. I was *alonenotalone*." He said it like it was one long word. "See?"

"Not really. Why don't you explain it to me?"

Venice closed his eyes, trying to piece it together. "I'd walk down the street, and it was like everyone I saw, they were all together, they were part of one big thing, the same thing, or something."

"And you weren't?" Bentley asked quietly.

His voice was soft now. "And I wasn't. I couldn't feel what they felt. The together thing."

"Ah," said Bent. "That thing." Strangely enough, she knew almost exactly what he was talking about.

He opened his eyes. "I've never known what that feels like. And the only thing I could feel was *that*, the feeling of not feeling it. The feeling that I wasn't one of anything."

"Which didn't help, I'm guessing." *Because it doesn't.*

"Of course not. So I just kind of gave up. I stopped fighting it. I knew I was *alonenotalone* because I lived on the other side of the wormhole, the wrong side for everyone else. The *alonenotalone* side. I accepted that. Even with my friends, even with my family. I just gave up." He shrugged again. "Probably sounds strange."

"Not entirely."

He slid his hand closer to hers, until their pinkies were almost touching.

"Sweet B, that's a bad place to be. Take it from me. You end up in a place like that and you start convincing yourself it's better to be plain old alone. You tell yourself that at least actually being alone is real, you know? At least you're not imagining it's any different."

"I guess not," Bent said.

"But it's not true. You can't figure everything out all by yourself. Sometimes all you can do is all you can do. Sometimes, you gotta let people help you."

He reached for her hand, and she let him take it.

It was still Venice's hand—no matter how annoyed she was at him—and she still felt better holding it.

"You think so?" she asked.

He smiled at her. "Yep. Even when your sister's marrying a punk or your brother is running a poker game. Even when you're stuck on some crappy television show that makes you out to be someone you're not. Even when your mom is scary as . . . well, scary."

Bentley looked at him for a long moment, then squeezed his hand. "I guess I should have known you'd recognize me sooner or later. It's your crazy memory thing. The way you see every single detail of every little thing."

He laughed. "That. And also, because of your crazy face thing."

"My what?"

Venice was still grinning. "You know what I'm talking about."

"I seriously don't."

He shook his head. "Do I really have to spell it out for you?"

"Yeah. You actually kind of do, I guess."

"Because, Bentley. Because you have the most unforgettable face on the planet, and not just because it's in the news. Because you're the single most beautiful person I've ever seen in my life, inside and out. Because you'd be friends with a guy who wears the same hoodie every day for a year. And a table full of homeless dudes. And a librarian with a stick up his butt."

"You're delusional," Bent said, but she found her face turning hot and red, all the same.

"I'm not. And I never was. Not even when we were pretending, all that time. I know I should have said something, but I was scared. I was being selfish. I couldn't imagine how hard it must be for you to be yourself around people, and I didn't want to ruin what we had."

Bentley smiled. "Have," she said. "I'm pretty sure we still have it. You didn't ruin anything. You probably couldn't, even if you tried."

"I wouldn't be so sure about that." He ran his hand through his tangle of curls. "Here's the thing. You can't play their game, Sweet B. They don't care about you. You have to find the people who do, and stick with them. They're your team. No. Not team." He searched for the word. "Tribe. They're your tribe."

Bent looked at him doubtfully. "What if I don't have a tribe?"

"You do, Sweet B. You have a whole library full of them. Just like you have me."

"How do you know?"

"Because, B, I have you."

Venice reached into the pocket of his ragged hoodie and pulled out a crisp white envelope. "Don't open it now. It's for later. Something you might find interesting, that's all. If you need it."

"What? Why?"

"You ask too many questions, you know that?"

His eyes were bright and blue, she noticed. The light almost seemed to come out of them, even in the fluorescent-lit glass cube of the reference room.

"Fine." Bent smiled and reached for the envelope—and he caught her by the hand again.

"Not so fast, B." He shook his head.

"What is it, Venice?"

"You gotta do one thing for me."

"Yeah?"

"Start talking."

"Venice—"

"You gotta talk to someone. A person can't survive on their own for that long. Not even when they're *alonenotalone*. Not even when they're stuck on our side of the wormhole."

She locked her fingers in his. "I can't. Everything's wrong. My brother—"

"The card shark." He nodded.

She sighed. "The card shark is out of control."

"That's not good," Venice said.

"And my mother is either pretending to be a mother for the first time in her life or having actual feelings—I don't know which of those things is scarier."

He winced. "I'd say they're both terrifying."

"Then my sister is in love with her fake fiancé."

"Okay, that sucks."

She nodded. "I don't know how to fix any of it, and I don't even know how to talk about it." It was true. Not Bach, not her family, not even Dr. A. knew the kinds of things she was keeping to herself now.

Venice smoothed back a strand of her rainbow-tipped hair. "But this isn't the zombie apocalypse. Like I said, you can trust me, B. You want to know how you can tell?"

"How, Venice?"

"Because you already do."

And as Bent looked at him, the guy in the ratty hoodie, the one she'd only ever hung out with at the computer table in the public library with their homeless crew, she knew he was right.

She could tell him anything. Probably everything.

And so she did.

Sixteen

NOTHING'S FREE
March 2018
Rampart Division, LAPD
(110 North to West Sixth Street, DTLA)

The Monday after Porsche's *pinksplosion* of a bridal shower—not to mention a different kind of fireworks at the library with Venice—Bentley was faced with an even bigger blowup.

As Bent and Bach walked into the front hall of school, they saw some kind of police officer—maybe a detective, the kind who wears a cheap suit and a badge, rather than a uniform—standing idly by the Mulholland Hall headmaster's office.[72]

He was tall and serious-looking, with a leathery, lined face, like someone who spent all his time outside.

"Wow," Bent said.

"I know. That's a first." Bach looked spooked.

"A bust at Mulholland Hall. *Kids today,*" Bent said lightly.

Bach moved next to the crowd that was rapidly forming around the cop; Bent followed. "Cheating? Or drugs?" She stopped to ask the nearest Mulholland-holic, Brynn Meyers, from her English class.

---

72 Per JG: The school would like a few of its Emmy-winning parent screenwriters to do a polish on this chapter before it prints. Y/N? ☺ —D

"Nobody knows," Brynn said. "The kid's in Cumming's office getting busted now. It's, like, the biggest deal *ever*. He'll probably get *expelled*. His life is *over*."

Bach was ahead of Bent, and she was looking at him the moment his face went dark. By the time Bent pushed through the crowd to catch up with him, she saw why.

Through the glass pane of the closed door to Cumming's office, she could see one face. It wasn't a pleasant one, and it wasn't one that meant anything good for her brother.

It was the face of Jake Morgan, who was almost as bad at cheating as he was at poker, and who was even worse at keeping his mouth shut. The same Jake Morgan who had been playing at her brother's regular poker games all year.

Bach stared. "I'm getting busted, Bent."

She tried to stay positive. "You don't know that. It's probably nothing. Maybe he cheated on something. Again."

Bach shook his head. "The cops wouldn't be here for cheating. Everybody cheats. They'd have to arrest the entire school."

"So he's getting busted for something else. This isn't on you."

"Unless maybe he's not getting busted at all," Bach said quietly, his eyes still on Jake. "Maybe he's in there talking his head off. Maybe he's a really sore loser—sore enough to rat out the rest of his game."

"You think he sold you out?" Bentley grabbed Bach by the arm. "I thought you said the Poker Club was a legit school activity."

"It was. Just not the part where we gambled with real

money. During real school hours. And especially not the part where Jake wanted *his* money back." Bach sounded grim.

"Okay. Yeah. That's not so good," Bentley said. She turned to look at her brother, but he wasn't there anymore. *Crap.*

He was making a beeline for his locker, though she could already see it was too late. The cop was standing there waiting for him. And worse, there were at least five kids recording the scene on their cell phones.

"What are you doing to my locker?" Bach stopped in his tracks when he noticed the crowbar in the cop's hand. Bent caught up to him.

The detective looked at Bach. "You Maybach Royce?"

Bach nodded.

"Detective Harry Connolly. You can just call me Harry." He held out his hand. Bach looked at him strangely, and then shook it. "Excellent timing. Why don't you do me a favor and open your locker, Mr. Royce?"

"How do you know my name?"

"I'm a detective. We know things. It sort of goes with the job." He rapped on the locker. "Now open it."

Bach remained still. He didn't unfold his arms. "You don't have the right to open that. You don't have probable cause."

Harry smiled again. "How about you *probably* should stop talking, 'cause this is going to be opened."

But Bach wasn't smiling now.

Bentley could see his face, and could see how angry her brother really was. She didn't know why she hadn't seen it before.

He was full of rage.

This wasn't Bach; at least, it wasn't who he used to be.

This was just where his life had dragged him.

Bent knew the feeling herself, and she also knew how desperately she didn't want to feel it.

Harry waited for a moment, then shrugged and held up his crowbar. "Suit yourself. I could probably use the workout, you know?" He pried the locker open within a matter of three seconds. It popped off like the lid to a Pringles can.

"Now, what do we have here?"

The locker was all but empty; nobody at Mulholland Hall ever used their lockers for books. Most of the students didn't study enough for that, and the ones who did were so nerdy, they carried everything on them. The lockers were the no-man's-land of the school; nobody wanted to be there, and nothing good happened there. Better to keep away.

Bentley had thought Bach knew that as well, but apparently not, because there was something in his locker.

Only one thing.

A bag she hadn't seen in years.

"Look at that." Harry pulled it out and held it up: an old black mini duffel. Prada. Small. Very used.

And very familiar to Bentley, because in ninth grade, it had been hers.

"What the . . . ?" Bach looked startled.

"You stole my bag?!" Bentley jumped in, all guns firing. "What the hell, Bach? How many times do I have to tell you to leave my stuff alone? I swear to god, I'm getting a padlock on my door."

Harry unzipped the bag. "So this is your bag, Ms. Royce? Then maybe you could tell me where you got all this cash?"

He pulled out a thick roll of money—Bach's gambling winnings—followed by a black notebook. If she knew her brother, it was probably some kind of detailed accounting of the Poker Club's dealings. (Bach had problems, but a lack of organizational skill wasn't one of them.)

Harry flipped open the book, studying neat rows of entries—with dates and dollar amounts and, if she wasn't mistaken, something that looked a whole lot like betting odds.

Bentley looked at Bach questioningly.

"Bent," he said.

"Shut up," she said, cutting him off.

He didn't have to tell her. She'd known before he'd said a word.

He wasn't only into poker.

He was a bookie, just like a certain demolition derby bookie they both knew. One who used to run the most profitable operation in all of Sanpete, Sevier, and Beaver Counties.

Don't think about it. Not now. Not yet.

The detective looked up from the book. "You running some kind of gambling ring here, Bentley? Where'd you get all this cash?"

Bach looked away.

Get it together, Bent. You can do it. Well, not you.

You know who you need right now, don't you?

Bad Bentley took a deep breath. "Where did I get all

that cash?" She shook her head. "Why don't you tell me, Harry? Since you're probably the guy who put it there. Or is Headmaster Collins the one on Lifespan's payroll now?"

"That's enough." Harry frowned. "I think it's time we take a little ride, Ms. Royce."

She smiled. "They always have a guy, Harry. Don't you know that? Did you really think you were the first?"

A reflexive murmur rippled through the crowd around them. She knew how the story would go, and how much bigger it would be by the end of the day. Bad Bentley was a pro at these things. She'd seen it all.

"Bent," Bach began.

But Bent grabbed her brother by the arm and squeezed as hard as she could.

Shut up.

Besides, it was true. The backpack really was hers. A long, long time ago. But it was also true that Bach was her little brother, and her person.

Her one always person, even in her *alonenotalone* world.

Venice would have understood.

Bent took another breath, a deeper one. She looked at Harry and held out her wrists. "Come on, Harry. Let's do this."

Bach was red-faced and shaking. He actually looked so stricken, Bentley thought he might throw up. Harry pulled her hands behind her back to cuff her. "I've got this, Bach. But do us both a favor? You probably shouldn't call Mercedes."

The cuffs went on without another word.

Half the class had the footage up on YouTube by the time the police car reached the Rampart station downtown.

Bentley didn't know who had tipped off the paparazzi, but they were there waiting when the squad car she was riding in got off the 110 North at the Sixth Street exit. When she saw that Mac and Ted and JoJo were standing with their handhelds among the throng of cameras, she was almost relieved.

It was the final confirmation of what she'd suspected all along.

She knew exactly who had set her up.

She pulled her sweatshirt up over her head as they led her inside. It only made them shoot her more.

The next time she saw him, Harry was reading a magazine in the interrogation room. "Did you know you can surf without even a beach?"

"Excuse me?" Bent sat up and tried to look at the picture he was studying, but she was handcuffed to a bar that ran along the edge of the table, and it was impossible to move too much in any one direction.

Harry looked up. "Ah, sorry about that." He leaned over and stuck a key into her cuffs, pausing only to look her in the eye for a moment. "You're not going to try to kill me, are you?"

"No. I'm really not," Bent said. "Too tired."

"I hear you." Harry sat back down and picked up his magazine again. "This says the best waves are out in the middle of the ocean where nobody can even see them."

Bent raised an eyebrow. "If nobody can see them, then how do you know they're the best?"

"Good point. You can't always believe everything you read in a magazine, can you?" He held up his copy of *MovieSt*r*. "I guess if you're rich enough, you buy a yacht the size of an aircraft carrier, and then you spend all year long trying to find them. The waves. If it's this time of year, you park it outside the Marshall Islands.[73] Where there are no beaches and no hotels." He tapped on a towheaded surfer's tanned face, on the middle of the page. "Only this poor loser."[74]

"He's not poor if he's on a yacht the size of an aircraft carrier," Bentley pointed out. She was too exhausted for this conversation.

"Yeah, really. I guess you're right." Harry laughed. "Whoever that poor loser is, he's not as poor as a cop—or even a detective."

She nodded. "Anyway, like you just said, that stuff is all lies, you know?"

"Yeah, well, everyone lies. Mothers, kids, cops. You don't need a tabloid for that." He laughed and put down the magazine.

Tell me about it, she thought. Then she looked at Harry.

---

73 *Jeff is curious—who owns an aircraft-carrier-size yacht? Sting? Tom Hanks? Spielberg?* —D
74 *Per JG: "Is it me?"* —D

"Speaking of lies, you don't really think I have anything to do with that junk in my bag, do you?"

"It's in your bag, isn't it?"

"It sure is, Detective." Bent yawned. "You did a *bang-up* job making sure of that. Especially for a new guy. Where'd you find it, my closet? What, did you send someone from Wardrobe after it? Speaking of which, who hired you—Jeff Grunburg? Pam?"

Harry looked at her. "Let me give you some advice."

"Please don't."

"It's free," Harry said.

"Nothing's free," Bentley said.[75]

"It's possible that I was asked to make sure your brother's stash found its way into your bag."

"Possible?"

Harry shrugged. "But you have to understand, they did it for your brother."

Bent raised an eyebrow. "When they sent me to fake rehab, was that for my brother?"

"Look, kid. One of Maybach's unhappy customers ratted him out to the school. That's not a fake problem."

"I know." She sighed. "I mean, I figured."

"The people who hired me just thought you could take the hit, you know, deal with the trouble better than he could."

"Yeah, Bad Bentley. I get that a lot." Dealing with the trouble was all she had ever known.

---

75 Per JG: "And if it is I don't want it, am I right?" ☺ —D

Harry nodded. "Well, you may be a bad Bentley, but you're a good sister. Misguided, but a good sister." He rubbed his hand through his hair. "I'm not supposed to say this, but I'm going to. Screw Grunburg, he's a little tool."[76]

Bent was surprised.

Harry sat up in his chair. "The thing is, you're not doing your brother any favors by taking the fall. You might think you are, but you aren't."

"Is that right?"

"Yeah. Consequences. That's the one thing nobody in this town ever wants to know about. But you do the crime, you should do the time."

"And then you say that line." Bent rolled her eyes. "Are you going to let me go? They usually let me go after a few hours."

Harry looked serious. "Not this time. This is a legit bust, not trumped-up evidence. I gotta figure a way through this. I can't toss you into jail for something you didn't do, but someone has to take the rap for running an illegal poker game."

Bent looked at him sympathetically. "Don't worry, new guy. You'll figure it out. The guy sitting in your chair always does."

"Yeah? Because from this side of the desk, it's not worth the twenty-five grand."

"Twenty-five? You should get a better agent," Bent said.

Harry laughed.

---

76 Per JG: "Little!?" ☹ —D

"Hey, don't I get a phone call or something?" Bentley pointed to Harry's phone.

"Only in the movies."

"Really?"

"Nah. I'm just pulling your chain." He dropped his phone on the table in front of her. "Knock yourself out."

Bentley hit a series of buttons from memory and then waited on the line. "Hi, Dirk. Is he in? It's sort of important."

"What are you doing?" Harry hissed.

"Don't worry. I'm not going to get you fired," she hissed back.

Then Bent pressed SPEAKER and held up the phone. She didn't even have to try to bring Bad Bentley back up to the surface now. Not for this phone call.

A voice crackled on the line. "This is Jeff."

"Hi, Jeff. It's Bentley—and Harry."

"Hi, Jeff," Harry said anxiously, looking at her.

"Hi, Bentley. Who the hell is Harry?"

Bent rolled her eyes at Harry. "Your new guy. Down at Rampart. He's great. We love the Harry."

"I don't have a guy at Rampart."

"Yeah, yeah. I got it. Funny stuff, Jeff. *Anyhoo*, we're calling from the precinct to let you know the deal. After talking it through with Harry—again, *great* choice—I've decided to take the heat for Bach on this one. Full press cycle. Print, digital, limited live interview if I have to. Your call." She winced. "Well, maybe not the blonde at *Entertainment Tomorrow*. Otherwise, your call."

"And?" The voice on the speaker sounded interested. Harry looked surprised.

Bent smiled at Harry. "As much as we both know you'd love to play the gambling-addiction story out, we also both know you can't afford for him to actually get arrested for . . ."

She looked at Harry. Harry wrote a word on the notepad between them.

"Racketeering." She gave Harry a thumbs-up and mouthed *thank you.*

"Go on," Jeff grunted.

"So I take the heat, and my brother goes . . . let's call it backpacking . . . in Europe . . . Eastern Europe, somewhere with terrible reception . . . and by that I mean rehab, real rehab, for his gambling problem, which is also real."

The speaker crackled. "On hiatus?"

"Immediately."

The speaker crackled again. "Thirty days."

"Yeah, we're going to need sixty."

The speaker went silent, except for static. Bent leaned toward the phone. "Are you following, Jeff? Stay with me, buddy."

"Go on," the voice said slowly.

"He's going to need a sober companion. I've looked it up, I can send you a name."

"And?" asked the voice.

"That's it. You have twenty-four hours to think about it. I'd talk through it in more detail with you, but hey, it turns out I'm in jail, so that's awkward." She looked at Harry.

"And my good friend Harry? He's telling me that twenty-five g's isn't going to work anymore. He needs fifty." She looked at Harry again. "Fifty and a new suit. He'll call you back with the size."

The voice over the speaker began to curse as she hung up the phone.[77]

She exhaled.

Harry looked at her in amazement. "Wow. That was quite a performance."

"Bad Bentley?" She made a dismissive face. "That was nothing. You clearly haven't met my mother. Ten times scarier than I could ever be. It's, like, a superpower."

Bent handed Harry back his phone, stopping to stare at the photograph that he'd chosen as his wallpaper. "Is that Mexico?"

"Yeah. Good eye. Sayulita. I got a little place down there. A shack, really. Surfing town, just north of Puerto Vallarta."[78]

"No yacht in the Marshall Islands?"

"Yeah, don't I wish. Why do you think I took the Lifespan job? Next time someone hands me a million bucks, it's first on my list."

"Only one million? I don't think so. I hate to break it to you, but a million doesn't get you too far these days. And aren't you a little old for surfing?"

---

77 *Jeff feels several liberties have been taken with the retelling of this conversation. He'd urge you to closely re-read the passage to make certain it's accurate. And then delete it.* ☹ —D

78 *If you find your way down there, Jeff recommends the totopos at Las Ventanas.* ☺ —D

"Yeah. A lot old." Harry laughed. "And it feels that way too."

"But you don't care?"

"About what?"

"I don't know. About what people think. About what you're supposed to be doing. Old guys like you." She shrugged.

He laughed. "Nobody gives a rat crap what I do." It sounded like the truth, and Harry seemed fine with it.

As far as dirty cops went, this one wasn't half bad.

She looked up at him. "Can I get just one more call?"

The desk sergeant looked up. "Can I help you?"

Venice dropped the hood of his sweatshirt and looked around. "Uh, hi. I got a call. I'm here to post bail for a friend of mine."

"Name?"

"Bentley."

"Last name?"

"Royce."

"I got this one," a detective said, looking up with amusement from a row of seats near the door. He stood, holding a paper cup of precinct coffee.

"I'm Connolly. Detective Harry Connolly. You must be Bentley's phone call. The Santa Monica Public Library. I didn't really believe it when she told me. It's not exactly Fort Knox." Harry held out his hand. "And you're . . . Venice? What kind of name is that?"

Venice clasped Harry's hand. "I don't know, just a name. What kind of name is Harry?"

"The kind your mother gives you when she's setting you up for a lifetime of playground beatdowns." Harry smiled. "She had a thing for British royals."

Venice looked at the detective. "Is Bentley in a lot of trouble?"

"She just got busted for running a high school gambling ring, so yeah, I'd say so."

Venice raised an eyebrow. "I think you've got the wrong Royce."

"Yeah, I hear you. I don't make the big calls. These things are complicated." Harry shrugged. "Bail hearing's set for tomorrow. Might not stick, but you never know. Have to prepare for the worst."

"Is she all right?"

"She's hanging tough. Poor kid." Harry shook his head. "I really don't get this Hollywood stuff."

"Me neither." Venice nodded and reached into the frayed pocket of his hoodie. He pulled out a blank check. "For the bail bond. Do I give this to you?"

Harry took it. "You sure? Like I said, the bail hearing isn't until tomorrow. It could be a big chunk of change."

"I'm sure."

Harry whistled. "You got it bad, kid."

BIG SLAM ON CAMPUS—
BENTLEY ROYCE BUSTED, BACH ROYCE BAILS

AP: Beverly Hills, California

Via Celebcity.com

The trouble only continues for teen television personality Bentley Royce, as footage posted on social media today confirmed that she was picked up by two Los Angeles Police Department officers at her tony hillside school, Mulholland Hall.

Video of the arrest has been virally shared across global transmedia sites in over thirty-eight languages and nearly fifty countries. More than a quarter of a million people have viewed the footage since this afternoon.

[See linked video.]

Further details on the arrest are unavailable at this time, but some connection to Royce's ongoing battle with addiction is said to have been involved. (Bentley and her sister, Porsche Royce, have been attending AA meetings locally for more than a year.)

Mulholland Hall is the fifth-ranked independent school in the country, boasting nationally competitive equestrian, golf and fencing teams, as well as a sister school in Geneva, Switzerland.

Bentley's brother, Maybach Royce, has reportedly fled the family drama and enrolled as a fledgling student naturalist in a highly respected, government-sponsored backpacking program in a remote area of the Italian Alps.

No one in the family has issued a comment on either of the two younger Royce children.

The youngest sister in the Royce reality television dynasty's troubles have been well documented on the family show, *Rolling with the Royces*. The Lifespan Network could not be reached for comment at the time of posting.

(Disclosure: Celebcity is a fully owned subsidiary of the Lifespan Network, which is itself a fully owned subsidiary of DiosGlobale.)

Follow @celebcity for breaking details,
or www.celebcity.com.

Seventeen

The past sixty days had flown by.

While the rest of the Royces prepped for the wedding, Bach left LAX a Lifespan pariah and arrived home a rock star. Jeff Grunburg was pleased with how his story line was converting, in terms of the numbers. Fans of the show had followed his (fake) eco-reports from the trail as if Mother Nature herself were starring in a global soap opera. Dirk had done an impressive job with Being Bach—even Bent had to give him that.

Sixty days of private time, and nobody was any wiser.

Except, hopefully, Bach.

And Lawrence—the only person on the planet Bent would entrust her brother to—who reported that Bach was really "learning to soar," whatever that meant. Judging by the way they had said good-bye at LAX, it seemed like it had something to do not just with the birds but also, possibly, the bees.

Bent just wanted her brother to be happy.

She'd insisted on picking him up at the airport herself. They didn't stop talking from the moment he got off the plane until the moment they got to the gates of Trousdale Park.

"Holy crap," was all he said. There was no cultured Italian saying for the circus outside their windows. The crowd that had gathered was too large for any car to drive through. There were so many photographers and journalists and cameras and vans that if they tried to swing open the gate, somebody would be crushed. Fans, reporters, neighbors, and even the occasional stalker had begun camping out for the wedding days before.

"Security will be down here in a minute. They're on the monitors twenty-four seven now. I guarantee you, Mercedes is shrieking in the kitchen, yelling, *'MY BABY IS HOME! MY BABY IS HOME!'*" Bent slipped her arm through his.

"Come on, Bent. I've only been gone sixty days, not sixty years."

"Sixty-two days, with travel time. I counted." She smiled.

"Fine. Sixty-two days is still not enough time to invent a personality transplant worthy of Mercedes Royce."

"I don't know, she hasn't been herself for what, six months now?"

As they waited in the backseat of the black town car, they watched the zoo outside the window. This was exactly how Bent had imagined it, the chaos of Porsche's wedding. The people and the traffic and the pileup of cars wherever they went. It wasn't only the journalists who were trampling the landscaping and peeing in the porta-potty of the remodel across the street. The hard-core fans were out in full force, wearing their handmade Team Porsche or Team

Whitey or Team Royce T-shirts (also popular: I ROLL WITH THE ROYCERS) or holding their handmade signs (MY OTHER CAR IS A ROLLING ROYCE; IT'S NOT REALITY UNLESS IT'S ON TV)[79] or staking out their turf with little pup tents and fleece blankets, usually printed with Porsche's and Whitey's faces.

And for every person like that, there were at least three more people wandering among them, if only to sell pizza or phone chargers or batteries or Wi-Fi service or *Duke of Ducks* socks, to hand out religious tracts or chapter samplers of books based on Lifetime shows or the occasional yoga DVD.

Now that word had leaked out that the rehearsal dinner was tonight, and the wedding itself tomorrow, nobody was going anywhere.

Tomorrow is the wedding, she thought.

You're running out of time.

It's now or never.

You know what you have to do.

Bent heard a rap on her window and looked at Bach. "Are you ready for this?"

He nodded. "I was always ready. That's what Larry says."

"Larry?" Bent smiled. *Go figure.* Then she took a deep breath and opened her door.

There they were, the unsmiling faces of the *RWTR* security team: nearly a dozen guys who had to weigh three hundred pounds each, holding black blankets over their

---

79 *Some of our top sellers, Jeff notes. Great product placement!* ☺ —D

heads. What emerged was a long black tunnel that snaked through the pedestrian door of the front gate—which would allow them through while still keeping everyone out.

This is what it had come down to. Working this hard to find a way back into a place where they barely wanted to be—and where it didn't feel all that much like home.

She looked at her brother. He was tanned and happy, with a good extra ten pounds of pasta weight on him. He'd never looked less like an Angelino, and it agreed with him.

"We've got this," she said.

"Totally," he agreed.

She nodded. "And just so you know, we're not going to let that wedding happen tomorrow, B."

"Not a chance in hell, B." Then he winked, and she smiled, and it almost felt like the old days. "Do we have a plan?"

"We don't have a plan, Maybach. We have several. We have plans within plans."

"Ah, yes," Bach said, grinning. "Those are my favorite kind."

She looked back at the crowd outside their car. "We'd better get this over with."

He sat up. "You want me to go first?"

Bent nodded. "Let's roll, Royce." Then she took a breath and followed him out into the light as the crowd went wild.

The outfits were laid out on the beds like a family of invisible people. The rehearsal dinner would not be televised, but at this point it almost didn't matter. There were so many countries live-streaming the red-carpet arrivals at Soho House—the dinner venue—that it might as well be the Oscars.

Bach and Whitey wore Tom Ford for Gucci—separates, not suits; the stylists had gone back and forth on this for months and decided that youth was more important than tradition. Even Mercedes's traditionally chic white tux was Gucci.

Bent, as the wild child of the family, had the edgiest dress—one of fifteen candidates, each custom made at the expense of a great design house. She couldn't understand how there could be so much fuss for only the rehearsal dinner, and for only the sister of the bride, but clearly she was as wrong about this as she had been about almost everything else that had happened in regard to this wedding.

Bent soon found herself being wrapped in a series of stiffly starched, pleated ruffles the size of massive ceiling fans, each layered on top of the next until they created a kind of immense, deconstructed single ruffle that wound around the length of Bentley's body like a massive paper snake. A deflated white bag dragged on the floor behind her, which one stylist claimed was a *gesture to a bridal train*, or a *comment on origins akin to an amniotic sac, or a chrysalis.*

"Stunning," said the first stylist, shooting Polaroids as if she knew how much they would be worth later. (She probably did.)

"Avant-garde," said the other, who was kicked out of the room when she tried to draw geometric eyebrows on Bent's face.

"A real statement piece," agreed the second-camera wedding videographer (Oscar nominated for *Dante: Retracing Exile to Inferno*, which was reviewed as "arty" and "viscous to the point of opacity").[80]

Bentley stepped into the stacked white acrylic boxes that were allegedly some sort of shoe, picked up the rubber section of tire that was allegedly some sort of clutch, and waddled over to look in the mirror.

"Don't put your arms down—it will crease the—what are those, sleeves?"

"More like flaps, really? Or bits of capelet, maybe?"

"Just as long as she doesn't sit."

"Ever?"

"Of course not. Look at it."

"How will she get to the party?"

"We've ordered a party bus with a pole, so that she can ride standing. She'll have to cling to it and hope that she can stay upright around the curves."

Bentley stopped listening sometime after the stripper pole revelation.

If this was a *statement piece*, the *statement* was some kind of joke, and possibly one that did not translate well from the original Japanese. She looked like an origami earthworm trying to wriggle out of a cocoon. (Not that earthworms had cocoons, and she wished that the designer had known that.)

Bentley Royce was the most ridiculous thing that even she had ever seen.

---

80 *Jeff thinks you're describing a gummy bear. (But—an amazing one!)* ☺ —D

By the time she stumbled out of her room and wiggled down the stairs into the front hall, the boys were waiting.

They did not look like origami worms.

Tom Ford for Gucci had worked magic. Bach looked like a cover model for *GQ Magazine*, and Whitey looked like a cover model for—*what? Hot Redneck Thug (with Great Arms) Weekly? Guns and Buns Weekly?*[81] *Impostor Marrying Your Sister, Esquire?*

To Bach's credit, he stopped laughing shortly before getting to the point of convulsing so hard that he threw up.

To Whitey's credit, he agreed to be the one to hoist Bentley up the stairs to her empty party bus stripper pole.

As Bentley clung to the pole, she looked at the sweating groom now moving back down the stairs. She reached out and hit the button on the side of the bus—and the doors slammed shut.

"Whoa—"

When he looked over his shoulder, the sister of the bride just smiled sweetly.

Twenty-five minutes later, the massive black party bus rolled up to the red carpet outside Soho House. Helicopters circled overhead, flying so low the humming noise of the chopper blades nearly drowned out the chanting crowds of #Roycers held back by just as many police.

Bentley emerged from the bus first, holding her head

81 *Per JG: "Do we have this? Can we?"* ☺ —D

high. The crowd roared at the sight of her disastrous dress, and it was only as she made her way to the door that she realized they were chanting "GA-GA! GA-GA! GA-GA!"

At least they aren't chanting "origami worm."

Bentley decided to go with it. She blew monster kisses to the crowds.

As she entered Soho House, the bus pulled away.

The groom was still on board, which was where he remained for forty-five minutes.

He stopped at a 7-Eleven for a 64-pack of Donettes and a Slurpee, and then a liquor store for something to pour into it.

The groom currently known as Whitey was just getting started.

Jeff Grunburg stood on the curb outside Soho House as he shouted into his cell phone. It was hard to hear over the news choppers circling Sunset Boulevard.

He raised his voice again. "I don't care which camera it is, Pam! Just make sure it's on me when I walk in! I don't want to spend five more minutes with Frankenstein's Bride and Groom than I have to—"

Tallulah tugged at his sleeve, interrupting. "Are you coming inside?"

He covered the phone. "Five minutes, hon. Go stand by the door. You might get yourself on *Celebpretty*."

Tallulah rolled her eyes.

When Jeff went back to his call, Pam had already

disconnected. Still, he swore into the phone a few more times before he made a big show of pretending to hang up on her. *Gotta model these things for the kid. How else will she learn how to grow up and run a studio?*

"Can we go in now?" she asked.

Jeff stared at his daughter. Tallulah wore a filmy gray minidress that he privately thought made her look like a handful of elbows wearing a wadded-up scarf—and he didn't mean that in a negative way. "Yeah. Let's get in and get out, all right, Lulu?"

She studied his face before answering. "Why are you so *obsessed* with hating that guy, anyways?"

Jeff sat down on the curb next to where Tallulah stood. He knew he was probably sitting in drunk vomit, but for the moment, he was too tired to care. It had been a long year. "Sometimes I forget you're only thirteen, you know that?"

"I figured." She looked at him. "You're old and I never forget that. Sorry."

"I figured." Jeff sighed.

"Answer the question," Tallulah said. "Why do you hate Porsche's fiancé? Are you jealous?"

"No," Jeff said, trying not to laugh.

"I mean, of the attention?"

"No," Jeff said again. He watched the cars speed down Sunset as he considered his answer. "You know how your mom sat you down and told you all about the birds and the bees, in Urth Caffé that day? Back in fourth grade? With the book with all the pictures?"

"Sex, Dad." She rolled her eyes.

"Yeah." He nodded. "That. Well, there's a whole other set of things people don't tell you until you bring it up. And that talk isn't about sex. It's about rage and loathing and spite and fury. Jealousy. Competition. Hate. And it's kind of like the birds and the bees—"

"Sex."

"Sure. That. Because it's irrational and instinctive and mammalian. And there are certain things, certain feelings, that you come to realize have lived on this planet a lot long longer than you ever will."

"But why *that guy*? What makes you hate that guy so much?"

He looked at his daughter. She was still wearing a necklace with an ice-cream cone on it.

He gave up.

Even he didn't really know the answer anymore.

"You know what? Let's go inside and see if we can pop some of those two-hundred-dollar balloons." Jeff pulled himself back up off the curb, felt in his pocket—and pulled out a KitKat bar.

Tallulah looked like she was going to pass out. "Are you *kidding* me?"

He shrugged. "Don't tell your mother."

She took his hand and let him pull her to her feet.

Just then, a van swerved up and Whitey stumbled out. His shirt was torn, and his breath smelled of alcohol. Jeff's face turned bright red. He could feel his veins bulging on either side of his forehead.

"Whoa, whoa, whoa." Jeff grabbed Whitey by the arm. "Where do you think you're going?"

"Inside?" Whitey slurred.

Jeff stepped in front of him. "No way, not like this, buddy. I don't know what kind of stunt you're trying to pull here, but you have some nerve, showing up like this. Do you know how many cameras there are here tonight? You're this close to destroying the entire show, do you realize that?"

"Hey, man, back off a little," Whitey said. Jeff's face was inches from Whitey's. He could smell the booze more strongly than his own aftershave.

"You don't tell me what to do, Whitey Trash." Jeff leaned even closer. "Now, listen to me—"

In one swift, blurry moment, Whitey raised his fist and—for the second time since they'd met—drove it into Jeff's face.

Jeff stumbled backward, stunned.[82]

Then he straightened up, smiling cruelly. "I hope you're happy with what you just did, Mr. White," he growled. "Because it's the last thing you'll ever do in this town."

"WHERE IS HE?"

Porsche Royce was pacing inside her dressing room at the club. She had come hours early with her team—Hair,

---

Makeup, Hair, Makeup (it was all about the layers, she maintained)—at the venue, but the joke had been on her when the groom never showed up for his cue. She had made her way alone down the red carpet to the door, only to beat a hasty retreat from the screaming crowds with no Whitey in sight.

This was not what anyone had rehearsed.

"I'm sure he'll be here any second," Bent said again, giving up on her dress and flopping down on the couch in front of her.

"*STOP SAYING THAT!*" Porsche was losing her mind.

"I'll go call the driver again," Bach said, taking the opportunity to disappear. (Bent had noticed that Bach now employed different strategies in response to the anxiety his family caused him. The one that seemed to be working best, at least for tonight, was not being around them at all.)

Mercedes stuck her head into the dressing room. "Anything?"

"Royces!" Jeff waltzed in with an almost manic air about him. "It's team huddle time."

Everyone just stared at him, blinking. Jeff had never been part of a *team huddle* in his entire life. In fact, he'd never said those words before.

"Nobody freak out—don't overreact—but I think it's time to write Whitey off the show. Cut our losses. He's deadweight. Awful guy. He's dragging you down. I know we have this whole wedding story line, but it'll be fine, we'll make the rest of the season be about Porsche finding new love—bring in a Jonas brother, or even better, a Hemsworth! Look, before you say anything—"[83]

"I love it." Mercedes clapped her hands together. "Porsche?"

Porsche looked at the two of them as if she were deciding which head to rip off first. Then the screaming began:

"ARE YOU FREAKING KIDDING ME? HE'S LEFT ME AT THE ALTAR?! MY LIFE IS OVER! EVERYTHING IS RUINED! THE WHOLE WORLD WILL BE LAUGHING AT ME—"

"Good news!" Bach interrupted, sticking his head through the door. "Tracked down the driver and had him bring back our groom. Sounds like Whitey just stayed on the bus. As of two minutes ago, he is back on the premises and in the bathroom getting cleaned up." He smiled. "You're welcome."

"Oh . . ." Mercedes said.

"AND WE'RE BACK! MAKEUP! I NEED MAKEUP!" Porsche dropped into her chair in front of the mirror, her crew materializing out of the hallway, where Bentley suspected they had been hiding.

Bach coughed. "Do you want the bad news?" His smile wavered.

"Spill," Bentley said, her eyes flickering toward the bride.

"Bach?" Porsche's eyes shot lasers at him, even through the mirror.

---

83 *Jeff is volunteering to play himself in this scene. He feels he'd make a good Jeff.* ☺ ☹ —D

"Apparently the bus has been parked at the liquor store down the street—and the groom is, well, plowed. See ya!" Bach ducked back behind the door, safely out of the bridal blast zone.

This time, screaming could be heard on Sunset Boulevard, even above the sound of the choppers.

Out in the vast dinner hall, Mercedes was greeting the guests, who seemed to be suddenly arriving all at once.

She knew everyone (that mattered) and remembered everything (that mattered), including the Mayor, who had once ridden in the car in front of her in a Tournament of Roses parade that time she was (deputy) honorary honoree for the city of Beverly Hills. The Studio Heads who (normally) never returned her calls. The Stars who (mostly) froze her out at industry functions. The Recording Artists who (uniformly) made fun of Porsche's debut single. The Designers who (utterly) mocked her style. And of course, the Agents who (best) understood the worth of her family, and fought (dirty) to gain her respect or at least attention, over and over again.

As the bride floated into the sea of tables artfully covered in burlap and tulle and a thickly twisting double helix of white peonies sourced from three continents, the scene was almost perfect.

Everyone who was anyone worth anything was here in this room, right now. Everyone, that is, except the groom.

By the time Whitey did stumble in, everyone was already seated, including the bride—and all he could do was make his way—very carefully—to the one table that Porsche had made certain was visible from every seat in the room.

Mercedes Royce had her eyes fixed on him the entire time.

It was not a look of love.

Neither was the look Porsche Royce gave him when he finally dropped into the chair next to her. The one her fiancé was supposed to have been in the entire night.

The resulting fight began with whispers, escalated to hisses, and soon developed into full-blown screaming.

"It's our rehearsal dinner. You're not just supposed to *be here*. You're supposed to *not leave my side*. We're supposed to be *in love*. This is supposed to be the eve of *our wedding vows*. This is supposed to be the *night before the happiest day of our lives*."

"If that's true, then why am I drunk and why are you crying?"

"Because," Porsche said, "you've become a different person. You're a stranger. And tonight, you're acting like a giant ass."

"People change," Whitey said with a sullen shrug. "Which makes me think," he continued, only pausing to let a belch fly, "that this whole damn thing might be a giant mistake, *Sweet Thing*."

As he spoke that last unfortunate (and really never very

clever) nickname, the nine-hundred-dollar-a-plate dishes began to fly.

"*I HATE YOU—*" A salad plate went whizzing past Whitey's head.

"*YOU'VE RUINED MY LIFE—*" Cutlery hit his chair like a dartboard.

"*I CAN'T BELIEVE YOU'RE DOING THIS TO ME—*" A half-empty gravy boat sailed across the table.

"*I'LL MAKE YOU PAY—*" Only Bentley seemed to see the pained look on his face as the groom crawled to safety beneath the table.

Thank god.

In many ways, the evening was considered a huge success.

The rolled caviar-and-blini cigars were called *daring* (especially when they emitted tiny puffs of actual steam).

The tiny hand-worked *burratas* formed in the shape of rosebuds were widely hailed as *inventive*; guests seemed to particularly enjoy their edible gold thorns.

The cold lobster cereal, served in lobster-shell bowls, was declared *whimsical*.

The boba micro-meatballs, speared with a single straight pin, were *triumphant*, and the single thread of spaghetti wrapped around them, an *inspired touch*.

And no one, no one had believed the *incroyable* artisanal *baguettes-minces*. The baguette toothpicks, no larger than a slender child's even-more-slender pinkie finger, were the subject of more illicit Instagram photos than the bride herself. *(SO THIN! SO INCREDIBLY DELICATE! AND YET—SO IMPERTINENT—TO SERVE BREAD!)*[84]

It was, in so many ways, an *exquisite* evening.

If it weren't for the fact that the bride had gone missing for a full half hour in the middle of the sorbet course, or that the groom and his mother-in-law-to-be were overheard screaming at each other inside the Sub-Zero, where they thought they couldn't be heard, or that Jeff Grunburg had fired the entire valet staff after they couldn't locate his Land Rover, then called in a temp agency to replace them, you might not have wanted to change a thing at all.

Bentley stood outside the back security exit to the venue with her mom and brother while her sister curled up into a weeping, quivering ball on the cold cement.

Whitey stumbled up behind them, smelling like the bathroom at a biker bar, especially now that he had thrown up in the bushes just next to the valet.

Bentley looked at her mother and brother. "What are we going to do, guys? You want the bride or the groom?"

"Get her home and get him out of my sight. We can figure the rest out in the morning," Mercedes said.

"Okay, but who's taking which sad sack, and in what car?" Bach asked. "I call the sobber, not the puker."

Porsche wept harder.

"No one's takin' thissad sack anywhere," Whitey slurred,

---

84 *Gluten-free? JG asks.* ☺ —D

"I'm goin' home and gettin' far away from you people, okay? Mister Valet! I got my card righ' here."

He waved the blue cardstock ticket in the air, and the valet plucked it hesitantly from his hand.

"You can't drive!" Bentley laughed bitterly. "You're beyond wasted." She looked to her family for backup. Porsche only cried. Bach looked at the ground. Mercedes shrugged.

"He's fine to drive, as far as I'm concerned," Mercedes said. "I hope he drives off a cliff. See if I care."

"This family is a very special type of dysfunctional," Bach said, feeling in his own pockets. "And on that note, I left my valet ticket inside. I'll be right back." He disappeared inside the club.

As he did, the valet drove up in Whitey's sparkling white Audi R8. The rear window had even been painted with the words *JUST MARRIED*. Whitey lunged for the keys before anyone could stop him.

"No!" Bentley shouted. "You can't let him drive! Whitey, stop!" She picked up her ridiculous gown and hobbled toward him. "I'll drive you home."

"Oh, no you will *not*," Mercedes protested, gripping her daughter's shoulder.

"Are you kidding me? We don't have to *like* the guy, but I'm not letting him drive off to his death, all right?" Bent shook her mother loose and hurried into the driver's seat, slamming the door shut.

"Bentley, no!" It was Porsche this time, standing up out

of her catatonic state. "Get out of that car right now. You're not going anywhere with that pig."

"God, Porsche, I'm not taking his side, I'm just keeping him alive. Let me just get him home safe, and I'll Uber home. It's not like he even lives that far."

"Seriously?" Mercedes yanked off a shoe and for a second, Bent thought she was going to throw it at her.

"I'll be home in an hour, and he'll be taken care of, all right? Let's get this over with. Then we can put the whole thing behind us." Bent rolled up the window, glanced over at Whitey—now passed out soundly in the passenger's seat—and hit the gas.

"Bentley!" Porsche shouted.

Bach looked up as he walked back to the valet.

The car didn't stop.

Their sister's silhouette in the darkened Audi window was the last Porsche and Bach saw of Bentley, before they awoke to the news that the very same Audi had been found at the bottom of a ravine.

HOLLYWOOD MOURNS, WHOLE WORLD WATCHES
BIGGEST RATINGS IN NETWORK HISTORY
AP: Beverly Hills, California

Via Celebcity.com

Today, Hollywood mourned the loss of its own—in true Hollywood style. Early reports indicate that a record-shattering number of viewers tuned in across the globe to see grieving would-be bride Porsche Royce lay to rest not just her fiancé, music industry exec T. Wilson White, but also her only sister, reality celebrity Bentley Royce.

At Porsche Royce's side throughout the Beverly Hills invitation-only (and packed to capacity) memorial service were mother Mercedes Royce and brother Maybach Royce. While overwhelming crowds gathering behind the police barricades at times threatened to shut the proceedings down entirely, the steady flow of celebrities into the chapel itself was nothing short of dazzling.

So, too, was the program; Bentley Royce's close childhood friend (and former Teen Choice Awards Breakout Pop Star of the Year) Justa Beatbox opened the service with "Amazing Grace," while readings and reminiscences were offered from many of Royce's "young Hollywood" peers, including Zoey Deutch, Alden Ehrenreich and Thomas Mann, as well as multiple musicians from White's record label. Eulogy was given by Jeff Grunburg, an executive of the Lifespan Network with whom both Royce and White were said to have close personal ties.

White's coffin was draped with his signature black ban-danna, as were the shoulders of his former fiancé. Lifespan may not have gotten the chance to broadcast the *RWTR* dream wedding, but even while forfeiting the allegedly multimillion-dollar live television event, the network should still come out on top; insiders predict that with exclusive rights to broadcast the memorial service, Lifespan will actu-ally be back in black for the balance of the season.

(Disclosure: Celebcity is a fully owned subsidiary of the Lifespan Network, which is itself a fully owned subsidiary of DiosGlobale.)

Follow @celebcity for breaking details,
or www.celebcity.com.

One Week Later

DETECTIVE ON THE CASE

Eighteen

Porsche Royce was frustrated. Harry knew the feeling, but that didn't mean their work here was done. And it didn't mean she was being straight with him.

"You don't get it. Something's wrong. Something doesn't make sense."

"It seems your sister and your fiancé pulled over on the side of the road for some time. We have two eyewitness accounts who can put a white sedan on Mulholland during the hour after they left you at the club."

"Why would they have pulled over? He could barely speak, and she was exhausted. She was just trying to get him home."

"Once again, you weren't fighting with your sister? Only the groom?"

"I've said it a thousand times. The last time I saw her, my sister was kinder than she's ever been to me in my entire life."

This time around, something about the bride's sob story slid a millimeter to the side—finally snapping into place in Harry's mind.

He raised an eyebrow. "Ever?"

"What?"

"Were you being literal? Was that actually the nicest your sister ever was to you in your entire memory of your entire life?"

Porsche thought about it. "Well, actually, we'd been getting along a lot better the last few months, but that night things just felt different. It felt like the trailer days. I mean, except for all the tear-filled rage."

"Trailer?" Harry asked. *How is that not in the files?*

"The network doesn't like us to talk about it, so you won't see it online, hardly anywhere. But we—Mercedes and me, and the babies—we used to be pretty dang happy in a double-wide." The *dang* just sort of slipped out.

"Where was this?"

"Southern Utah. Richfield. Sevier County. Prime sheep country. Until Mercedes realized she was distantly related to some pretty fancy people, including a congressman." Porsche shrugged.

"And?"

"So we moved when I was eight. Bentley was two, and Bach had just been born. Mercedes—my mom—says she looked at him and said, 'This is not a boy who will make it in a trailer park.' But I also think it had something to do with a falling-out between Mercedes and our dad, who she never, ever talks about."

"Anything else you can recall?"

"I don't know. Just stuff. There were raspberries in the summer. The dirt was red. We ran around in bare feet and played with the other kids in the trailer park."

"And you were nice to each other?"

"Yeah, but it was different then. The babies were just babies."

"And as best you can remember, aside from happier days in the trailer, your last conversation with your sister was the easiest moment of your relationship?"

She looked up at Harry.

Maybe she was getting it too. You never know. Either way, he could already tell that starting her talking was going to pay off.

Thank god for the good old days and the raspberries and the bare feet and the babies. Everyone has their own way of telling it, but it always gets to the same place.

Now Porsche looked stricken. "You think she was— saying good-bye? You think they drove off that cliff *on purpose*?"

"That's what we're here to talk about. You tell me. You were there—I wasn't."

Porsche's eyes immediately began to well with tears. "Can I see my—Mercedes now?"

"Soon, Ms. Royce. The way we do things is, I gotta talk to the three of you separately."

"But you've already done all that."

"And now I'm doing it again." Harry shrugged. "Things change."

She shivered when he said the words, but even then, she didn't look at him.

"I wish people would stop saying that. I don't want anything to change. I don't want them to be gone." The tears were flowing freely down her face now. "And it is my fault, you know."

"What's your fault, Ms. Royce?"

"All of it," Porsche said glumly.

He slid his hand beneath the thick steel table and pressed a hidden switch. If she thought she was at fault, he was ready to hear why. You never knew when the ex was going to start talking, and Harry had learned the hard way that it was better to be prepared.

"All of what?" Harry asked.

The green light at the top of the room, next to the clock, flashed on—and the session was now being recorded.

"I pushed him too hard. I fell in love with him, or at least I thought I did. It wasn't supposed to be like that, and everyone kept warning me. Bentley more than anyone. But I just didn't want to see it."

"And?"

"And I guess I drove him away. It was the night before what was supposed to be just a TV show, really. And I acted like it was our wedding, our real wedding."

"So it wasn't real?"

"No, it was. I mean, legally and everything. It just wasn't supposed to matter. Not to us. Not like that. We were going to split up." She sighed. "That would have been our guaranteed ticket to season seven, I guess. Not that it matters now."

"But that all somehow changed?"

"For me." She bit her lip and looked right at Harry. "I get it now. It only changed for me."

"I see."

"I don't think you do—I drove him away. I was being selfish, and desperate, and I just wanted him to feel what I felt, even when he didn't."

She pulled a tissue from her bag and balled it up against her eyes.

"And?" Harry pressed.

"And then I punished him for it." Porsche shook her head. "He had to drink a bottle of whiskey just to get up the nerve to tell me something I already should have known. That it was a fake wedding. That I was a fake bride. That we didn't have to pretend it was something it wasn't."

Harry checked his notes. "It says there was some throwing of china and cutlery, is that correct?"

She nodded. "That's putting it mildly. I think I jammed a tiny baguette up his nose, actually."

"I see."

"I'm not proud. I sucked him into my twisted little reality television world under what turned out to be false pretenses, and then I humiliated him in front of everyone we knew. I might as well have killed him myself."

Harry reached down and pressed the button beneath the table. The light by the clock switched back to red, and then died out. "Did you douse the car in gasoline and roll it off a cliff, Ms. Royce?"

"No."

"Then it's not your fault, ma'am." He leaned back in his chair, studying the girl. She seemed legitimately torn up.

Harry felt a pang of guilt. He'd known it was going to

be like this when he'd called them all back in today, but he didn't really have another way around it.

The case was the case, and now the case had changed.

The Royce family was plenty messed up, all right, but he didn't think they were criminals. Not yet, anyhow. He studied his list. Persons of interest? The thing that was the most interesting was the idea that the people on this list were all there was.

Somehow, Harry doubted it. He had begun to sense that there was more to Bentley Royce than anyone realized.

Harry tossed the paperwork on his desk. The case was thin. The details were suspect. He'd spoken to the teen in question himself, and she'd seemed perfectly normal—balls of steel, but normal. Something was off.

There had to be more than this.

Harry Connolly, senior detective, head of the Homicide Special Section task force, was sure of it.

He would bet his career on it. And in fact, he was. So he picked up the file and began to read again.

PERSONS OF INTEREST
LAPD HOMICIDE SPECIAL SECTION
RE: BENTLEY ROYCE, MISSING PERSONS

- Dave Nagao, Nobu, apprentice sushi chef
- Dr. A., therapist
- Maureen Reynolds, Mulholland Hall, Honors English teacher
- "Venice," probable transient, frequenting Santa Monica library
- "Chicago Bulls Cap," probable transient, frequenting Santa Monica library
- "Spots," probable transient, frequenting Santa Monica library
- "Fox," probable transient, frequenting Santa Monica library
- Joshua Lee, Reference Desk, Santa Monica library
- "Lawrence," meeting leader, Santa Monica Seventh Street meeting, AA
- Porsche Royce, sister
- Mercedes Royce, mother
- Maybach Royce, brother
- Guadalupe Flores, housekeeper
- Jeff Grunburg, Lifespan Network president
- Razz Jazzy White, head of Whiteboyz music label, father of T. Wilson White
- Pamela Pearson, *Rolling with the Royces*, producer
- Ronda Mahoney, CAA, agent/manager

- Tracey from Hair & Makeup, freelance, frequent home visits (according to sister)
- Brad B from TryCycle, instructor, three times weekly
- Ileana Raku, skincare facialist, Friday appointments
- Louis from Barneys shoe department, friend (note: self-described)[85]

Harry turned the pages in the file and kept reading. To his dismay, the sworn statements weren't much help either.

"Two vegetable soybean rolls, extra shiso, two spicy tuna, one tofu special. Cold soba noodle salad. She used to come in with her brother every night and pick it up. I think she liked me." **—DAVE NAGAO**

"Miss Royce was a deep thinker with college aspirations. I wasn't expecting that. I wasn't expecting much. Not from her, not in my class. You know celebrities. I mean, you probably know celebrities. Can't swing a dead cat without hitting one at Mulholland Hall's Upper Campus, right?"

—MAUREEN REYNOLDS

"Always on time. And a great, full brow. Really natural. I just cleaned it up, really can't take any credit for the shape."[86]

—TRACEY FROM HAIR & MAKEUP

---

85 Production Note: Licensing is thinking about other directions. Could we spin Bentley as a Maxxinista? Or similar. —D
86 Production: Is she a Visual Asset? Jeff is asking for more VA's and fewer VP's. (Visual Problems.) ☹ —D

"I don't know anything about that missing actress from the news. Why would a famous reality television personality come into a library? And wouldn't you think I'd notice, if she did? And if she was famous, why would she even talk to me? In fact, why are you talking to me? Don't talk to me. This is a library. In fact, just don't talk."

—JOSHUA LEE

"Bentley? No puedo hablar ahora. Mi jefe me va a matar. Usted no sabe Mercedes Royce. Ella es una perra fría."

—GUADALUPE FLORES

"Bentley's been with us for six seasons. She's no Porsche, of course, but then who is? Her presentation was getting better. We were encouraging her to spin, to take care of herself. The attitude needed a little work, to be honest, but we have people for that. She played Bentley Royce perfectly, we never once thought about recasting. We'd even talked about giving B her own story line. But I think we all know how that turned out." **—PAM PEARSON**

"Doctor-patient privilege. All I can say is, she liked animals."

—DR. A.

"Something was wrong. She had eaten shellfish, and possibly nuts, during the last week. She tried to deny it, but I could see it in the pores on her forehead. It was like her skin wanted me to know, you know? And while I can't say she herself was smoking, she was definitely letting herself be smoked on. There was clear blockage, borderline pre-blackheads. It was absolutely tragic."   **—ILEANA RAKU**

"Was Bentley Royce a member of our Pack? I really couldn't say. Was she taking her journey with us? You'd have to ask her. Celebrity client privilege. At TryCycle, we take that very seriously. This isn't SheWheel, for god's sake. We don't just light a candle, toss you a water bottle, and give you a mini cupcake on your birthday. We give you a vegan, gluten-free one."   **—BRAD B.**

"Do I know a Bentley? AA doesn't stand for Alcoholics All-Identified, for the public's gossip-mongering pleasure. If I knew her, I'd probably tell you she was a person, and she was hurting, and she was determined to stop living in the problem and start living in the answer. But I'm not saying I know her. You get me?"   **—LAWRENCE**

"Are you going to finish that cake?"
                    —VENICE AT THE LIBRARY, LAST NAME UNKNOWN

PORSCHE ROYCE COMES CLEAN IN ROYCE-WHITE CASE: 'I DROVE HIM TO IT'

AP: Beverly Hills, California

Via Celebcity.com

THIS JUST IN: Reality television celebrity Porsche Royce, who has been in the headlines ever since the Mulholland Drive discovery of the wrecked Audi allegedly carrying her sister Bentley Royce and fiancé T. Wilson White, has made a full statement to the LAPD task force investigating the case.

While the details of such statements are not available to the general public, sources familiar to the case indicate that the would-be bride cited the pressures of a global television event as well as those inherent in every wedding ceremony.

Royce reportedly spoke only of remorse and regret for allowing her fiancé and sister to leave the Soho House rehearsal dinner the night of the accident while pre-wedding (and pre-season-finale) tensions were running at an all-time high.

While no new charges have been filed in the case, recent conversations appear to be moving the course of the investigation increasingly toward the Royce family itself.

(Disclosure: Celebcity is a fully owned subsidiary of the Lifespan Network, which is itself a fully owned subsidiary of DiosGlobale.)

Follow @celebcity for breaking details,
or www.celebcity.com.

Nineteen

Mercedes Royce thought he was an idiot. That much was clear from their first five minutes together—when she'd all but called him that. And also, the rest of the minutes, when she'd called him just about everything else a person could be called.

He had to admit it. She was a firecracker, and she could hold her own in a police precinct—that was for damn sure.

She was rolling her eyes at him now, and he couldn't even remember why.

This time.

"Let's get to it, shall we? I'm not my children, Detective. I'm not as generous as they are, not as optimistic, and not as naive."

"What's that supposed to mean, Mrs. Royce?"

"It means, I know the ever-despicable Jeff Grunburg has you on his payroll. I know that, in fact, because he has me on his payroll. I also know that because it's my show, and I see every dollar that comes in or out of my budget, including your weekly check."

"There's nothing wrong with consulting on a show, Mrs. Royce."

"I know, I know. You worked on *Blown*, and it was the best five minutes of your crappy little life. I get it. Believe me, I've sung that song, Detective."

"Harry." He smiled, in spite of the abuse. "Call me Harry." She was a piece of work, Mercedes Royce. Now he could see why that little rat Grunburg was always so paranoid about her.

She nodded. "Harry, then. And I'm Mercedes."

"Mercedes." He smiled. "You gotta love German engineering."

She stared at him. "So, let's not waste time. I'm guilty. I'm the one you're looking for, but then, you knew that, didn't you?"

"Not particularly." He sat back in his chair, studying her.

"I'm more than just the guilty party, actually. I'm also the judge and jury. I convict myself and everyone around me of a thousand crimes, sins, lapses of judgment, questionable decisions, bad calls, wrong answers, moral turpitudes—"

Harry looked up from his yellow legal pad. "Can turpitude be plural?"

She raised one eyebrow. "Do I look like I went to college, Det—Harry?"

He narrowed his eyes, not really knowing how to answer.

"Anyway, I do all that before you make your coffee in the morning, Harry."

"I don't drink coffee," Harry said.

Mercedes looked at him like he was absolutely insane. "Who doesn't drink coffee? What *cop* doesn't drink coffee?"

"Ulcer." He nodded. "My gut."

"Ah. Stress. It's a killer." She sighed. "I suppose next you're going to tell me your wife doesn't let you eat doughnuts anymore."

"No wife," Harry said. "Not now, anyway. Apparently I wasn't marriage material, according to my ex."

She shot him a withering look. "When did this confession become about you, Harry?"

"Confession? Is that what this is?"

"I told you. I put them in the car together. I left my one daughter to be destroyed by that monster—to take care of my other daughter, who that same monster had already destroyed."

"But you're not the monster."

"Of course I'm not the monster."

"The monster is the monster."

"And are you an idiot, *Harry*?"

"I'm just trying to point out, *Mercedes*, that when you talk about that night, the person doing the attacking isn't you, it's Mr. White. He's the monster."

"This is Hollywood, Harry. Do you really think there's *ever* just one monster in the room?"

"Why don't you walk me through it, Mercedes? The last night?"

"Bentley was being her usual . . . charming self."

"Would that be more or less charming than usual?"

Mercedes thought about it. "She was more charming,

actually. She hated her dress, but she shut up and wore it, which isn't like her."

"That bad?"

"The dress? It was spectacularly ugly but very chic, and someone had to wear it. It's an origami designer Jeff wants to do his daughter's bat mitzvah, so one of us had to take the bullet, and Bentley got the short straw, I'm afraid."

"How often is that? That Bentley gets the short straw?"

"What's that supposed to mean?"

"I'm just asking. You're telling me she was more charming than usual on a night when another person might reasonably have been less charming than usual."

Mercedes's eyes were blazing. "Is my missing daughter's *charm* really the most powerful weapon in your crime-solving arsenal, Harry? What happened to DNA? Trace evidence? Fingerprinting?"

"Of course. We'll get there. Her phone records are being pulled now. Her room, you saw how quickly that was bagged and sorted. We have Tech taking apart her laptop. Detectives crawling over every inch of her school."

"And still nothing?"

"Well, our focus has been the crime scene, until now. And look, you have to give us that. We did pretty well figuring out that gasoline was used as some kind of accelerant for the fire. Which means, of course, arson."

She shook her head. "Who intentionally lights a *seventy-five-thousand-dollar* car on fire?"

"Folks have different reasons. Insurance fraud. Concealment of evidence. Homicide."

The last word seemed to stay in the air longer than the rest, and Harry immediately regretted saying it.

"None of that means anything right now, of course. That's why we're starting over again with all of you."

She nodded.

"So. Rehearsal dinner. Bentley was charming."

"She was."

"And she wore the dog of a dress."

"She did."

"Anything else?"

"She was kind to Porsche while I handled the party and Bach tried to track down Whitey's driver."

"And Whitey? He was . . . less kind."

Mercedes raised her head. "He was despicable. I had seen it coming. He was jumpy, secretive. You never knew what his motivations were. He either seemed too in love with my daughter, or totally ambivalent."

"And on the night in question?"

"Drunk. Completely obliterated and totally rude. By the end of the night, Harry, I wanted him gone." It was the truth, and she had no problem saying it.

As far as Harry could tell, her problem was with what came after.

"And now he is. I got what I wanted. He's gone and I'm left to feel guilty about that every day of my life."

Harry put down his pen. "Why is that, Mercedes?" He didn't reach for the button beneath the table.

He was transfixed.

When Mercedes looked at him now, her chin trembled.

"Because I got what I wanted—but he took my baby girl with him. And I would have thrown him off that cliff with my own hands, if I could have kept him from doing that."

Now the tears came. They leaked out of her eyes from behind her glasses, dripping down the front of her black suit and across her folded, manicured hands.

"There's a difference between feeling guilty and being guilty, Mercedes."

"Not to a mother," she said.

The tears still ran, unchecked. She didn't even try to wipe them. Harry reached into his pocket and pulled out a folded handkerchief, offering it to her.

"That's disgustingly unhygienic, Harry."

"That's what my ex used to say." He smiled, and she took it all the same, blowing her nose so loudly, the table rattled between them.

Harry sighed. "Did you douse the car in gasoline and roll it off that cliff, Mercedes?"

"No. I suppose not. Not like that."

"It's not your fault, ma'am."

Harry sat back in his chair and wondered, for the thousandth time, whose fault it really was.

MERCEDES ROYCE—MULHOLLAND MOMMY DEAREST? MAMA ROYCE PLAYS WEDDING EVE BLAME GAME

AP: Beverly Hills, California

Via Celebcity.com

BREAKING: Did the mother of the bride all but toss her future son-in-law over the edge of a cliff? In the second Royce sighting this week, the celebrity matriarch of television's beloved *Rolling with the Royces* made an unusual visit to LAPD's Rampart Division, to speak with Detective Harry Connolly, the head of the task force investigating the death of her daughter Bentley and would-be son-in-law T. Wilson White.

Royce's appearance downtown follows her daughter Porsche's conference with the same detective. Observers point to the flurry of recent family activity as indicative of new evidence in the Royce-White case.

A controversial figure, even for the world of reality television, Mercedes Royce has long functioned as the head of the Royce entertainment dynasty, and as a leading figure in the world of televised docu-follow programming. She is reportedly hailed as "Mercenary Royce" by friends and rivals alike.

(Disclosure: Celebcity is a fully owned subsidiary of the Lifespan Network, which is itself a fully owned subsidiary of DiosGlobale.)

Follow @celebcity for breaking details,
or www.celebcity.com.

Twenty

"Ah, Maybach. The prodigal son returns."

"Here I am, Detective."

"Harry," Harry said. "Please. Call me Harry. We might as well get comfortable with each other. We have a lot of catching up to do."

"Then let's do it." Bach nodded. "Seeing as I am the son, Harry, and I have returned."

Harry tossed his yellow legal pad to the table. "This is when, if you're anything like your mother and your sister, you tell me how guilty you feel and how torn up you are about Bentley, and then I tell you that it's all your imagination and you really aren't to blame at all."

"Yeah? I hate to disappoint you, but you sound like a pretty crappy detective, Harry. And if that's what you're expecting, you're way off the mark."

"How is that, Bach?"

"First of all, I'm nothing like my sister or my mother. And second of all, unlike both of them, I really am guilty. Bentley's death was my fault; I have the gasoline, and I know things about the last night of my sister's life that only her murderer would know."

Harry nodded, glancing up to the green light flashing on the wall near the clock.

He didn't have to hit the button this time.

He'd already hit it, the moment Bach had walked into the room.

"Why'd you do it, Bach? Was it the gambling? Did he have something on you, something that could have gotten you into even more trouble than you were already in? Or was it your sister who was the problem? You were angry, because she was the one who arranged to ship you off to Europe, while she took the fall for you?"

"All of the above."

"That's what a real man does, hey, Bach?"

Bach sighed. "Let me lay it out for you. Whitey was the douche bag who was ruining my family. I had to do something. I guess I just did the wrong thing."

"Because of your sister, you mean?"

For a second, the kid looked genuinely terrified. "I had no idea Bentley was in the car, and that's the honest truth. She was collateral damage in all of this. Maybe she always was."

"Collateral damage?"

"Sure. The middle child. The peacemaker. The one who sucks it up. Whatever it is that the shrinks like to say."

"Why don't you tell me, Bach? What the shrinks say?"

"My mother's a narcissist. My older sister is her clone. I was the spoiled baby, and the only boy. Bentley, well, she got whatever was left over from all of that. Let's just say it's no accident that she was the one who got stuck in the car with the drunk loser she happened to hate, even more than the rest of us did."

"How do you know?"

"What?"

"That she hated him?"

"I just do. Everyone hated him. It wasn't exactly a secret."

"But you just said she hated him most of all. I wrote it down, see?" Harry held up his pad.

Bach's eyes were red, and he looked exhausted, but he wasn't done. Not yet.

Harry knew something was about to go down.

Something big.

You could usually see it in their faces, if you looked closely enough.

"I know lots of things about my sister and Whitey that nobody else knows. That's why I decided to kill him."

MAYBACH ROYCE CONFESSES TO
ROYCE-WHITE KILLINGS;
ROYCE COLLATERAL DAMAGE, WHITE WAS TARGET

AP: Beverly Hills, California

Via Celebcity.com

DEVELOPING: Maybach Royce, the youngest son in the Royce television dynasty, and brother of the missing Mulholland crash victim Bentley Royce, has reportedly confessed to involvement in the alleged murder of his sister and T. Wilson White, his future brother-in-law.

The third member of the Royce family to visit LAPD's Rampart Station this week, Maybach has not been seen leaving the facility since his arrival earlier in the day.

The streets immediately surrounding the precinct have been closed to traffic due to media congestion. The sound of news choppers overhead has been deafening, and more than one area resident has been arrested for firing at the sky in frustration.

Mercedes and Porsche Royce have not made themselves available for comment.

The Lifespan Network is also not commenting at this time.

The hundreds of journalists and television crews camped outside the police precinct have been waiting for some sort of official confirmation of the day's surprising developments, but news from inside Rampart has been slow in coming.

More to come as the story develops.

(Disclosure: Celebcity is a fully owned subsidiary of the Lifespan Network, which is itself a fully owned subsidiary of DiosGlobale.)

Follow @celebcity for breaking details,
or www.celebcity.com.

Twenty-One

It wasn't until the next afternoon that Harry had Bach brought into the interrogation room again. This time, he threw a newspaper at the boy before he could say a word.

"Son, what are you doing?"

"Trying to confess to a murder, Harry."

"Stop messing around, will you? Be straight with me."

"I am."

"The case is about to close, Bach."

"Because of me?"

"Not because of you. Because of nothing, and nobody."

"I don't get it."

"There are no bodies, Bach. No genetic material whatsoever found in the wreckage. No bodies, no murder. There's nothing left to investigate, except for maybe destruction of private property."

"What about missing persons?!" Bach looked genuinely confused.

"Get out of here." Harry unlocked the door and yanked it open. "Go on. Get. Before someone changes their mind."

Bach shook his head. He didn't even stand up. "Harry, come on. Be reasonable."

"I just opened the door and invited you to walk away. Sounds pretty reasonable to me. And it goes without saying, we don't make that offer all too often around here, friend."

Bach was getting redder and redder. "You don't understand. I need to confess. It needs to be in the papers."

"It was in the papers. And now, the fact that it was all a stinking pile of horse manure is also going to be in the papers—with both of our names on it."

Bach looked miserable. "Then that's it. We're screwed. We're never going to find her. A trial was the only way to get her to come back. At least, the surest way."

"Come again?"

"She would have come back for me. She wouldn't let me go to jail for something she did. My sister's just not like that. She's not capable of that."

"I see. It only works the other way around?"

Bach sat up. "Exactly. And that's why I have to do it. I have to show her I'm not that jerk anymore. I wouldn't let her take the rap for me, not anymore. I know how to stand up, and someone in my family has to start acting that way."

"Someone?"

Bach's eyes began to water, and he rubbed at them with the back of one hand. "Someone besides Bent."

"Sorry, kid."

"Don't give up on the case, Harry. I swear, it's for real. I'm not sure what the exact crimes are, but I promise you almost everyone involved is kind of a criminal."

"Too late. The paperwork is filed. This goose is cooked. Or should I say, this duck has hit the deck."

Bach cringed. "Wait. You know about that?"

Harry shrugged. "I'm the show's consultant, remember? Why do you think I got assigned to this task force in the first place, my good looks?"

"Not really." Bach stared at him. "Are you any good, Harry? As a detective?"

"Sometimes. I have my moments."

"Okay then. We move to plan B. We find her ourselves."

"Hold on, pal. I've seen the evidence. It's not looking good. Whatever else her talents may be, your sister was thorough. She'd have a good career, if she was at all interested in a life of crime."

"It's not just her alone, though. She was working with someone. More than one person."

"How's that?"

"Let's go get my backpack. I can explain everything."

Harry shot him a look. "Nothing in your locker, right?"

Bach sighed, annoyed. "I promise, there's nothing incriminating inside. I'm clean as a whistle, I swear. Mother Teresa here."

"If I had a dime for every guy who sat in that chair and fed me that line . . ."

"Yeah? Really? Because the 'if I had a dime' line is so original?"

"Yeah, yeah. You know, you remind me a lot of someone we both know." Harry grinned. He had to admit, he was starting to like the kid. He had the mother's spunk and the kid sister's mouth. "Shut up and follow me."

When Harry handed him his backpack, Bach pulled out a dark object wrapped in a plastic bag. "Here. I was holding on to it, in case Bent ever got herself into trouble and this would help."

"Not here," Harry said, looking around the hallway outside the evidence room. "Let's go get a burger."

Bach smiled.

There was something satisfying about studying a cell phone that had been lost at a fancy exercise class while chowing down on cheeseburgers and fries and chocolate shakes.

Harry stared at the dead phone in front of him. "So you're telling me she ditched her own phone and then reported it stolen?"

"Exactly."

"Because there's something on this phone she couldn't risk anyone seeing?"

"That's what I'm guessing, right? I mean, none of it had uploaded to the cloud or whatever. They had to wipe the whole phone."

"Wiped, huh?"

"Yeah, that's the thing. She had Pam, our producer, kill the phone remotely. But you're the LAPD, right? You have to be able to do something with a wiped phone, right? Even if a regular person couldn't?"

"I don't know. Maybe. It might take a while, though. Or involve another federal agency. And then again, this case was declared dead the moment the labs could prove that there were never any bodies in the car. All we can do now is open a missing persons investigation."

Harry shrugged. It wasn't going to be easy, even if he could get it done. He didn't want to give the kid false hopes.

He picked up a battered leather notebook. "You found this in her locker?"

"That's right. After she left. I thought"—now the kid looked embarrassed—"I thought she might have left me a note or a clue or something."

"You thought she wanted you to find her?"

"Something like that." Bach sighed. "There's another part."

"Part of what?"

"Of the story."

"Yeah?"

"It's not just about where she lost it, the phone. It's also about what I saw on it before it was wiped. There was one number in the phone. I didn't recognize it until later—but I have a thing for numbers."

"Yeah, so I hear. Face cards too."

"It was Whitey's number. I'm sure of it. And if you can un-wipe that phone, I bet you'll find out whatever they were talking about."

Harry didn't look too surprised. "So your sister called her future brother-in-law. That doesn't mean anything."

"You don't get it. She lost the phone before we'd even met Whitey. Before Porsche even said a word about it to us."

Harry took a moment to let this sink in.

"Yeah." Harry looked at Bach. "You might have led with that."

"They were in on this thing, whatever it was. They must have faked it. Whitey and my sister." Bach shook his head. "The whole time."

"Ho-ly crap." Harry rubbed the grease off his hands and onto his pants. "Well, if the phone story holds up, you could be right—believe it or not."

"Why would they do that?" Bach frowned.

"Maybe they had a thing?" Harry looked at the kid. He felt bad for him, but someone had to say it. "I mean, there was that whole canoodling incident."

"No way. She couldn't stand the guy."

"A canoodle's a canoodle. But your sister and your mother said the same thing. Why?"

"I have no idea. She thought he was even faker than we did. It just got worse and worse, after a while."

Harry nodded. "So something about their deal was changing. Whatever it was. Someone has to know."

"She didn't exactly have a lot of close friends, my sister. It's sort of a family trait. Or, you could say, curse."

Harry snapped his fingers—almost upsetting his shake, or what was left of it. "What about that boy who was so stuck on her? The skater kid?"

"Skater kid? What are you talking about?"

"You know, the kid from the library. Kind of street-looking. Not a bad-looking kid, if you could get past the rough edges. The one with the hoodie, and the dark curly hair. You know the one I'm talking about. They were close. Like, real close."

"My sister? Close?" Bach looked at Harry. "I know Bent hung out at the library, but she never mentioned any skater dude."

Harry nodded. "Ah, see? The kid brother doesn't know everything."

Bach looked frustrated. "I mean, I know there were some homeless guys. But I think they were, like, old veteran types. Army vets, she said. She felt bad for them, for whatever had happened to them."

"Like the rescue cats. And the dead rabbit. Your sister had a real thing for strays."

Bach shook his head. "So you've been doing your homework, I guess."

"You gotta remember, I was on your family's case even before there was a case."

"Because of Lifespan." Bach nodded. "I forgot."

"The kid from the library, though—he wasn't a Lifespan problem. He's on the persons of interest list, seems he was a kind of secret friend of Bentley's. Which is funny, right? Seeing as he seems to have slipped under everyone's radar, even yours?"

"I guess," said Bach.

Harry kept thinking. "What was his name? It was Huntington. Manhattan—Venice. That was it. The kid went by the name Venice."

"My sister liked a boy named Venice who hung out at the library?"

Harry hit his head. "God, I am such an idiot. Not just a kid named Venice. A kid named whatever name is on that check."

"What check?"

"The one he used to pay her bail when she got locked up. The day she bawled Jeff Grunburg into sending you on an all-expenses-paid Italian vacation."[87]

He was on his phone before he finished the sentence—

Reaching for a napkin—

Searching his pockets for a pen—

Covering his other ear so he could hear in the crowded burger joint—

Until there it was.

Bach stared as he wrote it out.

A S A

"Asa? I remember that guy. She only met him once. At a party, at the Chateau Marmont."

"I see. Thanks. Appreciate it."

Harry clicked off, looking like he'd just solved the entire *New York Times* Sunday crossword.

"Venice is a kid named Asa. And not just any kid named Asa." He sat back in his creaking chair. "You're not going to believe this, but I'm pretty certain I know where Bentley is. Come on."

"Where are we going?"

"To pick up your sister and your mom. And to maybe pack some sunscreen."

"Sunscreen?"

"We're going on a little trip."

---

87 *Jeff feels "bawled" may be an overstatement here. Soften? —D*

Eleven Months Earlier

Twenty-Two

Bent was still furious about not being allowed into the room. It had been one day since the season six green-light meeting, and she knew she was running out of time. The network decision would come at any minute.

It was now or never.

Bent made the call from her bedroom, the one place where she knew Mercedes would never find her. Mercedes avoided all three of her children's bedrooms like the plague; she said it was because she was a *Cool Mom*, and she didn't want to see all the incriminating evidence, but in reality Bentley suspected the rooms were just too personal for her. As in, they just didn't have that *intimate* of a relationship, the kind where you could just walk into a room that had dirty underwear on the floor.

That was a different sort of Cool Mom, Bent told herself. In other words: she's just not that into you.

She turned the worn paper rectangle over in her hand.

It doesn't matter. They're your family. You have to do whatever you can to help them, or you have to live with knowing that you walked away. And if you play this right, you might just get everything you want too. A college education could be in your future after all.

It was no longer a decision.

It was time to call Yoda.

It was a United States cell phone number, but when the person on the other end of the line answered, he answered in Spanish. *"Hola?"*

Bent froze. She wanted to hang up, but she didn't. *Come on. You said you'd do anything. Now do it.* So she took a breath. "Is this, um . . . is this Senor . . . Senor . . ." She was tongue-tied, embarrassed.

The voice paused. "I'm a senior, yes? Who wants to know?"

What do I say to that? She almost hung up right then—but the man on the other end of the line started laughing. "I'm sorry, so sorry. I'm just joking with you."

"Oh, right. Hilarious." Bent tried to laugh.

"But really, could you speak up? I can't hear you very well."

It sounded like the old man she'd met in the lobby, but she couldn't be sure. Judging by the noise around him, the person on the other end of the line now was in some kind of dive bar. Wherever he was, there was lots of cheering and shouting.

Whatever.

It didn't matter if he was in a bar or a church. She didn't have a whole lot of options. It was now or never.

"This is Bentley Royce," she began again, this time

practically shouting. "I don't know if you remember me. You met my brother and me in the lobby of the Lifespan building yesterday?"

"I did?" Mr. S. sounded confused.

Her heart sank. "Yes."

A pause. "In San Diego?"

She sighed. "Beverly Hills."

Another pause. "Dark hair?"

Another sigh. "Blond. Rainbow on the tips."

When Bent mentioned the hair, the voice began to laugh on the other end of the line. "Ah, yes! The Troubled One! *Por Que, Bentley, Por Que?!*"

"That's right. I mean, that's not right, but that's me."

"I remember. The ax."

"Yeah, well, that's sort of what I was calling about." As she spoke, there was more cheering in the background, and then a blast of music that drowned out her last few words. "Is this a bad time?" Bent asked.

"Of course it is," he answered.

"Do you want me to call back?"

"No, no. There is no good time. Old men must be happy with whatever time we have." He paused melodramatically, and she couldn't tell if he was joking or not. She decided not to laugh, just in case.

"When I saw you, you had just come from meeting with Jeff Grunburg at Lifespan. Do you remember?"

"Tall?" Mr. S. guessed.

"Short."

"Brown hair?"

"Bald, actually."

"Friendly fellow?"

"You're joking again, right?"

Senor S. burst out laughing. "Now you're getting it."

"Great." Bentley was beginning to think he was drunk. *Do old men get drunk?*

"*Sí*, I met with Jeff and his team. They didn't seem like much of a team, but that's what he called them."

"And you were pitching them about Mexican wrestling, you said. You were looking for a distributor."

"That's right. *Luchadores*."

"That's your business."

"Not just a business. A *passion*, Bentley."

"Got it. The thing is—going back to the whole problem of our show getting the ax—"

"That is a problem, yes."

"I wondered if I could ask you a personal question?"

"Perhaps. Try me."

"Did you get it? The deal? For your wrestling?"

"My monthly licensing and distribution meetings are now the answer to your ax problem?"

"Not exactly. I just wanted to know if your pitch worked. Were you able to talk Jeff Grunburg into putting your wrestlers on the air?"

"Why?"

"Because you looked older than the other suits I saw in the room that day."

"Is that supposed to be a compliment?"

"Yes. Completely. Because if someone else could do your

job, they would already be doing it, since this is Hollywood. Hollywood hates old people. Jeff Grunburg's no different."

The old man laughed.

Bentley went on. "Also, you were dressed up, which usually means you're less important. So the way I see it, there you were, the oldest and least-senior guy in the room."

"And?"

"And you were in the room! Do you know how miraculous that is? Do you know how many times I've been stuck in the lobby with the Dirk? You got into the room at your age, which makes me think you know what you're doing."

He laughed again.

This was by far the craziest phone call she had ever made, and yet somehow she could tell it was working.

She tried again. "So tell me, did you get the deal? Did your pitch work?"

The old man paused, this time for much longer than a moment.

"You're an odd duck, Bentley Royce."

"Please. No ducks."

"Ah, yes." He spoke slowly and deliberately now. "While I can't answer your question specifically, due to the nature of my conversations with the network, I can tell you that I was very satisfied with the outcome of our meetings."

"So, in other words, yes."

"Just so long as those are your words and not mine."

She took another breath. This was it—why she had called, why she had thought of him. Her last hope, and her only plan.

"So here's the thing. The wrestling pitch. I wanted to know if you could teach me how to do it," she said.

"To wrestle?" He sounded delighted. The guy really was some kind of wrestling fanatic, she thought.

"To pitch. My family won't survive if I can't make another season happen. I want to be able to walk into Jeff Grunburg's office and pitch him something so killer, he'll have no choice but to keep us on the air."

"You do?"

"Yes. I want to say the magic words—whatever they are—that are going to get us renewed."

She could almost hear his *hmmmmm* over the phone as he thought about it.

Finally, he answered her. "They're not words, Bentley."

"I just mean I want to nail the pitch."

"It's not about a pitch. It never is."

"I don't understand."

"Three moves ahead. Just as I told you. You don't need the words that will give you another season. You need the season that will give you the right words."

"You mean, an idea?"

"Nobody can walk away from an idea that can't be walked away from."

"But the idea is just our family."

"No, it's not, Bentley. Think."

"*Young, Rich, and Beautiful,* that's what Jeff says. That's the only idea."

"But that's not true, is it? It's not the only thing."

"What else is there?"

"You tell me. How about—what's the last book you read?"

"*Love in the Time of Zombie Cholera,*" Bent said.

"Fine. So, we have love. How about the book before that?

"*Death in the Time of Zombie Cholera.*"

"All right, then. Now we have death. And the one before that?"

"*Zombie Cholera Apocalypse Wars.*"

The old man laughed.

Bent was embarrassed. "What? It's a series."

"I'm sure it is. I'll put it on my list. But there you have it. Love, death, and conflict. *That's* the season you want. All you have to do now is put *that* season into words. Your words. Does that make sense?"

"I think so. But what if I'm only thinking about those things because I just happened to be reading the Zombie Wars Saga?"

"If I had asked you for more books, would they all have been about zombies?"

"No. The last book before that was about Black Widow. She's an Avenger."

"And?"

Bent thought about it. "Love, death, conflict. Check, check, and check. All of the above. Yeah, okay, I see your point."

"Play the game you want to play. Use the cards you have. If you don't have them, find a way to get them. Just control the game."

"I want to. I think I have to."

"Of course you do. It's your game, Bentley. Nobody is going to care about your game more than you."

She wasn't sure she understood exactly what he was saying, but she had enough to go on. "Thanks, Señor S. Can I call you back? To try something out?"

"Absolutely. Anytime. I'm just here at the arena today."

"Arena?"

"*Luchadores.* You have to come to a match with me sometime. Talk about love, death, and conflict." He whistled.

She smiled. "I would probably like that. But right now, I have some thinking to do."

"Yes, you do. And then?"

"And then I want to pitch you a hot season six."

"You do that, and I'll try to help you find a way to get your ideas to Lifespan's ears."

"Deal," Bent said.

Thirty-five minutes later, she called Yoda back.

The pitch was hotter than either one of them had imagined.

So hot, a person could get burned.

So could an entire family.

It was Tallulah who had set it all up. She knew everything that went on at Lifespan, and not just from the time she spent with her father per their joint custody arrangement.

She kept an eye on her father from a series of nanny cams that she had installed in every gift she'd ever given him—most recently figurines from Giant Robot, her favorite store in LA's Westside Little Tokyo.

She was like a middle school version of the mafia, and she negotiated her terms just as strictly.

"Let me get this straight. I put you in front of my dad. That's it. I just tell you where to find him, and you send a Pizza Hut Stuffed Crust pepperoni pizza to my school at lunch, every Friday for the rest of the school year?"

"That's right," Bentley said.

"You're not looking for more than that? Alarm codes? Net worth? Combination to his wall safe? Because even for a very *helpful* person, like *myself*, that would require a different level of . . . *commitment*."

"I hear you, Lulu." Bent pushed away a flash of guilt; the kid even sounded hungry over the phone. Tallulah's mom, Jeff's most recent ex-wife, had demanded her daughter be raised vegan. Bentley felt like she was bargaining with Charlie Bucket while he was still standing *outside* the Wonka Factory.

"And?" Tallulah was holding out.

"No. Really. I just need to find a way to meet up with him in private," Bentley said. "Though those options all sound great."

She heard a sigh.

Then—

"Give me five."

Her phone was ringing a second later. "Palisades Beach Club," Tallulah said breathlessly. "Massage room B, right off the men's locker room. He pretends to be getting a massage, but really he's watching his Korean soaps. Every day at four."

"Wow," Bentley said. "Thanks, Lulu."

"No problem. Like I said, I'm a very helpful person."

By the time Bentley hung up, her plan was fully formed, as was her admiration for Tallulah Kyong-Grunburg.

She'd make a great studio head someday, if she could ever master that damn origami.

Stanford would be lucky to have her.

Bentley slipped into massage room B at four P.M. sharp the next day. What happened during the next forty minutes has never been detailed, not to anyone.

The only thing that we can know for certain is that Bentley Royce drove straight to TryCycle, where she did two things.

First, she engaged in a lengthy conversation with Tomme Torres, an aspiring actor/TryCyclist whose arm workout really was way too hard.

And second, she ditched her cell phone by shoving it into the seemingly endless crevasse behind the hall lockers.

It was just her luck that her brother, Bach, saw her do it.

He pocketed her phone and began to keep an eye on her, beginning the very next day.

TALK ABOUT A SPIN MASTER; TRYCYCLIST FRAUD REVEAL WHERE'S WHITEY? WHITEY WHO?

AP: Beverly Hills, California

Via Celebcity.com

BREAKING: Porsche Royce was engaged to a fraud. If this is the American dream, how delusional are we?

T. Wilson White, so-called head of the Whiteboyz music label, was never involved with the music industry, never named T. Wilson White, and had no plans to marry the oldest Royce sister—until he auditioned for the acting gig. There is, in fact, no person answering to any of White's many aliases at any of his alleged addresses. So-called father Razz Jazzy White, who vouched for the individual known as Whitey when he first appeared on the scene, is reportedly on vacation in South America and not taking questions at this time.

The revelation came about when a devoted attendee of Tomme Torres's TryCycling class saw a close-up photo of the impostor calling himself by the name of White. She called TryCycle late yesterday afternoon; the fitness group then contacted the authorities. As it turns out, to masquerade as "Whitey," Tomme Torres dyed his hair from brown to blond, shaved his trademark goatee, and hid his tattoos with industrial-grade concealer.

Tomme Torres, who departed TryCycle to reportedly pursue employment as an actor, now seems to have disappeared off the face of the earth. Porsche Royce, White's onetime fiancé, could not be reached for comment. No members of the Royce family, celebrity stars of what has now rebounded back to being the number one reality program in the United States, *Rolling with the Royces*, could be contacted at this time.

Seventeen-year-old Bentley Royce is still missing since the night she departed her sister's wedding rehearsal dinner at Soho House, a popular Los Angeles members-only club.

(Disclosure: Celebcity is a fully owned subsidiary of the Lifespan Network, which is itself a fully owned subsidiary of DiosGlobale.)

Follow @celebcity for breaking details,
or www.celebcity.com.

Twenty-Three

"Listen to me. You're not thinking straight, Tomme." Bentley, awkwardly sandwiched into her voluminous paper prison of a dress, clung to the stripper pole as if her life depended on it—which, as the party bus careened down Benedict Canyon, it possibly did.

His voice was muffled and miserable. "My name's Whitey now."

She wobbled in every direction as the bus rolled onward. At this point, she was holding herself up by the arms (and the pole!) alone.

She sighed. "It's not, *Tomme*, and you know it's not."

Whitey sat on the bench across from her, his head in his hands. "What if you're wrong? What if I *am* thinking straight? What if this is the first time I've ever been thinking straight in my whole life?"

She shook her head. "No way. This wasn't the deal. You were never supposed to fall in love with my sister."

"Don't you think I know that?" He sounded desperate. "I know that's not why you hired me. I know our wedding was supposed to be fake. Just let me go through with it."

Bentley didn't relent. This was Porsche she was talking about, and Porsche was her sister—no matter what else.

She deserves better.

To marry someone whose name she actually knows, and because of who they really are, not in spite of it.

He wouldn't really have to be a music-industry mogul. But he would have to be real. From reality reality. Real reality.

Not just a figment of Bentley's imagination.

Not a ghost named Whitey.

How long could that have even lasted? And how heartbroken would Porsche have been when she discovered the truth?

No matter how much this hurts her now, it's for the best.

Bentley knew this was the right thing to do.

"No, Tomme. It's too late for that. I know the plan was for the divorce to be season seven, but we're going to have to go another way. I can't put Porsche through it."

"So don't. Forget the whole divorce thing."

"I can't. You two can't be together forever. You don't even exist! I only know you because you taught my spin class."

"Don't say that."

"Why not? It's true! I happened to know you from TryCycle, just like the actual head of Whiteboyz happened to owe a friend of mine a favor."

"It's not the same," Tomme insisted. "Razz Jazzy and I, we really hit it off."

"It's exactly the same, Tomme. And we both know Razz Jazzy isn't your father. Razz Jazzy never had a son."

Bentley sighed. On the one hand, it was hard to believe

they needed to have this conversation—but on the other, everything in the Royce reality had gotten so convoluted, she didn't exactly blame him either.

"Tomme, come on. None of this is real."

"I know. I mean logically." His eyes sank to the floor. "But none of this is very logical anymore."

She stared at him. It wasn't the answer she had been expecting.

When he looked up again, he was teary-eyed. "I've been thinking about it for a long time now. Trying to see a way out. I figure, I've just got to come clean. I'll tell her the truth about who I am, tell her that I love her. Then I'll get back down on my hands and knees—"

"It's just knees," Bentley said. She tried not to smile. "You don't have to get down on your hands."

"Whatever. I'll do it. And when I do, I'll ask her to marry me, the real me, Tomme Torres."

Bentley started to laugh. It had all gone to such a ridiculous place. But Tomme Torres, he of the killer arms and the even more killer choreography, proposing to Porsche Royce, she of the venomous tongue and drought-ravaged tear ducts—that was not something Bentley ever could have expected.

It was way, way better—and way, way worse.

"Don't laugh." His face was clouding over now.

"I'm sorry. I'll stop." But she couldn't. She could only laugh harder and harder, until her stomach hurt and her eyes were filling with tears.

"Come on, B."

It was the nickname that shut her up. Now she wasn't even smiling.

"You don't get to call me that, Tomme. You are not my family. You are not marrying my sister, and this ends now. Don't you understand? If you tell the world this has all been a farce, then the wedding is off. The endorsement deals are off. The Lippies line goes under. *Rolling with the Royces* gets canceled. Jeff Grunburg will sue the Manolos off my entire family.[88] We will be *homeless* and everyone will hate you. Everyone will hate *me* for making it happen. You can't tell the truth. You can never tell the truth."[89]

"But . . . Porsche loves me." Tommy refused to give up.

Bentley sighed. "Porsche doesn't love you. She loves the head of the Whiteboyz music label. She loves a guy with a custom McLaren sports car and a Harley. She loves the attention and the talk and the toys. She loves having a fiancé and being a fiancée, not to mention the golf-ball-size rock on her finger, the one that *I* bought her."

He shook his head. "But it's also real. I can feel it. That's why it's so confusing. What we have is fake, and what we have is real."

Bentley felt sorry for the guy, honestly. He wasn't the first person Porsche had cast her spell on—he was just the most recent. "Trust me. My sister does not do real. But more than that, she does not do TryCycle instructors."

Even now, he was plenty stubborn. She had to give him

---

88 JG: "And probably still will!" —D
89 Finally, Jeff says. The moral of the story! —D

that. "We can work it out. I'll just go to the papers and come clean."

"No, you won't." Bent tried a new tack. "You want what's best for my sister, right? I mean, at least that part is real. You love her."

He nodded, looking more and more like one of those wild animals with their foot caught in a trap—the ones who know they're going to have to gnaw off a limb, but who just can't bring themselves to start biting yet.

Bentley sighed, still clutching her pole. (At least one thing in her life was steady at the moment.) "So you won't go to the papers. You won't end the show like that. You won't ruin her, and you won't humiliate her, and you won't take away the one thing she loves more than anything else, which is being a celebrity."

He gave up. He nodded at Bentley, and she knew by the look on his face that it was over. "What else can we do?"

"Something we should have done months ago, Tomme—back when I first realized you were crushing on my sister, instead of just pretending to. We're gonna blow this whole thing up."

WHY, BENTLEY, WHY?
ROYCE SISTER MAY BE MISSING MASTERMIND
AP: Beverly Hills, California

Via Celebcity.com

BREAKING: Sources close to the White-Royce investigation are now reportedly saying that the mastermind behind the disappearance of both individuals may in fact be none other than seventeen-year-old Bentley Royce herself.

Royce, often referred to as the "troubled" daughter of the celebrity family starring on *Rolling with the Royces*—which has just completed a historic sixth-season run that culminated in the disappearance and presumed death of two recurring cast members—is now the most watched "docu-follow" reality program in the world.

The whereabouts of Bentley Royce and Tomme Torres are still unknown, though an LAPD task force meant to investigate the murder/disappearances has now been closed; no evidence of human remains were found at the crash site of Royce's car. The charred vehicle was discovered in a ravine off Mulholland Drive, in the early-morning hours following a Royce family event.

Developing . . .

(Disclosure: Celebcity is a fully owned subsidiary of the Lifespan Network, which is itself a fully owned subsidiary of DiosGlobale.)

Follow @celebcity for breaking details,
or www.celebcity.com.

Twenty-Four

"Man," Whitey lamented, "I really loved that car. Did we have to kill it?"

"Obviously," Bentley reminded him for the millionth time. "We had to give Grunburg an even bigger finale than the wedding. This is the only way."

"There you are. What took you so long, B? I've been waiting for you forever." The voice came toward them through the night fog. Bent heard it as she walked away from the taxi stand.

I know that voice.

Bentley stopped in her tracks. Whitey kept on walking. Bentley leaned forward, peering through the foggy night, trying to focus her eyes.

Trying to better see his face.

The face that belonged to that voice.

Asa?

Now?

After all this time?

His hair was slicked back, just as it had been that night at the Chateau. But tonight, it couldn't stay down. Tonight, the underside of his hair twisted into rebellious waves that almost rivaled Venice's crazy curls.

The longer she watched, the more she could see his hair fly in every direction, this close to the ocean and the runway.

He also had Venice's voice—warm and affectionate and sharp and funny.

But this couldn't be Venice.

He didn't have any of his other tells, wasn't wearing any of his clothes, wasn't hiding his head under his favorite (and apparently, only) hoodie.

In fact, he wasn't wearing his uniform black tattered hoodie at all—or shuffling around in busted-up Vans, or ripped-up jeans, or an old black T-shirt from a band tour she'd never seen or even heard of, usually.

This Venice wore well-cut jeans and a faded white button-down sewn from the good stuff, top-quality linen; she could almost see the thread count now, trained as her eyes had been from racks and racks of #RTWR couture offerings (even if they all were three sizes too small).

His shoes, his belt, even his watch—none of those things were Venice things. None of those things belonged to the boy who had stood by her when nobody else would. Who had listened to her on her craziest days. Seen her face in a newspaper and never forgotten her. Given her a nickname within a minute of meeting her, when nobody else in her life—other than Bach—had ever bothered. Bailed her out of jail, even though it had meant cashing in the only thing he had left from the family he'd left behind—his grandfather's watch.

Venice was the one who had helped her put together

this whole escape. She couldn't do it without him now.

She needed him. And she wanted him. And she'd always known that, even when she'd been temporarily distracted by the bright blur of a single smile, lit by one flickering match.

The boy who was more comfortable at the public library than the Chateau Marmont.

That was the boy she loved.

Not this one.

Even though, at that moment, his hair flipped back into his crazy almost-Afro, and she was absolutely certain—for the very first time—that Asa and Venice were one and the same.

I should have known.

Asa Venice jammed his hands into his pockets and looked up at her. Shy. Uncertain. Almost nervous, as if neither one of them knew what was going to happen next.

Because they didn't.

Bentley took ten steps toward him and stopped again. She shook her head. "Why didn't you tell me?"

He approached her now, until they were standing face-to-face. They didn't touch, and even right there, she knew she had never felt farther away from him.

His voice sounded wistful, almost sad, when he finally answered. "How could I tell you when you didn't want it to be true?"

"You don't know that." She frowned. "How can you say that?"

"That you didn't want to see him in me?"

She nodded.

"Because you would have," he said simply. "The way that I saw you." He reached for her hand, grasping her cold fingers in his warmer ones. "Why do you think I even went to that stupid party? I hate those things. But I had been sitting by you in the library for so long, I had to get you to see me in another way."

Bent looked dazed. "You were already perfect. You didn't need to pretend to be something you weren't."

She could feel herself tearing up now.

He shook his head. "You didn't think of me like that. Not when I was just Venice. Not until after you met me as Asa."

"That's not true."

"Really? Why didn't you tell me the plan was a go? This plan?"

She rubbed her eye with the back of her hand and picked up her backpack. "I was trying not to involve you. You had already done enough, just helping me figure all this out. How did you know we'd be here?"

Asa Venice grinned. "How could I not know? I came up with this plan, remember? FedEx jet? Corporate cargo deliveries? Late-night paperwork, with tired border controls? A friend of a friend who could hook us up? This ringing any bells?"

Now Bent's mouth twisted into a frown. "Funny. The way I remember it, *we* came up with this plan."

"I was doing the planning. You were too busy mooning

about some blue-eyed guy with a book of matches." He shrugged. "It was hard to listen to frankly."

Bentley rolled her eyes. "Mooning? *Please.* Who was mooning? What even is that?"

Asa Venice pulled a book of matches out of his pocket and held them up. "I think you know." She stared at the matchbook as if it was her own personal shooting star. Then she smiled at him and he caught her hand, drawing her toward him.

Bent shrugged. "There might have been a *little* mooning."

Asa Venice smiled and spun her in front of him. Suddenly they were dancing. "A little?"

"To be fair, I had a hard time figuring out *which* blue-eyed guy I was mooning about."

Asa Venice spun her again. "Yeah, well, speaking for *both* blue-eyed guys?" Now he dropped her into a low dip. "That is exactly how I like it."

He lowered his mouth to hers, and she let him kiss her the way she had always imagined it should be. At first warm and safe and soft—and then, a few heartbeats later, none of those things at all.

"Uh, guys?" Tomme shifted his backpack as he stood up ahead of them, by the front of the airstrip office, still drunk and smelling of whiskey. "We're supposed to be on the run, remember? So maybe we should get . . . running?"

Asa Venice pulled back. "Don't go. Forget the plan. It was a bad plan."

Bentley smiled. "I thought it was *your* excellent plan?"

"I've got a new plan. It's even more excellent. Forget whatever you had in mind. Come with me instead."

"I don't care where we go, so long as it's off the grid."

He nodded, a sparkle waiting in his eye. "How deep?"

"Deep."

"Even better. I know just the place."

"Done." She picked up her pack again. "Tomme and I just need to lie low for a while."

He took it from her. "And then? After that?"

She sighed. "I haven't really thought much about after that."

"That's okay," he said, starting to walk.

She looked at him. "We won't disappear forever. Just until the media fallout ends."

"I know."

She smiled at him. "Don't you have, I don't know, a boardwalk to skate or waves to catch?"

He shrugged. "Venice isn't the only beach in the world, you know."

"You barely know me."

"You're the most regular date I've ever had. One hundred and three Wednesdays now."

"You counted?"

"You didn't? I thought it was important." He smiled.

"Wednesdays? They were for me. I didn't know you thought so. Then again, we barely know each other," Bent said.

He raised an eyebrow. "Do you really want me to do this right now?"

"I always want you to do this right now." She smiled.

He took her by the hand. "I know your favorite books. Your favorite cake. How you drool when you nap, at least, until the library security guards wake you up. I know the real you, Sweet B, and from what she's like, I can't wait to know the rest."

He was right, Bentley thought. He did know.

It wasn't the Bentley Bible.

It was the truth.

She looked at him sideways as they walked. "You really should be a lawyer."

Asa stopped walking. "Come on, Sweet B. I just handed you that whole touching, romantic speech and you come up with lawyer?"

She shrugged. "This is new ground for me. Give me one hundred and three more Wednesdays to practice, and I swear I'll come up with something."

"Deal."

Then they were kissing again, and walking, and laughing—and then Asa pushed open the gate to the hangar and gestured with one hand.

"I couldn't get a pumpkin carriage, but you don't really seem like the rescue-the-princess type, anyways."

It wasn't a carriage.

It was a Gulfstream G650.

ROYCE FAMILY ROLLS SOUTH OF THE BORDER; TULUM RESPITE DESPITE MISSING TEEN?

AP: Beverly Hills, California

Via Celebcity.com

The Royce family just keeps rolling.

Earlier today, Mercedes, Bach and Porsche Royce were seen boarding a Gulfstream Jet. Flight plans filed with the FAA list Tulum, Mexico, as the destination.

What's going on? Why Tulum? Why now? Could they possibly be heading south of the border to catch up with missing sister Bentley Royce, now rumored to be hiding out in an undetermined location somewhere outside the United States?

If so, what happened to the missing boy toy formerly known as T. Wilson White, who claimed to be a music-industry mogul, but was ultimately revealed to be an impostor, a TryCyclist instructor known in reality as Tomme Torres?

Could this story get any stranger, or the show's ratings any higher? Does the world even care that the only consistent truth to this family is their predilection for deception?

Only time will tell.

(Disclosure: Celebcity is a fully owned subsidiary of the Lifespan Network, which is itself a fully owned subsidiary of DiosGlobale.)

Follow @celebcity for breaking details,
or www.celebcity.com.

Twenty-Five

A ROYCE FAMILY REUNION
June 2018
Long Beach Private Airfield, Long Beach, California
(The 405 South exit at Long Beach Airport)

"What the—"

"That, Harry, is a Gulfstream G650. If you really want to know."[90]

Mercedes had been busily narrating the finer points of private air travel since Harry had parked his police cruiser at the hangar. For someone who didn't actually own a plane, she sure had plenty of opinions about them. On the other hand, Bach and Porsche hadn't said a word, and Harry didn't blame them. This whole week was only getting stranger and stranger. The Santa Ana winds were back, and the combination of the heat and the investigation and the media and the whole hectic pace of the last few days was starting to catch up with all four of them.

Which is why he hoped the small white jet in front of them now would lead them where he thought it would.

"I guess this is it," he said, double-checking the directions he'd gotten over the phone.

---

90 *Jeff says he does. He really does. —D*

Mercedes dragged her Vuitton bag toward him. Porsche and Bach followed a few yards behind her.

"You realize how strange this is? That we're just trusting you," Mercedes said, looking at Harry.

"Well, I am LAPD," Harry said. "Got a badge and everything."

"Says the dirty cop." She sighed.

He laughed. "Ouch."

She looked annoyed. "We could be kidnapped and held for ransom."

"I guess. You're not much more of a kid than I am, though," Harry said, winking.

Mercedes pretended not to hear him. "You could be selling us on the black market."

"I could try." He shrugged. "You'd be surprised. It's really a buyer's market now."

"You could harvest our organs."

"Guess it depends on the organ," he said, elbowing her. "You can probably keep that Hollywood liver."

"My liver is in excellent condition," Mercedes said, stopping to glare. "You, on the other hand, could be a madman."

He stopped next to her. "Well, I can't argue there. Do you want me to roll that for you?"

She shoved the handle of her bag at him. "We could all wake up in a bathtub full of ice."

He took it, and they began to walk again. "Not in this weather."

Now the two of them were staring up at the steps leading to the open doorway of the plane.

Even Mercedes looked impressed. "But I have to say, whoever your generous benefactor is, at least he has good taste."

"Well, there you go. What's an organ or two, if the plane is nice. Right?" Harry smiled. Mercedes smiled. They just didn't smile at each other, exactly.

Not yet.

"I think you got a little something in your teeth," Harry said. "Little black thing, like a peppercorn."

"It's chia." Mercedes froze. Then, almost automatically, she smile-grimaced to show her teeth. "Where?"

"Over one."

"There?"

"Now up."

"Is it gone?"

"You want me to get it?" he finally offered. "I might have floss in the squad car."

Mercedes's cheeks went pink, as if she'd only just now realized what she was doing and who she was doing it with and where she was. "Don't be disgusting. I barely even know you."

As if for emphasis, she grabbed her bag from his hands and tried to lug it up the first step to the plane.

It ricocheted off, bouncing back down to the ground.

"I'll get it," he called.

"I can manage," she huffed, shoving her bag back up onto the stairs. Her face was bright red, like some kind of alarm system had just gone off, somewhere in her body. She was radiating like a stoplight.

Harry looked back at Bach and Porsche, who looked as confused as Harry was starting to feel. "Is she always this much of a kick?" Harry asked Bach.

"A *kick*?" Porsche asked.

"Sure," Harry said. "A kick. A hoot. Hot tamale. Splash of Tabasco."

"Pretty much," Bach answered.

Harry nodded and straightened his sun hat. "I can see why folks watch."

The SUV had been waiting for them when they landed.

Now it curved down a long, winding road fringed with wild palms—taking them from the beach to a mountain overlooking it—and then the sea, of course the sea, on every side.

"Tulum," Harry mused. "I've wanted to get down here my entire life. But you want to know something wild? Before today I'd never even been past Cabo." He shook his head. "Things don't exactly turn out the way you think they will, do they?"

Mercedes said nothing. Her face was glued to the window, although Harry could see in the reflection that her eyes were squeezed tightly shut.

He suspected she was thinking about her kid, as any mother would be. Porsche and Bach were quiet in the backseat, as well.

The only sound was the constant hum of loose gravel spinning beneath their tires on the asphalt road.

He let them have the silence.

A lot had happened to this family.

The rest was going to be up to them.

Bentley Royce took a deep breath. It had been a quiet week, if not a calm one. But now that time was over.

Now came the storm.

She braced herself for the fighting and the blame. She waited for the judgment and the fury. She wasn't expecting to be forgiven. She was expecting the worst, but also expecting to tough it out, one way or another.

She knew she could, and more than that, she knew she would.

After all, she'd come this far—hadn't she?

And she was a Royce—wasn't she?

And Mercedes Royce's daughter could handle anything—including herself—couldn't she?

I can.

And this time it's me who can handle it.

Not Bad Bentley.

Real Bentley.

It was true. Real Bentley was a survivor. She'd learned that the hard way—which she now knew was the only way anyone ever learned anything at all.

She stepped out of the shadows of her villa doorway and went to face the bright afternoon light.

Bach reached her first.

His arms were around Bent before she could get a word out, his face buried in her shoulder.

Before Bent could say a word, Porsche piled on top of both of them, leaping up onto her little brother and sister as if they were once again wrestling on their old couch-cushion fort.

Muscle memory being what it was, Bentley went for her sister's armpits, while Bach kicked the backs of his sister's knees—until Porsche collapsed into a hysterical heap, a squirming, ticklish tangle of family.

Bentley looked up from the dog pile.

"Mom?"

Mercedes stood a few feet away, watching her children be with each other in a way she never had been, and never could be.

"Mom?" Bentley repeated the word. She reached out her hand.

Mercedes took it. "Baby B."

Mercedes tried to smile, but she stumbled over her words, and then everything inside her ruptured into what felt like chaos and fire and the end of the world—but turned out only to be tears.

Tears that came out, slowly and shyly at first, then uncontrollably, and without any sign of stopping.

Mercedes Royce cried at her children.

She cried because she missed them, and she cried because they missed her.

More than anything, she cried because she didn't know how to say it, or what to do about it.

Then her own children swarmed her, and as it turns out, she didn't need to know how to do anything more than stand there and let them.

Harry watched, satisfied.

He'd seen lots of families before, in lots of different pieces. Before and after. Together and apart. Some eternally fixable, some forever broken.

The Royces, they were all of those things.

One big piece of work, that family.

It was a good one.

It was finally Diego Sanchez, standing in his pressed white suit, who cleared his throat. "Welcome, Mercedes. Porsche. Maybach, of course." The old man smiled at Bach, whose eyes widened at the sight of him.

Bent stood up and took Mr. Sanchez by the hand. "Mercedes, you know Mr. Sanchez, right?"

Mercedes just stared.

Bent smiled. The Diego Sanchez name, especially for Lifespan employees, was no different from Willy Wonka. She also knew her mother, almost better than anyone, and Mercedes Royce was not used to being a mere Oompa-Loompa.

Yet here they all were.

Because Diego Sanchez, majority shareholder in DiosGlobale, parent company to Lifespan Network, owner of *Rolling with the Royces*, the top-rated reality program in the world, was Yoda himself.

The old man from the Lifespan lobby, whom she and Bach had met when he refused to pay thirty-eight dollars for a parking validation in his own building.

When he told them how to really play the game.

When he taught her how to pitch her own family, and her own life, not just her show.

When he listened to her crazy idea about a TryCycle instructor who wanted to be an actor, and who looked like ready-made ratings (especially in the bicep region).

When he set her up with the head of a record label who was only too happy to help out his largest principal investor—for an even bigger investment (especially if it meant taking an extended holiday at the Copa Palace on Rio's fabled Copacabana Beach).

When he'd watched and advised from afar as the season exploded—only intervening in the case of one right hook to the jaw.

When he'd welcomed her into his home, and—miracle of all miracles—stood by her side as he hugged his long-lost grandson for the first time in three long years.

Because Asa's story was every bit as long and convoluted as her own.

Because Asa was bound and bound again with her life, in so many different ways.

Because Asa was Diego Asa Sanchez III, son of Diego Sanchez II, grandson of Diego Sanchez himself.

Asa (Venice) moved out from the shadows of the immense oak tree to take Bentley's hand. His grandfather slid his arm around his shoulders, smiling at both of them.

When he spoke, he spoke directly to Mercedes.

"Bentley is my friend, Mrs. Royce. She's not just a remarkable person. She brought my only grandson back to me."

Bentley looked at Asa, and he intertwined his hand with hers. She spoke slowly but clearly, as if she'd just woken up from a long sleep—which in a way maybe she had.

"I was just trying to keep the show going, at least in the beginning. And, to be honest, I was hoping to build the show around Porsche and Whitey so that no one would notice when I went off to college next year. But I—"

"Wait, you got into college?" Bach asked.

"Yep." Bent beamed, glancing briefly at her mother. "A few of them, actually. My essay explaining that all my Get Bent behavior was a ruse to help my family was apparently *super* touching."

Mercedes covered her mouth with shaking fingers.

"But after everything with Bach and the police and the wedding," Bentley continued, "and Porsche falling for someone who didn't even exist in real life—I panicked."

Asa squeezed her hand.

She took a breath and looked at her family. "I'm sorry. I know you must have been worried out of your minds. It's just, I knew it was my mess, and I knew I had to fix it.

So I ran, and I got Tomme to come with me. I thought that was the only way I could help, but Asa convinced me I was wrong."

He nodded. "We made a deal. First we'd face my family. Then we'd face hers."

Mercedes raised an eyebrow. "And she somehow talked you into coming back to rough it on eleven acres of beach-front real estate, with a dock and a chef and more villas than I could count as we drove in? I can't imagine the hardship."

"No families are easy, Mrs. Royce." Asa smiled.

Mercedes waved him away. "Oh, *please*. Nobody calls me that. Mrs. Royce was my mother. Call me Mercedes."

Porsche snorted. "Last time I checked, your mother was Lucille Blatter from Blatter's Gas and Go, in Richfield—also known as the Gateway to Southern Utah."

Mercedes turned red—but other than that, she took it all in remarkable stride. Bentley realized then that the past months had changed her mom more than she would ever know. And she reached out and grabbed her mother's hand.

Mercedes looked at both daughters, equally surprised, but all she said was one word. "Lucille?"

Porsche nodded. "I read my birth certificate when we went to get our marriage licenses. Lucille's name is on it, as my grandmother. And it looked like she was the only witness to my birth."

Mercedes shrugged. "Well, of course she was. It was her gas station."

"What happened?"

"We had a falling-out, and I picked up the three of you

in the middle of the night and ran away." She looked up at the bright sky. "I can't remember why, of course. That was sixteen years ago now. But I've been thinking about it a lot lately. As you might imagine."

Her eyes were bright and shining. There was more, so much more, Bentley knew.

But not for today.

For today, there had been enough.

Diego sighed happily. "So you see, Mercedes. You have your family again, and I have mine. Bentley reunited me with Asa, and I owe your daughter everything."

"Did she?" Mercedes said, looking from Bentley to Asa.

Then she looked at Diego and smiled. "Do you?"

"Mercedes—" Bentley said. It was a warning, and like all warnings issued to Mercedes Royce, it went entirely unheeded.

"When you say, 'owe her everything,' Diego," Mercedes purred, "could you be a little more specific?"

Diego smiled. "Perhaps over *café*?" He nodded at Harry, who was mopping his brow with his sun hat. "Would your gentleman friend care to join us?"

"Gentleman friend?" Bent whispered to Bach.

Bach shrugged. "It's new. I give it five minutes." His eyes flickered over to Asa. "Speaking of new . . ." He lowered his voice. "Is it serious?"

Bent smiled. "You know what they say. Never underestimate a Blatter."

"I never do."

Bent put her arm around her brother and pulled him

close. "I'm sorry I couldn't tell you, Bach. And I'm sorry I left. And . . . I missed you."

"I get it. It's just . . . well . . . I'm starting to think you Blatters are just a bunch of big softies."

Bentley shoved him.

He laughed.

Asa cleared his throat. "Hey, is that your wallet?" he asked awkwardly, pointing to the ground next to them.

Bach looked down and nodded, picking it up from the grass. "Thanks. Guess I dropped it."

Bent saw that it was made entirely out of red duct tape. She smiled, because she'd made it for him.

"It's pretty cool," Asa said. "I guess."

Then he pulled out his own wallet.

It was made entirely of silver duct tape.

Both boys laughed.

From then on, Bent wasn't worried at all.

Porsche Royce walked across the lawn to the swimming pool, where someone was practicing his nearly perfect front crawl.

When he came to the edge of the pool and burst up from the surface of the water, gulping in air, her face went pale, and then red.

She dropped her handbag, kicked off her Chloé flats, and threw herself into the pool, Isabel Marant sundress and all.

Before Tomme Torres knew what had hit him, Porsche Royce was kissing him as hard as she could, two arms flung around his slippery, well-muscled torso. (*And the arms! Those infamous arms!*)

The fighting would come later.

So would the explaining, and the apologizing—and the story of a well-meaning fitness enthusiast slash actor, who had gone looking for a big break but found only a broken heart.

Now wasn't the time for that.

Now was the time for kissing and crying—for both former fake fiancés.

Or formerly former fake fiancés.

What did that make them now? What had they become?

Actual *real* fiancés?

As they sank below the surface of the water, Porsche knew there was nothing fake about the way either one of them was feeling.

And she knew something else.

She could do more than just love.

She could do forever.

ROYCE RETURNS, EXPRESSES REGRETS; STUNT WAS NOT 'RESEARCH' FOR UPCOMING ROLE

AP: Beverly Hills, California

Via Celebcity.com

The reality television celebrity, now sensation, has made her first statement regarding her recent disappearance. Short, sincere and sorrowful, the televised apology—broadcast via the Lifespan Network, and filmed on location in Tulum, Mexico—has been widely hailed as one of Bentley Royce's greatest performances.

A record number of viewers tuned in to the live press event, which is reportedly the highest-rated celebrity apology in a crowded field this year.

Wearing boyfriend jeans, rustic leather sandals and little makeup, the fresh-faced Royce daughter seemed a changed person. Gone were her signature rainbow-tipped locks, as the young celeb debuted a chic-but-carefree pixie chop. When asked who was responsible for her new coif, the cryptic answer was "The scissors were from Home Depot Mexico, I think."

Royce's message may have been brief, but it was emphatically apologetic. "I know there's a rumor out there that I was researching an upcoming television role, but that's not actually true. If I've researched anything this year, it's who I am when I'm not on any screen."

Royce went on to take full responsibility for the bizarre events surrounding her disappearance earlier this month. "I hurt a lot of people, and I'll be doing everything I can to make up for that from now on. All I can say is that I'm grateful for my family and friends and for second chances."

At the conclusion of Royce's statement, her mother, Mercedes Royce, stepped forward to clarify the future of the show. "Of course the Royces will keep Rolling. A Royce always Rolls!" As a result, the hashtag #RoyceRolls is now trending worldwide.

(Disclosure: Celebcity is a fully owned subsidiary of the Lifespan Network, which is itself a fully owned subsidiary of DiosGlobale.)

Follow @celebcity for breaking details,
or www.celebcity.com.

Twenty-Six

LAX was a zoo. It smelled like a bowl of cigarettes left outside in the sun too long. That, and gasoline and flowers. They'd left the world of private jets and private airports behind with the rest of their families, who were staying for a particularly good *luchadores* event the next day, per their host's insistence.

Ah, it's good to be home, Bentley thought as she stood at the traffic light next to Asa Venice.

The comforting surge of Latin Asian Americans rolled past her, pushing off the curb and crashing into the oncoming traffic. Everything was dirty. Everyone was a mess. Still, the sun shone weakly and the sky above the potholed streets was an almost startling blue—way more blue than the Santa Monica Bay had been in years and would ever be again.

In this horribly imperfect paradise.

A lone, scraggly palm tree on the far side of the taxi zone tried not to give in to the desolation of the never-ending concrete construction around it. Beneath it, hunted, exhausted-looking smokers snuck cigs, ducking away from the cops while Bentley watched.

The cops didn't care. Wearing their fluorescent-yellow vests, they were too busy waving along the lurking cars and bully cabs, knocking on hoods and windows.

Yeah, yeah. This is LA. You've seen it.

Now get on the freeway and haul your butt into that slow-crawling traffic.

In other words, she was home.

Bentley was back.

Asa Venice looked at her. "You're sure you're ready for this?"

The light changed colors.

She nodded, taking his hand, dragging her carry-on behind her until they reached his car, which he'd kept in long-term parking for the better part of a month now. When Bentley had expressed shock that anyone could live in LA without a car, Asa Venice had just looked amused. "We have a bus. We have a train. We even have city bicycles. Why do I need a car?"

When Bent saw his car, she understood; an old Mustang with a ripped convertible top, it didn't exactly look like it could handle the daily abuse of rush-hour traffic. The back was full of wet suits and dirty laundry and rank-smelling, mildewed, still-damp towels. Mercedes would have a heart attack if she knew her daughter was about to even stop in front of it, let alone ride in it.

Bent shook her head. "I can't believe you had a car this whole time."

"Not much of one," Asa Venice said.

"And an apartment."

"With only the one broken window covered in cardboard. The rest are actual glass," Asa Venice said.

"And a family."

"Yeah, that's sort of an as-is situation," Asa Venice said.

"And here I was worried about you living on the *streets*."

"Well, uh . . ." His cheeks turned red. He didn't have a comeback for that.

Bentley smiled as he pulled open the car door for her, which only took three tries. "It's okay, Venice—or I mean, Asa. I still like you. With or without the car."

"It's not like it's a fancy car or anything," he said, slamming the door after her. "It only runs, like, sixty percent of the time."

"What do you do the other forty percent?" Bent asked.

He slid behind the steering wheel, reached up to the dashboard, and retrieved a plastic card. "I told you. It's called the bus."

"Bus? I don't believe I'm familiar with that word." She examined the ripped passenger seat. Foam padding was busting up through a slit in the faded leather.

He handed her his bus pass. "It's like a big car with lots of people on it at the same time. You should try it. It's great."

"I'll add it to the bucket list."

"Then you should look into trains. They're like roller coasters, only slower. And hopefully without the loop-the-loops."

"Do you happen to have a third secret life as a worker for the Department of Transportation?"

"Don't even joke. No more secret lives, B."

"Well, that frees up a lot of time," she said.

He twisted the key in the ignition, and the car coughed and choked to life. "Come on. We don't have to go straight back to your mom's house. I'll show you around my LA. I love this town." He reached out to ruffle her hair with his tanned hand.

She leaned her head against his outstretched hand. "I already know plenty about this town. Too much, you could say."

He smiled. "Nah. Not my part of town."

She looked at him. "Palm trees. Sunshine. Taco trucks. I got it."

"You ever see the murals beneath a freeway overpass? Float a boat on the Silver Lake Reservoir? Take the Red Line to Chinatown? Hang in Union Station while a commercial's being shot?" He moved his hand against her cheek.

"Can't say I have."

"Downtown it is. We can hit up the Pantry. Never closes. Or Philippe's, for a French dip sandwich the size of your head."

Bent sat up in her seat.

"Philippe's? That's where those matches were from?" Her eyes welled up with tears. "It's a *sandwich* place?"

Venice looked at her shining eyes, not understanding. "Whoa, okay. You don't like French dip? How about pastrami on rye? So big, it takes two days to get it down? What would you say to that?"

She stared at him, trying to let herself feel it.

Happy. I can do happy.

Finally, she smiled, kissing the hand that still caressed her cheek. "I guess I'd say, what are we waiting for?"

"Beats me." Asa Venice grinned. "All I've been waiting for is y—"

Her lips met his before he could finish the sentence.

WAITLISTED, NOT D-LISTED;
BENTLEY ROYCE BECOMES A BRUIN!

AP: Beverly Hills, California

Via Celebcity.com

One of the latest twists in what has to be the strangest story of this year is also one of the most encouraging: Bentley Royce, youngest daughter of the tempestuous Royce family—who rose to fame with their hit reality show, *Rolling with the Royces*, and then to infamy with the alleged Royce-White murder investigation—has finally gotten some good news.

Bentley Royce, as of September 2018, will become a UCLA Bruin. The future freshman appears to have been admitted to one of the top public schools in California, as well as the nation, just off the waitlist this week.

In a rare statement posted via her verified Twitter account @TheBentleyRoyce, Royce had this to say:

"Don't give up. Find your tribe and hold on, they're out there. Also: the world is not a totally sucky place. Go UCLA BRUINS CLASS OF 2022!"

A highly placed source familiar with the Admissions Department, while unable to comment officially on any one case, noted privately that the Royce Personal Statement was reportedly one of the more compelling that the school had ever seen. Other sources believe that the essay itself has now been optioned by the Lifespan Network, in an attempt to cash in on what is widely regarded as the most successful scripted reality season of all time.

Alumni Trustee Diego Sanchez, a personal friend of Bentley Royce, has publically denied any involvement with the Royce admission decision.

(Disclosure: Celebcity is a fully owned subsidiary of the Lifespan Network, which is itself a fully owned subsidiary of DiosGlobale, of which Diego Sanchez is the majority shareholder.)

Follow @celebcity for breaking details,
or www.celebcity.com.

Twenty-Seven

BEST SEASON EVER
June 2018
The Lifespan Building, Century City
(Avenue of the Stars at Little Santa Monica Boulevard)

Jeff Grunburg sat at his six-thousand-dollar midcentury modern desk, staring at the collection of miniature plastic robots that sat in a row along the farthest edge.

They were a present from his tween daughter,[91] though he had no idea what fandom or universe they were from, or even why she'd chosen them.

With Tallulah, you never knew.

Each one had a heart etched in the center, which he suspected she had intended to be some kind of ironic inside joke with his ex-wife.

Happy Father's Day, to the man with no heart.

It wasn't true, of course, and Jeff's was beating like crazy at this particular moment. He couldn't catch his breath, and if he hadn't been forty-seven years old, he might not have even noticed.[92]

---

91 Per JG: "TWEEN? TALLULAH?" Also: Jeff wonders if anyone ever uses that word without flinching? He suggests SUB-TEEN or PROTO-TEEN? (Could shorten to PREEN?) ☺ —D
92 Jeff wonders if Production could get that number down in the next draft? (Spiritually, he feels he's more of a 36. He says 34 would also work.) ☺ —D

He did today.

Today, Diego Sanchez, the CEO of DiosGlobale, was coming to see him. And then, if things went as Jeff suspected, to fire him.

He reviewed his argument.

Really, as far as *RWTR* was concerned, six had been his best season ever.

The numbers were crazy good.

Ratings were way up.

Product sponsorships had more than tripled.

They'd had to get a new manufacturer for just the *GET BENT* merchandising alone, *hadn't they*?

And Jeff had done the impossible, *hadn't he*?

Sure, six hadn't quite worked out as anyone had planned, but did it *really* matter? *Sure*, the season finale was supposed to be a celebration of love and family. *So what* if the network had gone with an exploitation of scandal and debauchery? They hadn't had a whole lot of choice in the matter, *had they*?

When it came right down to it, was there really *that* much difference between a TryCycle instructor and the head of a music label?

He rubbed his hand against his still-aching jaw as he considered it.

And *so what* if the most celebrated memorial service in modern television had been a sham? So what if the groom and the little sister had totaled a *seventy-five-thousand-dollar car* along the way? Was any of that in the network's control?

All Jeff had done was play with the cards he was given. Could anyone blame him *for that*?

He wasn't the one calling the shots.

The girl was.

This was *her* story line, and only hers.

Jeff shook his head. He was starting to sweat. He had to get himself under control, before he had to change his shirt again.

He couldn't even bring himself to *think* her name.

She always was trouble.

If Sanchez wants to fire someone, he should fire her.

Those were all things he found himself saying to Señor Diego Sanchez within the first five minutes of their meeting.

No matter what Jeff said, though, the old man just raised his eyebrows and followed up with another irritating question.

Just as he was doing now.

"So you're saying responsibility for the entire wedding story line falls on the shoulders of a seventeen-year-old girl?" Sanchez asked, sitting back in a four-thousand-dollar chair. (The nicest chair in the room should always be the one behind the desk. Jeff had read that in a book somewhere, and taken it to heart.)

Jeff nodded. "That's exactly what I'm saying."

"And you expect me to believe that a *teenage girl* engineered this whole circus, without any guidance from your production staff, your writers' room, your development team, yourself?"

"The kid went rogue, I'm telling you."

"Interesting" was all the man said.

"Right?"

Now Sanchez stared at him. "Some could argue that a wedding is meant to be a private affair. A family time."

"Do you have any idea who you're talking about? *Mercenary Royce?*" Jeff shook his head.

On the other side of his desk, another eyebrow jumped in response. "Enlighten me."

Jeff thought about it. "Family time? They're not a family anymore. I'm not sure they ever were."

The old man looked confused. "Tell me then, Señor Grunburg, what are they?"

"They're a distribution channel. They're a content-delivery machine. Don't you get it?"

"I'm afraid not."

"It doesn't matter how they feel, or what they say. It almost doesn't matter what they do. It matters what they look like, what they wear, what they drive. Their water. Their shampoo. Their underwear."

Jeff pushed back his chair. He mentally prepared himself for what was about to come. Then he stood up.

"Go ahead. Fire me. Fire me because you don't like me. Fire me because you think I've jacked up your company. Fire me for the ten thousand times I've acted like the biggest jerk in the room."

The man tried to interrupt. "Mr. Grun—"

"But you can't fire me for what I've done with my show."

"Your show?"

"Our show. Your show. It doesn't matter what you call it. Six? This season? We killed it. Knocked it out of the park. Wait until Emmys. I'm—you're—going to clean up."

He took a breath.

"Are you done?" Sanchez looked at him.

Jeff nodded.

He wondered if he needed a box, or if they'd give him one. He wondered if they'd let him leave on his own, or have Security walk him out.

If so, he should get ready—he had a few things (well, one) he'd need to take with him. He tried to mentally prepare himself now, but it suddenly didn't seem as easy as it had previously looked, from over on his side of the table.

Jeff glanced at his doorway, dreading the inevitable sight of Lifespan Security Specialists. He always had the Dirk (*and Security!*) walk people out after he fired them, but he suddenly had a new understanding for why that seemed like a Dirk move.

Sanchez opened his stitched leather briefcase and slid a folder across the desk. "I've enjoyed our conversation. You're an entertaining man, Mr. Grunburg. Truly."

"I am?"

"Very funny indeed."

"Funny how?"

"Fire you? Who said anything about firing you?" Diego Sanchez smiled, his teeth bright white against the warm brown of his face. "I'm here to *promote* you. You just delivered the biggest numbers the network has ever seen."

"You are?" Jeff was amazed. The panic receded like an ocean wave. "That's wonderful." He began to do the mental math. Run the numbers. What he wanted. What he'd take. What he could get. Why he was being robbed, no matter how good the numbers were . . .

The old man tapped the folder in front of him on the desk. "Starting immediately. Get your things."

"My—what?" Jeff snapped back to attention.

"You might need a box. Do you have a box?"

"Why?" Now he was really confused.

"Perhaps Security could help you?" Sanchez nodded encouragingly.

Jeff felt ill. "What the hell are you talking about?"

"Mexico City, of course. I can't waste a man of your talents at a small-time cable network. You have four more years on your contract, and I want you to spend every day of them with me."

Jeff was stunned. He found he couldn't form a sentence. Not even a word.

"*Luchadores*, Señor Grunburg. *Lucha Libre.* Mexican professional wrestling. Tag team and *trios.* El Santo? Blue Demon? Man of a Thousand Masks? That's where the *real* drama is."

Jeff began to laugh. "Are you out of your mind? I have a house in the Palisades. A month of golf booked at the Riv." Now he was spluttering. "Sure, I'll take a weekend at Las

Ventanas, but if you think I'm spending the next four years babysitting masked men in tights—"

"Ah." The old man beamed and pulled a thick stack of paper from his briefcase. "Ironclad, Señor Grunburg. Your contract. Especially your non-compete clause. If you don't work with me, you won't have a job for five years. A very long time, in this town."

Jeff sat back, stunned. Sanchez was right.

Five years?

Five years in Hollywood might as well be fifty.

Sanchez stood up. "Don't worry. You're going to love it. And you can take as long as you like—so long as your things are out by tomorrow. I have a new network head starting, and I don't want to keep her waiting."

"You do?" It was the final insult.

The old man winked. "Let's just say you don't want to make her angry. I hear they call her *Mercenary Royce*."

Jeff Grunburg looked up.

Of course.

Now it all made sense.

There she was, standing in his doorway, towering over the room in four-inch heels and head-to-toe white.

Mercedes Royce, looking like she already owned the place.

And behind her stood her youngest daughter—the one who probably planned the whole thing just to get rid of him—the one he hated more than all his ex-wives put together. She was smiling, really almost laughing, at him.

Bentley Royce.

Right there in the hall, right behind her mother.

Just like always.

That was when he knew it.

He was *dunzo.*

He could cry about it later, but there was one thing he had to do first, and he had to do it quickly.

It was time to activate plan B. *B* as in *BE SURE YOU HAVE AN INSURANCE POLICY FOR YOUR INSURANCE POLICY.*

Even *Darth Vader*'s ship had an escape pod.

Jeff lunged for his wall safe. It was hidden beneath a poster-size photographic print of himself shaking hands with Lin-Manuel Miranda—it had cost him five grand at a charity auction for some stupid New York orphanage, whatever—which now tumbled to the ground, cracking the glass across both faces. He fumbled as he tried to remember today's seven-digit code for the keypad. (He changed it at least one digit daily, privately distrusting anyone with a man-bun, including Dirk.)[93]

D-A-Z-Z-L-E-D

There.

He pressed ENTER—but the light flashed red when it was supposed to turn green. Something was wrong. It wasn't working.

What the—

He hit ENTER again and again until he found himself smashing the front of the safe with his fist. "Come on!"

---

93 *I really don't either.* ☹ —D

"Are you looking for this?" The old man held up a DVD in a translucent sleeve. Written across its surface in black Sharpie were the words *HOPE ≠ FLOAT*, followed by more exclamation points than he would ever have publically admitted to writing.

There it was.

The only remaining evidence of the ill-fated D-day shoot.

Of all his hours of collected B-roll footage, across all of his shows, this particular DVD was the one he had always thought would pay for his retirement.

Thanks to plan B: *B* as in *BLACKMAIL.*

But now, Jeff's shoulders sagged as he watched his escape pod blow itself up in space.

He was stunned.

"How did you get into my safe? Nobody knows that code. I change it myself, every day."

Security Supporters (that was what Jeff had insisted they be called, as part of the New Positivity) appeared on either side of Diego Sanchez now.

The old man pocketed the DVD. Then—still flanked by Security Supporters—he slowly reached down and hung the cracked poster back on the wall.

"Safe? What safe? All I see is a picture of you and a man I deeply admire." He tipped his hat to the face of Lin-Manuel Miranda. "And I guess I don't like to waste my shot either."

By the time Jeff Grunburg and his plastic-hearted robot collection were escorted out to his Tesla, he was already plotting his revenge.

At least, that was how it looked to Mercedes as she watched from Jeff's old window—the one he'd had installed especially to spy on the parking lot. She wasn't too worried. She'd dealt with worse. Jeff Grunburg wouldn't have lasted two rounds at the Sevier County Demolition Derby, and his odds would have been terrible. Nine to one, tops. Still, she knew him well enough not to count him out for the whole gig. "He'll be back."

"Jeff?" Bentley said, her feet already up on her mother's new desk. "Oh, I'm sure he's coming for us. He'd burn the channel to the ground before he'd walk away from it. Tallulah gives it six months."

Mercedes sat in a chair across the desk from her daughter. "If we're lucky."

"Not a worry." Sanchez shrugged. "We also have some openings in Bogotá? Cartagena? Medellín?"

"No, let him try." Mercedes said, her eyes on the Tesla as the aerodynamic driver's door slammed shut. "I can't wait."[94][95]

---

94 Per MR: Mercedes wonders if we could bring some writers in to do a polish on a more rousing "moment of victory" speech? Maybe the Mullholland Hall guys? Or similar. ☺ —D
95 Per MR: One more thing—Mercedes says to ignore all the previous notes! ☺ ☹ —D

Epilogue

GET BENT
A Word from Bentley Royce

As posted on the GET BENT blog and
reposted by www.CelebPretty.com.

It's been four months since I was sentenced to community service for my racketeering charges, and I've loved every minute of it. Having the opportunity to serve the community has taken a gigantic weight off my shoulders: it's made me feel a part of humanity instead of dangling precariously above it, and here's what I've learned.

Not all fakes are phony.

Some of it goes deep, way deep down, and all the way through.

I'm surrounded by idiots. And I'm an idiot too. Because these idiots love me, even when it seems like they're incapable of loving anything except their own flat belly buttons.

I don't know why I didn't see it before.

Love, no matter who or where it comes from, is a game changer. The highest of high concepts, as Production would say. A real *name in lights* moment.

You're not too good for love.

Nobody is.

At least I know I'm not.

Love is legit. It's the only legit thing, maybe. Even here in Los Angeles, my so-help-me-god home. The city of bony blond angels.

Let me put it in terms my people will understand.

Love is pearly-whiter than brand-new white AG jeans. More golden than the most expensive Clarins self-tanning gel. More fun than an Audi convertible with a top that never goes up. Sweeter than an Arnold Palmer minus the iced tea.

Love is bread without carbs. A body without hips. A butt without cellulite. A vegan prime rib. A Barneys sample sale without other shoppers.

It's better than a Raquel Allegra sweatshirt right out of the dryer. Than the self-righteous buzz of waking up on an empty stomach. Than knowing you can eat all the freaking breakfast you want, and no one can say a word.

Not even you.

I love my awful, horrible mess of a family, and my awful, horrible mess of a family loves me.

Whether or not they can say it, whether or not they can even know it.

Mercedes, Porsche, and Bach.

And now Asa Venice and Harry and Tomme and Sanchez?

I don't know what it is, but it's something.

And I'm in.

Maybe sometimes the people who mess you up are the same people who fix you up. Maybe it's all just two sides of the same old stupid mess, anyway.

The way I see it, we're all going down in this ship together. Why else have a ship? Why else have a together? To be in this catastrophe, with these people, is an honor. It's a privilege.

My privilege.

We're a family.

A messed-up disaster of a family.

Which is how you know one thing, the only thing that matters.

That it's real.

[Fade out.]

ACKNOWLEDGMENTS

Getting **ROYCE ROLLS** into the hands of readers was a (JOYOUS!) labor of (UNBRIDLED!) love that I had the (INCOMPARABLE!) honor of sharing with my (RIDICULOUSLY!) rock-star team at Freeform.*

Here is how it happened: I started writing it for fun, because writers do that sometimes, out of slight madness (*see: writers*) and also because all LA writers have at least one good LA story in them. **Raphael Simon** & **Melissa de la Cruz** (GLEEFULLY!) read the early chapters. **Hilary Reyl** (MORE GLEE!) listened in the car on the way to **Eunei Lee**'s place (COMPOUND!) in Maine. **Veronica Roth** (CHEERILY!) said *keep going you weirdo*. **Virginia Stock** (KNOWINGLY!) said *this could be a show*. My agent at the Gernert Company **Sarah Burnes** (UNFLAPPABLE!) said *well, why not?* Editor-in-Chief & Associate Publisher **Emily Meehan** (MEDIA MAGNATE!) at Freeform said *I don't know what this is but I think I like it. . . .*

And from there it went like this: **Emily Meehan**, **Kieran Viola** & **Heather Crowley** (MASTERFULLY!) edited it. Many, many times. **Patricia Callahan**, **Meredith Jones** & **Dan Kaufman** (PAINSTAKINGLY!) copyedited and proofread it. **Mary Ann Zissimos**, **Seale Ballenger** & **Andrew Sansone** (BRILLIANTLY!) publicized it. **Holly Nagel** & **Elke Villa** (INGENIOUSLY!) marketed it. **Marci Senders** (ON FLEEK!) designed it, and **Sara Not** (DOUBLE FLEEK!) created the art for it. At Freeform Network—Go

Karey Burke (FEARLESS!)—Simran Sethi (& PEACHES!) thought of using it on the air, and Kirsten Creamer (INDEFATIGABLE!) made that happen, while Dalia Ganz & Amina Ahmad pulled off the (EPIC!) cover reveal. Sam Roach (TEEN PRODIGY!) shot the trailer for my fictional—(TERRIBLE!)—*ROLLING WITH THE ROYCES* television show, with the help of Shane Pangburn (SHANE OF ALL TRADES!) on graphics. Melissa de la Cruz, Curtis Sittenfeld, Veronica Roth, Daniel Handler, Ransom Riggs, Marie Lu, Maureen Johnson, Jesse Andrews, Brendan Reichs, Kami Garcia & Danielle Paige gave me (TRULY AWFUL!) reviews for the Royces' (AGAIN, HORRID!) show. Tori Hill (FUTURE POTUS!) put together my social media, tour promotions, and the book's launch. Susanna Hoffs (TINY YET EMPHATIC!) laughed in all the right places at my earliest draft.

And my family, Lewis, Emma, May & Kay Peterson; Dave, Sara, Jake & Charlie Stohl; Burton & Marilyn Stohl; plus as a bonus Jackson Roach & Alex Kamenetzsky (not to mention Jiji & Kiki) listened to me stress about it all (INCESSANTLY!) from start to finish. Sometimes they laughed. Sometimes they ignored me. Either way, I'm truly grateful for all of the above—and I know exactly how lucky (VERY!) I am. XO

*Side note: Kids, when you're figuring out what you want to do when you grow up, ask yourselves these questions: 1) Would I do it for free? 2) Would I do it with these people? 3) Would I

keep doing it? 4) If things went south, would I say to myself, like any good sea commander, **"It is my honor and privilege to go down with this ship"**? If the answer is yes to all of the above, you're right where you're supposed to be . . . like me!